DANGER SIG

ROBERT
has rep
abroad.

Now a ... ives with his wife and two so ... rgan.

His first ... ovel was *Angels of Death*, also available in Fontana.

Also available in Fontana Paperbacks

Angels of Death

ROBERT PEART

Danger Signal

Fontana Paperbacks

First published by Fontana Paperbacks 1985

Made and printed in Great Britain by
William Collins Sons & Co. Ltd, Glasgow

PROLOGUE

The man shuffled nervously in the mountain clearing as he waited for the cable car to appear. The air was cold and heavy with the scent of edelweiss which only thrives at such altitude. Snow was packed hard around his high Alpine boots.

He wore a one-piece hooded rubber suit and a gas mask with an antiseptic filter. No part of his body was exposed. Behind him the ambulance waited. It was more than ten years old, a mid-1920s design with thick spoke wheels, a running board and a high back which would bounce on the hard suspension.

The man turned and walked cautiously to the boarded-up terminus. He climbed onto the wooden platform built out over the precipice.

'There.' He pointed to the mountain on the far side of the abyss. The cable car's shadow slid over the snow, which seemed blue in the moonlight.

He turned towards the ambulance. 'It's on its way.'

Two men climbed out. They were dressed identically to the first. They joined him and waited.

The cable car hung before them, rocking slightly.

'Hold it steady.' The leader's voice crackled through his mask as he slid back the door. He played his torch beam inside.

There were four large canvas bags, like bulky hammocks. Each was tied like a kitbag with a rope threaded through metal loops at one end and knotted tightly.

'Move,' snapped the leader, sensing the men's reluctance.

The bundle sagged in the middle when they lifted it. Only then was it obvious, by the shape it took, that it contained a human body. The bend of the trunk and knees was unmistakable.

They moved crablike to the ambulance and dumped the corpse in the back. Then they fetched the other three.

The leader watched the cable car climb back into the night. From this place in the Italian Alps the rough track could go no further. Yet above it the mountain still rose. High above him he could make out the flickering pin-points of light from the up station on the ridge below the summit.

He shuddered suddenly, but blamed it on the cold.

'Let's move it,' he called as he eased himself into the ambulance's cab alongside the others.

The ambulance pulled away slowly, its old engine straining in first gear as it began its descent. The track was narrow and dangerous. The slightest error would have put them over the edge, and it was more than a thousand feet until they reached the tree line. Not even Italian mountain pine could survive at these heights.

The engine began to hiss steam as they reached the trees, but the track, still strewn with boulders, was wider. The leader watched carefully for the chosen spot. The others sat in silence.

'It's around the next bend,' he said at last.

The ambulance slowed until it came to a gap in the tall trees. It swung off the track and into the forest. The wheels dug deep furrows as, revving wildly, it swerved between the tall trunks. Above, the pine branches met to shut out the light from the moon.

Then they came to the clearing and once more saw the stars. The ambulance parked on the edge of the trees, its headlamps lit the clearing.

The leader got out and paced the ground. He selected the spot.

'Here,' he called. 'And make it deep.'

He watched as the others responded warily. They unloaded the canvas bags first, then rolled out four black metal drums. Each drum was painted with a yellow skull and crossbones.

Armed with snow shovels the men began to dig. Their leader noted with satisfaction that they worked tirelessly, the sound of their heavy breathing exaggerated through the filters of their mole-like masks.

Damp earth piled high around three sides of the deep pit. Then the men hauled themselves out.

'The mixture first,' the leader said.

One man rolled a drum to the edge of the hole and carefully opened the tap. A stream of thick white liquid poured into the pit. It bubbled into the earth and sent a haze of fumes into the air.

The leader nodded. His men tossed the first canvas bundle into the gurgling mixture.

Two more drums were emptied for the next two bundles.

'The last one,' came the order.

'Thank Christ,' said the man as he took the shoulders, his companion the feet. They swung the bundle to give it the momentum to clear the drums still pouring their mixture into the pit.

On the third swing the bundle jerked to life.

The canvas fell loose as the shape inside began to thresh.

'Get it in the pit,' screamed the leader, but the warning was too late.

The man holding the legs was thrown back, as they kicked out in desperation. His arms windmilled as he tottered on the brink of the pit. A scream choked in his mask as he tried to lean forward and regain his balance. Slowly he tipped backwards and was gone.

'Move, man,' he yelled to the other and dived for the ambulance cab. The machine pistol was on the seat. By the time he'd cocked it he saw a hand shoot from the canvas. The fingers grabbed wildly for his companion's mask. The shape inside the bundle now screamed in anguish. The hand tore the mask from the man's face. He yelled in terror and fell to his knees.

The leader, unable to move, watched the shape free itself and was aware of the stench that pervaded his mask.

It was a young man, thin and naked with arms extended like a figure from the cross. His rib cage and pelvic bones pressed from his skin. He was covered in black circular weals and broken blisters.

The leader's fingers tightened around the trigger as the young man, arms extended and mumbling, moved towards him.

He fired.

The young man bent double, blood gushing from his mouth.

He fired again. The second burst threw him into the air, onto the bank piled on the side of the pit. Slowly he rolled into his grave.

He saw his kneeling companion's look of gratitude change to sheer terror as he raised his pistol for the third time. The man raised his arms protectively to his head.

Then he fired.

'You let him touch you. You stupid bastard,' he mumbled as he pushed his companion in with the others. 'I had to kill you. All of you. There was no choice.'

Then he poured part of the last drum of corrosive and frantically began to refill the grave. He sweated, but dared not remove his mask.

He finished his task as dawn broke. An orange tinge crept across the Alpine sky as he moved the last drum to the place where the men had struggled. He turned on the tap and watched the pungent liquid eat through the blanket of pine needles.

It bubbled as it seeped through the damp soil.

CHAPTER ONE

The threat of a war where he would be forced to take up arms against his own father's people filled Bruno Rossi full of dread.

He also knew that a graveside vow would be broken and saw his life's dream swept aside by the hate.

He twisted open the throttle in anger.

The motorcycle leapt the humpback bridge with both wheels off the ground. The flock of sheep in the road ahead scattered for the safety of the common.

Crouched low, as if on a race track, he eased back on the grip and braced himself. He smelt the sear of burning rubber as the tyres scuffed the road and pressed his knees tight against the chrome tank. He felt the back wheel flip and leant to one side for balance.

The bike weaved.

Again he twisted the grip, and powered the bike back into a straight line.

Once back on course he slowed to walking pace, sat upright in the saddle and guided the Brough Superior with one hand. Its 1000 cc engine rumbled hoarsely in protest. He wiped the insects from his goggles and pushed them up onto his leather flying cap. It left two white circles on his dusty face. One hand rested on his knee.

Bruno Rossi felt the tension ebb. He'd guessed it would. Riding the bike through the Cambridgeshire countryside always helped. That's why he'd invested a major part of his salary as Lecturer in Research Bacteriology at King's College in the Superior. It was the best bike on the market.

The tension had gone.

But not the anger.

Because of it Bruno found it impossible to concentrate.

For Bruno Rossi was the Welsh-born son of Italian immigrants. And that morning in April 1939 Mussolini had invaded Albania. Britain, the BBC said, would introduce conscription in weeks.

Bruno knew that war between Britain, the land of his birth, and Italy and Germany was inevitable. Bruno's world would be turned upside down, and there was nothing he could do about it.

He wondered if there would be time to realize his dream before the fighting started. A professorship had already been hinted at. It was no more than he deserved. Bruno Rossi was brilliant.

He had been the youngest member of Alexander Fleming's team which discovered penicillin. A professorship would be a giant stride along the path to his dream. He wanted to produce the wonder drug in powder form. Next month he was due to publish a paper.

It would revolutionize medicine for all time. Mass killers like diphtheria, meningitis and pneumonia would be wiped out by a simple injection.

'Catch pneumonia and die,' was a feared phrase from Bruno's childhood. His brother, Aldo, caught it; and died. That was when Bruno first had his dream.

It was a strange dream for the ten-year-old son of an immigrant café owner. But at Aldo's funeral Bruno made a vow. One day he would find a cure for the 'germs' that had taken away his brother. He had never forgotten the dream. Now it was threatened by war.

Aldo's death was the only scar on a childhood he remembered with affection. At times he knew he idealized it.

Bruno's parents, like thousands of their countrymen, came to Wales to escape the cruel poverty of their native Italian mountains. Most chose the mining valleys to set up their cafés and ice-cream parlours. They found no hostility. Welsh values were similar to their own, the family was venerated, so were women and music. They slipped on their adopted culture with the ease of a second skin and were accepted without question. They worked hard, put in long hours and never seemed to get into trouble.

There was not a town or village in South Wales that did not boast its own Italian café.

Alfredo, Bruno's father, used to joke: 'At home they were carpenters and cobblers. Here, suddenly, we are all chefs.'

Alfredo Rossi, Tuscan peasant, chose to open his café in the damp dockside town of Barry where terraced street above terraced street of brick houses looked down on the Bristol Channel. The menu was all chips and no pasta.

Bruno, like his brother before him, was born in the small flat above the café. But even there the everyday fare was solid British. The table creaked under the weight of roast with two veg, meat pies and suet puddings. English was also the language of the home, Italian was never spoken, unless his parents wanted to discuss things they didn't want Bruno to understand.

'Why can't I speak Italian?' Bruno would often ask.

'Because we are British now. This is where you were born so this is what you must speak. Italy is now in the past,' Alfredo replied.

And it was. Except for Sundays. Bruno Rossi loved Sundays best of all. It was the one day he could be Italian.

The café would not open and after mass they would join other Italian families for a celebration. Sometimes they would catch a train to the Rhondda Valley or Swansea. But wherever they met the day would be the same.

Lunch would last until early evening, the food was Italian, so was the wine. The women would gossip, the men reminisce over grappa and sing old songs with tears in their eyes while the children played around their feet. In English. Bruno never understood why.

His parents had never returned to Italy. The break, for them, had been clean and final.

Bruno had, thousands of times. It was easy. All he had to do was go to his room, close his eyes, and pretend. Presto.

The only thing wrong with Bruno's Italy was that everyone spoke English.

That was when Bruno first started to call on the Vacaris. Mr Vacari made ice cream in a shed in his garden and his wife gave music lessons.

'You want to learn the violin?' Mrs Vacari asked the eleven-year-old Bruno.

'No. Italian,' he replied.

Mrs Vacari made a quick calculation. When Bruno was twenty-one her daughter, Gina, would be seventeen. And Bruno showed all the signs of wanting to get ahead. He'd already won a scholarship to the County School. Everyone said he had a brilliant future – university perhaps?

Two years later Bruno was fluent. He could hold his own with the men at the Sunday gatherings. His father Alfredo pretended not to notice. His mother beamed with pride.

It was after one of these gatherings that Bruno told his mother of the vow he'd made at Aldo's funeral.

'I am going to find a cure for pneumonia. It won't bring my brother back but I'm going to do it,' he said. And he'd spoken in Italian.

She'd wept and smiled at the same time. From that time on Bruno spoke to her only in Italian. Yet when his father was present she always replied in English. Except when, years later, Bruno announced, 'I've won a state scholarship to King's College, Cambridge.'

'So you really are going to keep your promise,' she said in Italian as she smothered him with kisses.

And the paper he was to deliver on his antibiotic drug was just another step along the path to fulfilling the vow.

He looked up over the handlebars of the Brough Superior and lowered his goggles. In the distance he could see the spires of Cambridge rising out of a landscape as flat as Holland. God, how he missed the mountains. Only his work could compensate for the loss of freedom he felt without the challenge of a sheer cliff face. It didn't matter if the climb was a coastal cliff near Barry or the formidable crags of North

Wales. He ancestors were mountain men. Their blood ran thick in his veins. That day he felt in need of mountain peace. Still, the powerful motorcycle was some compensation.

Bruno eased back the throttle and let the machine have its head. As it surged forward he bent over the tank and watched the speedometer rise.

Thirty.

Fifty.

Seventy-five. Rising.

The engine screamed out for more. The countryside became a green blur as the trees seemed to suck in the fields. When Bruno threw the machine through the bends sparks flew as the footrests scraped the road.

Ninety.

Ninety-eight.

The wind scorched his face. His skin burnt as Bruno experienced a growing freedom and found it exhilarating. His blood pumped in time with the massive chrome engine beneath him.

One hundred and ten. More if he wanted it, just for the asking.

Sheer freedom.

It was almost as good as mountaineering.

Almost.

He twisted the grip as he kicked down through the box. The machine responded obediently and slowed as he crossed the River Cam. Traffic was light as he swung onto the Roman road and headed for the university city.

Ten minutes later he hauled the Brough Superior onto its stand outside King's main gate. The exhausts were still red hot. It looked out of place alongside the line of student cycles.

Bruno bounded through the gateway. It was as if he had absorbed the very energy from his bike. He had work to do.

A promise to keep.

He did not look back as he strode across the quad towards the ancient building. If he had, he would not have given a second glance to the black Humber saloon parked on the other side of the street. Or the fat man in the back seat eating thin slices of salami who noted Bruno's arrival on the pad beside him.

Bruno had disappeared past the porter's lodge by the time the man got out of the car and walked towards the college gates.

Bruno, head bowed, worked furiously on his paper. The anger had been replaced by urgency now. The casualties of war would heighten the need for penicillin. Keeping his vow was never more vital. He was sitting at his desk in front of the lattice window overlooking the cloisters.

'Sod it,' he cursed.

There was a knock on the study door. Bruno rose. He was in his early thirties, young for the position awaiting him. His hair was dark and fell unfashionably long about his ears. His Tuscan ancestry showed in his features, firm and dark. An unexpected cleft in his chin was softened by his green eyes. His accent rang of Wales, was deep baritone and reassuring to girl students who held him in awe.

Bruno made for the door. His study was small and cluttered with an arched Tudor ceiling. Books lined every wall and there was an old Chesterfield and a scruffy club chair where students sat for tutorial. He opened the door.

It was Alan Seldon.

And he'd been drinking.

The grin that greeted Bruno was from ear to ear. Seldon held up two flagons of cider, his shirt was open and hung out of his brown corduroy trousers.

'You're missing one hell of a party, old son. Even Miss Ironknickers-bloody-Watson has been at the sherry, so bring your tin-opener and let's go. C'mon.'

Bruno banged his forehead. 'I'd forgotten.'

'Brilliant.' Seldon pushed back his blond quiff. 'You forget his farewell drink and you've been tipped to get the old bugger's job.'

'A lot could happen between now and then,' Bruno said soberly. He gestured Seldon inside.

Seldon twisted his head and hunched his shoulders. He shuffled into the study with an exaggerated limp.

'Most ungracious of you as my potential successor not to pop in and say cheerio,' Seldon lisped.

Bruno laughed. It was a perfect impersonation of Professor Norman Langslow.

'But what can one expect from a Grammar School boy?' Seldon added limping to the window. 'The man is a foreigner you know, a Welsh Italian. Can't depend on them.'

'It just slipped my mind.'

Bruno rummaged through the invitation cards on his desk. It was a jumble of notes and papers. At last he found the card. He should have guessed. Langslow's party was not due to start for another hour.

He chuckled and took the flagon of cider Seldon offered. He noticed his friend had tucked in his shirt. Bruno knew he should have recognized the act the moment he'd opened the door. Seldon used it often, to great effect. He'd pretend to be drunk. This meant he could be outrageous, push social conventions to the limit and flaunt the rules. Next morning he always pleaded drunkenness and craved forgiveness.

'It's amazing what you learn about people if they think you are a harmless drunk,' Seldon once told him. But Bruno guessed there was a lot of the real Seldon in the drunk act.

The man was Bruno's closest friend. It was a friendship that had lasted more than ten years. Their backgrounds could not have been more different. Bruno, the son of an immigrant dockland café owner whose willingness to extend credit meant he'd never be rich. Seldon's father was. He ran a City of London law firm and sat on the boards of a dozen companies. They were the kind that display discreet brass plates on the doors of their offices. In the City the smaller the plate usually meant the richer the company.

Yet both men had hit it off from the day they'd met. They'd shared a love of rugby football, supporting Wales and

England respectively. Yet when it came to soccer Bruno rooted for Italy.

'It's only because the bloody Welsh can't play soccer,' Seldon often chided.

'You just can't take losing to my lot at both codes,' Bruno would reply.

The friends had even shared the same women. And they'd never had a serious argument. For Bruno knew he had Seldon's respect. It cemented their relationship. Seldon could satirize Bruno's background with impunity because Bruno knew it was done without malice.

Although Bruno could handle the jibes with aplomb now, deep down inside him they hurt. He found the motivation behind such attacks an affront on the intellect.

As a freshman it had been worse. A nightmare. Cambridge was another planet, unlike anything Bruno had ever known. His associates left him in no doubt they felt him to be an outsider with no right to be among them.

Except Seldon.

It was only later Bruno realized that Seldon had gone out of his way to be his social mentor.

'If you want me to come to your dreary little thrash then you must invite Rossi too,' Seldon always insisted, as a girl once told Bruno.

Things were different now. Bruno's work won the respect of those around him. But socially he knew the gap would never be bridged, but as long as it did not interfere with his work he didn't give a damn.

He uncorked the flagon of cider as Seldon searched for glasses. 'How the hell you ever find anything in this mess beats me,' he complained looking under the desk.

'It's like a palace. We keep pigs in the kitchen at home,' Bruno quipped, 'and we can use these. They are clean.'

He held out two cocoa mugs. One had a broken handle. Seldon took the flagon and poured.

'How do you rate my chances of getting old Langslow's post?' Bruno asked seriously.

'Should be in the bag, if you learn to knot a bow tie.'

'I've heard Maxwell's in the running.'

'The prig is a buffoon. And he's queer. Langslow loathes Nancy boys.'

'He's got a good mind.'

'But not as good as yours.'

'Maybe.' Bruno sounded genuinely unsure.

'For God's sake don't plead that scholarship waif bit. You know the moment you deliver that paper they'll be falling at your feet.' Seldon held out his arms and, still clutching the mug, bowed low. 'Hail the new wonder brain,' he wailed.

'You're right. The paper is good. Bloody good.' There was no conceit in the voice. Bruno was stating a fact.

'It had better be. If the news from Europe is as bad as they make it sound we'll all be shooting at each other by the summer term. Your drug is going to be in great demand. You can retire to the Bahamas on the loot. I could be your butler.'

'Don't make light of it.'

'No alternative, dear boy. If we didn't joke we'd all go around the bend.' Seldon's tone changed. 'It must be even more difficult for you.' He paused as Bruno shifted.

'You mean having Italian family.'

'Yes.'

Bruno sighed. Every day there was talk of rounding up foreign nationals and putting them in camps. He shuddered as he tried to imagine his father behind bars. Or Mr Vacari.

Seldon asked, 'If it came to the crunch would you fight?'

'Let's hope the situation never arises.'

'But if it did, would you?'

'Yes,' Bruno said firmly, 'I would. The Fascists must be stopped.'

'Good.' Seldon clicked his tongue thoughtfully. 'That is good to hear, Bruno.'

Bruno sank his mug of cider and moved to the window. He held out the mug and Seldon refilled it.

'Are you going to change before going to Langslow's do?' Seldon asked.

'Yes. Into an Anglo-Saxon public schoolboy. It might improve my chances.'

Both men laughed. Bruno sensed Seldon was as pleased as he was that they'd changed the subject.

'We'd better finish this and make tracks.' Bruno raised the mug.

'Nonsense,' Seldon said. 'There's another flagon. You know I can never face that lot without a few jars inside me.'

They polished off the second flagon.

'I wonder if it's true?' Bruno said as they made their way down the winding stone stairs to the cloisters. Langslow's study was on the far side of the quad.

'What's true?'

'That Ironknickers Watson is one of the perks that goes with Langslow's post.'

'If it was everyone would still be undergraduates. She's too high a price to pay for advancement.'

They entered the porter's lodge.

'Excuse me, Dr Ross . . .' coughed Shapcotte, the porter.

He does that on purpose, Bruno thought.

He said, 'Rossi. Dr Rossi. You left out the last syllable.'

Shapcotte leant out of his window. He wore a grey woollen pullover under his shiny black blazer. His grey moustache was tinged brown by cigarettes.

'There was a person asking for you, Doctor. I said you was busy and he'd 'after make an appointment. He was a foreigner.' Shapcotte rolled his tongue over the word foreigner as if it was a contagious disease.

'Was he now?' Bruno said.

'He was.'

'No need to worry, dear fellow,' Seldon said. 'He was only one of the advance guard of Hitler's fifth column.'

'A what?'

'A spy. Come to steal the boat-race plans for Hitler's navy, shouldn't wonder,' Seldon quipped.

Bruno chuckled as they crossed the quad. The cobbles were worn smooth with age. Ivy clung to the walls on all sides and covered some of the lattice windows.

'That's something you'd probably be very good at if war broke out,' Bruno said.

'What?'

'Catching spies.'

Seldon laughed wolfishly.

Soft jazz seeped from under Professor Langslow's study door. There was polite laughter and the tinkle of sherry glasses.

'Oh God,' Bruno groaned as he knocked on the door.

Seldon had already untucked his shirt. He'd put on his ear to ear grin. Bruno sensed him swaying behind him.

The door opened.

Bruno looked down on a vision from the past. He felt his knees weaken as she smiled.

'Lucia,' he smiled and reached out for the black-haired girl.

She jumped back.

'Jessica,' the girl said apprehensively. 'Jessica Mexted. I think you may have mistaken me for someone else.'

Bruno took the long white hand and shook it politely. He stepped from the darkness of the doorway into the room. He recognized his mistake at once.

The girl was beautiful, but she was no Lucia. The skin was too pale. It should have glistened like a pale olive. The eyes were dark, not black. And they didn't sparkle.

'I'm sorry,' Bruno said. 'I thought for a moment you were someone else. I'm Dr Rossi.'

'So pleased to meet you. I've heard so much about you.'

The accent wasn't soft Italian either.

'Jessica will be joining us in the autumn, won't you dear?' Miss Watson placed herself between them. She was tall and thin with stringy hair and rimless specs. She held a tray of sherry glasses.

'Do have one,' she said.

Bruno loathed sherry. Before he could refuse Seldon lifted

one from the tray, took Jessica by the arm and steered her towards the corner of the study.

'Dreadful young man,' Miss Watson's voice was high pitched, 'his manners are atrocious, always prying. It's very rude. Sweet or dry?'

'I'd prefer something else,' Bruno said.

'If you must. The punch is over there.'

Bruno made for the table. It was covered with a white tablecloth. There were plates of thin sandwiches with the crusts cut off, small cubes of cheese and pineapple, cocktail biscuits and a celery dip.

Bruno ladled himself a glass of punch. It looked like a purple fruit salad and tasted of sherry.

'Most gracious of you as my potential successor to pop in and say cheerio.' Professor Langslow limped towards him. He looked like a hunchback heron.

Inwardly Bruno chuckled.

'Must say I think you are just the fellow for the job,' the professor added.

'That's very kind of you.'

'Not at all. You can count on my support all the way. If – when, I mean – you are appointed, what are your priorities going to be?'

'Penicillin,' Bruno replied simply. 'Given time I want to make it as common as aspirin.'

'Do that, dear chap, and they'll give you a knighthood.'

I just want to keep a promise, Bruno thought.

He said, 'I wouldn't regard that as important.'

'Good heavens,' Langslow sounded shocked. 'Every Englishman would jump at such an honour. If you know what I mean.'

Bruno did.

'I hear young Howard Florey is working along the same lines as you. He's making remarkable progress, so they say,' Langslow continued. 'Let's hope he doesn't pip you at the post.' He chuckled.

That was a put down, Bruno thought.

'We must have a longer chat later. Must circulate, you know. Help yourself to more punch.' He limped off.

The study was beginning to fill as more guests arrived. The staff held court in small groups of nodding students. The wives formed their own circles.

Bruno could see his rival, Maxwell, at the far end of the room. He was a round, red-faced man and wore a pink bow tie with black spots. Two languid young men listened to him adoringly.

Bruno saw that Langslow avoided the group. It was a good sign. He looked for Seldon. He was with Jessica in the corner going through his witty drunk routine. Jessica loved it.

God, the girl did remind him of Lucia. The thought made his mood sag.

He'd first met her at a party in London. Lucia Corso was the most beautiful creature he'd ever set eyes on. She was doing a year's medical research at Guy's Hospital. She had not been allowed to complete it.

Bruno felt a knot of anger. He would have married the girl, but she'd gone. He'd been too late.

For Lucia Corso was Italian.

At first Bruno thought her a shy girl, quiet, with a way of lowering her eyes that drove him to distraction. He soon learned she had a strength of spirit that was wild and free.

That first night he'd expected her to say no when he asked her to leave the party with him.

'Just go? Why not?' she'd said.

'Good. There's something I want to show you.'

'What?'

'Mountains.'

It was nine thirty that August evening when the Brough Superior roared out of London. Bruno still remembered the way she held him around the waist, skirt billowing and squealing with a mixture of fright and sheer delight.

They saw the day break in the mountains of Snowdonia in North Wales. They bought breakfast from a farm and cooked it over an open fire.

From then on they spent all their free time together in the mountains. They had both inherited their forefathers' feel for the rugged isolation. Problems shrank into perspective when seen against the scale of the mountains.

When Bruno had tried to make love to her she'd refused. He understood and she respected him for it. Yet all the time he ached for her. And she him.

Yet she could not. She never told him why. Content to wait, he did not press her. He thought the time would come and when it did the wait would have been worth it.

But it did not come. In that October of 1938 Mussolini annexed Libya and brought down Bruno Rossi's world.

The British reacted by expelling Italian nationals. Among them was Lucia Corso.

'Marry me,' Bruno said, 'then we could stay together.'

She said no. She would not risk the career that meant so much to him. He'd told her of his dream.

'I would be an impediment for you,' she'd said.

He rode to London to get her to change her mind.

She'd gone.

Bruno wrote to the Rome address she'd given him. The letters were returned 'not known'.

He'd lost her. All other efforts to trace her failed. It was as if she did not want to be found.

Bruno was jolted back to the present by Seldon's dig on the arm.

'Jessica wants to thank you,' Seldon said. 'I've told her she'd never have met me if it hadn't been for you.'

Bruno could have cursed him. He felt himself colour. What the hell was Seldon playing at? He knew they'd agreed never to discuss it. It embarrassed him.

'I thought that was taboo.' There was a defensive edge to Bruno's voice as he raised it.

'Nonsense. I wouldn't be here without you.'

If this was part of Seldon's act then he was overdoing it, thought Bruno. Perhaps he was drunk.

'Cut it out, Seldon,' Bruno said through his teeth.

'You're too modest, isn't that right, Jessica?'

'I said cut it out.' Bruno was angry as Seldon waved him aside. As he climbed onto a chair and called for attention Bruno headed for the door. He was seething.

'Listen everybody. I'm going to tell you why your new professor, Bruno Rossi, is a bloody hero.'

The words echoed in Bruno's ears as he closed the study door behind him.

Bruno had cooled down. He killed the Brough's engine and ambled into King's. It was dark and there was a chill in the air.

Earlier he'd ridden into the country, found a pub and had a few halves of bitter and a pork pie. He'd played a game of darts with a farm hand and won.

He reasoned Seldon must have been drunk. He could think of no other reason he'd have brought up that hero nonsense. He realized he had overreacted. Perhaps thoughts of Lucia had sparked him off. He'd be expected to apologize, and he would.

A light burnt faintly in the porter's lodge. There was no sign of Shapcotte.

Bruno took the winding stone stairway to his study. He fumbled for the keys. He could never remember in which pocket he'd put them.

He stopped dead.

His study door was ajar.

He pushed it open with his foot. The iron hinges creaked with age as the door slowly opened.

Bruno hesitated, waiting for a response from inside. None came. The room was pitch black. Someone had drawn the curtains. He'd left them open.

Cautiously he moved forward, uncertainty in every step. His hand felt the wall for the light switch. Then he stopped.

He saw the red glow from the tip of a lighted cigarette. Someone was sitting in his club chair. Waiting.

Bruno hit the switch.

The man was fat. He sat motionless, the cigarette hanging from his full lips. The ashtray on the wine table beside him was full. Next to it sat a sheet of greaseproof paper. On it were thin slices of salami. Still the fat man said nothing. Just stared as he drew on the cigarette. His paunch rose and fell in rhythm.

Bruno's mind raced. Physically the man did not present a problem, a glance around the study showed nothing had been touched, yet the full ashtray indicated that the wait had been a long one.

Bruno moved to the centre of the room. The man's eyes followed.

'Who the hell are you and what in God's name do you think you're playing at?' The tone was slow and firm. 'Get up.'

The man leant forward and pressed his hands on the arms of the chair to raise himself. Bruno noticed his bald spot. He was short with wild frizzy hair, his lightweight suit, though expensive, fitted badly. The baggy trousers folded in creases at the ankle, too long for his stubby legs. The man's eyes darted now, avoiding Bruno's fixed stare. His nostrils flared, whether with malice or nervousness Bruno was not sure.

'My name is Verdi. Enzo Verdi. Forgive the intrusion, Dottore.' He fished into his top pocket. 'My card.' He spoke in Italian.

Bruno took it. Verdi was simply a 'businessman'. He had two addresses, one in Rome, the other in London.

'This tells me nothing.' Bruno replied in the same language.

Verdi half smiled. 'It's suitably vague. You could say I'm a kind of broker, I fix things.' He indicated the chair. 'May I?'

He sat before Bruno could reply. Bruno's eyes flashed with anger. He pointed to the door.

'Out. Before I throw you out.'

To his amazement Verdi raised his hand to quell him. 'I think you should hear what I have to say first. I have a proposition to put to you.'

He spoke with a rapid Roman accent. It filled Bruno with mistrust, as it would his peasant ancestors.

'I said out.' Bruno fought not to shout. Inwardly he fumed.

'How much do you earn, Dottore?'

Bruno was dumbstruck.

'Eight hundred a year? I can increase it fourfold. Maybe more.'

A commercial pimp, Bruno thought. A talent poacher. He felt contempt and it must have showed. Verdi's expression changed. He shrugged.

'I did not mean to insult you, Dottore. I apologize.'

'Just what the hell do you want?' Bruno moved to the chair and leant forward. He smelt the salami on Verdi's breath.

'You.'

Bruno straightened.

'In return I can offer you a research team of your own choice with unlimited facilities at the University of Bologna. Money, of course, will be no object. Appealing, no?'

Bruno was thrown. Bologna. The oldest university in Europe with standards on a par with Cambridge.

'Who sent you?'

Verdi shrugged. 'It's not important at this stage. Let's just say every facility at Bologna would be at your disposal.'

'I already have that here.'

'But for how long?'

'What the hell are you driving at?' Bruno said angrily.

'If things go on as they are in Europe then people with your background are going to feel the backlash. In Italy we look after our own.'

'I was born here.'

'An accident of birth. Italy has need of your services.'

'You mean Mussolini needs penicillin?' There was contempt in Bruno's voice. 'And I work for science, not flag-waving mobs.'

Verdi hunched forward and clenched his hands between his knees. He sucked his cheeks thoughtfully. 'We would respect your wish to carry on your research in that field but it is not what we had in mind. There is another project bigger, far bigger, than anything even you could imagine, Dottore. Far bigger.'

'Rubbish.' Bruno felt insulted. 'I think you had bettter leave before I do something I'd regret.'

Verdi hauled himself to his feet. He postured absurdly as he made for the door. 'You will be in touch with me. Perhaps sooner than you think.'

He left the door open. Bruno slammed it shut. Verdi had left an unpleasant feel to the study and Bruno was aware of the mistrust the man's rapid Roman accent had aroused when he'd first spoken.

Bruno realized his forefathers would have felt it when a landlord or tax collector visited the village.

Verdi bore the menace of officialdom.

Bruno felt suddenly threatened.

'Ah, Seldon. How nice of you to pop down from Cambridge to see us.' Dolman rose from behind the oak desk. Not a steel-grey hair was out of place. He looked fit and tanned, much younger than his sixty years.

Seldon shook the firm hand. 'You did say it was rather urgent, sir.'

'Everything is at SIS these days. Please sit down.'

Seldon sat. He looked expectantly at his control officer. They were in Dolman's first-floor office in the Special Intelligence Service overlooking St James's Park.

'How long have you been with us now, Seldon?'

'Almost five years, sir.' Seldon wondered if he'd done anything wrong. He was never called to London. His job was to be the Service's political eyes and ears at Cambridge. The thinking at Cambridge influenced government. SIS wanted to know what the government would think before it thought it. Seldon told them.

'Your report on young Anthony Blunt and his chums, the Apostles, has ruffled a few feathers over at MI5,' Dolman said. 'They seem to think they are quite harmless. A bunch of well-meaning idealists.'

'They are communists, dedicated and dangerous,' Seldon said quietly with conviction.

'I'm with you all the way,' Dolman said, 'but then I didn't go to Eton.'

Seldon felt relieved. It was short-lived.

'Now what about this chap Rossi, the one that's up for a professorship?'

Seldon's stomach churned. 'The man is above reproach. He is not a political animal but he has a healthy loathing of Fascism. He is a close friend and I can vouch for him personally. He has my one hundred per cent trust.'

'But you did feel it necessary to send us details of his foreign visitor and the car he drove?'

'I saw it as part of my duty, sir. I did not intend it to be taken as any reflection on Dr Rossi,' Seldon said defensively. It was still the same xenophobia. When would they ever learn?

'Good.' Dolman paused. 'The car is registered to the Italian embassy. The visitor's name is Enzo Verdi. His cover is businessman with an address in Covent Garden. He is a member of the OVRA, Mussolini's secret police. We have had an intercept put on his telephone and mail.' Dolman chuckled. 'The man has an enormous sexual appetite.'

Seldon found nothing to laugh at. Why the hell hadn't Bruno told him?

He said, 'I'd still stake my job that Rossi's clean. I know the man like a brother. He'd never chance anything that would risk his career at Cambridge. He is the most dedicated person I know. He lives for his work. The man is almost married to the damn place. Nothing would prise him from his research. Nothing.'

'Oh, I know all that,' Dolman said. 'And that is part of the problem.'

'Sorry?' Seldon did not understand.

'Since we put on the intercept we've learned Verdi tried

to entice your friend Rossi to go to Bologna University. They are prepared to offer him anything he wants. They want him badly. The thing is, Rossi has turned him down. Gave him a flea in the ear by all accounts. Verdi's chums in Rome are none too pleased.'

'End of problem.' Seldon felt he could breathe easily again. Until he saw Dolman shake his head.

'Wrong. We want him to go as badly as they do.'

'Utter madness.' Seldon could not contain himself. 'Rossi is one of the best medical brains in Europe – the world. We need him for what he is about to do with penicillin. It could save us hundreds of thousands of lives on the battlefield.'

Dolman checked a file on the desk. 'It seems Rossi is not alone in the penicillin field. A Professor . . . let me see. Florey. Howard Florey is working along the same lines. We are way ahead of the rest of the world without Rossi. He is dispensable.'

'That sounds sinister,' Seldon said. 'The man is brilliant.'

'Maybe so. But we want him in Bologna.'

This was total madness. Insane.

Then Dolman said, 'I do not ask lightly what I want you to do.'

Seldon eyed his superior with a sense of dread.

Dolman spoke slowly. 'I want you to get Bruno Rossi drummed out of Cambridge, branded as a Fascist and a traitor. He will not, and must not, be made a professor under any circumstances. I want the stink associated with his name so strong that he will never find another job in this country. He will go to Bologna because no one else will touch him with a bargepole.

'You will have a free hand. You will be above the law. If you have to break it, break it. You will hound the man out of his wits. Hit him where it hurts, his family if necessary. I want you to break him. I want him to end up hating your guts, this country's guts. His hate for us all must be such that he runs. Blindly. To Bologna. I want him running and I want him scared. Finish him.'

Seldon was on his feet. This was more than insane. It was evil.

'No,' he yelled at the top of his voice. 'I will not do this.'

'There is no choice.' Dolman's expression was grave. 'Wait here.'

Seldon watched him walk to the door. His contempt was turning to hate. 'For Christ's sake, don't you understand? I cannot do this to this man. Not to him.'

Dolman eyed him sadly. 'Just wait.'

Seldon slumped back into the chair as the door closed. He slammed his fist down on the desk.

He would rather cut off his own arm than do this to Bruno Rossi. The man was more than just his friend. He owed him his life.

Seldon could still feel the swing of the rope. He could see the details of the rock face as it flashed before his eyes. Then, at that moment, he had known he was done for. On that crag, high in the mountains of Wales.

The crag was called Rhiw o' Farw, the Ridge of Death. For Seldon it almost was.

Bruno led the climb. He was experienced and good – a natural. Seldon was raw and afraid. His reluctance to try the climb was overcome by Bruno's persuasiveness.

'It can be like making love to the most beautiful woman in the world,' Bruno said.

They were almost at the summit when Seldon fell. He had swung to and fro into the abyss like a pendulum. Below he could see the jagged boulders and certain death.

Above him he saw the rope that held him to Bruno had twisted around an outcrop. With every swing of the pendulum Seldon saw fragments and strands fray. When it severed he would fall to his death.

He watched helplessly as Bruno came back down the face. He came slowly, inch by inch. Just as Seldon saw Bruno take the rope below the outcrop it snapped.

Seldon dropped sickeningly for an instant then jerked to a halt. The rope burnt into his waist as he dangled in the void.

Bruno had held him. Seldon felt the pendulum action begin again. Bruno, face straining, swung him towards a narrow ledge. On the first attempt to reach it Seldon hit the face. He felt his ribs snap.

The third attempt made it. He was on the ledge. He could not move because of the pain.

'Just lie still and trust me,' Bruno yelled. In minutes he was on the summit. Ahead of him lay some of the wildest terrain in Britain. It was desolate and uninhabited. Bruno began his walk as the night gathered.

Seldon did not know how long it had taken. He blacked out with pain.

When he came to, Bruno was beside him on the ledge. A rescue stretcher was strapped to his back.

Above them Seldon heard voices. They were speaking Welsh. Bruno strapped Seldon into the stretcher and launched them both from the ledge. Seldon blacked out again.

He came to in hospital in Bangor.

'I almost killed you,' Bruno told him. 'I should not have persuaded you to go. I was stupid to do so.'

'You saved my life,' Seldon replied.

'Then we are even. We'll never tell a soul.'

But Seldon had. At Langslow's party.

He knew there were people there who sneered at Bruno. They thought he had neither the character nor background for the professorship.

Seldon put them right.

Now he was being asked, ordered, to ruin Bruno. Make him flee to Bologna.

He would disobey.

He looked up and saw Dolman had returned. He carried a file.

'Read this,' he said quietly. 'We have received the photographs it contains from a man called Fulgoni. He is one of the wealthiest men in Italy. He also hates Mussolini's guts. Fulgoni has already begun to organize partisan cells to form a resistance movement when the time comes. We are going to help.'

Seldon took the file.

'When you have read it you will understand why you must do what I ask. Must. There is no choice. This is what they are doing at Bologna.'

Seldon looked at the photographs. He winced. The horror was appalling.

'Read on,' Dolman said.

Seldon did.

He began to shake as the colour drained from his face. Surely no human being could plan a scheme like this? Nothing could be more evil, not even in the annals of hell. Seldon fought for breath as his throat tightened. The stench seemed to leap off the pages at him. He let the file fall. He could read no more.

'Now do you see?' Dolman spoke in no more than a whisper.

Seldon could only nod dumbly.

'Bruno Rossi must be our man on the inside. But he must never know that, until the time comes when we are ready to destroy this obscenity. They will not be able to break his cover because he will not have one to break. He will be in the field blind. He will be what they think he is. There is no other choice. Not if the human race as we know it is to survive.' Dolman walked to the window. 'Well?'

'As you say, we have no choice,' Seldon mumbled. 'May God forgive me.'

'He will,' Dolman said.

Seldon walked to the door.

Bruno Rossi's world was about to come crashing around him.

CHAPTER TWO

Lucia Corso dreamt of the mountains of Tuscany. The air was cool, cypress trees and vines clung to the hillside, constantly changing in the limpid light.

From the hilltop she could see a cloud of dust moving along the road in the valley below. It shimmered like a mirage. Then she heard the song of the motorbike's engine, like a distant bee.

Lucia kicked off her sandals, gathered up her skirt and ran towards the road. The grass felt soft under her feet. The drone of the bike grew louder. She paused for breath, cupped her hands to her mouth and called his name.

'Bruno.'

The echo rang through the valley.

She reached the road, its warm dust felt like sand. Lucia never wanted to leave this place. She, they, would stay forever. Lucia waved her arms and ran headlong.

The bike neared. She could see him clearly in the saddle, the sun glinted on his goggles. There was so much she wanted to explain. Nothing would part them now.

All days would be like this.

She looked up to the red-roofed villa at the head of the valley. There were orange and lemon trees, all in neat rows. That's where they would live. There was a charcoal oven on the patio. After dinner they would walk the mountains.

The bike was getting closer, flashing its headlights.

In winter they'd burn logs and ski to the village. There was an inn where old men sat and talked. It would be a good place to grow old. Together. Above her a lone goat bleated.

And all days would be like this.

Then the stranger at her side began to snore.

Lucia slowly opened her eyes. She felt terrible, her mouth

was dry and her head throbbed. The silk sheet felt soft under her skin.

She realized with horror that this was not her bed.

Lucia lay still, not daring to move. The sound of breathing next to her grew. So did her sense of dread. She closed her eyes and bit her lip.

She tried to remember where she was, how she'd got there. She remembered a trattoria, strange faces and strange tastes in her mouth. She sucked her tongue. It still stung. But nothing more.

The stranger turned over, drawing the sheet from Lucia. She opened her eyes and glanced sideways. A wave of revulsion swept her.

He was in his fifties, fat and totally bald with a head like a melon. She moved cautiously to the edge of the bed, then peered around the room.

It seemed larger than it was. The twin bedside tables were woven cane. They matched the high-sided chairs. There was an art nouveau bedside lamp of pink glass and a crystal chandelier hung from the ornate ceiling. A large Renaissance tapestry of a hunting scene covered one wall. A blond wig stood on its stand in front of the mirror, angled to give a full view of the bed.

Louvre doors opened in from the balcony.

Lucia carefully set her feet on the floor. The terrazzo felt cool. She stepped over the empty bottles of Spumanti and tiptoed to the balcony.

The garden was enclosed by a mellow sandstone wall covered with vines. Gravel paths wove among statuettes and small fountains. It was an oasis of ornamental shrubs. There was no garden gate.

Lucia had to get out. She slipped back into the room. Her dress lay in a heap on the floor. Quickly she put it on, then her pants and sandals. She snatched up her bag from a chair and stole onto the landing.

Her head swam and she felt she was going to be sick. For a moment she saw double. She shook her head clear.

A large curved staircase swept down to the high entrance hall; and a door. The house was still, except for the tick of a grandfather clock at the foot of the stairs.

Lucia drew a deep breath and ran.

Seconds later she was on the street.

The Strada Maggiore, Bologna's wide avenue of crenellated mansions. The rich merchants who built them after the time of Leonardo modestly called them mansions. Homes fit for the kings of commerce and art.

She glanced back at the house. God knows how she got there. The revulsion returned. She ran, blindly.

Her long legs stretched out along the pavement. It was compacted earth, hard and dusty. Kerbside palms grew fat like giant pineapples.

It must be Sunday, Lucia thought.

Families were strolling in the sun after mass. They parted as she ran headlong. Her dress, damp now, clung tightly to her lithe body. She began to cry. People stared.

They think I'm mad. Mad, she thought.

She stumbled into the cobbled Piazza di Porta Ravegna and almost collided with an ice-cream cart drawn by a large dog.

'You're crazy,' the owner yelled after her.

Lucia, exhausted, reached the steps of San Petronio's basilica. Her breathing was ragged. She looked up at the cathedral, hesitated, then turned away in desolation.

She realized no priest could help.

Lucia leant on the rim of a fountain in the centre of the ancient square. The centrepiece was Neptune, the sea god. Trident in hand, he stood astride four sirens, water gushing from their breasts. The spray was cool and she was grateful.

Suddenly she yearned for the peace of the sea. She thought of the times she'd spent on the Adriatic, the Valli Comacchio where fishermen net eels at dawn and dusk.

She was sane then.

Lucia looked at her reflection in the fountain. She saw a stranger.

The face in the water was twenty-three years old. The ripples moved over the high cheek bones and her hand brushed back a strand of long black hair from the corner of the full mouth. She looked into the eyes and saw only torment.

Then the face on the water began to change. The reflection became her mother's.

She remembered the last time she'd seen her. The torment on her face as the male nurses carried her struggling to the waiting ambulance.

Lucia gripped the fountain's rim as she heard her mother's screams. She breathed in and smelt the drink on her father's breath. It was as if he had left the grave and was standing next to her on the piazza.

Pawing her. Touching her. Stroking her.

Her mother's child.

No man had touched her since. She needed time.

Then she thought of the snoring stranger.

She tried vainly to remember. But there was nothing. Only the foul taste in her mouth remained.

Perhaps THEY were right.

She was going mad. Losing her sanity. Just like her mother.

She lifted her face to the fountain. The water felt cool as it ran over her skin and spread through her hair, sweeping it back over her shoulders. The droplets tingled as they ran down her neck.

I'm not mad. I'm not mad. She forced the words into her mind.

But THEY were convinced she was. That's why they pumped her with the injections. Lucia clasped her arm and felt the needle pricks.

But I'm not like my mother, she told herself. I'm not.

Yet no one would believe her.

Then she remembered why.

She alone knew what they were doing.

'I'm not mad,' she shouted at the top of her voice.

Heads turned. Lucia saw the looks of amazement on their faces, suspicious smiles – pity.

Lucia laughed loudly. 'I'm sane,' she yelled.

Then she turned and ran.

Tears began to fall down her cheeks.

Lucia shut the door of her rented room. She pressed her back against it and closed her eyes. Drops of water fell onto her shoulders from her wet hair. They seemed to soothe away her last doubts.

Finally she whispered, 'I'm not insane.' Her words were soft and confident. She repeated them reassuringly. Her confidence grew. She opened her eyes, kicked off her sandals, unhooked her dress and stepped out of it.

The room was small and sparse. An unmade bed sat under the only window, there was an old wardrobe and a gas ring next to a sink with one brass tap. Above it hung a crucifix, books were piled on a small table, dozens more were stacked on the floor. It was just like any other room in a city of students.

Lucia went to the sink and washed her face. The soap was scented. It smelt of pine, she noted with satisfaction. Her senses were returning. She began to feel in control again.

There would be no more visits to the pyschiatrists, she vowed. No more injections. Never again. Never.

The visits had begun two weeks after she'd found the photographs. She found them in her professor's desk. Professor Pini was head of the Department of Tropical Medicine.

The photographs were the most horrific she had ever seen. That was when Lucia's nightmares began. Then the crazed images started to come to her when she was awake. There was no respite, asleep or not, she could not rid her mind of the horror.

Repulsive.

The photographs did not represent medicine.

That was not research.

It was genocide.

No wonder the doctors thought her mad.

She'd told Maria Balbo. And Maria was dead.

Lucia also told Rosa Mori. Two days later Rosa left Bologna never to return.

Now she alone knew Pini's secret.

Pini, one of the most powerful and respected academics in the whole of Italy. Who would take her word against his? The word of a girl everyone thought mad.

No one.

Except the man she'd been forced to leave.

Bruno Rossi.

She knew he had written but she returned the letters unopened. That hurt her. Yet she felt she could still not risk the career that meant so much to him. And ruin his dream, the dream he had spoken to her about so passionately.

But things were different now. The obscenity of the photographs made it so.

Yet war loomed. When Mussolini joined Hitler where would Bruno's loyalty lie? she wondered. The land of his father or the land of his birth.

She prayed neither. This horror was above such things. It was too great, too terrible, for such considerations. He would have to help. There was no one else.

Lucia turned for the bed, removed her damp pants and lay on the unmade sheet. The window above her was open but the shutters were drawn, their pattern covered her with shadows. She thought of the letter she must write.

She moved onto her side, hand supporting her head. On the chair next to the bed she saw a bottle of mineral water, glass upturned over the neck. She didn't remember putting it there. But there had been a lot of things she'd failed to remember recently.

Lucia took pad and paper, the pen hovered uncertainly. Would he think she was mad?

She poured a glass of *minerale* and took a sip. Her tongue stung slightly, she gulped the glass and put it aside.

How could she begin?

She crossed out the first attempts. It was difficult. On paper the whole thing sounded so crazy. The ramblings of a mad woman. Her mouth dried.

She poured more *minerale*. It was bitter. Her mouth burnt.

Her head began to swim.

Just as it had at the Trattoria Luigi the night before. Now she remembered.

She felt the tears well as she saw herself walk into the trattoria. She had sat alone, unable to stop crying.

A hand closed on her shoulder. She looked up and saw Professor Pini. He took her to join his friends. He gave her wine. It tasted bitter, stung her tongue. Just like the *minerale*.

Then she remembered the villa on the Strada Maggiore. Pini had gone. But not his friends.

They made her dance for them, clapping, drooling. There was loud American music. Jazz. She was passed from one lap to the other, hands explored her, strange tongues were in her mouth.

Then they made her dance for them again. Like a marionette. Everyone laughed at her.

Lucia rose from the bed and ran for the sink. She was sick. The room began to turn. She stumbled for a chair and sat in front of the table. She sat motionless for several minutes. Linnets sang in a cage outside the window. They helped steady her.

At last she picked up the pen and willed herself to write. The hand was a spidery scrawl, almost that of a child.

She began 'Bruno, please understand. As I write this I feel my sanity slipping away . . .'

She wrote feverishly, the nib of the fountain pen scratching, blotting the paper as her writing became larger. Words merged becoming barely legible.

Then she was done. Without reading what she'd written Lucia put the letter in an envelope, addressed and sealed it. She addressed it to his home.

There was a knock on the door.

'Telephone, Signorina Lucia.'

It was her landlady, a round Sicilian widow, Signora Bellini.

Lucia stumbled to the door. She grabbed her raincoat from the hook and put it on.

As she opened the door Lucia reeled backwards. She felt the old Sicilian reach out and steady her.

'Are you all right?'

Lucia nodded.

'Please take this. Post it for me. Please promise.' Lucia thrust the letter into her hand. 'Promise.'

'Of course, my child. You should lie down.' She tried to lead Lucia to the bed.

Lucia shrugged free.

'The phone,' she mumbled. She began to sway. She pointed unsteadily at the bottle of *minerale*. 'Please take that away.' Then she shouted, 'Get it out of here. It's poison.'

'*Si.*' The old woman sounded puzzled. She picked up the bottle and followed Lucia from the room.

The pay phone was in the hall.

Lucia drew the raincoat tight and picked up the receiver, holding onto the coin box for support.

'Lucia?' a woman's voice asked. It was faint and distant.

The girl nodded dumbly.

'Lucia?'

'*Si*,' she mumbled. The wall seemed to be spinning.

'This is your mother.' The voice laughed.

Lucia dropped the phone. The receiver swung on its cord, laughter echoing hollowly from the mouthpiece.

'You're DEAD,' Lucia screamed. 'DEAD. DEAD. DEAD.'

Lucia let the raincoat fall and ran to her room. The rag doll she'd kept from childhood was on her bed. It was a tattered thing in a blue dress with blonde plaits. She grabbed it and held it to her breasts as if to shield it from the walls of the room. They seemed to be closing in to crush them.

Lucia screamed.

Signora Bellini was in the doorway.

Lucia's eyes darted defensively, her hair was tousled. She backed past the Sicilian.

'My baby is not going to be like her mother,' she mumbled. 'And no one is going to take her away. No one.'

The naked girl ducked as the woman reached out for her. Tiny drops of perspiration flecked her skin, her shoulders heaved as she paused at the open front door.

Then she was in the street, rocking the doll in her arms. The street was narrow with no pavement. Plaster peeled from the walls of the medieval houses.

A small group of nuns emerged from a courtyard gate.

'Don't you stare at me,' Lucia yelled.

They stepped back as one. Lucia felt fingers, plump and hot on her shoulder. Signora Bellini was panting.

'My child,' she said softly.

Lucia raised an arm as if to fend off a blow and ran.

The narrow streets were empty. Through the gaps in the houses Lucia could see the turrets and the city towers and campaniles. They oppressed her. She yearned for the mountains. She would be safe there. She ran on, faster. In the back streets of Bologna she could smell the mountain air, fresh, clean, scented.

The smell changed to roasting coffee. It came from the crowded pavement cafés. Lucia was unaware of the astonished faces as she stumbled between the tables.

A woman screamed as Lucia lurched towards the tram rails which ran down the centre of the Via Ugo Basi.

It was then she dropped the doll. It flew from her grasp as the tram bore down on her. Lucia dived after it.

The tram's brass rail caught her on the thigh and threw her sideways. Blurred faces gawped at her from the tram windows as it flashed past. She remembered sparks from the metal wheels as the driver hit the brakes. The sparks seemed to set her skin on fire. Then she realized she was skidding across the cobbled street on her back.

The pain left her. She thought of the doll and began to crawl blindly, calling its name.

'Angelina. Angelina.'

Her fingers closed around the doll's plaits. She smiled.

She smelt the mountains.

But then came the bitter taste of the *minerale* in her mouth. It mixed with blood.

Her head spun. Boots pounded towards her.

Then nothing.

The two men looked down at the problem in the hospital bed. Lucia was unconscious, her left eye bruised and top lip swollen. Her legs and arms were swathed in bandages.

'It's a pity she didn't kill herself,' Professor Pini said. 'It would have been easier all round. I thought she might have tried after all the medication we have pumped into her.'

The big man at his side drew hard on a cigarette. He wore the uniform of the OVRA, Mussolini's security service. The gold insignia denoted the rank of colonel.

'Drugs,' the colonel snorted. 'My people find castor oil more effective. Pour it down their throats and they shit themselves until they die of dehydration.'

'At least we have had her certified insane. She won't walk the streets again for a long time.'

'How much does she know about the project?' The colonel's brow furrowed.

'Enough to make life difficult.'

'And the others?'

'One girl is dead. The other is where she can do no harm.'

The colonel reached out, held Lucia's chin and turned her head. He would have liked to have simply thrown her out of the window, or under another tram, and have done with it.

But there was a problem. That's why he'd taken charge.

To have faked the girl's suicide seemed the answer. They'd convinced the world she was mad. She was an orphan, brought up in a convent, so there was no family or relations to worry about.

Then the colonel's minions had checked the girl's bank account. She was wealthier than any research student should have been. Every month someone paid a sizeable draft into her account. They failed to trace who. That someone had also paid for the girl to go through university. The bank refused to give details. That meant whoever paid the draft was powerful.

And the girl never touched the money. She existed on the paltry sum the university paid her.

One reason for the colonel's rapid rise in OVRA was that he never made a move until he knew every strength and weakness of his opponents. He never dealt with unknowns.

And somewhere, Lucia Corso had an ally, rich, therefore powerful, but worst of all anonymous.

The colonel removed his hand. 'I can't risk killing her at this stage,' he said.

'That leaves one alternative,' Pini said.

'Do it. The Alpine air will do her good.'

A look of terror flitted across Pini's face.

It passed and he found a weak smile.

CHAPTER THREE

Bruno's paper earned him a standing ovation. He felt desolate.

Maxwell had been given the professorship over his head. Langslow had told him over the sherry. Bruno felt as if his throat had been cut.

After the rapture his paper received Bruno thought it was in the bag. The audience had stampeded to grab copies of the paper from the table at the back of the packed hall before he'd sat down. Even Professor Howard Florey had grabbed him warmly by the hand in congratulation.

'Brilliant, just brilliant,' he'd enthused.

But Ferguson, the college Dean, had not joined the applause. Neither had his assistant, Abernathy.

They had glowered darkly.

That was when Bruno first suspected that something was wrong.

'I'm afraid the matter is out of my hands, old chap. You were my choice of course,' Langslow said.

'But why?' Bruno was flabbergasted.

Langslow would not look him in the eye. 'I'm sorry but it is entirely out of my hands.' Then he said, 'I think the whole thing is disgraceful, quite disgraceful.'

Then he limped off.

Bruno thought that there must be some mistake. People were crowding around him. They jostled to shake his hand and pat him on the back.

'Magnificent paper.'

'It was a sensation.'

'Marvellous.'

The plaudits rang hollowly in his ears. He didn't want praise and empty congratulations.

He wanted the professorship. The chance to put his theories to the test. The chance to keep his vow.

Bruno elbowed his way to the far side of the hall.

Ferguson and Abernathy glared at him.

Unsmiling. Hostile.

'I would like to speak to you in private,' Bruno told Ferguson.

The Dean looked uncomfortable, shifting his weight from leg to leg and toying with his sherry glass.

It was his assistant, Abernathy, who replied.

'We would also like to speak with you.' He spoke with a low Scottish accent. 'But I hardly think this is the time or place.'

'I do,' Bruno spoke with determination. 'I think I'm owed an explanation.'

'An explanation?' Abernathy's voice rose incredulously. 'I think it is you who owes us an explanation.'

'What?' Bruno gritted his teeth. This was an insult.

'What the assistant Dean means, Dr Rossi, is that you will be able to put your case at the appropriate time and place. I think you . . .'

'Case? You make it sound as if I am on trial.'

'Be that as it may. Before you interrupted I was going to say that King's has decided to hold a special college court. Certain allegations have been made against you. This is not the place to discuss them. Good day.'

They turned their backs and walked away.

'A college court,' Bruno mumbled.

It was a modern Star Chamber responsible to nothing except itself. Its power was absolute. It could break a man. Ruin him. There was no appeal.

Bruno stormed from the hall.

There was no sign of Seldon.

Bruno sat alone in the bar of the White Hart. It was their local pub. The Dean's words echoed in his mind. They mystified him. And frightened him.

What accusations? He had done nothing to merit this. Unless presenting a paper that would change medicine was a crime. He lifted his beer, realized he was shaking and put the glass down.

The pub was beginning to fill. Students in striped blazers thronged around the bar like a row of deckchairs. Their laughter and banter made him feel even more alone. He thought one or two stole quick glances, then looked hurriedly away.

'It's my imagination.'

But he knew it was not.

They were talking in whispers. About him.

Then he saw Seldon.

Thank God for that. He was beginning to feel as if he had two heads.

'Seldon. Over here.'

Seldon responded with an unsmiling nod. He placed his beer mug on top of the piano before coming over to Bruno's table.

Bruno sensed his friend's hostility. It threw him.

'I didn't get Langslow's job,' he said quietly.

'If you're looking for sympathy from me then forget it. Your kind deserve everything they get.'

Bruno leapt to his feet. He was still wearing his academic gown over a tweed sports coat and twills. Seldon, the taller, thinner man, wore open shirt and slacks. White faced, Bruno began to shake in anger. Heads turned at the bar and conversation hushed.

Seldon spun on his heels, Bruno grabbed him by the elbow and pulled him back.

'Sit down, Alan,' he said deeply, 'and for Christ's sake please tell me what the hell is going on.' Seldon's blue eyes bored contemptuously into his own. Never had Bruno experienced such loathing. He released his grip and slumped back to his chair.

Seldon placed his hands on the table and pushed his face close to Bruno's.

'In future I'd prefer it if you kept well out of my way.' He clenched his teeth as he spoke.

Bruno banged the table. 'This can't be happening.'

'It's a little late in the day for all this feigned innocence, old chum. You've been bloody rumbled. I must have been a complete idiot not to have spotted it sooner.'

Bruno threw his hands into the air. It was like a bad dream. 'Spotted what?' He clenched his fingers with frustration.

'You should have been on the stage. But I suppose that little art is a prime requisite for your kind.' Seldon stood back.

Bruno was dumbfounded.

'In future I shall have to be more careful of the company I keep. It's a piece of advice you should have followed.' Seldon turned away, then added, 'If there is anything more I can do to help bury you and your kind, don't hesitate to ask. It'll be a pleasure as well as a duty.'

Seldon made straight for the door and was gone.

Bruno remained fixed to his chair, his head swimming. He needed time to think. Bruno thrust into his coat pocket for his motorbike keys. He felt the hostile eyes follow him into the narrow cobbled street.

Minutes later he stood outside the ornate gateway to King's College. There, parked at the end of a line of student cycles was the Brough Superior. Bruno mounted it, kicked it to life, stabbed it into gear and rode it off its stand. With his gown flowing behind him he roared through the narrow streets until the city was behind him.

Bruno lifted the gargoyle knocker. Then he let it fall. He pushed open the door to the Great Hall and walked in without knocking.

There were five of them.

Ferguson, the Dean, Abernathy, Baillie, Hughes and Langslow. They sat at a long polished table in front of the Tudor fireplace. Above them hung a shield bearing the college coat of arms.

This side of the table was a single chair.

Only the Dean looked up. He indicated the chair.

The others fidgeted with the folders in front of them.

Bruno stared at the Dean until the man lowered his eyes. He felt strangely calm, no knotted stomach or dry mouth. It was as if he was detached from the figure standing in front of the table.

He felt he was doomed. He sensed the decision had already been made. He was to be kicked out.

Bruno took the initiative. He would not go without a fight.

'Why are you going to fire me?'

The men behind the table glanced apprehensively at each other, shuffling the papers in front of them. Ferguson coughed.

'Why?' Bruno raised his voice. 'My work?'

He paused, almost relishing the silence. It was the men behind the table who should feel guilty. He had done nothing.

'No, gentlemen. Not my work. I defy you to fault it.'

He searched the faces for an answer. He saw only their unease.

'No, Doctor. We cannot fault your work,' Ferguson said.

Abernathy whispered into the Dean's ear.

Then he said to Bruno, 'We are responsible for the good name of this college. But certain things have been brought to our attention.'

'What?' Bruno said coldly. This was a farce. He wanted no more of it.

'Are you, or have you ever been a member of the British Union of Fascists?' Abernathy asked.

Bruno could not believe his ears. 'No.'

'Your parents are Italian?'

'My mother is dead. My father is a British citizen.'

'Ahh. Does he contribute to the British branch of the Italian *Fascisti*? Many Italian exiles do.'

'Don't be ridiculous.'

'But he does sympathize?'

'No,' Bruno protested.

'Do you?'

'I won't dignify that kind of nonsense with an answer.'

'Then we can take it as read?'

'No, you bloody well cannot.'

'Please, gentlemen,' Ferguson said. He asked, 'Your work on antibiotic drugs. It would have tremendous commercial applications?'

'Of course. But that does not interest me. I have openly turned down approaches to join drugs companies.'

'British ones?'

'Yes. And American and Swiss.'

'Italian companies?'

'No.'

'Have you had any approaches from the Italian government?'

'Regime,' quipped Abernathy. 'One can hardly call it a government.'

'Is all this really necessary?' It was Langslow. 'I wish it to be made known I find this whole affair scandalous. Dr Rossi is a fine and able member of this college. We have no right to treat him in this way.'

Abernathy ignored him. 'Answer the Dean's question. Have you received any approach from the Italian government?'

'No.'

'Do you know a man called Enzo Verdi?'

Bruno felt his first twinge of doubt.

'I have met him. Once.'

'Does he work for the Italian regime?'

'I have no idea.'

'No idea? Have you not entertained this man in your study?'

'Entertain is not the word I would use.' This was getting out of hand. Bruno shrugged in disbelief. His stomach was knotted now. His world was about to break up around him. The years of hard work – all for nothing.

There was nothing he had ever wanted outside his work. It was his life. Now these men were about to take it from him. They were going to smash every ambition he'd ever cherished to bits.

Verdi.

The name loomed in his thoughts.

That's when things began to change. The day Verdi came to his study.

'What did you discuss with Verdi?' Abernathy drove home his point.

'He offered me a job. I turned him down,' Bruno mumbled. He fought vainly to take control of himself.

'Turned it down? Was it a job with the Italian government? A country with which we could soon be at war?'

Ferguson said, 'Under the circumstances I feel I must ask for your resignation. A decision on whether we accept it or not will be made when certain investigations have been completed.'

Investigations? What investigations? Bruno thought. His head spun. This was a nightmare. Yet he was awake. The injustice of it all sickened him. And there was nothing he could do about it. There seemed no point anymore. He turned and stormed for the door.

'I must protest. It's disgraceful.' Langslow's lone voice trailed after him.

'Perhaps he can get a job in Bologna.'

Bruno froze at Abernathy's words.

How in hell could the man know about Bologna? Bruno had mentioned it to no one.

Yet this man knew.

He had to seek out Verdi. He still had the man's card somewhere. He had to confront the Italian. Perhaps he could then sort things out.

He saw no other choice.

He rushed from the hall and came face to face with Alan Seldon.

Neither man moved. Seldon in flowing gown, books tucked under his arm, stood motionless in the cloister. The only sound came from the spray of the stone fountain in the centre of the quad.

They stared into each other's eyes.

Then Bruno thought: He knows. This is the bastard who knows why.

Seldon glowered, hard, accusingly.

'I warned you about the company you keep, Rossi.' His lip curled.

Bruno fought to control himself and turned away. He took one pace, then something snapped. He swung around and punched Seldon hard on the jaw. Books went flying as his former friend crashed backwards onto the floor. His mouth bled.

Bruno looked down at the prostrate figure, then turned his back and made to walk away. A group of students, amazement on their flushed faces, began to run towards him.

Then he heard Seldon yell out. 'Fascist,' he screamed at the top of his voice, 'you filthy Italian Fascist bastard.'

The taunt echoed through the cloisters.

Bruno spun towards Seldon, who now leant back on his elbows looking up. He spat at Bruno's feet.

For the first time in his life Bruno Rossi kicked a man. He was still kicking when the students pulled him away.

Verdi lived in Hanover Street.

Bruno arrived at one in the morning. He decided La Piccola Italia was sordid. It formed a concrete oblong of restaurants and clubs set in narrow streets and alleys between Charing Cross Road and the elegant façades of the Strand. Faint gas lamps hissed and cast a yellow-grey glow over the overflowing bins on the pavement. Trade had fallen off badly among the once prosperous family-run restaurants. Owners blamed the lack of customers on Mussolini. Their protests did not stop the nightlife tide drifting on to Soho and points west.

Bruno noticed all the nightspots were already closed, paint peeling from the drawn shutters. He parked his motorcycle next to a pile of crates in a narrow alley and stuffed his goggles into his pocket.

Hanover House blended perfectly into the district. It was a five-storey, grim-faced, red-brick Victorian mess. Iron spikes were set on each window ledge, whether to keep the occupants in or intruders out, Bruno was not sure. Three stone steps led to an arched door with a large brass knob. It was unlocked. Bruno pushed it open.

A naked light lit a dim hall of cracked black and white tiles. A push bike stood against one wall next to a pram. It smelt damp. Bruno moved towards the bare staircase. He placed his hand on the wooden banister when someone grabbed him roughly by the shoulder.

'Where the hell do you think you're going?'

The owner of the gruff voice looked like an ex-wrestler. He wore a dirty white vest and baggy trousers with a wide leather belt. His arms were still muscular but the rest had turned to flab. He reeked of rum.

'Suite 25A,' Bruno said removing the hand on his shoulder.

The big man looked nonplussed.

'You police?'

Bruno shook his head.

'Some bloke's already been asking for him tonight. Talked real posh he did.'

Bruno smiled reassuringly. He took out his wallet and removed a ten shilling note. He watched the man's eyes widen.

Bruno said, 'I'm a friend.'

He pressed the note into the large hand and watched it close around it.

'Sure, here you are.'

The man unhooked a key from the bunch on his belt.

'You never got this from me, mind?'

'Of course not.'

'Top floor.'

Key in hand, Bruno took the stairs.

No light showed from under the door. Quietly he unlocked it and pushed it ajar, stepped inside and pressed it shut with his back. The only sound came from the tick of the clock on the mantelpiece. The curtains were open and Bruno could see the front of the bed through an open door. He inched silently towards it and pushed it back fully with his foot.

The double bed was empty.

'Verdi,' Bruno called loudly.

No reply. Only the sound of the clock.

Bruno took in the room. It was sparse, a high wardrobe and small wicker table. The bed covers were thrown back to reveal creased sheets. A man's silk dressing-gown was draped over the bedstand next to a pair of woman's stockings and a petticoat.

He moved back into the sitting room. Amid the smell of stale cigarettes he caught the faint whiff of perfume.

He moved back to the door and flicked on the light. A dress and a shirt embraced on the floor. The remainder of the couple's clothing laid a trail to the empty bedroom. A high-backed settee with feather cushions faced a low table and an unlit gas fire. Two empty glasses flanked a half-drunk bottle of white wine.

In front of the window was a heavy desk. Amid the piles of neat papers was a phone. Bruno crossed the room. He glanced at the papers and his jaw dropped.

He picked up an old school photograph held to a sheet by a paper clip. The young face smiling proudly back at him through time was his own. The snap had been taken the day he'd won his state scholarship to Cambridge.

The neatly typed information on the paper confirmed the details, dates and grades of the examinations he'd passed. Bruno turned cold. He let the paper fall. He began to sift through the bundles on Verdi's desk. They were a complete catalogue of his academic life. Bruno wiped his forehead, gathered up a bundle and slumped onto the sofa. He arranged the papers on the table and huddled over them. It was uncanny as he began to pore over episodes of his student days that he'd long forgotten, all recorded by someone. Recorded and filed away neatly, accurately, unnoticed until this moment on the desk of a man called Verdi.

'How?' Bruno asked aloud.

Suddenly Bruno felt unclean.

An hour later he'd finished. Now he felt sick. It was as if he'd read his own obituary. Bruno loosened his collar.

Now he asked the question 'Why?' in no more than a whisper.

Someone had opened a file on him the day he'd won his scholarship. It had been kept meticulously up to date. Verdi even had the previous day's cutting from the *Cambridge Evening News*. It was a terse two-paragraph statement, without comment, announcing the suspension of Bruno pending inquiries by the college court.

Bruno replaced the bundles on the desk. He glanced down at the message pad next to the phone. He saw his own number, underlined, the number of his father in Wales and one in Rome. He copied it, and placed it in his wallet.

He drew back a floral curtain hung on a wire to reveal an alcove which housed a small kitchenette. Dishes were piled high in the sink, the saucepan on the small stove contained a mixture of Milanese sauce and coils of cold spaghetti. A chunk of rock-hard Parmesan cheese sat on the single shelf amid unwashed coffee mugs. Verdi, a meticulous keeper of records, was a sloth. Somehow it made Bruno feel better, even though he decided against a coffee. He let the curtain drop.

The bathroom, Bruno decided, must be through the door on the far side of the room, behind the settee. He opened it and pulled the cord. The bulb above the bath came on.

Water lapped around the bath's rim. Bruno looked down in horror at the girl's eyes gazing back at him from beneath the surface. Her dark hair floated over Verdi's shoulders. He lay face down, their legs interlocked. His face was buried in the girl's breasts. The single bar electric fire rested next to the girl's face. The flex was still plugged into the wall socket. It had blown black.

Bruno inched forward and hesitantly reached out and touched Verdi's white back. The cold flesh felt like putty. At Bruno's touch Verdi shifted slightly and a thin line of bubbles floated from the girl's lips. Bruno leapt back.

He bounded into the sitting room and picked up the phone, hesitated, then replaced the receiver.

Bruno's instincts told him to run.

He needed time to think.

Bruno considered calling the police. Then decided against it.

He followed his instincts.

A lone light burned in Dolman's office at SIS. He put down the phone and looked across at Seldon.

'That was Special Branch,' he said. 'Bruno Rossi has just left Verdi's flat. He made no attempt to report the murder.'

'Good,' Seldon said.

'Where will he run to?'

'South Wales I should think. His father's place.'

'Can you get there by tomorrow?'

'No problem.'

'I think you should arrange a welcome home present for him, don't you?'

Seldon said nothing.

He felt like the lowest form of life.

CHAPTER FOUR

Bruno changed trains at Cardiff. His wallet contained the money for the Brough Superior motorcycle he'd sold to a dealer in South London. The exchange was favourable, but no compensation for the loss of his machine.

After the sale he'd caught a bus to Victoria, booked into a small Irish-run hotel, and remained in the single room until early afternoon. Then he walked up to Hyde Park, and along Oxford Street where he bought a copy of the three evening papers. There was no mention of Verdi and the woman.

His curiosity overcame the advice of detective fiction writers and he found himself walking past Verdi's flat. There was no sign of any police activity, no constable outside the door, no crowds of newspapermen. Nothing.

He spent the night alone in his rented room then caught the train from Paddington next morning. None of the papers carried news of Verdi's death either. It was as if it had never happened.

Bruno walked under the subway to the branch line platform and the last leg of his journey to his father's home in Barry. It was early afternoon.

The local train was full, compartments crammed with day trippers to the seaside from the mining valleys. Pale children, faces sticky with sweets, clutching buckets and spades. Their mothers all seemed vast and had brought winter coats as a precaution against the Welsh weather. Outside the temperatures soared. It was going to be a glorious summer day. Bruno stood. He hung onto a strap and opened the window for air. It was stifling. On the platform a platoon of Territorial Army reservists lolled in the shade: their ill-fitting uniforms had scant respect for shape or size.

'Better get to the beach before that lot mine it,' joked a

mother with a crying child on her knee. Everyone roared.

'Not funny,' complained her husband. 'It's going to be serious. War is just around the corner, you'll see.'

Bruno noticed no one paid heed to the man. He shuddered.

The small tank engine blew its whistle and steamed slowly backwards from the station, hauling the brown and white coaches through the dingy terraced suburbs. It crossed the estuary mud flats and left the city for green fields and wooded hills. It took the coastal route along the cliffs hugging the Bristol Channel, and stopped at every tiny halt as people piled out for the beaches. The names were a catalogue of delight from Bruno's childhood.

Penarth – day trips on a paddle steamer from the pier; St Mary's Well Bay, the rock pools of Sully. And Lavernock, most of all Lavernock. It was from a small farm there that Guglielmo Marconi sent the first radio message over water. A place of constant pride for the young Bruno Rossi. Marconi, the student from Bologna.

'Bologna,' Bruno said to himself, and thought of Verdi's face down in the bath. Now, somehow, that ancient seat of learning had a sinister ring.

But as a boy, it had been different.

'You could be another Marconi,' his mother used to say. He remembered fondly the day he won a scholarship to Barry's prestigious County School, only one of two boys from his junior school to do so. His mother had proudly hauled the reluctant eleven-year-old to the local tailor to be fitted out for uniform.

'Congratulations,' Mr Radok beamed as he measured the green blazer, 'and what will you be now? Work hard and the world is at your feet.'

At eighteen Bruno was back in Mr Radok's shop. This time he'd won his state scholarship to Cambridge.

'To read medicine,' the tailor beamed as proudly as if Bruno had been his own son.

'Then research,' Bruno reassured him. 'That is where the

solution to all cures lies.' He spoke with a conviction beyond his years. He did not add that he found a strange beauty in the abstraction of it all. Its purity of pattern, its sheer poetry of mathematical logic. When Bruno Rossi looked into a microscope, he did not see the minutiae of life at its most basic. He closed his eyes and heard the geometry of Johann Sebastian Bach play inside his head.

Now someone had broken the harpsichord.

The train jolted and began to slow. It pulled into Barry Dock Station. Bruno was the only one to alight. The platform was empty except for half a dozen Somali seamen with empty black faces waiting for the Cardiff train and another ship. There was no sign of his father.

Bruno had phoned from London. He thought it strange the old man was not there to meet him. He'd expected him, complete with the familiar battered old trilby and grey walrus moustache.

He made for the exit.

The newspaper billboard hit him like a knee in the groin.

LOCAL MAN KICKED OUT OF CAMBRIDGE.

ACCUSATIONS FLY.

It could have been worse. The accusations did not include murder. Yet.

That was something.

He dug his hands into his pockets, looked down, and strode into the street. It was a short, brisk walk to his father's café.

It was closed. Normally it would have been packed, tables filled with hungry dockers and sailors. Bruno felt a twinge of apprehension. He peered through the window. Chairs were stacked on tables; clean dishes piled high on the counter. His father had not opened up. That was unheard of.

Bruno sensed something was wrong. He let himself in by the side door. The place was silent. He called up the stairs to the flat. There was no reply.

'Papa,' he called again as he moved cautiously up the stairs, hands on the wall. He began to dread what he would find, like the day, that first college leave, when he tried to wake his mother from her afternoon nap and couldn't. The heart attack had been fatal.

'Papa.'

This time he yelled and bounded up the rest of the flight. He burst into the living room.

It was a shambles. A lifetime of family memories lay in ruins. The furniture, some upturned, had been slashed to ribbons. The Welsh dresser with its set of fine Italian china had been toppled, the pieces smashed.

Someone had urinated in the corner.

Bruno looked up at his mother's photograph on the wall, as if it might provide answers to the questions flying through his mind. It was missing. In its place was daubed the slogan: TRAITOR.

Bruno screamed with rage.

'Lying bastards.' He thumped the wall with a clenched fist.

He turned and raced for his father's bedroom. The broken china crunched underfoot. Bruno flung open the door.

The old man was still in his pyjamas. He knelt by the bed, eyes closed, rocking to and fro, clutching his wife's photograph. Bruno eased it from him. The glass had been smashed by a heel.

He helped his father to the bed and held him to his shoulder. Bruno could find no words.

At last his father said, 'Why?' and looked down at the photograph. 'Why?' he asked again. 'Because we are Italian?'

Bruno thought: No. Because I am Bruno Rossi.

Then just one word. Bologna.

The hate welled inside him. He had never hated before. Somehow it felt sweet. It soothed the bitterness.

Bruno faced his father across the scrubbed kitchen table. The breakfast kettle steamed on the hob of the blacked iron range behind him and the room still smelt of freshly baked bread. Just as it had when he was a boy.

'We should have told the police. I speak with Inspector Grabham. He's a good man. He'll know what to do.' Alfredo pushed away his untouched coffee.

Bruno shook his head. He dare not risk the phone. 'Let it rest. Whoever did this was not from this town.'

And that frightened Bruno. He now feared his father was also at risk. Why, in God's name, was this being done to him?

'Bruno.' His father leant across the table. 'What you done?'

'Nothing. I swear it.'

'On your Mother's grave.' Alfredo crossed himself.

'On Mother's grave.'

'Then why the papers say such things? They print the denials that you were going to sell your research to a foreign drug company. The denial is just a clever way of saying that was just what you was going to do.'

Bruno could have willingly killed the lying bastard who leaked that to the press. He knew he could never work for any university again. And what firm would employ him after a story like that? That was if he ever got the chance to apply.

He'd been home almost a week and had not set a foot outside the door. He could not bring himself to face his friends. It was almost as if he had begun to believe the lies himself. He despised his own vulnerability. He was beginning to fall apart. Every knock on the door or ring of the phone filled him full of dread. He expected it to be a policeman with a warrant for his arrest for Verdi's murder. It was all that was needed to complete his destruction. He held his head in his hands.

'Bruno.' He felt his father's hand on his arm. 'Soon everything is going to be OK. I fix it. You got no need to worry anymore.'

Bruno looked up. He never ceased to be amazed at his father's use of English, even though he'd spent more time in Britain than Italy. He couldn't help a smile.

'Now you promise me not to be angry,' the old man said earnestly.

Bruno shook his head.

'I telephoned my brother Gino's boy, your cousin Enrico. I called him all the way to Roma. He is a very big man now. He works high up for the government. Very powerful. He's gonna help you.'

Bruno had never met his cousin Enrico Rossi. His father had still kept in touch by letter. Bruno did not see how a civil servant could help, or want to.

'Why should he care? He doesn't know me from Adam.' Bruno's lack of interest was clear.

His father banged the table. He looked hurt. 'I'll never understand you,' he snapped. 'He cares because he is your family.'

'Papa,' Bruno concealed his exasperation and spoke softly, 'this is not the old country. You are the only family I've got.'

The old man pursed his lips. He raised a finger.

'I came here on a coal boat, from Genoa,' Alfredo said, his eyes vague. 'I was just seventeen. In Perino Maggiore, my village, I left my parents, six of your aunties and four of your uncles, including Enrico's father Gino. He was the baby. And my Rosa,' he crossed himself, 'your mother. You know why I leave, eh? Because I was starving.'

'Yes, I . . .' Bruno was cut short by the admonishing finger.

'No, Bruno, you don't know. Not hungry like here in the strike, or the big slump. Not soup kitchen hungry. I was starving. I came here to Barry and people have been very kind. First I sell ice cream on the beach from a tray. Then I buy a cart. In two years I make enough to send for your mother. Soon we open this place in Thompson Street. Sure it's the docks, not the smart part of town, but it's good. From dawn to dusk we sell food to dockers and sailors. At night we make the fish and chips. We were blessed with two sons. Now there is just you and me.

'You know I never see any of my family from the old place ever again. You don't know, but once I sent to Gino for his boy Enrico to come here, to give him the kind of start you had, but Enrico too had gone from Perino Maggiore, just like I did. Enrico got a good job. He was sweeping the floors at Fiat in Turin. You know how he got to Fiat? He walked across two hundred miles of mountains. That's how. He walked. So don't shake your head at me. It is you who does not understand why he now wants to help. I know.'

Bruno reached out and touched the old man's sleeve. 'This is another time, another country. What happens if we and the old country go to war?'

'The old country never kicked you out after you work so hard for it,' his father said defensively.

'It kicked you out,' snapped Bruno.

The moment the words were out Bruno wished he'd been born dumb. He looked appealingly at his father and the old man smiled.

'That's the truth of it. This is the place that gave us a home. Mussolini is a pig, but now not so many people leave their home. So what do you say? Italy is the mother, here is the wife, the home. If a man must choose between his mother and his wife then he must choose the wife. Let's not fight.'

Bruno was lost for words.

Alfredo wagged his finger again: 'But remember, people make countries, not politicians. Never forget your people or your kind. And when one of yours offers you a kindness in your trouble it is because he has your blood. You call him.'

'Perhaps,' Bruno said.

'What is the alternative? You wanna work in the café?'

The door bell rang. Bruno started. His nerves were shot. It was getting worse. He cursed himself. He had to pull himself together.

'The postman,' Alfredo said and made for the door.

'An airmail letter from Italy for you.' His father turned it over and squinted at the envelope. 'It looks like a child's writing.'

Bruno took the letter. The sender's name was on the back. The spidery hand was barely legible.

At last he made it out.

Lucia Corso. And the postmark was Bologna.

> 'Bruno, please understand. As I write this I feel my sanity slipping away and there is no one else I feel I can turn to. You must help me please, please, please. They must be stopped before it is too late, this is murder, not science and the victims are all mad. LIKE ME . . .'

He put the letter down on his bed. He must have read it a hundred times.

Lucia.

Perhaps she was mad. He looked at the page again. It made him ache. The scrawl became an illegible scribble in places. There were blots everywhere punctuated by child-like drawings of a doll.

He began to pace the room. First light showed through the thin curtains. Could the girl he had loved, wanted to marry, have written this?

In some ways it might have been more acceptable if she had lost her mind. If not, then what she claimed made everything else totally, criminally insane. He picked up the letter.

> 'Because of what I know, they are trying to destroy my mind in the same way as they destroy the patients in the experiments. They just want people to think I'm crazy to stop them listening to me. You will listen, won't you? . . .'

Classic.

Bruno was no psychiatrist. He did not have to be to read the paranoic warnings in the letter. They were making her mad in order to destroy her.

Casebook.

But wasn't that just what was happening to him? Someone was trying to destroy him too.

And she was in Bologna. A university offered to him by a murdered man.

There had to be a link.

His mind swam.

He had to make sense of Lucia's letter. It was a jumble, a rambling, illegible mess. Yet he knew it was vital he understood everything she was trying to tell him.

Bruno tried to put what facts he had in order.

He began to recite as he paced.

'One. Lucia thinks she is being driven insane.

'Two. This is because she has discovered secret experiments being carried out at Bologna University under a Professor Frederico Pini.'

Bruno paused. He knew Pini by reputation. A brilliant man. This was crazy.

'Three. The experiments are carried out in conjunction with a German university. We do not know which one. Just that it's German.

'Four. The experiments are carried out on human beings.'

Bruno felt the bile burn the back of his throat. Ridiculous.

'Five. Because of these experiments the patients have all died. Lucia has seen some photographs. These people died horrific deaths. She says in agony. But she does not say from what. Damn. What the hell would be the point?

'Six. All these patients were mentally defective. Mad. Just like the woman I wanted to marry.'

Bruno realized he was shouting.

An anger swept him.

It mixed with shame.

He felt unclean. Ashamed.

He suddenly needed space.

He slipped silently from the house, taking care not to awaken old Alfredo. His push bike leant against the outside toilet. Bruno mounted and began to punish the pedals, swaying slightly, until he got up speed. Head down, he rode the bike, passing cloth-capped dockers on their way to meet the needs of the morning tide.

Faster – he needed space, the sea, the cliff. Faster. Bruno headed west. Suburbs of mock-Tudor semis with neat lawns.

Then he reached the bay. A long strip of empty car park between a rising cliff and curved pebble beach. It stopped at the Bull's Nose. Two hundred feet of rock as resolute as the animal after which it was named. It had been pounded by the seas since its creation and still it stood.

Bruno dropped the bike and raced across the beach and stood at the foot. He could hear the pebbles behind him rattle as they were swept by the encroaching tide. It had advanced between him and the tarmac strip. The only way was up. He stood, legs apart and head raised to study the cliff. The limestone ran in jagged strata, the first thirty feet slippery with green sea slime.

Bruno thought: Are you trying to kill yourself? He knew it would make things simpler. Then he thought: Fool. But he realized the question contained a grain of truth.

A wave crashed, sending foam racing around his ankles. Bruno reached for a ledge and hauled himself upwards, fingers straining until his feet were sure. He inched sideways, then higher, carefully, aware of the slime. Dry rock now, cold, hard, cut sharp by wind and sea.

He could taste the perspiration that ran down his face and stung his eyes, and he dare not wipe them.

Higher he climbed, searching out handholds, testing and tugging them, gently at first, then harder to see if they'd hold his weight, his life. His mind emptied except to receive and respond to the feel of foot and finger.

He passed fifty feet, sixty feet, and his eyes burnt and fingers bled as the rock sliced into the skin. The pain increased as he climbed higher. It stabbed down his spine, tore through his hip joints until it seemed it would sever his knees.

At two hundred feet he froze, his limbs just locked, spreadeagled on the rock face. Above him he smelt grass and heard the gulls' cry. Below him the grey sea beckoned.

Don't look down, he thought.

But he couldn't stop himself. The swell, streaked white, rose and dipped as it lashed out viciously at the cliff trying to shake Bruno free. He could feel the rock shudder.

The wind sang.

The girl is mad. Demented. Let go. It's easy. Just let go.

'NO,' Bruno screamed at the waves.

He began to climb now, sure, steady, from crevice to crevice, as if glued to the cliff. Unshakeable. Ozone filled his lungs and flowed to his limbs.

The cliff began to flatten until he could scramble to the top. Exhausted he threw himself on the cushion of springy turf. He closed his eyes.

The anger had gone. So had the shame he'd felt earlier. He'd denied her.

It didn't matter if Lucia's letter came straight from a psychiatrist's casebook. And he reasoned it must have done. No one could do what she'd claimed. Exterminate people.

For what? It *was* crazy.

He sat up and clasped his knees. He looked out over the sea. The grey hills of Exmoor rose out of the heat haze on the other side of the channel.

Things were clear now.

Lucia needed him.

He also needed Lucia. For the first time in weeks his brain was working. It felt great.

His mind slipped into gear.

His career had been wrecked. They had denied him his dream.

Damn them.

He would *not* let them break his graveside vow.

He would *not* let them hurt his father. Not because of him.

There was nothing left for him in Britain. Except to face charges for a murder he did not commit. If Bruno Rossi had been told a month ago he risked a hangman's noose he would have laughed like a drain. But a month ago he thought he was going to be made a Cambridge professor.

His father was right. It made sense. He would ring his cousin Enrico Rossi.

Bruno took the cliff path back to the beach. Now he didn't

need to climb. He thought of Lucia. It pained him.

Bruno finished his call to Rome. It had taken three hours to get through and Enrico Rossi was out.

Bruno slugged a glass of his father's rough grappa. He needed it. The number he'd rung was the same number he'd found on Verdi's pad.

It was the office of Mussolini's OVRA. His father had been right. Rossi did hold high rank in government service. He was a colonel in a Fascist secret service.

Bruno had spoken to Rossi's deputy.

The thing that frightened Bruno was that the man had been expecting the call.

Everything, it seemed, was already arranged. A position awaited Bruno at Bologna.

He'd get a professorship. He could carry on his research into penicillin. The funds would be open ended. But that would come later.

First there was a project which was too sensitive to talk about on the phone. His cousin would explain. In Bologna.

Then the phone rang. Bruno jumped and lifted the receiver.

'I'd like to speak to a Dr Bruno Rossi, if I may.' The accent was London. The voice gruff. It was the call Bruno feared.

'He's not here. I get him to ring you.' Bruno aped an Italian accent. 'You tell me what's it about.'

'A routine inquiry into the death of an Italian person and a female. We would like him to account for his movements.'

'I get him to ring you. You give me the number.'

'Whitehall 1212. Scotland Yard. Ask for Inspector Morris.'

Bruno hung up. He was shaking.

'What's the matter? You look ill.' Alfredo was standing in the doorway to the flat. He wore an apron and wrung his hands in a dishcloth. 'You ring your cousin Enrico like I say?'

Bruno nodded.

'And he help you?'

Bruno mumbled 'Yes'. He saw his father's expression change.

'Something's a wrong. You tell me.'

'Nothing's wrong. You were right. I got a professorship at Bologna. Fantastic.' Bruno forced a grin. Inside the butterflies in his stomach collided.

He could see the old man was not fooled.

'So you go. You know, I got a premonition ever since you come home.'

Bruno saw his father's eyes fill.

'I don't think I am ever going to see you again.'

'Nonsense.' Bruno embraced him. But the look in his father's eye told him it was more than a premonition.

It was a conviction.

His father was convinced he was never going to see him again.

Ever.

And for that someone was going to pay.

Dearly.

The Golden Arrow steamed into Dover Harbour Station on time. The growing crises in Europe meant everyone passed through dockside embarkation for inspection.

Bruno joined the queue for the cross-Channel ferry.

The plainclothes policeman spotted him at the barrier. PC Higgins recognized him right away. Bruno's head in the photograph he held in his hand had a ring pencilled around it. He was standing next to Seldon on the day they'd both graduated.

Higgins watched Bruno cross the damp yard to the ferry. He carried two cases.

The policeman waited until Bruno had passed through customs then walked to the Harbour Police office. He did not knock.

'Can I help you, sir?' asked the desk constable.

Higgins produced his warrant card and watched the constable inspect it with a knowing nod.

'Anywhere I can use a phone in private?'

'Anything to oblige our colleagues from the Special Branch.'

Higgins rang the Yard and asked for Inspector Morris.

'The bugger's just got on the boat train travelling on a British passport. You can tell Mr Seldon that he booked a one-way ticket to Bologna.'

'Was he alone?'

'Far as I could see.'

'Good riddance to bad rubbish, I say. Tell me, Higgins, why is it Cambridge always seems to produce his sort?'

'Don't ask me, sir, I never even went to grammar school.'

CHAPTER FIVE

Bruno Rossi had dozed fitfully through the night, stretched out on the compartment seat and covered by his overcoat. Seven hours earlier his arrival on Italian soil was heralded by swirling drizzle from the northern Alps. The Italian dining-car attendants failed to appear. Bruno, tired and hungry, closed his eyes and slept. He stirred at first light. The train had just passed through the grim industrial outskirts of Modena and the Maserati car plant. The factories had given way to open country dotted with whitewashed houses with terracotta-tiled roofs. It was magnificent.

The sun had lifted over the horizon and turned quickly from deep crimson to pale yellow. Bruno noticed the heat haze begin to shimmer over the vast plain of Emilia Romagna. The houses became fewer as the train picked up speed through fields of vines that stretched into the distance. It should have been a monotonous landscape, Bruno thought. But it was not. He realized the light was constantly changing its whole texture. It should also have been unfamiliar. Yet Bruno Rossi felt he'd known it all his life.

Then there were the mountains on the far side of the train. The Apennines. They halted the plain's advance west without ceremony, rising like a huge painted backcloth. These were his father's mountains, stark and uncompromising, the spine of Italy. He could see tiny villages clinging to the higher reaches that went on forever.

He rose and folded his coat and stepped out into the rattling corridor as bells rang when the train flashed past a level crossing. A laden donkey headed the small queue of traffic.

The smell of fresh coffee and roasted tobacco hit his nostrils. Bruno smiled broadly and walked in the direction of the buffet car and the noise of an Italian mother yelling at her child.

Suddenly, Bruno Rossi had the strange feeling he was home.

The train was on time. Crowds swarmed through Bologna station like ants as disembodied voices from several different speakers vied for attention. *Carabinieri* swaggered in pairs, holsters on hips with machine guns cradled in their arms.

Bruno scanned the moving sea of faces.

A tall thin man emerged holding a placard. On it was written Bruno's name.

'I'm Dr Rossi,' Bruno told him.

'Please.' He indicated the exit and picked up Bruno's suitcases.

The man wove through the crowds, Bruno at his heels, and out into the mid-morning sunlight. Bruno held his hand to his eyes, it was dazzling.

A large white Lancia stood waiting. Bruno stepped in and settled back in the vast leather seat. There was a glass partition between him and the driver. Conversation was through a speaking tube. Bruno picked it up.

'Where are we going?' he asked.

'Villa Marco, out near San Luca,' the driver replied.

They drove west, left the city behind them and headed towards the church of the Madonna di San Luca. It stood high on a hill approached by a mile-long portico of white arches.

The Villa Marco lay off the portico. The Lancia swung off the road and bounced up an unmade track cut through a lemon grove. The pair of large wrought-iron gates were open and a gravel drive twisted down to the villa at the foot of a slope. Steps led to a harp-shaped swimming pool alongside the tennis court. There was a liberal display of marble statues in classical Roman poses.

As the Lancia stopped a man appeared in the shadows of the villa's front door, feet apart and hands buried deeply in his jacket pockets so he seemed slightly round shouldered. As Bruno got out of the car he moved towards him, hands still in his pockets. He was smiling broadly.

Bruno instantly recognized the features of his own bloodline.

Enrico Rossi was larger than Bruno. His eyes, determined, were steel blue. He walked forcefully, yet with no hint of swagger. His suit was tailored and elegant, his watch gold, shirt and tie silk, the shoes were soft handmade leather. He wore the trappings of the rich and powerful with cool assurance. He removed his hands from his pockets. They were enormous and despite the carefully manicured nails, the hands of a mountain peasant. Hands like Rossi's had evolved through generations to till the reluctant earth and drive stubborn oxen before the plough.

Enrico Rossi paused. He clasped his hands.

So this was his cousin Bruno. He looked more like a footballer than an academic.

Rossi smiled broadly. This was the moment he had planned for. His cousin Bruno was going to make him one of the most powerful men in Italy.

Bruno would succeed where Pini and the others had failed. And he, Colonel Enrico Rossi, would take the credit and the riches. He deserved it.

He had not done badly for a kid who once swept the floor at Fiat. He knew then he could not afford to miss a chance. That was why he told his foreman that one of the machine minders was fooling with the man's daughter. Next day the machine was his. Rossi was not cut out to be a machine minder for long, especially when the foreman was selling company parts.

Rossi did not tell the company. He told the union organizer who was local president of the newly formed *Fascisti*. Rossi became foreman. Then local party president. That was how he met his wife Paola Grazziani. Her father was head of the OVRA.

Now Rossi wanted the power that went with his father-in-law's job.

He would get it through Bruno.

He had followed his cousin's career closely through the letters his Uncle Alfredo sent. He'd even opened a file in case one day he might need it.

He had.

When the Wildfire project at Bologna ran into trouble it threatened Italy's influence in the Pact of Steel with Hitler. But if Wildfire worked then Italy could even control the German dictator.

And Rossi knew Bruno could make it work. Rossi went behind his father-in-law's back to Mussolini himself.

'Get him,' Mussolini said.

Rossi sent Verdi.

He was panic stricken when Verdi failed. So much depended on it.

But he needn't have been, he thought. The British had secured Bruno for him. The bloody fools. He could not believe his luck when his Uncle Alfredo had phoned in response to the letter he'd sent offering to help his family.

Now Bruno was here.

Wildfire would work.

Bruno felt the huge hands tighten around his shoulders, then pound his back as his cousin embraced him in a bear hug.

'Welcome,' Rossi said, his accent still rang of the mountains. 'My Zio Alfredo's son here in Bologna.' He shook his head as if he could not believe it, then laughed heartily.

Bruno was steered into the villa. The floors were marble and the furniture classical antique. He was ushered into the drawing room.

It was vast with a high ceiling and views of the church.

'This place is at your disposal,' Rossi said. He gestured around the room. 'Not bad for two kids whose grandfather couldn't read.'

'Let's get to the point.' Bruno sat in a winged chair. 'Why do you want me in Bologna?'

Rossi smiled. Mechanically. He shrugged and lifted his hands. 'Why Bruno, you are . . .'

'Don't give me that family bit.' Bruno cut him short. 'Did you send Enzo Verdi?'

'Yes.' Rossi's eyes bored into his. The smile had gone.

'He's dead.'

'He should have learned to control his habits.' Rossi showed no emotion.

Bruno thought: You are a ruthless bastard.

He said contemptuously, 'Verdi said Bologna was working on something that made penicillin seem insignificant.'

'At least he got something right.' Rossi walked to the window, his back to Bruno.

At last Rossi said, 'I wanted you to come to Bologna because I think you are invaluable.'

'For what?'

The directness of the reply threw Rossi. He hadn't expected it.

'Your mind.' He paused. 'And the ultimate safety of every man, woman and child in Europe.'

'What?' Bruno sounded incredulous.

'Bruno,' the name rolled off Rossi's tongue seriously, 'how many people have died from the Black Death, bubonic plague?'

Bruno stiffened. 'Twenty-five million in the fourteenth century.'

'Try this century,' Rossi interrupted.

Bruno frowned.

'In the first decade more than ten million died . . .'

'What is all . . .' Bruno began but was cut short.

'And the British are developing a strain of the Black Death as a weapon of war.'

Bruno leapt up. He felt sick. 'Rubbish,' he yelled.

'Why do you think they killed Verdi? The British knew he was trying to enlist your help. They wanted to prevent him.

That's why they tried to blacken your name.'

Bruno thought of the phone call from Scotland Yard. Would they have gone that far?

'It's too fantastic,' he said.

Rossi turned and held up a hand. 'What if I could show you a sample of the strain and give you proof?'

'Then it would have to be stopped,' Bruno mumbled.

'Prevented,' Rossi corrected. 'Which is why I wanted you to come to Bologna.'

He moved to the grand piano next to the fireplace and opened an attaché case. He thrust a bundle of papers under Bruno's nose.

'Read these.'

Bruno took them. The top sheet bore the crest of the Vatican.

Bruno began to read, his face masked in horror.

He learned that an Irish Roman Catholic priest called Padraig O'Hagan had taken sojourn from his Glasgow parish to go sea fishing in Stornoway on the Isle of Lewis in the Outer Hebrides. Priests of his faith being thin on the ground in that part of Scotland, the local police had called him to administer last rites to a Catholic called Watson.

Watson was in an isolation ward at the local cottage hospital. He'd been brought there from a rocky outcrop called Fiagha, ten miles west of Sula Sgeir in the North Atlantic. On his deathbed Watson unburdened himself. He told the priest he was a Royal Signals operator attached to a team of army scientists who, against all conventions, were developing germ warfare projects, among them anthrax. Watson had broken radio watch to hunt for matches for his pipe. He'd picked up a box in an out of bounds but unguarded laboratory. He was in the laboratory just two minutes. It was enough for him to have contracted anthrax.

The priest forgave him.

Three sleepless nights later the troubled Father O'Hagan caught the Liverpool ferry to Dublin. He then took a train west and visited his brother, a bishop. After great deliberation and soul searching, his brother decided Watson's last confession should be brought to the attention of higher authorities. He drafted a letter to the Vatican.

Six weeks later an Italian submarine rose in the swell off the Isle of Fiagha. Six specially trained navy frogmen put ashore. They returned with test-tube samples stolen from the unguarded laboratory.

The samples were analysed at Bologna University.

Anthrax was confirmed.

So was a mutant strain of the Black Death.

It was codenamed Wildfire.

Bruno put down the report with horror.

It was common knowledge in university circles that experiments were being carried out with anthrax. Bruno thought that despicable.

But bubonic plague!

If that report was true then everything else, including his dream for penicillin, passed into insignificance.

'So you see, we have samples of the strain. I want you to produce an antidote. Science has so far failed to find one. You must,' Rossi said urgently.

'How can I be sure that report is genuine?'

'You can't,' Rossi said. 'But you also can't take the chance it is not.'

Bruno knew that was true. The whole concept of using the Black Death in germ warfare made him retch. Millions would die. There would be a new Dark Age. The plague was no respecter of international borders. The scientist in him began to relish the challenge. With an antidote the weapon would be useless. People could be immunized.

Then Rossi said, 'You will be working with Professor Pini. You know of him?'

Bruno nodded. Pini.

He felt a bead of cold sweat run down his neck.

Revulsion.

Images from Lucia's letter raced through his mind.

He suddenly felt like a fly in a web.

Enrico Rossi was the spider.

Bruno was alone. He sat on his bed and scanned the phone book. He had to get hold of Lucia. Talk to her. Find out the truth.

She was not listed. His spirits sagged. Why the hell hadn't she put an address on the letter?

He'd call the university. He picked up the bedside phone and dialled. It was a direct line.

'Medical research. Lucia Corso. Professor Pini's department.'

There was a delay.

'Research,' a woman said.

'Signorina Corso.'

There was a pause.

'Who?' she asked.

Bruno repeated the name.

'One moment.'

He heard her put down the phone, walk away, and a door close. A minute later a man came on the line.

'Who is calling?' he asked.

'It's personal. I want to speak with Lucia Corso,' Bruno said.

'You have the wrong number.'

'That is Professor Pini's department?'

'Yes.'

'Then I have the right number,' Bruno said. He could hear whispers in the background. Hushed. Conspiratorial.

'You must be mistaken,' the man said, 'there is no one here of that name.'

'But this is the number I was given,' Bruno protested. A strange feeling stirred uneasily inside him. 'She is a researcher,' he added.

'I'm afraid not. There is no Lucia Corso working here. Or ever has been for that matter. Goodbye.'

The man slammed the phone down.

Bruno's mouth went dry. He dialled the main university switchboard.

'Student registry,' he asked.

'Registry.'

'*Buongiorno*,' Bruno said. 'My name is Dr Mario Fantoni of International Pharmaceutical Products of Geneva. We have received a job application from one of your researchers and I would like to confirm her qualifications before offering her an interview. Could this be done over the phone? It would save a lot of time.'

'Certainly.'

'Her name is Lucia Corso.'

'One moment.'

Bruno waited anxiously. Perhaps Lucia's claims were nothing more than the wild imaginings of a deranged mind.

The voice came back on the line.

'You did say Lucia Corso.'

'Yes.'

'We have no record of any such person.'

This was nonsense.

'I'm afraid she has misled you. There is no record of her ever being an undergraduate at Bologna or anywhere else in Italy.'

Bruno, open mouthed, put the phone down. This was like a bad dream. He loved the girl.

Now he was being asked to believe that she never existed.

His stomach turned. Bruno needed air. He moved to the window and opened it. He breathed deeply and looked up towards the church on the hill.

The sun glinted on something in the lemon grove.

Two spangles of light danced from amid the trees. Then they were gone.

Bruno looked hard.

He saw a yellow shape move through the trees.

It was a jacket. The man wearing it was ducking low and moving up the hill towards the portico.

A pair of binoculars were slung over his shoulders.

The man had been watching the villa.

Dinner was taken alfresco on the terrace under an arbour of vines and dry reeds. The wine flowed freely.

Bruno eyed Pini across the table. He was reptilian. His smooth skin sallow, as if bathed in formalin. His eyes, Bruno noted, seldom blinked behind his round glasses. He'd eaten daintily, frequently brushing his lips with his tongue. He wore a cream lightweight suit and a panama hat.

Rossi picked up a carafe of wine and carelessly filled their glasses.

'Right, gentlemen,' he said, 'to business. You all know the Black Death once changed the course of history. It brought the Middle Ages in Europe to an end and killed one in two of the population. You men of science would know the whys and wherefores better than a simple policeman like myself. But I know that dying from the Black Death is not a pleasant end . . .'

Bruno felt Rossi's huge hand close around his arm, the fingers tightened on his flesh. From the corner of his eye Bruno noticed Pini peel an orange. He felt Rossi's breath on his face as his cousin bent towards him.

'Pini tells me a man begins to shiver first and his temperature rises, it's as if he has a common cold. His neck comes up in lumps, then his armpits and groin. His skin breaks out in black sores. Twelve hours later he's dead. And in that twelve hours he has damned to death every man, woman and child he's come in contact with.'

Bruno felt his grip tighten and saw beads of sweat on Rossi's forehead.

'Take a city like Naples, even Rome. Just imagine what would happen if there was an outbreak as a result of germ warfare. Just imagine.'

Bruno did.

It made him shudder.

'You must help us,' Rossi said urgently. 'You must. We have to know how we can stop this Wildfire strain. But so far we've come up with nothing.'

Rossi glanced at Pini who was carefully cutting his orange into neat segments and arranging them carefully on his plate.

'Explain to Bruno in words of one syllable that even I can understand,' said Rossi.

Pini sighed, his face expressionless, the overhead light reflecting on his glasses.

He had the air of a man scornful of those less gifted than himself and envious of those who were.

'How much do you know about the plague?' Pini asked.

'I've never made a study,' admitted Bruno, 'but I assume it's similar to other bacterial zoonosis.'

'What?' Rossi interrupted.

'A disease from animals,' Pini said, then turned to Bruno. 'We received samples of the Wildfire strain about ten months ago. Examination showed it to be an artificially induced form of *Yersinia pestis*: the Black Death. In normal circumstances the bacteria live in rats. Fleas bite the rats, suck their blood and themselves become carriers of the disease. They then bite humans and infect them. Just two or three bacilli are enough to prove fatal. Three bacilli among the countless billions of cells in the human body and in twelve hours the unwilling host is dead.'

'Fine,' interrupted Rossi. 'But fleas can't infect millions of people. It's just not possible.'

'They don't have to,' Pini said enthusiastically. 'Once into the human blood stream the bubonic bacillus starts multiplying and changing. Basically, there are three forms of the disease, straightforward bubonic, septicaemic which causes the body to break out in black sores and lastly, the pulmonary plague. This affects the human lung and here we have our killer. It is passed on by droplet spread, breathed out in microscopic particles. This cannot be prevented by any known vaccination. This is the basis of the Wildfire strain, an airborne plague, with no way of stopping it.'

Bruno said to Pini: 'What has already been done?'

'Everything,' he said forlornly. 'We've tried the lot.

Intensive protein and carbohydrate cultures have an effect on the basic bacillus, but . . .'

'Which is why I've asked you to help,' Rossi snapped. 'Can you?'

'Perhaps,' Bruno answered.

'I'm going to need more than perhaps,' Rossi rasped as if he felt excluded from the men of science. 'You have got to come up with an antidote.'

'Science isn't that simple,' Bruno said. He resented his cousin's tone. He added, 'Before I help you I want to see this strain in laboratory conditions. I have to examine it and be given full access to papers relating to previous experiments.'

'As good as done. When do you want to start?'

'Tomorrow. I must see everything.'

He saw Pini hesitate, his eyes flickered briefly.

Bruno would wait before he asked about Lucia.

CHAPTER SIX

The three Rhesus monkeys were bald. Their bodies had been completely shaved smooth, except for the fur on top of their heads. They sat in separate glass tanks built into the wall of Pini's research laboratory. With a passing glance, even a man of Bruno's experience could have been forgiven for mistaking them for human babies.

Their skin was pink, creased to chubby rolls in places. Their tiny buttocks were red. Even the nails on their fingers and toes were perfect. Yet he saw the fear in their listless eyes as they lolled on the floor of the tanks.

'When were they injected with *Yersinia pestis*?' Bruno asked Pini.

'The first two were injected twenty-four hours ago. The third hasn't been touched.' He pointed to the last tank.

Bruno could see it was connected to the other two by separate red rubber tubes.

'They provide the droplet spread from the injected pair,' Bruno said.

Pini, hands behind his back, nodded.

Bruno moved closer to the tanks. He saw the first Rhesus had already broken out in open sores which the animal had been scratching until they bled. The second monkey leant against the corner of the tank, head between its knees. Great lumps appeared on its neck from swollen glands. Black boils covered its arms and thin legs.

Bruno's eyes ran along the length of tube to the third monkey's tank. It was in a worse state than the others. It lay curled in a foetal position, its ulcerated arms positioned protectively over its head. It convulsed in a spasm. Bruno turned away. It was obscene. Yet he knew the obscenity would be greater if a human baby had breathed the air in that sealed tank.

'This is the Wildfire strain,' Bruno said.

'Yes. You can see just how quickly it transmutes into the airborne pulmonary version. That animal will be dead within the hour.'

The prospect of what he saw repeated outside the laboratory relegated any reservations Bruno had about assisting Rossi and Pini. All that mattered at that moment was that he should find a way of destroying the horror he'd witnessed. He had always had the ability to concentrate his mind on a problem until he'd solved it. Bruno could shut out all matters except the one in hand. Some saw it as a trait of single-minded arrogance, others selfishness. They were wrong.

It was total dedication.

He would apply this dedication.

'Show me the culture,' he told Pini and allowed him to lead the way from the laboratory. He paused for Pini to open the heavy sealed door and looked back at the third tank.

Behind the thick glass wall he saw the monkey writhing on the floor, its mouth opening and closing in silent screams.

Bruno pressed his eye against the microscope and adjusted the focus. Beneath the lens was a glass slide. In it was sealed the agar, a jelly-like culture of protein which played host to a single bacillus of the Wildfire strain. Because it was so lethal the authorities had constructed a special underground laboratory away from the main campus of Bologna, in a small valley five miles from the city and sealed by a high fence. *Carabinieri* guarded the gate with slung rifles. Strict security meant no one got in or out without a pass. It was unlike any university research unit Bruno had ever seen. But as he focused the microscope he knew why. The single mutant bacillus of *Yersinia pestis* came into view.

Bruno stood back from the eyepiece. He wore an antiseptic mask, even though the slide was sealed, and filled a pipette from a tray on the bench. It contained a concentrated protein preparation.

Carefully, he squeezed the pipette into a tube which ran through a sealed bung in the agar culture. He looked into the eyepiece and beheld total wonder. The life forms began to move in time with the music of Bach that played in his head. He saw a form of death in motion and could only marvel at the miracle.

The bacillus was rod shaped, adorned at the edges with fine threads which floated rhythmically as it moved through the culture. There was a cautious but purposeful relentlessness about its movement as if it was aware of its own deadly strength. It stopped suddenly as the drops from Bruno's pipette spread across the agar. Minute globules left the parent body like reconnaissance scouts as other, larger blobs followed in their wake like advance raiding parties.

The bacillus tensed as they approached and, uncertain of their intentions, began to retreat slowly, changing shape until it faced the intruders like a pair of bull's horns. The globules entered the arc of the horns. Then the bacillus whiplashed in one violent movement scattering all before it.

It was no longer cautious. Convinced of its own invulnerability it began its systematic destruction of the opposition. Its ribonucleic acids began to act, searing down the centre of the rod-shaped bacillus, dividing it into two identical parts. It began to give birth to itself, creating life to produce death, in a frantic unending microscopic ballet. Its sting was victory. Final and complete. Unopposed it would recreate itself a millionfold.

Bruno looked away.

'It's awesome,' he said.

'Lethal,' Pini added, with a note in the tone of his voice that Bruno found disturbing. He could not think why.

Bruno rose, hands behind his back, and walked to the door leading to the other laboratory. With Pini at his shoulder he looked into the third monkey's tank.

The creature had died. So had the others. Bruno stood in

silence. He studied the look of sheer terror on the animals' faces.

At last he said: 'I want to study all your research papers and experimental findings.'

'I'll have it seen to,' Pini said.

'Now,' Bruno said. 'I have work to do.'

'Let's drink to it,' Rossi beamed when Bruno told him his decision to stay. They were sitting with Pini around a table on the villa terrace.

Rossi bellowed, 'Bring some grappa and brandy.'

The caretaker's plump wife Rosa put the bottles and glasses on the table. Bruno returned her smile. She cooed at him as she would an infant, then waddled back indoors.

'This evening we relax, later I have a treat for you,' Rossi said getting to his feet and filling the glasses with grappa.

'Brandy for me,' Pini said.

Rossi waved the request aside and gave him grappa.

'This is a man's drink,' he said.

Bruno saw Pini screw his face as he took a sip.

'Now,' Rossi said, 'we'll have a real celebration. Did my Zio Alfredo teach you mountain songs?'

'Some,' Bruno said, 'a long time ago.' He thought wistfully of Welsh Sundays when men cried at thoughts of home. He realized, ironically, he was thinking of his home for the first time since he arrived in Italy.

Rossi began to sing. His voice was strong and clear, it carried with feeling on the night air. His repertoire was mixed. Work songs from the fields and vineyards. Bawdy songs about randy goatherds and willing girls.

'Do you know this one?' he asked but launched himself into it before Bruno could reply. Even Pini, Bruno noticed, nodded in appreciation at the fine quality of the voice. He'd also secretly exchanged his grappa for brandy.

Gradually, the songs became gentler.

'This is one of the greatest love songs I know,' Rossi said. 'I sing it to my wife Paola.'

Bruno recognized the haunting melody and noticed Rossi sat quietly when he'd finished, as if he had nothing left to top it.

No one spoke as he filled his glass with grappa and sat looking at the outline of the Apennines against the night sky. Deep in thought. Distant.

Bruno saw his chance. He took it quickly and engaged Pini in small talk. Trivial university talk, between one academic and another. Pini even smiled thinly at times and each tried to top the other's stories.

'Ah, Bologna, the city of students,' said Pini as Bruno plied his glass with brandy, 'and the bella Novella d'Andrea. She was one of the most beautiful creatures ever to grace the earth, she gave her lectures from behind a curtain so as not to distract her students.' He laughed for the first time that evening. 'But that was in the thirteenth century. There is no one like her at Bologna these days.' He pulled a face.

'But that's just not true,' countered Bruno lightly.

'You wait until you see them.' Pini had begun to slur his speech as he waved his hand dismissively.

'No,' Bruno smiled and wagged his finger, 'there was a girl from Bologna I met once in England.' Bruno clenched his fist and slapped the inside of his arm as he raised it symbolically. He felt cheap.

'Let me see,' Bruno stretched the sentence. 'Lisa something. No. Lucia, that's it. Lucia Corso.'

He noticed Pini's smile fade. He retreated instantly behind his reptilian mask.

'No,' he said quickly. 'The name means nothing. She has not been at Bologna during my time. You must be mistaken.'

Pini's face was blank. It betrayed nothing. But the throbbing pulse pounding the vein on his temple did.

'I must be mistaken,' laughed Bruno, knowing he had never been more right in his life.

The way Rossi jerked from his melancholy at the mention of the name confirmed it. He glanced quickly at Pini, but not quickly enough for Bruno to miss his fleeting concern.

He announced, 'It's late.'

Pini took his cue and glanced at his watch.

'Have one for the road,' Rossi insisted. But at the same time he took Pini by the arm and moved from the table.

'Another time,' Pini said as they drifted towards the villa.

'I'll see you in the music room for a nightcap,' Rossi said over his shoulder, 'it's getting chilly.'

Bruno grunted. He sat for a few minutes listening to the crickets. He rose when he heard the Lancia's engine start up and moved towards the open French windows.

Rossi was already waiting, a glass of brandy in each hand. Bruno took one.

'It's real French cognac,' Rossi said. 'What did you think of Pini?'

'Bit of a cold fish,' Bruno said, 'but capable.'

Rossi agreed. 'But I enjoyed the evening. It's good to sing the old songs to someone who appreciates them. Not like Pini, he has Roman water in his veins. If you need anything for your work then come straight to me – don't involve yourself with Pini's red tape. What you want you'll get.'

'I'm going to need it,' Bruno said. 'Those bacilli are the most virulent I've seen.'

'I know.' Rossi nodded with satisfaction. He'd spoken just as Pini had when he described it as lethal. Again Bruno felt disturbed. Then realized both had sung its praises.

Proud of it.

Like parents.

'Anything wrong?' Rossi said.

'I'm tired,' Bruno feigned a yawn.

Rossi's face fell. 'But I have arranged a real treat for us, something special.' He sounded disappointed.

Bruno put down his glass and waved aside Rossi's protest. 'It's been a long day,' Bruno said and made for the door.

Pini lied about Lucia Corso.

Her name had also jolted Rossi, Bruno decided.

He leant on the balcony outside his bedroom looking up at the church. It was oppressively hot and still. The double windows were open and he'd lit a small chemical burner. It gave off foul fumes, but killed the mosquitoes.

He saw the white Lancia return and swing through the gates.

Rossi's footsteps echoed in the hall, the door opened and he saw his cousin stride towards the waiting car. Two women got out.

The blonde was tall. She wore a tight-fitting white dress that fell below the knee, slit halfway up her thigh. A fur stole was tossed carelessly over her bare shoulder. She held an evening bag and stood with her weight on one foot, her hand on her waist to emphasize the curve of her hips.

The raven-haired girl wore a low-cut red blouse with layers of frills and puffed sleeves. Her make-up was heavy and she hovered uncertainly behind her companion.

Bruno stepped back from the balcony. He knocked over the insect burner.

He saw Rossi raise both arms in greeting. The blonde came forward, threw her arms around his neck and kissed him fully on the mouth, bringing her knee slowly up between his legs.

Bruno saw the other girl shift uneasily. He realized they were the surprise Rossi promised.

Rossi and the blonde were huddled in conversation, heads together. Bruno watched as she turned, walked back and spoke to the other girl. She seemed reluctant. He couldn't hear what was said, but there was much gesturing. At last the girls came forward. Rossi drew the other girl to him and kissed her as he had the blonde. Then one on each arm he walked back to the villa, laughing loudly. Bruno closed the window.

Then he stopped dead, caught his breath, and peered towards the open gates.

In the moonlight he saw the man clearly. But only for a second. Then the man ducked into the shadows of the lemon trees and vanished.

But not before Bruno had noted his wild black beard. Or the pale yellow jacket.

His unease grew. He knew he had to find Lucia Corso.

CHAPTER SEVEN

Bruno counted the death toll. He was in the laboratory.

In ten months Wildfire had accounted for two hundred Rhesus monkeys, eighty-four guinea pigs, and countless rats and mice. The results were depressing. None survived exposure.

Each experiment had been carefully cross referenced. He could follow the directions research had taken like a map. Nowhere did it point to experiments on human beings.

There was nothing he could find to back up what Lucia had claimed in her letter. If she was still in Bologna she would have made some attempt to contact him. That worried him. He had to find her.

Bruno re-read the papers. This time his mind was focused only on the problem of finding a way to stop Wildfire. He must. He pored over the research and he realized something was missing. There had been no experiments on the prime carrier of Black Death. Black rats. He made a mental note to get some.

He ploughed through the papers until early afternoon. In his glass-walled office at one end of the long laboratory he could see the research team at work on the long benches which ran down the centre of the room. Dressed in white coats they pored over culture samples or hunched over microscopes. There were twenty-eight – four teams of seven – at the main university. Twelve more worked here in the underground laboratory.

Bruno had not yet spoken to any of them. But he knew all there was to know about them, what schools they'd attended, their qualifications, personal details. Their files contained it all. Just like his own file he'd found at Verdi's flat.

He buzzed the intercom and called the project secretary.

Claudia Mattucci swept into the office. She was a ripe woman of thirty with flawless olive skin and full bust. She moved with a lithe sensuality and feline grace.

'These are the complete files of everyone working on the Wildfire project?' Bruno asked.

'It's what you asked,' Claudia said. 'If you need anything else just let me know.' She rounded her lips and offered them with a smile that left Bruno with little doubt as to what she meant.

'How about coffee,' he said. 'Care to join me?'

'Mmmmm.'

Bruno caught the draught of her perfume as she swished from the office. His eyes followed the motion of her hips as she moved down the laboratory, turning men's heads as she passed. She returned with two cups. Bruno took one and offered her a chair. She sat, instead, on the corner of the desk and delicately hitched her skirt.

Bruno sipped his coffee noisily.

'Just like an Italian already,' said Claudia.

They laughed.

Bruno waved his hand sweepingly to embrace the laboratory. 'Does all this excite you?' he asked.

'It's all above my head,' she said airily. 'But sometimes I think this place would come to a halt without me. They are all very sweet, but so disorganized. I wonder how some of them find their way to work each morning without a map. They are dotty.'

They laughed again.

'But not you,' she said suddenly.

'No.'

'Why did you want to see the personal files? Not even Frederico has asked for that.'

Bruno was not sure if it was the question which surprised him, or that a secretary should refer to her professor by his first name.

'Just to check their background,' he said casually, 'to see if I think they are up to standard.' He gathered up the files around him. 'You can put them back now.'

Claudia bent over the desk and took them, Bruno felt her fingers brush the back of his hand. They lingered briefly. He was tempted.

'Anything else?'

'Yes.' He watched her raise one eyebrow. 'How many people have left this project since it began?'

She paused. 'I'm not sure. I've only worked for Frederico for a month. I could find out for you.' she said eagerly.

He watched her pick up the phone. She put the question to someone at the other end, then covered the mouthpiece with her hand.

'This could cost you dinner,' she laughed.

'Done.' He smiled back.

'Uh-uh,' she nodded down the phone and hung up.

'Three. A man and two women.'

Two women.

Bruno stirred.

'Would we still have their files?' he said.

'Of course.'

'Could I see them?'

'That might just cost you supper as well.'

Bruno watched her wind her bead necklace around her index finger.

She returned at six with the three files. Over her shoulder Bruno saw the lab staff hang up their white coats and drift home, faces tired after another long and futile day.

'Remind me to order as many black rats as I can get,' Bruno told her without thinking.

'Charming.' Claudia threw back her head in mock indignation. 'I shift heaven and earth for these files and all you can talk about is rats. What about dinner?'

'Sorry,' Bruno grinned. He showed no sign of the urge he felt to get at the files she held under her arm. He was convinced one would be Lucia Corso's.

'You're forgiven,' Claudia said. 'I'll see you at eight in the

Trattoria Luigi. It's just around the corner on Via San Vitale.'

'Can't wait,' Bruno said and wished her gone. He clenched his fingers under the desk as she dropped the files in front of him.

'Till eight,' she said and left.

Bruno tore at the files, heart pumping. It had to be there. The disappointment spread over him like gloom.

There were three names.

None of them Lucia's.

One of the files had the word 'Deceased' stamped in red on the cover. It belonged to a Maria Balbo. He put it to one side. They'd kept a record on the dead. But not the living. Not Lucia.

Then he realized the other two would almost have certainly known Lucia. They were no longer part of the team and he would be able to talk to them without raising suspicions. He turned to the two files.

The man was a young doctor called Angelo Calvi. His photograph was fixed inside the cover. He'd worked directly under Pini at the security laboratory. But had emigrated to Argentina seven months ago with his wife and two children and now worked in the Italian hospital in Buenos Aires.

Bruno had drawn a blank. He slung the file on the dead girl's.

The girl in the third file was also no longer of this world. Rosa Mori, former medical student, had become a nun. She'd abandoned the Wildfire project and taken holy orders that June. Almost three months earlier. She would have worked with Lucia. She was now at the Holy Convent of the Sacred Heart. Bruno noted the address.

It was almost as an afterthought he checked the dead girl's file. He opened the cover and felt his pulse stop with a thump. Maria Balbo's photograph then made his heart pound again. Furiously.

He recognized the dead girl's face.

She had been very much alive the last time he'd seen her.

She was the raven-haired girl who came with the blonde to Rossi at the Villa Marco. A bar girl who hired her services.

Bruno's eyes were drawn slowly back to the file.

It said Maria Balbo had been a senior researcher. She was twenty-four. Her position had been under review at the time of her death because of her anti-government attitudes. She belonged to a radical student group. She'd died with a boyfriend when his car left a mountain road and plunged into a ravine.

That was a lie. As much a lie as the denials of Lucia's existence.

He had seen the girl.

She had slept with his cousin and a blonde.

Bruno gathered up the files and locked them in the desk. He had never felt less like dinner.

Even though it promised Claudia Mattucci.

Pini's project secretary.

Even though he wanted her.

'I am going to fire three of the research team,' Bruno told Claudia.

'Oh?' Claudia half tilted her head in surprise.

'They don't seem to have the dedication or application I need,' Bruno lied. He hated lying.

'When did you decide that?'

'This afternoon. After I'd read their files. They should never have been recruited.' It was vital he should be seen to justify his inspection now he knew Claudia was not only Pini's secretary. She was also his mistress.

She told him over the *frutti*. Then said, 'You are going to sleep with me tonight, Bruno, but we must take great care. Frederico Pini may not look it but he can be wild when he's jealous. It is better he never finds out.'

She'd laughed wildly. Throwing back her head on her long neck.

Bruno studied her. They shared a kerbside table under a palm outside the Trattoria Luigi. It was popular with university staff and students alike. Bologna's artistic set also used it. Actors rubbed shoulders with artists. Now Bruno wished they'd chosen somewhere more discreet. He felt guilty. He did not want to fire three of the team, but he did want to sleep with Claudia Mattucci.

She was beautiful, amusing and intelligent. All evening he'd resisted the temptation to reach out and run his hand over her smooth skin. He needed a woman. It had been months. A woman like her. He also knew she wanted him. She'd made that clear from the first time he'd seen her. Now her hand squeezed his knee under the table.

Behind him voices sang to the sound of a mandolin. Bruno looked over his shoulder. A group of student musicians moved among the tables of the trattoria opposite.

They caroused the customers and were dressed like seventeenth century street players of Bologna – the *Mezzentini*. They wore pointed hats with feathers, pantaloons and baggy jerkins with bright puffed sleeves. A girl collected the lire in a deep hat.

Bruno turned to Claudia. His jaw fell.

'What is it?' She touched his hand. 'You've gone white. You look as if you've seen a ghost.'

Bruno sat numbed.

The group moved off up the street.

Bruno leapt to his feet and knocked the tray from the waiter's hands. A bottle of wine and plates smashed on the floor. Bruno bowled between the tables, knocking the chairs aside as he tore after the students.

They turned and ran, scattering in all directions.

Bruno dogged the girl with the cap.

The young girl from the Villa Marco.

The girl with the face of someone who'd been killed in a car crash.

She threw the cap aside, scattering coins and notes over the road. Her arms flailed wildly. Bruno saw her fear as she stole glances at him over her shoulder.

He breathed deeply, gritted his jaw and threw back his

head. His feet pounded the street. He didn't see the street vendor, his tray of sweets and nuts around his neck.

They collided. Bruno stumbled and lost his balance. When he recovered the girl was at the corner of the Via Zamboni.

Bruno ran flat out and rounded the corner. He paused, heaving for breath, hands on knees. The girl ducked into a church. Bruno bounded after her.

The high wooden doors were closed. They led to the Cappella Bentivoglio, the funeral chapel of the family whose name it bore.

The doors closed after him with a heavy thud. It echoed. Then the church was still. Candles burned in front of the high altar. Bruno squinted into the gloom.

It was as silent and chilling as the tombs it housed.

Bruno moved cautiously towards the altar.

There was no sign of the girl.

'I am not going to harm you,' he called. His words echoed softly in the emptiness.

He inched down the nave and crossed the transept under the carved pulpit, where a bible was borne on a wooden eagle's open wings.

Bruno climbed the steps to the sanctuary and searched the clergy pews. He approached the high altar and lifted the crimson cloth.

No one.

He called again. Silence.

Bruno moved behind the altar into the ambulatory. It was deserted. Then he checked the small rooms off the ambulatory. Nothing. The rear door was bolted. From inside.

The place was deserted. The girl had just vanished. Bruno walked back to the door and waited.

She had to come out.

She didn't. Twenty minutes passed, then bewildered, he walked back to the Trattoria Luigi, felt like a fool, and wondered what he'd say to Claudia.

He needn't have bothered.

She'd left.

He paid the bill. Then found a small hotel and booked in for the night.

He slept badly.

Bruno lingered in the shower, allowing the cool water to wash over him, until he came alive. He shaved with a borrowed razor and nicked himself twice. He retrieved his socks from the balcony where they'd dried in the morning sun, dressed, then ordered morning papers. They brought *La Stampa*, *Corriere della Serra* and *Resto di Carlino*. The first two were published in Turin and Milan, he glanced at the headlines and put them aside. The third was Bologna's local paper. It would be more likely to carry stories the others would ignore, fatal car crashes, for example.

He called the labs, checked their work plans, cancelled them and gave fresh instructions. Then Bruno folded the local paper under his arm and ordered a cab from the hotel foyer. It dropped him outside the editorial offices of *Resto di Carlino*.

The ground floor windows were completely boarded up. The boards were daubed with graffiti and political slogans. Two armed police stood outside the swing doors. Bruno walked past them into the foyer a little uneasily. Armed guards at newspaper offices were outside his experience.

Once inside the foyer, he saw the reason. Two walls were charred and the ceiling was black with smoke damage. A sodden carpet was rolled and stacked next to the burnt-out office furniture. Temporary phone lines ran over a frosted glass partition marked EDITORIAL.

The reception desk was unmanned. Bruno slammed the brass bell with the palm of his hand. Moments later a young man emerged from behind the partition. He wore a short-sleeved pullover, baggy cord trousers and no tie. His hair was tousled. He acknowledged Bruno by lifting his head and eyebrows at the same time.

'Yes?' he said guardedly.

'I need your help,' Bruno said. 'Is it possible to see some back numbers and look through the cuttings library? I'll pay the fee.'

'It's possible but it wouldn't do you much good. They are just burnt paper now.' The reporter indicated the damage. 'A *Fascisti* fire bomb.'

Bruno showed anger. 'Why?'

'They didn't like something we wrote, perhaps. Who knows? They don't have to have reasons. They just remind us they're there now and again.'

Bruno shook his head. 'Thanks anyway,' he said. 'And good luck. Keep on writing.' He turned to go.

'Wait,' the reporter called, his tone warmer. 'What did you want?'

'Details of a car crash.'

'When?'

Bruno told him.

'Ah-Ah,' the reporter said knowingly.

'You remember it?' Bruno was surprised.

'The Manzini crash. I covered it.'

'Manzini?'

'He was driving. Manzini was a well-known student radical. He'd been to a party in the hills with his girlfriend.'

'Maria Balbo.'

'Right. You knew her?'

Bruno shook his head. 'Tell me about the crash.'

'Which version?'

Bruno looked puzzled.

'You're not Italian are you? I thought I detected a slight accent.'

'My parents were Italian.'

'You're American then.'

'British.'

The reporter nodded knowingly again. 'The official version was that Manzini lost control on a bend and went over a cliff. He'd had too much to drink. Unfortunate, but the authorities weren't going to shed a lot of tears. He was a thorn in their sides with student protests and things. It was an accident.'

'The other version?'

'Manzini didn't drink. Someone cut the brake pipes.'

The reporter left Bruno in no doubt which version he believed. He said: 'You saw the wreck?'

'I got to it with the photographer before the police.'

'And the couple were both dead?'

'Yes.'

'Are you certain?'

'I helped pull the girl out. She was dead.'

Bruno thought: Who was the girl I chased?

He said: 'You have been a great help. Thanks.'

'*Prego*.'

'Oh,' Bruno added. 'One last thing. Have you ever heard of Lucia Corso? She worked with the dead girl.'

'Lucia Corso?'

He shook his head.

The Convent of the Sacred Heart was a former hospice at the end of a cobbled cul-de-sac. Once it housed lepers. It was shielded from the narrow street by a high brick wall. The courtyard beyond had been torn up long ago. It was now divided into vegetable patches. The soil was sparse and the crops poor. The sisters it fed did not complain. Their needs were small and they asked for nothing more, except the strength to pray. It was here that the novice, Sister Rosa Mori, had chosen to spend the rest of her days on earth. Bruno had the order's permission to see her.

He tugged the wire rope at the door set in the outer wall. He heard a bell ring inside and pictured a hundred silent faces turn towards the sound. He waited.

At last the judas slid back in the door. Behind the iron grille he glimpsed a pair of eyes weighing him up carefully. The judas closed and he heard bolts withdrawn. The door opened.

The nun was bent with age and leant heavily on a twisted stick. She smiled faintly, held a bony finger to her lips and beckoned Bruno with a crooked arm. He followed the hobbling figure along the path between the vegetable gardens towards the old hospice. He smiled at a nun milking a goat which was tethered to a gnarled fig tree. She looked down.

The hospice was dark and fusty. There was no furniture in the large hall except a plain wooden cross on the wall, next to unlit tallow candles.

He followed the nun up a narrow winding stone stairway and along an unlit passage. It was low and he was forced to stoop. They stopped outside a door. He watched the old nun struggle with a large key, unlock it, and push it open for him. It closed behind him.

The flagstone floor was covered by a mat of reeds. There was a small window high in the wall. Under it was a bed of wooden boards, no pillow or blanket.

Bruno Rossi looked down on the most serene face he had ever seen. It was oval and pale with calm black eyes. Sister Rosa Mori closed them briefly in greeting. She sat at a table, an open bible before her.

'I need your help,' Bruno said.

She nodded.

'Are you allowed to speak?'

She nodded again.

Speech, Bruno realized, was a privilege not to be wasted lightly. He said: 'Mother Superior has explained why I'm here?'

Sister Rosa smiled faintly.

Bruno said: 'Did you work with Maria Balbo on the Wildfire research programme?'

Sister Rosa crossed herself and mouthed: 'May God have mercy on her soul.' She nodded.

'What about Lucia Corso?'

'Yes.'

Bruno felt the relief sweep over him like sunlight. He closed his eyes and experienced a rapid sequence of emotions. Satisfaction. Exultation. Joy. Anger because they'd tried to lie to him. Then fear.

'Do you know where she is?' His voice rose expectantly.

Sister Rosa sat impassively.

At last, she gave a barely perceptible movement that Bruno took to be a shake of the head.

'Were you her friend, please Sister, I need to know. Very badly.'

Again the nun would only nod.

'I came to Bologna because she wrote to me. Now she has vanished. And I swear by your God I must find her. Must,' he emphasized.

She bit her lip.

Bruno was baffled. The Mother Superior had agreed the girl could break her vow of silence. Yet she seemed bound by some great reluctance. He could sense turmoil behind the serenity.

She looked up into his eyes and he felt she had read his mind. It was uncanny. She brought her hands together and began to speak with a voice like a clear bell.

'They were both my friends. Lucia had a terrible secret which she shared with us. Maria was killed because of it.' She paused, yet her lips still moved. A silent prayer.

Bruno thought: And you ran here. It was a churlish thought and he hated himself for it.

The nun mouthed her Amen. Then continued: 'No matter what people may tell you Lucia was not mad. You see, she had no God. She had no priest to confide in, only psychiatrists.'

'I don't understand.'

'I believe Lucia was given medication to break her mind.'

'Hallucinatory drugs.' Bruno failed to conceal his scepticism. His disparagement was met by a patient gaze.

'Please do not make me waste words,' she said and raised her hand to ward off interruption. 'When Lucia told Maria and I she had proof that human beings were being sacrificed for medical research, we believed her. It was a truth. Maria told Gino Manzini and they were going to make politics out of it. Now they are dead. Killed. By that time I had already decided to serve our Lord here. His protection keeps me safe, though that is not the reason I took it. That left Lucia. She could not call on the strength that shields me. She went to doctors of the mind, not the soul. It was then, and only then, people feared her sanity was deserting her. Who would believe her stories now?'

'Did she tell you how she knew, or why such experiments were being carried out? Or where?'

She shook her head sadly. 'Find her,' she murmured.

'I've tried. I don't even have her old address.'

'Signora Bellini. Strada Giulio.'

Bruno looked down at the nun. He tried to picture her in another place, laughing at a party, walking in the woods or along a beach. He could not. This was her place, perhaps it always was. Then he thought of the dead girl.

'Sister Rosa,' he said softly, 'what if I told you I had seen Maria Balbo twice since her death? (He almost added – and she works as a bar girl for hire – but the words would not come.) 'Once I almost touched her but she ran away.'

'Then I'd say you saw Carla.'

'Carla?'

'Maria's twin sister.'

Bruno was taken by surprise. Before he could recover the heavy key turned in the lock behind him. He heard the door creak ajar and saw Sister Rosa fall onto her knees in prayer.

He turned.

The old nun stood framed in the door.

Bruno's eyes fixed on the knotted leather thongs she held in her gnarled hand. He watched in horror as she shuffled to the table and laid the thongs on the open bible. Sister Rosa continued praying.

The old nun motioned Bruno to follow as she moved from the room.

As the door closed Sister Rosa called quietly, 'You must help her.'

It was with torment Bruno Rossi realized the price the young nun had to pay for breaking her pledge of silence.

CHAPTER EIGHT

Half the deserted street was in shadow, the other baked by the afternoon sun, hot and white.

Bruno Rossi sat astride the Motto Guzzi motorcycle he'd bought earlier that morning. He wiped the sweat from his eyes, kicked the bike into gear and cruised the Strada Giulio slowly. He scanned the houses until he saw Lucia's old lodgings. Signora Bellini's name was painted in black scroll on the pink wall. He parked the bike in the shade and crossed the silent street. He knocked on the door.

It half opened moments later. A lined, leathery old face looked at him suspiciously through the crack.

'Signora Bellini?'

'*Si*,' her voice was cracked.

'I'd like to speak to you about Lucia Corso.'

The door slammed in Bruno's face. But not before he'd caught the look on the old Sicilian's face. It was one of fear.

'Go away,' she called from behind the door. 'She does not live here anymore.'

Bruno knocked again. He bent and called through the letterbox. 'Please, it's very important.'

He heard the old lady fasten the bolt with a thud.

'I am a friend of Lucia's,' Bruno pleaded urgently.

'That's what the man with the knife said. Go and leave me in peace.' Signora Bellini's voice trembled.

'Sister Rosa Mori told me where to find you. And I don't know anything about a man with a knife. I swear it,' Bruno said softly.

An old eye looked back at him through the letterbox. It was still cautious, but the fear had gone.

'What is your name?' she asked, her accent heavy Sicilian.

'Rossi. Bruno Rossi.'

The eye vanished and the bolt was drawn back slowly. Bruno straightened.

The door opened. Signora Bellini was swathed in widow's black. Her eyes darted as Bruno stepped inside. He followed her into the parlour. In it were amassed the trinkets of a lifetime. Faded photographs in oval frames, china figurines of saints. The furniture was old and shabby. There was a gate-leg table covered by a cloth of fine Sicilian lace. On it was a snapshot of Lucia Corso. Bruno picked it up.

Something kindled.

'Do you know where she is?'

The old lady shook her head. She reached out and took the snapshot from Bruno's fingers.

'They took everything else,' she said, 'but then you know.'

'No,' Bruno said. 'I don't know; tell me.'

The old Sicilian fixed him with an expressionless stare. She moved to a worn armchair without taking her eyes from him and sat. The silence seemed endless.

At last she said, 'You must know. The poor child was troubled. Greatly troubled.'

'Was she . . .' Bruno searched for a word other than mad. But the woman understood.

'No. She was not mad. Just greatly troubled by something. It drove her in fear, panic, from this house. She had an accident and was taken to hospital. I went straight to the hospital but she had been removed. They said she had been taken to a private clinic for the insane. They would not tell me where. I treated that child like my own. I know she was not mad. I know.'

'I believe you,' Bruno said.

The woman seemed gratified she was not alone.

'I'm glad,' she said. 'When they refused to tell me where she had been taken from the hospital I went and complained to the police.' She stamped her foot and snorted. 'They said there was nothing they could do and it was no business of mine. I was not family. But when I got home there were two men waiting. They said they were colleagues of Lucia from the university and would take her things for her. They cleaned out her room, took everything that was hers. They left nothing to show that she'd ever lived here. Nothing.'

'Can you describe these men?'

The old woman swelled with anger.

'One looked like a snake.' She spat the words.

Pini, Bruno thought.

'But it was the other, the charming one, who was poison. There are many of his kind in Sicily. You can tell them because they always smile, no matter what they mean or say. When they smile it is really to show you how sharp their teeth are.'

Bruno recognized the description of his cousin. But it was hard to believe that either man would have to threaten the old woman in the chair with a knife.

'These were the men who threatened you with a knife?'

The old woman threw back her head in a guttural scoff. It sounded like a death rattle.

'No, this man had *la paura*. That made him dangerous.'

Bruno knew the words meant more than fear. It meant the experience a man feels when he is dragged from his bed by strangers at dawn.

'He came like you,' she said, 'but with *la paura*. He said he was a friend and asked for help. But he smelt like a hunted animal. When I told him what I've told you he produced a knife. He held it to my throat and called me a liar.'

She spat into the empty fireplace.

'He pressed the knife, here.' Her fingers dug into her wrinkled neck and left a white mark against the brown skin.

'What did you do?'

'I cursed him.'

'And?'

'He took away the knife and knelt. He squeezed my hand and pleaded with me to tell him where Lucia was. I could not because I do not know. But if I'd known I would not have told him. He had *la paura*, the kind that makes the hunted hunters.'

Bruno understood.

'This man, what was he like?'

'Young,' she said sympathetically, as if it justified all. 'He was small and thin, with a black beard and eyes with *la paura*. His hair was wild.'

The man from the bushes at the Villa Marco, Bruno thought. The man who'd watched him.

'You know him?' she asked.

'No. But I think he knows me,' Bruno said.

'Then be careful.'

'Did he have a girl with him?'

'He was alone. His kind are happy that way.'

Bruno doubted it.

'Signora,' he asked, 'may I see Lucia's old room, if you have not re-let it?'

The Sicilian shot him a glance that cut.

'Her room will always be waiting. No matter how long,' she said as if no other thought had ever crossed her mind. 'But as I've told you; they have taken everything of hers.'

'Please,' Bruno insisted.

The old lady mumbled to herself and Bruno followed her upstairs.

She unlocked the door.

'See,' she proclaimed. 'Nothing.'

Bruno brushed past.

The old woman seemed right. The room looked bare.

Bedclothes were folded neatly on the mattress. The wardrobe doors lay open to reveal empty hangers and shelves. The bookcase was bare, light squares on the faded wall showed where pictures had hung. The patch above the sink was shaped like a crucifix.

The tap dripped into the sink. A glass stood upturned on the draining board. Bruno picked it up and turned on the tap. The water gushed rust from the lead pipe.

'Not for drinking,' the old woman said.

Bruno turned off the tap.

'So they left nothing at all?'

'Nothing except the bottle of *minerale* Lucia gave me. She said it was poison.'

'Do you still have it?'

'I think so. I'll go and see.'

She returned with the bottle.

'May I taste?' Bruno asked.

The woman nodded.

Bruno poured a glass and took a sip.

He spat a mouthful into the sink. It had tasted bitter and pungent. He recognized it instantly as NKV, a mildly hallucinatory compound used in the treatment of manic depression. But if taken by someone not suffering from the illness then it would create the symptoms. Inwardly he cursed Pini.

Then he turned to Signora Bellini and squeezed her shoulders.

'No,' he smiled, 'Lucia Corso was not mad.'

Bruno sat in the medical library. It was on the first floor of the university main building, overlooking the Via Zamboni. He sat alone at a table in shadows, away from the shafts of strong sunlight that sliced through the lattice windows, when the peace of the library was shattered by the crash of breaking glass.

Bruno ducked as the stained-glass window in front of him caved inward. Coloured shards rained down like arrows. A large fragment of paving stone glanced off the polished table. The remains of the window followed, dragging the thin lead frames with it.

Women screamed from the street outside.

Bruno moved to the gap where the window had been. He peered out.

The scene was utter chaos.

Below he saw students streaming from the main entrance of the university and into the street. Most ran, arms waving, to swell the ranks of the crowd milling outside the theatre opposite.

A few students moved in the opposite direction to join the chanting mob. The majority were dressed in the black shirts of the *Fascisti*. They linked arms and swayed in time with their growing chant. Some carried banners, others were armed with sticks and pick handles.

Each group taunted the other and hurled stones.

A loud cheer went up as a group of *Fascisti* set fire to a captured student banner which read: 'No to Mussolini, Hitler and War.' It burnt fiercely.

This seemed to incense the students. They charged. The remains of the burning banner were torn from the men holding it aloft. They were knocked to the ground and kicked. People screamed and scattered in terror as the burning petrol spread amid them. More fire bombs came from the side street. They were followed by baton-swinging Blackshirts.

They clubbed men and women alike without mercy. Bruno was appalled by the viciousness. He heard the police sirens with relief. It was short-lived.

Police in full riot gear appeared at the end of the street to cut off the students' line of retreat.

They advanced in a line beating the students back towards the *Fascisti*.

The air was heavy with black smoke. Broken bodies were being trampled underfoot as people screamed and wept with panic.

It was then Bruno saw the dead girl's sister again. Carla Balbo was being dragged along the ground by her hair. Her nose was bleeding though she kicked and struggled to free herself from the Blackshirt's grip. He responded by pausing to kick her in the ribs with his heavy boots. Her screams were lost among the countless others as the students were put to rout by police and mob.

'Stop it, for Christ's sake, stop it,' Bruno screamed from the broken window. He felt totally helpless. 'You bastards,' he yelled at the top of his voice. He began to shake with rage.

He saw Carla Balbo thrash wildly as a second man kicked

out at her then tore at her shirt. Then the man doubled under a rabbit punch which chopped the side of his neck.

If the young man with the wild black beard had *la paura* when he'd seen Signora Bellini then it had left him now. He punched the second man three or four times in the kidneys until he crashed to his knees.

Then the young man butted the man holding Carla's hair. He caught him smack on the bridge of his nose. The butt was enough to send him reeling back. Bruno saw the blood pour from between his fingers as he covered his face with his hands.

Bruno put his hands to his mouth and called Carla's name as the young man hauled her to her feet. She slung her arm over his shoulder and used him as a crutch. More bottles and stones fell about them thick and fast. The couple began to push their way up the street.

Bruno yelled her name again. It seemed to be lost in the din.

But the young man suddenly stopped and turned his head towards the broken window. The two men's eyes met. The young man's were angry and black. Bruno saw a ruthless vengeance; the kind that can wage a blood vendetta over generations. Although his expression was as cold as stone his mouth was carved in contempt.

He spat.

Then dived back into the milling crowd hauling Carla with him.

Bruno was taken aback, shocked at being hated by a man he'd never met. A man he did not know.

As a cloud of tear gas billowed below Bruno saw the couple duck low and race across the street.

More gas grenades exploded and they were enveloped by a rolling cloud of bitter smoke.

But not before Bruno had seen where they'd fled.

The funeral chapel of the Bentivoglio family.

The same sanctuary Carla had chosen when Bruno first chased her.

Bruno saw the great doors close behind them.

Police wearing masks began to round up the students and throw them into the vans.

Further down the street the Blackshirts began to chant. They formed a column and, banners aloft in triumph, they marched away to the tune of a patriotic hymn.

But Bruno stayed at the window, his eyes fixed on the funeral chapel.

Half an hour later the Via Zamboni was free of people, empty except for debris of riot, broken bottles, stones and used gas grenades.

Bruno's eyes remained on the chapel door.

'Are you all right?' a voice asked.

It was one of the library clerks, a meek man with rimless glasses. Bruno motioned him to his side and indicated the chapel.

'Watch that for me until I get to the street. Tell me if anyone leaves.'

The clerk looked puzzled but agreed.

'Bloody students,' he mumbled as Bruno bounded from the room.

Minutes later he was on the street. The air still smelt of rancid gas.

'Anyone?' he called to the face in the window. The clerk shook his head.

Bruno entered the chapel and closed the great door silently behind him. At first it seemed as before.

Cold. Dark. Empty. The only light came from the flickering candles. He stood rigid, aware of the sound of his breathing in the silence.

Then he heard it. So faint at first he almost missed it. The second gasp was louder and followed by a long and gentle moan.

It was made by a woman.

Bruno took off his leather shoes and put them carefully aside. Cautiously, he moved down the aisle in his stockinged feet towards the sound of the woman. Her moans grew longer, broken by a soft sob as he heard her draw breath deeply. The sounds came from the sacristy behind the high altar. He saw the door was ajar and inched silently towards it. The cries from inside quickened urgently. Bruno eased back the door and his gaze rested on the face of Carla Balbo.

Her eyes were closed and she bit her lip as her features contorted in ecstasy. Her torn shirt fell open around her large white breasts which heaved in time with her writhing young body. Her skirt lay discarded at her feet. Kneeling on it was the man with the black beard. Carla stood with one foot resting on a chair, her fingers entwined in her lover's hair as she pressed his face deeper between her thighs. Her hips swayed in time to the rhythm of his tongue as his hands cupped and kneaded her firm buttocks.

'No, please Franco, no,' Carla cried and tightened her fingers in his hair as he teased her by pretending to pull away. 'You know I need this. It is the only way after action. Please,' she said and opened her eyes. The mist in them cleared.

She screamed.

Bruno, mouth agape, stood rooted and stunned in the doorway. He was lost for action and words. This was the last thing he'd expected.

Then he saw the flick knife in Franco's hand. Bruno backed away, arms held defensively, as Franco crouched before him. Bruno's eyes followed the knife as Franco switched it from hand to hand. His legs bent at the knee as he closed slowly on Bruno.

'Bastard,' Franco hissed.

Bruno leapt back as the knife scythed before him. He crashed back against a door.

Franco smiled coldly. Bruno searched for the handle and frantically turned it. He realized in horror it was locked. He braced himself as Franco shifted his weight to the balls of his feet, then screamed as he lunged at him. Bruno threw himself sideways as the blade flashed through the air. He heard the dull thud as the tip sunk into the door beside him. It was only a split second later when he felt the damp warmth of his own blood run down his side that he realized he'd been stabbed. The pain came as he grabbed Franco by the throat and brought his knee up viciously into the man's groin with all the strength he could muster.

Franco's scream pierced the chapel. He released his grip on the knife's handle and tried to tear Bruno's grip from his throat. Bruno's fingers closed and as both men fell to the floor he began to shake Franco's neck until the colour left his face. His rage was blind and total and the back of Franco's skull banged repeatedly on the flagstone floor as Bruno sat astride him ignoring the burning pain in his side where the knife had sliced through him.

He felt only Franco thrashing wildly beneath him as he tried to claw at Bruno's eyes then tear his face.

From the corner of his eyes he saw the silhouette of the half-naked girl standing beside him, her breasts now heaving with anger. He looked up as she brought the long candlestick down on his head.

Then there was nothing except darkness.

His head felt like lead. The wound in his side was aflame. A rough flex cut into his wrists and ankles where they'd bound him. Bruno shifted in the darkness and tried to sit up.

'Christ,' he called out in pain as the movement caused his side to bleed.

There was a loud crack and he screwed up his eyes as light dazzled him. A burning brand was thrust under his nose, he drew back his head and looked up at the painted face of a clown. The greasepaint under the false red nose gave his mouth a mournful expression. He wore a cone-shaped hat with a white satin suit with black fluffy buttons. Shadows from the brand danced across his face. In the distance behind him Bruno heard music and laughter. He heard the tread of dancers' feet thud on bare boards in unison.

'Shout out and I'll kill you,' the clown said as he placed the brand in a bracket on the wall in front of Bruno.

Bruno nodded and watched the clown vanish into the

shadows and walk towards the distant music.

From the light Bruno could see he was in a tunnel or passage. The rough walls reeked of age and damp. He peered into the gloom as he heard hushed voices and saw the beam of an electric torch bob towards him.

It died and Carla came out of the darkness into the circle of light where Bruno lay. He looked up at her. She wore her long hair loose with a light floral dress which swayed below the knee. She held an automatic pistol fitted with a silencer in her hand. He sensed in her the zeal of a wild tigress.

Bruno winced with pain as she tossed her head and dug him in the side with her foot. He rolled over and struggled into a sitting position.

'Why?' he asked looking up at the stone-faced girl. 'Why all this, Carla? I came to you for help.'

He saw the surprise on her face at the mention of her name.

'So Mussolini's jackal has a tongue,' she said and raised the pistol. 'Nothing would give me greater pleasure than blowing your head off, you murdering bastard. I owe my sister that at least.'

Bruno's stomach churned. For the first time in his life he experienced terror. He shivered, then began to sweat. The sound of Carla pulling back the pistol's hammer danced in his brain.

The girl laughed contemptuously.

'Don't worry,' she mocked, 'you will be given as much chance as your kind gave Maria and Manzini. But first you are going to tell us about the project you are working on for your filthy regime. You will tell us why your work is so important my sister had to die because Lucia told her about it.'

The pistol was still pointing at Bruno. But he noticed the grip was unsteady and had begun to shake. He saw Carla's eyes well with emotion.

'I am a scientist,' Bruno said reassuringly, 'I had nothing to do with your sister's death. I sought you out because I want to find Lucia Corso.'

Carla shook her head. She was on the verge of tears.

'Oh no,' she said slowly. 'I know you by the company you keep. You and that pig Rossi from OVRA killed her. For that you will both die.'

'Carla, leave him,' a voice called from the darkness. Running footsteps echoed down the tunnel. Breathless, Franco and the clown appeared in the flickering light from the spitting brand. There was a young woman with them. She carried a doctor's bag.

Franco positioned himself protectively between Bruno and Carla.

'*Mia bella*,' Franco said gently as he slowly reached out and took the gun. He gave it to the clown, drew the girl to him and held her tightly. 'We have orders not to harm him,' he added.

Bruno shifted as the young woman opened her bag and knelt beside him. He cried out as she tore his shirt from him. The blood had caked to the wound.

'How long has he been like this?' she snapped at Franco, ignoring Bruno completely.

'Thirty-six hours,' Franco replied.

Bruno caught the look of disapproval on the woman's face. She began work on the wound and the gash on his head.

'This won't hurt,' she said as she splashed Bruno with iodine. It did.

'You are lucky,' she told Bruno and shot another disapproving look at the trio behind them. 'Another few hours and this infection would have been out of hand.'

Her voice seemed to grow fainter. Bruno felt himself slipping away.

'Loss of blood. Loss of blood.' The voice trailed away.

He remembered, as in a dream, being lifted and carried by his arms and legs along the passage. There was music again, much louder, and laughter. There was also pain. He willed his mind blank.

When he came to he was in a theatrical dressing room. He looked at himself in a mirror edged with light bulbs. He was gaunt and pale. He was lying on a couch surrounded by theatrical costumes.

Franco and Carla sat opposite. The clown, his make-up removed, was heating a saucepan on a gas ring. He poured the contents into a mug.

'Here, drink this.'

Bruno took the offered mug. It contained beef broth. He drank eagerly.

'I still say we should have killed him,' Carla said.

Bruno noticed she spoke as if he was not there.

'You'll obey orders, that was made clear to you when you joined us. The Cavaliere Fulgoni wants him alive. He wants to see him now,' Franco said firmly.

'Why?' Carla protested.

'He didn't say and it does not concern us,' Franco replied.

'We should have killed him first, then told Cavaliere Fulgoni,' snorted Carla.

Bruno watched her leap to her feet. He returned her stare with as much venom as it was given. She stormed from the room.

'She's passionate,' Franco said laconically. He lit a cigarette, striking the match between his thumb and finger-nail, and handed it to Bruno.

Bruno shook his head. He was intrigued by the complete transformation in Franco. Earlier the man had tried to kill him. He was now following orders not to harm him to the letter.

'Do you feel fit enough to travel? It's a fair journey,' Franco asked.

Bruno grunted. 'No thanks to you.'

Franco shrugged his shoulders. The lips beneath the wild beard parted apologetically.

'Who is . . .' Bruno was cut short by a girl who burst into the dressing room. She wore a skin-tight leotard and dancing pumps.

'*Carabinieri*,' she blurted. 'There are four of them in the foyer with two plainclothes men. They stink of OVRA.'

Bruno was strangely relieved. He'd never thought he'd be glad to see secret policemen. At least they would not harm him. He wished he felt the same about Franco and his cohorts.

Suddenly he was hauled to his feet. Franco's breath was hot on his face.

'I was told not to harm you,' he grimaced, 'I won't unless you put my life in danger. If you do that I'll kill you.'

Bruno was shoved forward from behind by the clown. He lost his footing and stumbled against the girl in the leotard. She reached out to steady him. He felt her fingers sink softly into his arm as she smiled reassuringly. It comforted him. He looked down and winked. The girl blushed coyly. The place seemed less hostile for it.

'Let's go,' he told Franco.

He followed him down the corridor, past the dressing-room doors and down a flight of wooden steps. Franco turned his head and held a finger to his lips. Bruno nodded.

They moved between high flats of painted theatrical scenery and piles of discarded props. There was a roll of drums and an orchestra burst into life.

'Curtain up,' breathed Franco. They were on the side of the stage now. From the wings in front of them Bruno saw a bevy of dancing girls link arms and kick their way to the glare of the footlights. He turned and saw Franco motion towards him. He'd lifted a trap door backstage. Bruno followed down a ladder fixed to the wall and drew the door closed behind him. They were under the stage. It seemed the dancers above Bruno's head would come through the boards at any moment.

A beam of light from the torch in Franco's hand cut through the darkness and Bruno saw it light the passage ahead. It was the same place where he'd come to after being stabbed.

The men moved quickly along the passage. At last they came to a stone wall. Bruno watched Franco feel the roughly hewn stones, then heave against one. It flew open. They ducked through the gap and Bruno once again found himself in the sacristy.

Bruno sighed loudly. 'That's how Carla vanished when I chased her.'

Franco smiled. 'The theatre was once the palace of the Bentivoglio family. They were much hated. They built the passage so they could walk to worship without contaminating themselves by brushing shoulders with the common herd. I think they were afraid of being torn apart. Our group rediscovered it. It has many uses.'

Bruno caught Franco by the shoulder. He spun him around and held him firmly up against the wall. To his surprise the smaller man offered no resistance. But Bruno did not slacken his grip. He pressed his forearm against Franco's throat.

'I want some answers,' he said.

Franco nodded passively. Bruno eased his arm.

'Who are your group and who is this Cavaliere Fulgoni?'

'He will explain. He is Lucia Corso's father.'

Bruno stepped back in utter amazement.

CHAPTER NINE

The red Alfa Romeo left a trail of white dust as it climbed the winding mountain road effortlessly. From the passenger seat Bruno could see the Cavaliere Fulgoni's villa perched on the top of a distant peak. He thought castle would have been a better description. One wall, topped with battlements, rose from the rock face like a Moorish fort. Three towers were crowned with pointed roofs.

The uniformed chauffeur changed gear and the Alfa surged forward. Bruno welcomed the wind in his face. They had been travelling for four hours, and changed cars three times to make it difficult for any would-be pursuers. Franco had driven the first car to the outskirts of Bologna, then a girl had taken him by unmarked backroads to a mountain clearing. Fulgoni's chauffeur then took over for the last leg. Answers to Bruno's questions had all been met with a firm silence.

Great wooden doors set in the high wall swung open as the Alfa approached. It swept into the outer courtyard and through a gateway. The inner courtyard was bounded on three sides by Romanesque arches to give cool walkways in front of the main building. There was a white Rolls-Royce parked in the shade. The Alfa pulled up alongside.

A white-coated butler with a pale face and slicked hair appeared from nowhere and opened the door for Bruno, bowing slightly as he did so. Bruno followed him inside.

He was struck by the air of immense wealth. The kind of wealth that accumulates and grows over centuries. It generally placed its owners above and beyond the limitations of law and convention.

Bruno's footsteps echoed down a long corridor. Mirrors set between marble pillars added to the impression of size.

He allowed the butler to open the double full-length doors next to a Canaletto painting of Venice.

'Cavaliere,' he announced, 'Dottore Bruno Rossi is here.'

The doors closed behind Bruno. His eyes rested on the figure standing, hands behind his back, in front of the window at the far end of the vast room.

He was a bear of a man with massive shoulders and a shock of thick silver hair. Sunlight spangled off the gold rings on his clasped fingers. His suit was light grey mohair.

'Kind of you to come, Dottore.' His deep voice boomed and filled the room.

Bruno walked forcefully towards him. 'I was under the impression that I had little say in the matter.'

He saw the huge shoulders shrug. The mohair rippled. Bruno strode on as the Cavaliere looked over his shoulder then turned fully to face him.

'Still,' Fulgoni said, 'you came. For that I'm grateful.'

The voice seemed to come from the pit of his diaphragm. Bruno thought his face matched the tone. It was rugged and lined. Beneath the deep waves of furrows on his forehead black bushy eyebrows contrasted to the colour of his hair. His strong jaw line was still firm and his neck had held off the ravages of his seventy years.

Bruno thought: I'd not like to tangle with you.

For his size Fulgoni moved with an athletic grace. Two long settees faced each other over a low table. Fulgoni sat and Bruno accepted his gesture to do the same.

The Cavaliere radiated an awesome strength. If aroused he would be a lethal foe.

They faced each other in silence. Fulgoni leant back and draped his arm on the back of the settee. Bruno was aware the Cavaliere was studying him, watching closely for a sign of weakness or nervousness. A restless shift in position, interplay of fingers or a hard swallow to wet a dry mouth.

He saw none and, at last, said, 'A few days ago I sanctioned your death.'

Bruno remembered the look on Carla's face when she held

the gun on him. His blood ran cold. He studied Fulgoni and was puzzled. To order a man's execution you must hate or fear him. Fulgoni, he was sure, did neither. Bruno felt afraid again.

'Why?' Bruno asked coldly. He showed no emotion or anger. A distant expression glazed over Fulgoni's heavy eyes.

'Because of an old man's guilt,' he said sadly. 'A belated attempt to make up a lot of lost time.' He paused. 'Wasted years.'

'I'd like an answer that makes sense, not . . .' Bruno halted as Fulgoni raised his hand. It was the old man who now shifted uneasily.

'Almost a quarter of a century of wasted years,' Fulgoni mumbled and it was obvious that they pained him. 'That was when I first set eyes on Lucia's mother. Her name was Francesca and she was the most beautiful woman I have ever seen. I was with a hunting party out after a wild boar in the mountains. I tired of it and wandered off alone. There was this vision picking fruit. It was Francesca. I offered to help and she accepted. I still remember the sound of her laugh, the dress she wore. Everything. We sat and talked. The time flew and by dusk I realized I was in love like I never had been before or since.

'When the rest of the hunting party returned I stayed on at the lodge. I could not leave. I climbed the mountain to the spot where we'd met and she was there. Waiting. She came there every day for a month. After a week we made love. She was a virgin but I have never experienced anything as beautiful. It was lovemaking in the real sense.

'She was the only woman I have ever been able to talk to. Pure, simple and honest. I was rich and perhaps one of the most powerful men in Italy. To her it did not matter a fig. Yet she would never come to the lodge, only to our secret place.

'There was a problem. Her parents had arranged for her to marry a local innkeeper. The sleazy bastard drank and smelt. By village standards he was a prosperous catch. I pleaded and begged Francesca to be my wife. She could have had anything she wanted. Yet she would not disobey her parents. Peasants.' He shook his head with disbelief. 'She believed her disobedience would result in her frying in hell. Priests,' he said scornfully.

'I seriously considered removing Corso. I could have had it arranged with no problem. Then one day I waited at our meeting place but Francesca did not come. Nor the next day. My pride stung and I left. It was two months later before I returned here. There was a letter. It was posted the day I left the village. She was pregnant and was to marry Corso. I sent my aides, lawyers, friends to beg her to come to me. She would not.

'I bought the hunting lodge and installed my people so they could keep an eye on her. I received one more letter from her. She asked me to vow that Lucia would never know I was her father. I kept it.

'Francesca's life with Corso was hell. He drank, whored and beat her. She could not take it and her mind gave in.'

He paused. Bruno noticed his moist eyes. It was as if he was staring back into his wasted time. Bruno felt sorry for him. The poorest rich man in Italy.

Fulgoni broke his stare and looked expectantly over his shoulder, as if he expected someone to walk in. Ghosts past, Bruno thought.

'I thank you for your patience,' Fulgoni said.

Bruno could only nod. He would let the Cavaliere continue in his own time. He felt loath to press him. Somehow it seemed like an intrusion.

The Cavaliere continued, 'Francesca's memory haunted Lucia. She feared she would be like her mother. Feared,' he spat the word. 'If only she could have known.' His voice mellowed. 'When her mother died I did something I should have done the first month I met her. I had Corso killed. My people took the drunken oaf and held his head in a pond until he drowned. A not unexpected accident.

'I then allocated a sum of money to a convent. In return

they took in Lucia. From then on I saw she wanted for nothing. I took care of everything. Her education. The lot.'

'I'm sure she would have wanted a father rather than cash handouts,' Bruno said sourly.

'I gave her mother my word,' retorted Fulgoni loudly. 'And I never break my word. Never.'

'So where is she?' Bruno asked.

'Dead.'

The word rocked Bruno back.

'When?' he asked desperately as the numbness enveloped him.

'Who knows?' There was a bitter edge to the Cavaliere's voice. 'But there can be no other explanation. Those bastards from OVRA.' His massive fist smashed on the table between them and Bruno thought the whole room seemed to shake. 'They and that little weasel Pini. And they are going to pay. My power knows no limits. I own men body and soul everywhere. I have a network of organisations that spread from Italy throughout the world. Yet none of them could find my *bambina*. That means she is dead.'

'Not necessarily,' Bruno protested.

Fulgoni shook his head. 'I feel it in my bones. Someday I'll know how and by whose hand. I vow it.'

'Is that why you sanctioned my death? You thought I was with them.' Bruno's voice rose. 'Your daughter wrote to me for help because she had no one else to turn to. Not even her own father. And now you sit in this edifice and have the audacity to sanction my death because . . .'

'Enough, enough.' There was torment etched in the lines on his face. 'I know that now,' he said quietly. 'I know that.'

'How? You were almost too late.'

Again he noticed the Cavaliere look apprehensively over his shoulder. He turned to Bruno. 'I need your help.' His request contained the command of absolute power. It was as if he knew, expected, he would not be refused.

Bruno's question remained unanswered as the Cavaliere

continued to speak rapidly. As if time was running out.

He said, 'I want you to help me avenge Lucia. I do not want her to have died for nothing. I have already begun my vengeance. My vendetta for sanity.'

Bruno raised his eyebrows. 'Franco and the others? A bunch of idealistic troubadours.'

'They are called *Noantri*. It means we, the others. The alternative. The different ones.'

'I know what it means,' Bruno said. 'They are just young idealists. I sympathize, but most of them are going to end up dead or in jail if they go on the way they have been.'

'No,' Fulgoni said in a way that made Bruno uncomfortable. 'They are not just young idealists, although that's just what Italy needs at this time. They are well financed, well trained and well protected idealists. In them I have created one of the most efficient cells of the *Grupio di Azione Patriottica* – the GAP partisans. When the time comes we shall be more than ready for Rossi's OVRA thugs and the likes of Pini.'

'That's a long way to go to appease paternal guilt,' Bruno said. There was sorrow in the look Fulgoni shot him.

'It may have been once. Now it is much more, much bigger than that. You were not the only one Lucia confided in, Dottore Rossi.'

'You mean the dead girl, Maria Balbo, and Sister Mori?'

Fulgoni nodded gravely.

'Maria was a member of Franco's Gap cell. At that time they were just students and actors from the theatre. When Lucia vanished I sent my people to them.'

Bruno watched him rise and stride to a painting on the wall. It was a Botticelli. He removed it. It concealed a safe. Fulgoni operated the combination. Again Bruno noticed how he kept looking expectantly over his shoulder.

The safe was open. He took out a large brown package and laid it on the table.

His large fingers made short work of the knots that bound the package. He removed the contents. He placed a bunch of photographs face down on the table and laid a leather-bound book beside them.

'Franco removed these from Lucia's room an hour after her accident.'

'What are they?'

'Medical photographs. And Lucia's journal.'

Bruno's heart skipped. He reached for the diary. Fulgoni's grip enclosed his outstretched arm.

'First the photographs.'

Bruno took them. He laid them out in a row. As he did so Fulgoni glanced backwards, again.

Bruno gave a low whistle as he looked down at the set of prints. They were the kind used to illustrate lectures and textbooks. The sort laymen find disturbing and the medical profession take in their stride. Bruno recoiled. 'Jesus God,' he whispered.

Some were of corpses, men, women, children, stretched out on mortuary slabs. The naked, thin bodies were covered with sores. He recognized instantly the symptoms of Black Death.

The other humans in the set bore the same symptoms, yet they had been alive when they were taken. They were posed forlornly. Some sitting on beds, some standing against walls, others in various positions to reveal the extent of the pestilence.

Bruno fought not to throw up.

'Lucia was right,' he choked, 'I was a fool to doubt her, they are experimenting on humans.' He held his head in his hands and lowered it between his knees to prevent himself vomiting. 'The evil bastards,' he kept repeating.

At last he looked up at Fulgoni. The Cavaliere was staring over Bruno's hunched shoulders towards the door. Bruno lifted his head from his hands and followed his gaze, slowly turning his eyes towards the door. His jaw dropped and eyes widened in sheer disbelief.

'Seldon,' he gasped.

Alan Seldon, hands buried in his pockets, was leaning

against the door. He straightened casually, removed the cigarette from his lips and brushed his blond quiff from his eyes.

'Seldon,' Bruno repeated in utter amazement as if he could not believe his eyes.

'Hello, Bruno,' the English accent drifted lazily across the room.

Bruno turned to the apprehensive Fulgoni, then rose and turned to face the man he'd last seen when he'd punched him to the floor at Cambridge. The man he was convinced had conspired to wreck his career. His blood began to boil.

'What the hell are you doing here?' Bruno hissed through clenched teeth.

'I came to see you, old chum,' Seldon said.

Bruno clenched his fists and started forward. Fulgoni took him firmly by the elbow. 'Easy,' he said, 'I think you had better listen to what he has to say.'

Seldon drew tensely on his cigarette. He blew the smoke out through his nose. 'Fulgoni is right. Now Britain is at war we need . . .'

'War?' Bruno could not believe his ears. 'What the hell are you talking about?'

Seldon raised an eyebrow. 'Where have you been for the last week?'

Bruno spun on Fulgoni. 'Out of circulation.' His eyes blazed accusingly.

'I thought the *Noantri* would have told you,' Fulgoni said.

'Told me what? They would not give me the time of day.'

'The Nazis have invaded Poland,' Fulgoni said gravely.

'When?' Bruno was flabbergasted.

'Three days ago.'

The day after Franco knifed Bruno.

'The Germans have refused the British and French ultimatum to withdraw. They are now at war.'

Bruno looked stunned. His first thought was for his father. Alone in a foreign country at war. A potential enemy alien.

'What about Italy?' he asked weakly.

'No,' Seldon said. 'They have not thrown their hat into the ring yet. But we expect Mussolini to join Hitler as soon as he sees which way things are going. That is why I've come to see you. We need your help. We want Wildfire.'

'Just who the hell are we?' Bruno's mind raced in confusion. How did Seldon know about Wildfire? Why was he here, in Italy?

Seldon walked to the drinks cabinet. He poured himself a brandy from a crystal decanter. His hand shook. He was pale and nervous.

'Bruno,' he mumbled apologetically and threw back the brandy. He steadied himself. 'You are working on a weapon of war. The ultimate weapon.'

'Liar,' Bruno yelled. He remembered Rossi's Vatican report. 'I'm trying to find an antidote to the mutant stocks of bubonic plague some demented bastard in Whitehall has produced. And I'm doing it for the sake of humanity not a pissing power bloc.'

Seldon refilled his glass. 'I just wish it were that simple. You have heard of Professor Werner in Munich?'

Patronizing bastard, Bruno thought.

'Yes. He works in genetics.'

'Genetic engineering to be precise. He is working with Pini for Rossi. He will graft cells from the antidote onto the mutant Wildfire strain. Billions of the bloody things will be sealed in a bomb. A target will be isolated and attacked. Twelve hours later the entire population will be dead but the built-in antidote will destroy the original bacillus. It would then be safe to walk into the target area. The population will be dead but everything else would be left intact. Your work is going to be used to perfect the most hideous weapon ever devised by man.'

Seldon emptied his glass.

Bruno stared at him in disbelief. He glanced down at the photographs on the table beside him. Then at Fulgoni.

The old man nodded. 'It's true.'

Bruno turned to Seldon. 'And you want the weapon?' His

voice trailed in disbelief. Then he said, 'Bollocks.'

Seldon was ashen. He looked away, avoiding Bruno's glare. He said softly, 'The antidote is the reason we got you to Bologna in the first place.'

Bruno froze.

'Got me to Bologna?'

'It had to be done and I despise myself for it. I work for the Special Intelligence Service. I had no choice but to engineer your expulsion from Cambridge.' He picked up the photographs. 'These made it necessary. I'm sorry.'

Betrayal.

His best friend.

His wrecked dream.

'You bastard.'

Seldon looked pleadingly.

'My father's home? Verdi?'

'Yes. We had to get you on the inside. Now I must ask for your help.'

Bruno snapped.

He lunged at Seldon knocking the glass from his hand. Then he threw a wild punch. Seldon blocked it with expert ease. It fuelled Bruno's anger. He lashed out and grabbed Seldon by the shirt.

Betrayal.

His hands closed around Seldon's throat. He shook him.

'Bastard.'

The whites of Seldon's eyes rolled. He turned blue, fighting for breath. Bruno forced him to his knees.

Then Seldon hit him in the kidneys.

Bruno doubled in pain.

The second blow sent him crashing over the settee. Bruno leapt up, blind with rage. As he raised his fist an iron grip closed around his wrist.

'Stop this madness,' Fulgoni bellowed.

He loosened his grip as Seldon filled a brandy glass and held it out. Bruno took it and gulped.

'I deserved that,' Seldon offered.

Bruno glared.

'You must help,' Fulgoni said. 'Then Lucia will not have died in vain.'

'Bruno. You must give us the antidote.' Seldon was pleading.

Bruno snorted. 'Is that all?'

'No,' Seldon said quietly. 'We want to find out where they are carrying out the human experiments. That will be where they are developing the weapon.'

'Then we destroy it with the help of my *Noantri*,' Fulgoni said.

'Simple,' Seldon added.

Too bloody simple, Bruno thought. He distrusted Seldon. 'If the plan is to destroy it then why do you need the antidote?'

'As a precaution in case we fail,' Seldon replied.

Balls, Bruno thought. You want to make the weapon too. 'No,' he said.

Seldon looked nonplussed.

'I don't suppose I could appeal to your sense of patriotism?' he asked.

'Oh, piss off, Seldon,' Bruno said wearily. How could this man once have been his best friend? He had wrecked everything he held dear.

'Don't force my hand, Bruno. Please.'

'What could you do about it? Bump me off?'

'It is an option London has considered.'

Bruno realized Seldon meant it. He felt contempt.

'But there are other ways,' Seldon added.

'Really?'

'When Italy enters the war your father risks internment. If you help us you can save him from jail. He's an old man, Bruno.'

This time Bruno caught him. He brought his knee up hard between Seldon's legs.

Seldon sank to the floor, groaning in agony.

This time Fulgoni did or said nothing. He just looked at

Bruno who saw understanding in the old eyes.

'Don't let Lucia have died in vain,' he said. 'You owe her that.'

'We'll see,' Bruno said. The Cavaliere patted him on the shoulder. 'I'll get your driver to take me back to Bologna,' Bruno added.

Fulgoni nodded.

Bruno stepped over Seldon and walked to the door.

'Where the bloody hell do you think you're going?' Seldon yelled. 'That threat about your father was not an idle one.'

Bruno turned. 'You harm one hair of his head, Seldon, and I'll kill you. And that is not an idle threat either.'

He walked from the room.

There was a light on in Bruno's room at the Villa Marco. As they drove through the villa gates the light died. He didn't give it a second thought. His mind was on other things.

The journey from Fulgoni's villa to Bologna had been shorter than the one out. Bruno spent most of it following the BBC World Service across the dial of the car radio. The Poles were finished. He thought it a bad omen for what might lie ahead. It made him depressed. The depression was compounded by thoughts of Lucia. Could she really be dead as her father feared? Did he owe it to her to stay and fight? And what about Seldon's threat to his father? He felt trapped by dilemmas as he entered the villa.

He called out for the caretaker. Then the man's wife. The calls were met with silence. He thought of the light in his room and felt uneasy. He climbed the stairs.

No light showed now from under his door. He turned the handle carefully and eased open the door. He flicked on the light. He caught his breath when he saw her.

Claudia Mattucci lay full length on his bed. She was naked except for a black velvet choker around her neck. A transparent green silk negligee was draped by her side. Pini's mistress and secretary lay on her back.

Bruno closed the door. As he did so her lips parted in a

moist smile. Her hand wandered slowly across the sheet. She drew the negligee slowly across her breasts and shuddered visibly at the cool feel of silk. She raised her knee slightly and pressed her thighs tightly together as she dropped the negligee to the floor.

Bruno's throat had dried as he looked down on her. Claudia Mattucci had an animal eroticism. His eyes feasted on the ripe contours of her body. She delighted in the effect it had on Bruno. She lay back, arms stretched out above her head and twisted slowly on the sheet. Then closed her eyes. Her hips swayed as if in time with unheard music. Bruno watched as her movements became more sensual and uninhibited. She ran her long fingers the length of her own body and along the back of her raised thigh. They lingered briefly on the dense bush of blue-black hair as she raised her hips to meet the pressure from the palm of her hand. Her olive skin glistened with tiny pearls of perspiration in the heat of the room.

The swelling in Bruno's loins began to ache. He moved towards the bed, his damp shirt clinging to his back. She now seemed oblivious of his presence, totally immersed in her own sensuality. He halted inches from the bed as she opened her eyes. She ran her hands over her breasts and raised herself in the kneeling position.

Bruno opened his mouth but she stilled his words by raising a finger to her mouth. Light reflected on the painted red fingernails. She leant forward and unbuttoned Bruno's shirt. He felt the sharp points of her nails as she gently drew them over his skin. Claudia unfastened his belt and flies and he stepped out of his trousers. She drew him onto the bed.

Claudia held his face and kissed him hard on the lips, her tongue searching frantically for his as she explored his mouth, then bit him on the lip. He pushed her back on the bed and she drew his mouth to her breast and mewed plaintively as he caressed her rock-hard nipple.

The ache in Bruno's loins became unbearable as she reached down for him. It had been months since he'd enjoyed a woman. Claudia Mattucci more than made up for it. He wanted to bury himself in her, lose himself and, at least for a night, forget everything except her.

He kissed her on the mouth and she guided him inside her. He willed himself not to explode as she raised her knees and crossed her ankles behind his back. Her cries urged him on as her locked legs pumped the small of his back. Then, despite himself, the explosion came. Every muscle in his body tensed before melting into ecstasy and weakness engulfed him.

She still locked him to her and as they rolled onto their sides she continued the slight, almost imperceptible, rocking movement as her tongue played with his body until his blood burnt. Their glistening torsos entwined as they pleasured each other with mounting intensity until they cried out with fulfilment and fell back into each other's arms.

Neither had spoken a word.

Now Claudia said, 'I've wanted that from the first time I set eyes on you.'

Bruno smiled. He'd needed it. Within minutes he was asleep.

He slept through until morning when he was awakened by a dream. In it Bruno saw himself wandering through lush English countryside. Thatched cottages dotted the green landscape, cattle and sheep grazed in patchwork fields. There was brilliant sunshine and a cool breeze. He wished all days should be as such.

Then he came to a village. It was deserted. He knocked on doors and called out but no one replied. At last he pushed open a door in a timber-framed Tudor house. He stepped inside, then opened a door only to be faced with another across a small room. He opened it, then another, and another. This went on until he came to the final door. It led to a vast hall. There was a robed figure standing on the far side, a pointed hood covered its head. He walked cautiously towards it.

The figure raised its arms and the robe fell away. It was

a girl with long dark hair. She turned and he saw it was Lucia. He choked on his own scream as he recognized she was covered from head to toe with the marks of pestilence.

She pleaded with him to keep his distance but he was drawn irrevocably towards her. She backed away, her raised hands at arms' length, begging and screaming at him to stay away. He tried to reason with her that he must help, it was his duty, but she only screamed louder. He began to run but, although she only walked, he could not close the distance.

He glanced around him and saw dozens, then hundreds of hooded figures. They were descending on him. Sweating, he awoke to the sound of his own scream. He was alone in the bed.

Claudia rushed in from the bathroom. She wore one of Bruno's shirts. It hung open.

'What is it?' she asked. 'You scared the life out of me.'

'I'm sorry,' Bruno mumbled. 'It was just a dream.'

'Some dream,' she smiled, her white teeth flawless against her olive skin.

He swung out of bed and watched her cross the room and ease herself into a pair of flimsy panties.

'Breakfast?' she asked.

'Just coffee. The caretaker's wife will fix it.'

'I've sent them away for the rest of the week. I didn't want loose tongues wagging around Frederico Pini's ears.' She winked, half buttoned the shirt and breezed cheerfully through the door.

'We'll have it on the terrace,' she called back laughingly, 'and I mean the coffee.'

Briefly Bruno thought about Pini. He wondered how best to explain his absence. He went to the bathroom and as he shaved his mind switched to his dream and Lucia. Cavaliere Fulgoni's plea echoed in his head.

'Don't let Lucia die in vain. You owe her that.'

Bruno shuddered. He felt a dull ache at the thought of her. The black-eyed girl he'd met at Cambridge.

He shuddered again, wiped the razor clean, and tried to

will her image from his mind.

'It's ready,' Claudia's voice trailed up the stairs.

Bruno welcomed the diversion from his thoughts. He dressed quickly and went down to the terrace.

He saw Claudia was sitting under the arbour of vines. The table was set with a coffee pot, two cups, a jug of fresh orange juice and a basket of rolls and butter. Claudia picked a speck of butter from her thigh and licked her finger. Bruno returned her smile as he sat and poured himself some coffee. Strong and black, the way he liked it.

'That was quite a surprise last night,' he said.

'I like surprises. I take it you did not object.' Claudia laughed wickedly and threw back her head.

'I did not,' Bruno said, which was the truth.

'I should have been a famous whore and pleasured for profit.'

They laughed.

'How did you get in?'

'When the Professore is away this is one mouse that wants to play.'

Bruno pricked his ears. 'Away?'

'The old bore has gone to Venice. I wanted him to take me along too. But he wouldn't. It is another one of those endless discussions with the arrogant Professor Werner from Munich. I love Venice.'

'So do I,' said Bruno. The adrenalin began to rise although outwardly he appeared totally unconcerned. 'How long has Pini been away?'

'Almost a week.'

Bruno clucked his tongue. Now there was no way he would have to lie about his absence. It was then, at that moment on the terrace, that Bruno Rossi first thought about committing murder. Pini and Werner both regularly in Venice under the same roof. The thought flitted through his mind. It would not be murder. He remembered the Lucia of his dream. Fulgoni's photographs. It would be a service to humanity. Like penicillin. Then he realized just what he had thought. It frightened him. He dismissed the idea.

'Hey,' Claudia clicked her fingers in front of his blank expression. 'Are you bored with me already?' She spoke with exaggerated gestures.

Bruno grinned sheepishly.

Claudia smiled back. 'It's Venice I miss, not him.'

Bruno studied her across the table. It was impossible to think of her making love to Pini as she had to him. 'Why did you become his mistress?'

She looked quizzical, slightly taken aback by the directness of his question. Then she said seriously, 'I've told you, I should have been a high-class whore. I pander to his strange little habits because one day he is going to be a very powerful man. He may look nothing, but with his connections he is destined for high things. So is your cousin. He gave me to Pini.'

Bruno looked surprised.

'They are both political animals and power fascinates me. I could never have hoped to hold on to the colonel. Pini was next best.'

'Then why choose me?'

She bit into her roll, wiping the crumbs from her full lips with her tongue. The way she did so Bruno found faintly erotic.

'Because I thought you'd be good in bed.' Her expression changed. Her libertine air seemed to be chased away by a serious one, like the shadow of a cloud on a summer hillside. 'I need men like some women need children.' She used the word *bambinos* longingly. 'I waited for three nights between those sheets for you to return. That is the way I am. And that is why you must never get involved with me, except for the pure physical joy. It is cleaner that way. I want nothing more from you other than to enjoy you.'

Bruno was lost for words.

She laughed again, got up from the table. 'I am going for a swim,' she said. 'Then I want you to ravish me again.' She ran down the steps to the pool and, still wearing his shirt, threw herself headlong into the water with the freedom of a bird of the sea. Bruno watched her swim with a mixture of envy and sadness.

The noise of an engine distracted him. A post van pulled through the gate, slewed on the gravel as the postman tossed a tied bundle of letters through the van window, then accelerated back the way it came.

He rose, ambled to the bundle, picked it up, and undid the string.

The letter caught his eye immediately. The stamp bore the head of King George VI. The handwriting was his father's. He returned to the arbour, fanned through the remainder of the post and put it aside. He tore at his father's envelope cleanly. A folded cutting fell out and floated to the ground. He picked it up and smoothed it flat as Claudia screamed with delight in the pool and called him to join her.

The headline drowned her screams.

CAMBRIDGE LECTURER WANTED IN MURDER HUNT.

Bruno's stomach churned as he read: 'Police today said they wanted to interview a Cambridge Lecturer in connection with the murder of Enzo Verdi, an Italian civil servant, and Bridget Slattery, a known prostitute. Dr Bruno Rossi . . .'

He slumped back in the chair and held his head in his hands. Then he hissed, 'That bastard Seldon.'

Bruno knew that only Seldon could connect him with Verdi's death. He also knew that a return to Britain would mean arrest and, with Seldon's efficiency and stealth, an appointment with the public hangman. Seldon had checkmated him.

Bruno's mind changed gear. There had to be an alternative. His thoughts raced. He saw one.

He would get his father out of Britain, away from the risk of internment and away from Seldon's clutches. He would go with the old man to somewhere safe, South America perhaps. He remembered there was no extradition treaty.

Father and son would start life afresh.

Buoyed with new hope he took the letter his father had sent with the cutting.

> Dear Bruno,
>
> Please help me understand. Some people from the London Foreign Office come to see me last week. They say if you do not stay in Italy I am to be charged with accessory to murder . . .

He read no further, screwing the letter into a ball in his hand.

It was checkmate.

Even if he fled Bologna there was no way his father would survive a prison sentence at his age. He knew it would kill him. So did Seldon. Bruno was devastated.

He felt a pair of hands cover his eyes and the wet shirt Claudia was wearing press into his back.

'Let's go inside.'

Bruno took her hands away.

'I need to be alone.'

He picked up the letter and cutting and walked towards the white portico and the church of San Luca high on the hill above.

CHAPTER TEN

The silver half moon hung in the sky as Bruno emerged from the church of San Luca. He did not notice the chill in the air as he trudged forlornly down the hill towards the single light that burnt in the villa below. Bruno Rossi was now a prisoner. He was locked in a foreign land, and only Seldon had the key.

He cursed the war, he cursed the Wildfire project, but most of all he cursed the former friend who had turned his world inside out.

Bruno reached the Villa Marco and found the front door unlocked. He crossed the hall and into the drawing room. Claudia was curled up in front of the log fire which burnt with a crackle in the open grate. She wore a red brushed mohair sweater and tight white ski pants. Her attention was captured by the dancing flames.

'Claudia,' he called.

She turned, her face expressionless. 'Do you want me to go?'

Bruno shook his head. 'Stay,' he said, 'I need solace.'

She smiled as Bruno crossed the room and sat beside her. He indicated the fire. 'We always burnt coal at home,' he said wistfully.

'Your letter from home. Was it bad news?'

'Yes. It means I can never leave Italy.'

'Then, for me at least, it's good news. I don't want my fun stopped when it's only just begun.'

She amazed him. 'Aren't you afraid Pini will find out? Choosing me is not exactly tactful.'

'He won't find out and besides you give the adventure more spice. Does it worry you?' she asked.

'I don't give a toss anymore.'

'Good,' she said. 'But I always make his bookings so I know when he leaves and returns. He is like clockwork. He always stays at the Europa in Venice. Very chic. He took me once. But then I think Colonel Rossi forbade it.' She pulled a face. 'His meetings with that dreadful Werner are all supposed to be a big secret.'

A shiver shot through Bruno at the mention of Werner's name. He remembered Seldon's explanation of why the men met. To discuss progress on a plan that would kill millions. Progress that depended on him.

'What's the matter?' Claudia said as Bruno shifted and rose, the black look of doom on his face.

'Claudia,' he said, 'I am going to do something I have not done for years.'

She looked up expectantly.

'Get blind drunk,' he said. 'Blind bloody blotto.'

'Blind bloody blotto,' she mimicked the phrase he'd spoken in English. 'It sounds funny.'

'It is.'

'Then let's both do it.'

'Right,' Bruno said. 'They promised me anything I wanted. Let's find where they keep the champagne in this OVRA dosshouse. You find the glasses,' he called as he made for the door.

He returned carrying a crate. The wine was French. He put the crate on the floor and produced a bottle by the neck. 'I've never had Dom Perignon 1935.'

'I have,' Claudia said. 'And look what I've found.' She held an ice bucket. The glasses rested on the ice.

The cork shot from the neck of Bruno's bottle and sprayed them both with foam. He filled the glasses and they sat in front of the fire. Glass followed glass in rapid succession, most of them in Bruno's direction. He drank heavily, making light talk with Claudia. Her ambivalence fascinated him.

They were well into the second bottle when Bruno, who had not eaten, began to feel the effect of the wine. He was amiable and distant from his problems, as if floating above them. Yet he was aware that there was a slight slur in his speech.

'I've met a man . . .' He eyed Claudia unsteadily through the wine in his glass and hiccuped. 'Sorry. I've met a man who would have been good for you.'

Claudia, still sober, said, 'You'll do.'

Bruno waved the glass dismissively in front of his nose. He squinted as two Claudias, both beautiful, merged again as one before his eyes. Then he shook his head vigorously.

'No. No. No.' He grinned. Aware of the sound of his own voice, as if someone else was speaking his words. 'No.' He took a deep breath and held it. She refilled his glass. He downed it and held it out for more. She obliged.

He beamed like a full moon. 'This man,' he paused, 'is better, far better, than Pini and Rossi combined. Besides that he's a good man.' He confirmed it by shaking his head. 'A good man. He is richer and more powerful than those two put together.'

'Who?' She raised her hands. 'Tell me.'

'The Cavaliere Fulgoni. Your father.'

Claudia laughed. 'He's not my father. I just wish he was.'

'Oh, he is.' Bruno drained the glass. He was drunk now. 'You just do not know about it. Because he is a man of honour.'

'You are sweet,' Claudia said, 'but everyone knows he is childless. He has no heir. The papers are always writing about it.'

'Wrong,' Bruno waved the glass and dropped it on the rug. 'Wrong,' he echoed.

'You've had enough.'

'True. True. True.' The room seemed to turn. 'It's hot,' he added. His head fell onto his chest. He allowed Claudia to gently ease him onto his back. Expertly she removed his clothes.

He smiled as the glow of the fire warmed him. He opened one eye and saw her remove the red sweater. She wore no bra, or panties, he saw as she peeled off the ski pants. She lay across him and ran her fingers through the hair on his chest.

'You're sad,' she whispered. 'I hate that.'

She kissed his chest and he felt her lips and tongue move gently down his body.

'I'm useless. Too pissed,' he slurred.

'Nonsense,' she murmured. And reached her destination.

He groaned and was aware that he was slowly responding to her arousement.

She raised her head. 'See.'

He mumbled. Then he drew her to him and took her gently. It seemed timeless. At last she slid from him and wrapped her arms around his neck. 'Enough. Please,' she said softly.

'Lucia,' he said, 'I love you.'

He fell back onto the rug.

He thought, I just made love to a ghost.

Claudia remained at the Villa Marco until the eve of Pini's return from Venice. During those two days Bruno never made love to her again. Nino, the caretaker, handed him the note. She had no regrets. When the time was right she wanted him again. She finished with, 'I envy Lucia, whoever she is. The Cavaliere must be a proud father of such a daughter.'

That tore Bruno to the quick. He crumpled the note and tossed it into the wastepaper basket alongside his dressing table. He looked into the mirror. His reflection was gaunt and haggard. He told it: 'You are in love with a corpse.'

His own words made him feel cold, but at the same time he feared for Claudia if Rossi ever found out that she told Bruno about the meetings in Venice.

The days turned to weeks and the weeks into months and still he received no reply to the several letters he'd written to his father.

His consolation was his research. He worked endlessly. He collated the team results himself. This way no one, even Pini, was aware how each part fitted in the whole. Only Bruno.

The strain began to show. When he did eat it was irregularly. His staff finished work Saturday lunchtime. He worked through. He came in on Sundays alone.

It was on a Sunday that he first noticed it. Initially, the significance almost escaped him.

Tired and unshaven, his white coat grubby because he had forgotten to get it laundered, Bruno sat hunched over a microscope. A solitary figure in an empty laboratory. He adjusted the instrument's lens and brought it into focus. It was not dissimilar from thousands of cultures he'd studied. A single Wildfire bacillus on a lime-green agar jelly. He removed the slide, replaced it in the sealed rack and was about to remove another when he froze. The palms of his hands became clammy and he was aware of the sound of his own heart pounding through his rib cage. A look of sheer disbelief crossed his face as he cautiously reached for the culture slide he'd replaced. He lifted it gingerly from the rack and placed it carefully under the microscope. The beads of sweat on his forehead had turned to torrents and he wiped them from his eyes. He realized he was frightened to take a second look. Frightened he might have been mistaken. He was tired, he told himself. His eyes were mocking him.

He looked again and realized they were not. He studied the lethal rod-shaped bacillus that could wipe out a civilization. The fine threads at its edge which should have been propelling it through the protein agar hung as still as the fringe of a parasol without the wind.

'There's only one,' Bruno mumbled with astonishment. He looked up at the empty laboratory.

'The ribonucleic acids have not reacted.' He knew they should have, they always did, so that the bacillus could reproduce itself.

'It's dead,' he yelled at the top of his voice and threw his arms into the air. 'The bastard thing is dead.' He began to leap joyously around the room. He twirled in a frenetic solo dance laughing until his lungs almost burst. Then he collapsed into a chair and lapsed into silence.

'I've done it,' he said at last. He felt tears well as he rose and walked back to the microscope. He could not bring himself to look again.

He took the slide number and checked the formula for the agar in his files. He went to the far end of the lab, and began to reproduce it. When he'd finished he took a fresh bacillus from the lead storage safe and dropped it into the culture.

His elation turned to dread as the bacillus instantly began its reproduction cycle. He repeated the experiment with the same heartbreaking results.

Bruno pondered. That first bacillus had been destroyed. The question was how?

He returned to the first slide and took it into the sealed isolation room. He removed part of the agar and returned to the laboratory. There he began the painstaking process of analysing it.

He finished just after midnight. He checked the original formula with his own. The constituent quantities of a minor protein element differed. A researcher had made an error. The error was minuscule but it was the difference between life and death for countless millions.

Bruno, his adrenalin at full flow, worked like a man possessed. He reproduced the culture and began experimenting. By three in the morning he had a dozen dead bacilli.

He had done it.

He had destroyed Wildfire.

He had it done by accident.

But it was done.

His initial elation had vanished. That was the joy of discovery, of achievement. Now he had to face the consequences of that achievement. They were frightening. He paced the floor then climbed the stairs and let himself out of the underground building. The rain had stopped but there was a damp chill in the air. Bruno did not notice it.

He sat on the steps and lit a cigarette.

He drew deeply on the roasted tobacco. A sudden shaft of

light fell on him. It came from one of the *carabinieri*'s torches at the main gate. Bruno waved and the guard killed the torch.

Bruno thought long and hard. The pile of cigarette butts grew around his feet. Then he got up and went back to the laboratory. He gathered up the slides of successful agar and the dead bacilli. He took them to the incinerator room and fired the furnace. He threw in the slides when the dial registered white hot and destroyed them.

Back in the laboratory he replaced the other cultures and formulae in place. He pocketed his own then wearily rode home for a grateful sleep in an empty bed.

There was nothing in the laboratory to show that the deadliest bacillus known to man had been destroyed. Bruno had carefully seen to that. He rubbed his eyes and felt a sense of well being.

The tables had been turned. Now *he* had the key.

Seldon.

Rossi.

Pini.

Werner.

Now he had what they wanted. He smelt the aroma of freedom it would bring and liked it. Now he had to decide how best to use it.

Bruno arrived at the theatre. He had to see Franco.

He stopped in his tracks at the stage door.

'Closed by Government Order,' the notice in red, nailed to the door, proclaimed. It was signed by the city's Fascist prefect.

Bruno tried the door. It was unlocked. He pushed it open.

The place was cool and dark. An old man with a moustache sat feet up reading a newspaper. He adjusted his glasses and eyed Bruno curiously.

'We are closed. *Il Duce*'s orders,' the man said.

'When?' Bruno asked.

'Since the beginning of September. Where have you been?'

'The beginning of September?' He had lost all track of time.

His blood ran cold. Fearing for the safety of the Cavaliere Fulgoni's *Noantri*. The others. The different ones.

'Why?'

'They need no reason,' the stage doorman said with resignation. 'None at all these days.' He spat on the bare boards of his cubby hole. 'They raided the place and shut the show.'

'Did they arrest anyone?'

'Some,' he shrugged.

Fulgoni's well drilled group.

'What happened to them?'

'Who knows?' He gestured to the wall, fingers pointing at the bare brick. 'Do you know members of the company?' he asked.

'No,' Bruno blurted instinctively. 'No. Not at all.'

He backed through the stage door feeling like a minor Pontius Pilate. As he rounded the corner on his motorcycle he thought of Carla, the sister of Lucia's dead friend. A shiver rippled down his spine.

Bruno rode from the city, taking no particular route. The motorcycle seemed to run to the mountains. He followed where it led.

The car tailing him changed three miles outside Bologna. The tiny Fiat bug was replaced by a French-built Facel Vega with Turin number plates. The driver wore glasses. So did the girl in the back.

Bruno noticed it first on the Apennine road to Florence. The Facel Vega was bright yellow. He glanced at it as he checked his mirror before taking a dirt road which would lead him high to the heart of the mountains. When the car broadsided after him he felt uneasy. The car closed.

He opened the throttle.

The car accelerated and flashed its lights.

Bruno's unease turned to concern.

OVRA, he thought.

They know.

He threw himself onto the tank and let the bike have its head. He roared up the straight, hitting the brakes and dropping gear to take a right hand curve. He glanced behind and saw the car weave crazily in a cloud of dust, then again flash its lights.

Bruno took the bend.

The back wheel hit a pothole in the road and threw him out of true. The bike bucked. It glanced off the rough cliff and spun in a complete circle. He faced the car as it rounded the curve, then slewed back to the open road. He fought to hold it, fighting the handlebars. He came back to true and looked back over his shoulder.

The car was closing.

The sound of its horn carried above the scream of the Motto Guzzi. He looked ahead. The road curved wickedly, this time to the left.

He eased around the bend – then saw the herd of goats. The bell on the lead billy swung soundlessly. He must have led twenty nannies and kids.

Bruno kicked down through the box. His left hand pumped the clutch, his right the brake. As the bike slithered at an angle, he saw the goatherd dive for the narrow verge.

The bike slowed.

He lost it as it slipped from under him and broadsided into the fleeing goats.

He landed on his feet, arms flailing. He tottered after the bike, then lost his balance. He rolled on his back and could smell the goats as they leapt over him in panic.

A hoof caught him on the side of the head. Behind him he heard the screech of brakes as the Facel Vega's wide chrome bumper bounced off the road. He knelt.

A car door slammed. Then another.

Footsteps ran towards him.

Dazed, he looked up.

A swarthy man and Carla Balbo looked back.

She took off her sunglasses.

'Cavaliere Fulgoni and the man Seldon want to see you,' she said.

Her face fuzzed.

Bruno passed out.

He came to on the back seat of the Facel Vega. Carla sat next to the man on the front bench seat. The goats had gone, the Motto Guzzi, undamaged except for twisted handlebars, was parked on the verge.

'Are you all right?' Carla asked. The question was rhetorical. She sounded unconcerned.

Bruno grunted. 'I did not know it was you.'

'I flashed my lights to signal you to stop,' the driver said.

'That still did not tell me who you were. I'd come from the theatre. You could have been OVRA for all I knew.'

'Should that bother you?' Carla said curtly.

Bruno eyed her cuttingly. She looked away.

'Next time you people want to get in touch use the bloody phone,' Bruno snapped.

The driver took off his glasses. 'Friend,' he said, 'the authorities arrested seven of our members when they raided the theatre. We have watched the police watching you. Today you were not followed, as far as we could see. But to have made a direct approach in the city would have been an unnecessary risk.'

He replaced his glasses. He gunned the engine and shifted the column change. 'I'll have your bike picked up. It will be left at the university.' The back wheels spun as the car roared off.

'Where do we meet Fulgoni and Seldon?' Bruno asked. He saw Carla glance at him through the driving mirror.

'A small dump of a village in the mountains. It is called Perino Maggiore,' she said.

Bruno's neck prickled. It was the village of his father. Seldon must have known. The bastard, Bruno thought.

'Why there?'

'The village is sympathetic,' Carla said. 'Most of them are in the mountains. They hate Mussolini and his *Fascisti*. We have established a base nearby to be ready when the time comes to fight.' She spat the last word with venom.

The signpost read: Perino Maggiore. 12 Km.

Something stirred deeply inside Bruno as the Facel Vega flashed past.

'Is this the only road into the village?' Bruno asked.

'Yes,' Carla replied.

Then his father must have walked it when he'd left his home for the last time. His eyes followed the road. It was narrow, no more than a twisting track. The surface was rutted. He closed his eyes and saw his father walking down it, his belongings tied in a blanket carried over his shoulder like a sack. Then he imagined his mother following much later. The flush of expectation at the prospect of meeting his father would have been tinged with sadness as she sat primly in the back of the donkey cart.

His cousin Rossi had trodden it too.

None of them would walk it again. These mountains were a cruel host to the generations they sheltered.

Bruno opened his eyes and saw why. The mountains rolled away to the distance like a rumpled sheet of granite. It was as if, when time began, some giant hand had torn the land in rage, crushed it, then cast it aside like a crumpled mantle of rock.

The first white caps of winter snow topped the peaks. This was a harsh and cruel vista, yet Bruno felt a strange magnetism draw him. He could not explain it, it seemed a force reached out and drew something from down inside him.

Deep valleys spread like fingers down the sides of the mountains. They had a grey-blue hue. The bare rock refused even the thinnest blanket of soil on the highest reaches. Lower down there were great sweeps of dense forest above terraced fields, cut from the stark undulating hillside. They were dotted with white flecks. Wandering herds of goats or sheep, Bruno thought.

Spirals of grey smoke curled from the trees. These must have come from the fires of the *carbonari*, the itinerant bands of charcoal burners who roamed these mountains. His father had often spoken about them. The only time people locked their doors was when they were in the area. His father said this was unjust as he'd never heard of anyone stealing anything. That, his mother had argued, was because people locked their doors. Bruno smiled sadly at the memory.

The signpost now read: Perino Maggiore. 4 Km.

Bruno looked ahead along the dipping road. It vanished into a small wood. He felt a certain trepidation at the prospect of seeing the village for the first time. Would it be as familiar as the image he held from his father's description?

The car slowed as it neared the wood. Then stopped.

'This is as far as we go,' Carla said as she got out of the car.

Bruno watched curiously as she kicked off her shoes and unhitched her skirt and petticoat. She flung them into the car, removed a coarse pair of men's trousers, jacket and boots from a paper bag and put them on.

'To the village?'

She shook her head. 'To our camp. They have installed a Fascist prefect. There is risk.'

Bruno was concerned. 'I thought you said these people were sympathetic to your *Noantri*.'

'The prefect is not the people, despite what the likes of Colonel Rossi tell you,' she said coldly as the Facel Vega pulled off the road and out of sight. 'Let's go.'

Bruno caught her arm as she ducked into the wood. 'I can't help it if you choose not to like me,' he said, 'but I will tell you for the last time I had nothing to do with your sister Maria's death.'

Carla shook away his grip. 'I don't dislike you,' she said, 'I just don't trust you.' Then she was gone.

Bruno plunged into the wood after her. It was moist and

soft underfoot. It smelt of moss. A blackbird cried a shrill warning as they began to climb deeper through the trees. Pale lines of light slanted off them.

Another blackbird called and a jay crashed through the foliage. Bruno halted as Carla raised her hand. Bruno sank to his haunches. Someone was moving through the undergrowth towards them. The branches and thickets snapped.

He saw Carla dig into her jacket pocket. Her glance said: Don't make a sound.

His eyes moved to the gun she held in her hand. The pistol had a silencer. Guns and Carla seemed to go together.

He noticed she held it with expert ease, crouching like some wild beast, eyes aflame. She swung her arm in a slow arc in front of her.

Another bird fluttered noisily from a tree. Then there was silence.

'It's all right, Carla.'

Bruno jumped from his skin as he felt a hand on his shoulder. The man had circled behind them.

He looked up.

Franco looked back.

He wore a cloth cap at an angle. His beard had grown. The jacket was coarse blue denim and like Carla's, his boots had heavy toecaps. A *lupara*, a hunting shotgun with sawn-off barrels, was slung on his shoulder, a cartridge belt around his waist.

He said to Carla, 'You must take greater care.'

She glared.

Bruno thought, She wants to claw his eyes out.

'I could have been *Milizia*,' he offered an olive branch. 'You are too valuable to lose at this stage of the game.'

'What are the *Milizia*?' Bruno asked.

'Mussolini's full-time private army. There are reports they have been scouring the mountains. Things are hotting up. Other groups have already begun destroying property. One blew up a railway bridge last week.'

Bruno looked up in disbelief.

'You won't read it in the papers. No more than you will that members of our group have been arrested. Then murdered.'

Bruno stood up.

'Do you remember Anna?' Franco added.

Bruno shook his head.

'The girl in the leotard who warned us the day they raided the theatre.'

'Yes,' he smiled now, 'the pretty one.'

'They arrested her. She's dead.'

'Bastards.'

'The woman doctor who treated you reported us. Luckily she did not know your name. Seven were arrested that day. They shut the theatre down. That is why we have all come to the mountains. The time has come to fight back.'

Bruno felt guilt. He remembered the girl's kindness to him and now, because of him, she was dead. Just like Lucia. Fulgoni had been right. Italy was under the heel of a pig of a regime. His guilt turned to a cold anger.

'I think it's time we went to Fulgoni,' Bruno said.

'*Si.*' Franco clapped him on the back. 'I think it is,' he said warmly.

They moved off through the wood in single file. Franco leading, Carla bringing up the rear. They moved cautiously.

'The camp is just ahead,' Franco said and Bruno smelt charcoal on the air. Voices called out to greet them in welcome. Just like a homecoming, Bruno thought.

If it had not been for their appearance Fulgoni's partisan band of *Noantri* could have been gypsies at their encampment.

He counted about twenty of them, all young men and women. They sat in small groups of two or three, gathered around a fire. An old iron cauldron hung above it. A few thin plucked chickens lay next to a line of rabbits and hares, victims of the *lupara* hunting guns that lay strewn on the short coarse grass. The smell from the cauldron Bruno recognized. His father often cooked it. *Cacciatore*, the Hunter's Stew, often enriched with spicy Bologna sausage or salami. Delicious. He felt hungry.

The group all wore the coarse denim with boots and cap, just like Franco. Some of the women wore plain headscarves. Their young features had already begun to weather to the colour of the peasants who now sympathized with, and harboured them. Bruno saw a strange dignity in their appearance. The same kind of defiant nobility he remembered from the faces that stared from newspapers in the great strike of 1926. Like the dockers and their families who blocked the port gates of Barry when he was a youth. Suddenly, he felt at one, part of this group – the *Noantri*. The different ones.

The smell of charcoal seeped from the encampment's perimeter. A circle of pits had been dug around the circumference. In them, logs burnt slowly covered by layers of ash and sawdust. There were also half a dozen primitive *baraccas*, crude huts built just like the *carbonari* would have done. The walls were roughly hewn planks of untreated wood with ill-fitting doors. The roofs were topped with turf. Gaps in the walls had been sealed with mud which had dried as hard as brick. Inside Bruno saw bedding heaped on the bare floor.

'Our camp of *carbonari*. These hills are full of them,' explained Franco, 'as they have been since the days of Rome. No one questions their presence. Not even the *Milizia* give them a second glance. It is our cover.'

'I hope it holds,' Bruno said.

Someone called out above him. There was a figure silhouetted on a ridge of a rocky hill face which rose behind the encampment. Thorn bushes sprouted between the bald boulders.

The figure waved an arm.

'The Cavaliere Fulgoni waits,' said Franco. Carla looked sullen.

She walked to the cauldron and filled a wooden bowl with

stew. Then sat cross-legged and ate without looking up.

'She has been through a lot. The girl Anna who died in OVRA hands was a close friend. Then there was her sister,' Franco explained as they picked their way to the waiting figure, *lupara* cradled in his arm.

'I feel bad about them, Lucia too,' Bruno admitted. The mention of her name still pained.

He felt Franco take him by the arm. 'Look. You can't carry the guilt. You did not murder the three of them. *They* did.' He spat.

'You're convinced Lucia is dead too?'

'She has vanished from the face of the earth. These days in Italy that means vanished for good. Like hundreds of others. Some bodies have been found, like Anna's. Others not. The fate is the same except the ones that turn up have the dignity of burial. Just give Carla time. She'll come around.'

'Do you love her?'

'We are lovers,' was as far as Franco would go. Bruno thought briefly of Claudia, then again of Lucia. As they neared the top of the ridge his limbs felt suddenly heavy but it was not because of the climb.

He was sad.

They reached the top. Bruno recognized the lookout as the clown from the theatre. He acknowledged Bruno by cocking his head. Bruno nodded. He looked down on the village of his father nestling on the opposite ridge on the far side of the valley.

It was just as it had been described. Once his mother sketched it for him. It had not changed. The narrow twisting streets, houses shuttered from heat and cold. The aged stonework, buckled walls and peeling plaster. Chickens and donkeys in the street. The red tiles of the roofs, some now green with the years. He noticed two oxen hauling a cart up the main street. A lump came to his throat.

'Welcome.'

He recognized the deep voice of Fulgoni and turned to face

him. The Cavaliere was not dwarfed by the mountain setting. He loomed above Bruno, standing on a rock. He was dressed in a leather flying jacket with its sheepskin collar turned up. He wore hunting trousers and stout mountain shoes. The gold on his fingers seemed incongruous. The rock on which he stood was on the edge of a steep ravine. There was no sign of Seldon.

Bruno took the Cavaliere's outstretched hand and shook it firmly.

'*Grazie*,' he said to Franco who returned down the hillside.

Then to Bruno he boomed, 'Come.'

The old man moved like a mountain goat down the ravine. Bruno had trouble keeping up with him as he sent loose stones and rocks showering before him. Halfway down there was an outcrop covered with a dense patch of bushes and shrub on the outcrop. Bruno watched Fulgoni tear them away with his hands. They covered the tiny entrance to a cave. Fulgoni clambered through, grunting with the effort. Bruno followed, then reached out and pulled the bushes back in place behind him.

It was dark. Pitch black. He saw sparks from a lighter as Fulgoni stumbled and cursed somewhere to Bruno's side. There was the pale yellow glow and smell of a storm lamp. It grew as Fulgoni turned it up.

Bruno found himself in a long narrow passage. He followed the light as it swayed. The passage led to others. It was a labyrinth.

'It goes for miles under these hills,' Fulgoni explained. 'There are several entrances – all concealed. If the *Milizia* ever discovered us we'd be as safe as houses down here.'

The air was cold. Bruno shivered and clapped his arms about him. He could see the vapour of his breath in the light of the lamp.

They ducked through the passages until they came to a large chamber. Bruno was amazed. There was a large table in the centre of the floor. By the glow of the lamp Bruno picked out a map. Coloured flags had been placed on it.

'Positions of villages with Fascist prefects,' Fulgoni pointed at the flags. 'The others mark *Milizia* positions and bases in these hills.'

Beside it hung a picture of Garibaldi next to an Italian flag. There were paraffin stoves, several military-style beds, sacks of grain and tins of food. There was a radio and transmitter.

Bruno noticed another passage. In it were stacked arms and explosives. He walked to it and picked up a rifle. It was an MI carbine.

'By courtesy of the British SOE through the kind offices of Seldon and his department.' Fulgoni grinned, his lion face creased in benign wrinkles.

'It's like a military headquarters,' Bruno said.

'It is.'

Bruno studied him. He saw a man with pride, unbent with the advance of years, erect and resolute. A man who did not break his word. A man who had sworn vengeance for a daughter he'd never met. A man who wanted Bruno to play a lead part in it. Against his own bloodline. How could Bruno, when he thought of Lucia, refuse him?

There was a bottle of grappa in Fulgoni's hand now. He produced it from behind the grain sacks along with two tin mugs. He filled them and set them each side of the table. Bruno sat and cupped his mug.

Fulgoni eased himself into a small chair opposite. 'Why did you go to the theatre?'

Because I've cracked Wildfire, Bruno felt like screaming at the top of his voice. Yet he remained silent.

Fulgoni raised his hand and indicated with his huge finger. Bruno saw a crude wooden ladder. It led to a sack which draped an entrance to the cave and fluttered slightly in the wind.

'Seldon's out there,' Fulgoni said, 'training my young women to kill with their bare hands. You must learn too.'

Bruno nodded. A few months ago such a remark would have filled him with horror and revulsion. Now he just gesticulated with his shoulders. Times were changing.

Bruno realized he was changing with them.

Fulgoni added: 'I think I should make it clear that Seldon is here as an adviser. He is helping to organize the GAP partisan cells. But I am in charge of this one, the *Noantri*. It is I who decides yes, or no. I want you to understand that, Dottore Rossi. Once Seldon may have had a certain say in your destiny. No longer. It is I who ask for your help.'

Bruno thought, You don't know Seldon.

Fulgoni's fingers closed round the mug of grappa. He threw back a draught.

'Now,' he said wiping his mouth with the back of his hand, 'why did you go to the theatre? A man like you does not waste valuable working time making social calls.'

'Because I believe the whole Wildfire project must be destroyed,' Bruno said slowly, toying with the mug. He saw satisfaction flit over Fulgoni's face.

'Then you have found the antidote?'

'If I had do you think Seldon and the British would allow you to destroy Wildfire? Used as a weapon it would be awesome. They would want it for themselves.'

'I said I run the *Noantri*,' Fulgoni said assertively. 'If I say destroy, then it is done.' He thumped the mug on the table and clenched his massive fist.

'Then destroy – now.' Bruno raised his voice.

'No,' Seldon's voice echoed around the cave. He pushed aside the blanket at the entrance and was climbing down the makeshift ladder.

Bruno stood up. Then Fulgoni. The tension sparked.

Bruno was confronted by Seldon. He was seething. He clenched his jaw.

'This is not a bloody medical research programme. We are not here to do humanity a favour and save it from the plague. These bastards are producing a weapon of war. Your sodding antidote is the key part of that weapon – the firing device. Without that they have no weapon. When they do, then we strike.'

Any doubts Bruno had that Seldon wanted the weapon

were now gone. 'You are as low as they are,' he said contemptuously. 'Lower.'

Bruno turned to Fulgoni as Seldon grabbed him by the arm. Bruno said, 'Wildfire is a mutant strain. The stocks must be limited. Destroy them and it's over.'

'And the people who control it,' Fulgoni said. His authority was imposing. He glared at Seldon who released Bruno's arm. Fulgoni gave a single nod of his head.

'If you try to go it alone, and I doubt if you can, I'll see to it you are stopped,' Seldon said quietly. There was a calculated menace in his tone.

'Then I'll have you killed,' Fulgoni said simply.

Seldon was ice cool. Bruno felt his blue eyes pierce him. 'You have more to lose than most,' Seldon said, then shot a glance at Fulgoni.

Bruno knew the threat was directed as much at his father as him. He said, 'You are never going to get your hands on that weapon. No matter what you do. Never.'

Seldon flicked back his blond hair and glowered.

'I am going to find the source of the Wildfire stock,' Bruno said, 'and wipe it from the face of the earth.'

'We'll see,' Seldon said. He picked up a lamp and moved off into the labyrinth. Bruno watched him go. He now regarded Seldon as much a threat as Rossi.

He felt Fulgoni's hand on his shoulder. He sensed the old man was troubled.

'Bruno,' he said, 'let's go up into the air.' He squeezed his shoulder paternally. 'There is something I want to tell you.'

Bruno moved towards the passage.

'Up there,' Fulgoni indicated the ladder, 'we'll be alone.'

Puzzled, Bruno climbed to the entrance. He stood on a small ledge and jumped the few feet to the ground. The view of the mountains was spectacular. This vast graph of a landscape as far as the eye could see. The backbone of Italy. Fulgoni jumped down and stood at his shoulder.

'I said I would not tell you,' the Cavaliere faltered, 'but there is something you should know.'

'Well?' Bruno's unease grew. Fulgoni took him by the shoulders and held him at arms' length.

'Seldon again tried to threaten you in there and you chose to dismiss it.'

'You mean my father.'

'Bruno,' Fulgoni lowered his eyes, 'he's dead.'

Bruno's knees gave way. Fulgoni supported him. 'They took him into custody. It was to be as a lever to put more pressure on you. He died of a heart attack. You were not supposed to know.'

Bruno gathered himself as a numbness swept over him. He felt empty. He turned and walked slowly to the ridge. From there he could see Perino Maggiore. He sat on a rock and gazed at it. The village of his father's birth. The numbness slowly left him. Yet still he sat and stared.

Then he felt the salt of his own tears.

For the first time in his life he felt hate. Pure hate.

He hated Seldon.

He hated his system.

And he hated the country that perpetuated it.

His country.

CHAPTER ELEVEN

Rossi wept when Bruno broke the news of his father's death.

'The British bastards,' he said.

Bruno agreed.

'That's why I want to help.'

Rossi looked up. He wiped his eyes. 'I don't understand.'

'I have found the antidote to Wildfire,' Bruno said. He had sat up all night making the decision to tell Rossi. He had decided neither his father nor Lucia should have died in vain. Wildfire, he reasoned, had caused both their deaths.

Now he was going to destroy it. With the *Noantri* he would also thwart Seldon.

He looked down at Rossi. His cousin was astounded. 'What?' He got to his feet. 'When? Why didn't you tell me before?'

'I had to be sure,' Bruno said.

Rossi rushed forward and held him in a bear hug. Bruno was lifted off the ground.

'Magnificent.' Rossi laughed. He rushed to the drinks cabinet. 'Let's celebrate.'

'Isn't it a bit early for that?' Bruno asked.

Rossi turned. 'Early?'

'I said I wanted to help. And I think you are going to need that help more than you realized.'

Rossi raised an eyebrow.

Bruno knew he had to take a chance.

'I know about Werner, the genetic engineer from Munich.'

'How?' Rossi's face fell. He looked menacing for a moment, then smiled.

'Pini let it slip,' Bruno lied. He did not want to mention Claudia Mattucci. He feared what Rossi might do. He also knew he dare not reveal what he'd learned from Seldon.

'Why does Pini meet Werner regularly? It can only be to discuss Wildfire.'

Rossi darkened. 'How much do you know?'

'Not a lot,' Bruno said. 'But logically I'd say you were trying to genetically engineer Wildfire. Why, I don't know.'

Rossi nodded.

Bruno could almost hear his mind ticking over. His cousin had two choices now.

Kill him.

Or take up his offer to help. But only Bruno knew the antidote formula.

'My father's death – murder – has changed a lot of things. I am asking you for the chance to avenge him. I want to get back at those British bastards. I think you can help me through Wildfire.'

Rossi flushed. His eyes pierced Bruno.

The phone rang.

He snatched it.

'Rossi.' The tone was curt.

Bruno watched his cousin's face change. He gritted his teeth.

'What?' he screamed. 'How many?'

He grunted.

'Shit.'

He slammed the phone down.

'There has been a raid on the Wildfire laboratory.'

Bruno's stomach churned. 'What happened?'

'Dead,' Rossi snapped. 'Two women. The rest fled. They did not get further than the main gate. The anarchist bastards.'

Seldon and the *Noantri*, Bruno thought.

He wondered about the girls. Carla?

Bruno's hand had strengthened.

'You need me. What would have happened if that raid had succeeded. You would have lost Wildfire. Everything.'

Rossi bit his lip.

Bruno could see his cousin's dreams of yachts, villas and a dozen Claudia Mattuccis fade.

Rossi punched the palm of his hand.

It was then Bruno knew his gamble had paid off. He had him.

'I want to be part of whatever you are planning,' he said.

Rossi scowled.

Doubt.

'It makes sense,' Bruno added. 'Without me you are in trouble. Only I have the antidote formula.' He touched his temple. 'And it's locked in here.'

Rossi stiffened.

'OK,' he snapped.

'What's going on?' Bruno was stoic. 'I must know everything.' He paused, then added, 'I am on your side.'

Rossi took a drink. Imported Scotch. He did not offer one to Bruno. He spoke with a great calm.

'I told you at the very beginning that if we went to war on Germany's side we would have to exert a great influence or be swept aside. We'd become Hitler's poodle. I cannot accept that. It is now certain we will go to war – against your country . . .'

'It is not my country anymore,' Bruno corrected.

Rossi shrugged. 'We must produce Wildfire as the ultimate weapon. That's why we needed Werner. He is a master theoretician and a cunning one. You will not be allowed to meet him. Ever. The man is a Nazi idealist. If you gave him the formula he'd make off with it. We just want his theories on how it can be done.

'The real work on the final grafting is being done by a Dr Zeiss. He is Swiss and like all his race his main interest is money. He can be bought. We have the money.'

'So Zeiss is the key,' Bruno added.

'You are the key,' Rossi said grudgingly. 'Zeiss has only been conducting the grafting experiments.'

Bruno thought of the photographs. Lucia's photographs. He said nothing. He thought, Evil little shit.

He said, 'And Zeiss does not know the antidote formula.'

'No. He has just been experimenting with your early culture formulae.'

'To no avail.'

'No.'

Bruno felt elated. Rossi had no choice.

He was on the inside.

'Where is Zeiss based?'

'We have a clinic. The Clinic Ascha. High in the Alps.'

'I could do with some Alpine air.'

'It might do you some good,' Rossi said. 'We can go at the end of the week.'

The small tank engine with a long stack toiled slowly through the darkness. It was hitched to a single wooden coach, the type normally used to take tourists high into the Italian Alps. The coach windows had been painted out with the same dull red paint as the bodywork so no light showed. The train slowed to a halt. From this place the railway could go no further. Yet the mountain still rose above, silent and steep, beyond the range of pine trees heavy with snow.

The door of the coach opened and Bruno and his cousin stepped out onto the observation platform.

Bruno felt the cold air burn his lungs as he inhaled. Next to him his cousin coughed.

There was a flurry of light snow. Through it a figure trudged and was lit by the beams of headlights which came to life and played on Bruno and Rossi.

Bruno held a gloved hand to his eyes and watched the figure come through the night snow. The figure was dressed in a grey boiler suit and boots laced to below the knee. The flap of a Russian-style cap covered the ears. A scarf was over the face.

Bruno looked down as the figure halted alongside the observation platform steps. The scarf was pulled from the face and the fur-lined cap pushed back.

He saw it was a woman. Her harsh face without make-up

and hair cropped short.

'Welcome to the Clinic Ascha,' she said and indicated the old high-sided truck behind the beam of headlights. 'They are waiting.'

Bruno noticed even Rossi shudder. He did the same. His cousin was strangely silent, as he had been the whole train journey which had begun from a disused halt just inside the Austrian border.

As Rossi descended the steps Bruno hesitated. His instincts cried – horror.

Rossi and the woman turned. He followed reluctantly, fearful of what lay ahead.

The cable swung precariously to a halt at a small wooden platform. It had borne Bruno, Rossi and the harsh woman from the down station, built where the mountain had run out of road. There was total darkness.

Somewhere a dog began to bark, then others, ferociously.

'Please wait,' said the woman. She swung back the car door and stepped into the snow-flecked night.

Someone flicked a switch and the car was bathed in light. It came from searchlights. They were set at intervals on high perimeter fences topped with coils of barbed wire.

Bruno looked down. Steps led from the platform to the ground. The cable car control was a wooden building with a flat roof. It was guarded by two men in boiler suits and balaclavas. Their rifles were slung and they held Dobermans on a short leash. He saw them part to make way for the woman who entered the building. The place looked more like a prison to Bruno than a clinic, and in essence he supposed it was.

As the woman re-emerged, a small electric tug came silently out of the snow. It pulled two small coaches which looked as if they had been filched from a children's fun fair. It swung around at the foot of the steps and the woman motioned Bruno and Rossi towards it. His cousin followed Bruno down the steps. Bruno nodded as the woman opened the door for them and saluted. It was the first time in his life anyone had done that for him. It felt odd. The woman closed the door, the searchlights died, and the tug purred up a slope, following the single ray of light from the lamp in the centre of its snub nose. The snow fell thicker, obscuring Bruno's view of the clinic. The tug pulled up outside a double glass door.

Bruno saw a reception party waiting in the foyer. It was composed of several men in white coats and nurses in starched white uniforms with flat white shoes which did nothing to flatter their legs.

Bruno pulled up his collar and got out of the coach. He glanced briefly upwards through the falling snow. The clinic was designed like a vast Alpine chalet. Four rows of windows were set in the sloping roof whose eaves extended to form a porch around the building. The glass door was engraved with the flourishing legend, '*Clinic Ascha*'.

It opened automatically as Bruno, Rossi at his heels, approached. He entered. The air was hot. He stood aside as Rossi greeted the reception party with a sweeping gesture of his arm which embraced them all. They nodded respectfully.

'Bruno,' Rossi smiled, 'I want you to meet Dr Conrad Zeiss.'

Bruno eyed the figure who stepped smiling from the group that promptly lined behind him like a row of toy soldiers for inspection. The whole place had a Teutonic rather than Italian feel about it. The walls and floor were white. It sparkled with cleanliness and, as Zeiss pumped his hand, Bruno looked in vain for an ashtray or a dirty coffee cup. He turned his attention to Zeiss.

'An honour to meet you,' he repeated, still pumping Bruno's hand. His perfect white teeth were set off by a deep tan. He was a well-built man in his late forties with matinée idol good looks. His hair was fair and slicked.

Bruno was propelled along the inspection line and introduced to the waiting senior staff. Some had French names, others German and Italian.

'These are the cream of the Swiss pharmaceutical industry,' Zeiss explained proudly as he dismissed them.

'Now, what would you like to do?' Zeiss asked.

'Sleep,' Bruno said looking at his watch. 'It's been a long day.'

'Of course. I'll get someone to show you your room. Everything has been prepared.' He clicked his fingers. A plump middle-aged nurse eased herself from a desk full of pot plants.

'There are some things I'd like to discuss. Tomorrow I have to return to Rome,' Rossi said.

'Then goodnight.'

Bruno followed the nurse up the corridor.

It had stopped snowing.

Bruno stretched, put down his coffee and walked out onto the balcony. He breathed deeply and the thin air made him light-headed. He looked out over the roof of Italy, then turned his face north. The distant Alps would be Austrian. He followed their line until he guessed that was where the Dolomites began their fall to the blue waters of the Adriatic.

He saw the clinic was enclosed by an inner and outer high wire fence. There was no gate. The only way in or out was by cable car to the road far below. Even so, the boiler-suited guards and their dogs kept constant patrol in pairs around the perimeter. Their barking had woken him several times in the night.

He counted six single-storey concrete buildings in the grounds. They were set in a row a hundred yards from the clinic. The electric tug came into view from behind the buildings. It pulled an open truck hitched behind a small coach. Bruno could pick out four indistinct figures in the coach. The tug wound down the road to the cable car control. The car itself, doors open, stood waiting. A mobile wooden hoist lift was positioned alongside the steps leading to the platform. The tug drew up alongside.

Bruno took a sharp breath when the four figures got out

of the coach. They wore one-piece hooded rubber suits and what, from where Bruno stood, looked like gas masks.

From the open truck he saw them unload two large hammock-shaped bundles and hoist them onto the platform.

There was a knock on his door.

'Come in.'

It was Rossi and Zeiss. They joined him. Bruno pointed as the men dumped the bundles into the car.

'What are they doing?'

'Burying the dead. Or rather, taking them for burial in a quicklime mixture. Work begins on a crematorium when the thaw comes in the next few weeks,' Zeiss said proudly.

Bruno gripped the balcony rail until his knuckles turned white.

Rossi left for Rome at noon.

Zeiss showed Bruno around the clinic. Earlier they'd spent the morning discussing the technical problems of genetically engineering the cells of the antidote into the mutant bacillus. Zeiss was enthusiastically optimistic of early success. He displayed great expertise. Bruno noted with detached respect that his mind was sharp, precise and analytical. Bruno found himself unable to concentrate, the image of the men loading the cable car would not quit his thoughts.

'Ach,' Zeiss waved his hand at Bruno's protestations, 'they were hardly human. Just like those we are about to see.'

Bruno passed through the door Zeiss held for him. It was a hospital ward.

'One of six in the clinic,' Zeiss explained as they walked down a corridor. The walls and doors were painted pale green.

'We find it has a soothing effect on the subjects,' Zeiss said.

'Patients,' Bruno corrected.

Zeiss flashed his smile. 'Hardly.'

Bruno watched as he drew back the judas on one of the doors set each side of the corridor. Bruno took up his invitation and took a look as Zeiss stepped aside.

He peered through.

The woman sat cross-legged on the bed, her back propped up against the wall. Her hair was crudely cropped and sprouted in tufts. She wore a coarse smock and played with her fingers on her lap.

'She's thirty-two,' Zeiss said.

She looked up. Bruno saw a face like old leather, lined and stretched. She smiled. He saw the few teeth that remained were black and stained. She nodded rapidly and made gurgling noises.

She swung her thin legs onto the bare floor and Bruno instinctively stepped back as she rushed to the door, arms outstretched like an oriental beggar pleading for alms.

There was no glass in the window.

Bruno saw a thin hand reach through, fingers moving in unison as if beckoning him, while animal noises came from the back of her throat.

He had to turn away.

'I told you so,' Zeiss said. 'They are no more than animals.'

'They are people. Sick people.'

'No more than animals. They have no sense or feelings. They are the worst cases from the mental asylums of Italy, Germany and Austria,' he shrugged. 'They have, for the most part, been institutionalized since birth. They have no family, no ties, nothing. At least they are some use here. For them death must be a sweet release.'

Bruno said nothing. Inwardly he seethed.

Zeiss added, 'Their ultimate fate is nothing more sinister than enthanasia.'

Bollocks, Bruno thought. It revolted him.

'The less severe cases are through here.'

Bruno pushed open the door. It was an open ward with beds along the side of each wall facing one another.

Like the woman, Bruno noted the patients all had their hair cropped, wore the same rough smocks and went barefoot. Some sat silently, others milled like demented ants.

Bruno had seen enough.

'I'd like to see the research facilities,' he said.

'Certainly.'

They walked towards the six buildings set in a row. The snow was crisp and hard. It crackled underfoot.

'As you can see, the buildings have concrete shells. They are, however, lead-lined for security,' Zeiss explained as they entered the first building.

There were five research teams. One to a building and all of Swiss nationality. No Italians or Germans. That puzzled Bruno.

Bruno spoke to all of them. They were thorough and dedicated yet utterly detached from the subjects they were experimenting upon.

Yet it shocked him when Zeiss said, 'Of course you realize the clinic is run as a private company.'

Bruno failed to conceal his surprise.

'I thought you worked for the Italian and German governments?'

'Financed by them,' corrected Zeiss. 'We will sell the final product.'

Bruno wondered what Rossi's stake was in the company as they entered the sixth building. It would give him power and wealth.

'The testing lab,' said Zeiss. 'You will have to dress accordingly.'

Bruno was shown into a small room. The hooded rubber suits hung in rows upon pegs. He put one on. Then the filter mask. He followed Zeiss down a stone passage and entered a room.

One wall was glass and on this side was a long table. On the other, three gaunt, naked figures were sitting on beds. One was a woman. They paid no heed to the people on Bruno's side of the room.

He sat next to Zeiss at the table. Three suited figures with clipboards and stop-watches sat alongside.

'We are about to introduce the droplet spread.' Zeiss's

disembodied voice floated from the face filter. 'We shall analyse the effect. There are only three more such experiments. The one after that will be with the engineered bacillus. Your brainchild.'

Bruno shuddered. This was sheer murder. He looked at the tormented figures rocking to and fro, their knees tucked under their chins as they sat on the beds. He noticed one's mouth move. It was the woman's.

Jesus, Bruno thought, she's singing.

The others began to sway in time to her soundless tune.

It's murder. Pointless murder. The results are obvious. There is no need for this.

He stood up and stormed from the room, Zeiss hard on his heels. He barged into the changing room and tore the mask from his face. The sweat was pouring from him. He unzipped the suit and stepped out of it. Zeiss, mask in hand, came into the room.

'You have no stomach for it?' he asked.

'Not that. It's pointless. You know they will die,' Bruno snapped.

'Knowing how they die is important,' Zeiss countered.

'But I do not have to watch it. All I am here for is to observe and assist in the antidote preparation.' Bruno paused for breath. He forced himself to say, 'When you are ready to try that with the engineered strain then I shall be only too pleased to watch.'

A look of incomprehension spread over Zeiss's face.

'I want to see where the Wildfire stocks are stored,' Bruno said quickly, cutting out any possible questions from the Swiss.

'There is a vault under the main clinic. I . . .'

'Show me.'

The images of the day haunted Bruno's restless sleep. He twisted and turned and threw off the covers. He could not rest, not after what he'd seen. The radiators in the room were on full blast. There was no way to turn them down. He threw open the balcony window and let the wind gusting off the snow chill him.

The light from his room fell onto the snow and, unseen in the darkness, the guard dogs began to bark. The sound echoed off the mountain.

Bruno pulled the window tight. He dressed and walked through the sleeping clinic. He passed the doors to one of the wards. They were locked.

He went down to reception. The plump nurse snored from amid the potted plants, her head on her arms which were folded under her on the desk.

As Bruno stood on the rubber mat in front of the glass doors they slid back. He walked out into the still night. A lone dog barked. He saw the cable car hanging motionless against the stars of a crystal-clear night sky. There was a thin sliver of new moon.

Bruno kicked at the snow sending a burst of powder into the night. He noticed a light still burnt in the testing lab. He wondered just how long the poor bastards inside would have to endure their inflicted agony. He hoped their death would not be long in coming.

At least he had one satisfaction.

He'd located the source of Wildfire.

He had infiltrated the Clinic Ascha.

He was on the inside.

The obscenity of it was worse than he'd imagined. He remembered the day when he'd received Lucia's letter. He was shocked then by the contents, yet he never thought it could be like this.

He rounded a corner of the building at the back. There was no path around the rear. The snow was knee deep. He hesitated and thought to turn back, then changed his mind.

Bruno trudged into the snow. The only light came from the thin moon. He looked over his shoulder and saw the mark he'd made through a drift.

He rubbed his face. Ice began to form on the stubble on his chin. The air burnt his lungs. He turned back.

An oblong of light fell in his path, pale yellow on the white. Someone had turned on a light on the second floor.

Bruno glanced up. He saw a shadow on the wall of the room. It vanished.

The window flew open and a figure leant out. The girl breathed the night air then looked down at him.

He looked up at a ghost.

The face of Lucia Corso looked back, a mask of total disbelief.

CHAPTER TWELVE

They looked blankly at each other, locked in silence. He saw her sway slightly and lean against the window frame for support. She pressed her head into the crook of her arm and began to weep, softly. Her bare shoulder rose and fell. She wore a chemise.

Bruno, up to his knees in snow, was dumbfounded. His jaw sagged as his mind emptied, except for realization she was alive.

She was here.

Lucia, face tear stained, turned her head. Slowly she began to shake it.

'You came,' she said and he saw her reach out for him. He noticed she trembled.

The sound of dogs barking drifted over the snow. Bruno stiffened. Countless questions flooded his brain. The answers would have to wait.

'Do you have clothes?' The whisper carried in the night.

She nodded, biting her lip as she half smiled.

'Get dressed,' he hissed, 'and put out that light.' He pressed his hands. They felt clammy.

Lucia just stood there, as if in a trance.

'Go on,' he urged through clenched teeth. 'We are getting out of here.'

She vanished. The light went out.

The dogs stopped barking. Bruno, his arms like pistons, ploughed back through his tracks in the snow. Nothing moved in the darkness. The lights still burnt in the testing lab. He was sweating now as he made his way back to the window.

Lucia appeared.

'Jump.'

She hesitated.

'Jump,' he barked.

She raised her hands above her head, closed her eyes and threw herself from the window. Her skirt billowed around her waist as she hit soft snow. She rolled onto her back as Bruno threw himself beside her.

'Are you hurt?'

He held her head to his chest as she threw her arms around him.

All she was able to say was, 'You came. I knew you would.' He squeezed her tightly.

All he had to do now was get her out. He lifted her to her feet. She wore a woollen jumper, skirt and flat shoes with no stockings. Lucia began to shiver, with cold and fear.

Bruno looked around him. The fences were stark against the clear Alpine sky. He was gripped by uncertainty as the scale of his task came home to him.

The fences were probably electrified. Scaling them without being seen by the patrolling guards would be impossible. If he, they, achieved the impossible then they still had the Alps to face. Even if they were equipped for it and had provisions, the chances of survival were almost nil. His mind raced with desperation. He cursed himself for acting on impulse. He should have waited, bided his time, until he had worked something out. But the sight of Lucia – alive – had triggered off his basic instinct. To take her and run. But how? He realized the cable car was the only way in or out.

'Don't move,' he told Lucia as he placed his hands on her shoulders. She nodded meekly, unable to come to terms with what was happening.

Bruno moved to the corner of the building. He saw the tiny glow of a cigarette. The guard smoking it stood chatting to his comrade outside the cable car control hut, their black outlines clear against the vast white backdrop of snow. One of the dogs at their feet lifted its nose and bayed at the pale moon. Its wail echoed down the valley.

The light still burnt in the testing lab. Bruno looked across to the row of buildings and clicked his fingers with delight.

He had it.

It was a slim chance. But it was a chance. The only chance. He galloped back to Lucia. She huddled herself, hands on shoulders, shivering.

Bruno yanked her by the wrist.

'Just do as I say.'

He hauled her to the far side of the building. They skirted it cautiously. The path was clear of snow under the eaves, it glistened damply. Their footfalls were softened by a high row of pine trees which acted as a windbreak to the icy east winds.

They reached the front corner of the clinic. He could see the guards still at the foot of the cable car. Rifles on their shoulders. Dogs at their feet.

Bruno realized he should have been afraid. He was not. He experienced a strange exhilaration. Almost like riding his Brough Superior around the green countryside of Cambridgeshire. He was aware of the haunting beauty of the Alps. Still. Silent. Majestic. The only taint was the obscene birthplace of Wildfire.

Bruno released Lucia's wrist. He kissed her on the forehead.

'Listen,' he said, his voice no more than a deep whisper, 'I want you to walk beside me as if we owned the place.' From the shadows he pointed to the guards. 'Just pretend they are not there. We are going to walk to the testing lab. When we get there,' he paused and held her arm, 'you may find . . .'

'Bruno,' she said, 'I know what's there.'

He closed his eyes, grimaced, and nodded. He felt her hand on his face. He kissed it. 'Let's go.'

They moved into the light from the reception area. The fat nurse still slept amid the potted plants. The electric clock above her read 2.25.

They walked between the banks of snow that had been shovelled from the path between the clinic and the laboratories. Bruno glanced at the guards. The dogs began to bark, straining on their leashes.

'Talk,' Bruno said through the corner of his mouth, 'say anything. Just talk.'

Lucia laughed theatrically. She began to recite from Dante's *Inferno*.

Bruno responded at the end of each stanza by rendering one line excerpts from King Lear's speech on the heath in Italian.

At the cable car a guard lit another cigarette as Bruno and Lucia's banter took them to the door of the test lab. Bruno pushed it open for Lucia.

Inside Bruno leant his back against the door and breathed deeply. Lucia looked haunted.

'Quick,' Bruno said. He ushered her through a pink-painted door into the changing room. He grabbed a rubber-hooded suit from a peg and tossed it to her. She caught it.

'Put it on,' he rasped as he tore a second suit from the peg. The filter masks were laid on a table against the far wall. Above the table was a rack. It contained four carbines, German Mausers, held in metal clips.

Bruno kicked off his wet shoes and tried to ease himself into the rubber suit. He saw Lucia hoist her skirt and tuck it into her pants. She wriggled into the suit. It was skin tight, her skirt bulged at the hips.

Bruno fastened the collar of his suit and pulled up the hood.

'Do you know the research staff?' he asked.

'Some,' Lucia replied.

He flung her a mask. She fumbled with it, Bruno took it from her and placed it on her head. He tucked her hair in and fastened it. He motioned Lucia to stay put and edged into the corridor. He crept up to the laboratory door and silently turned the handle.

It inched open.

He peered through the crack. The research team sat with their backs to him. There was no sign of the victims behind the glass screen. The clock on the wall read 2.35.

Bruno eased the door closed.

He had to wait for two men and a woman to die from bubonic plague.

Bruno looked at his watch. It was 3.55. Lucia, legs crossed and head bent, sat on the floor at his side. They had not spoken, not daring to break the silence. His back was pressed against the wall, the carbine held firmly in his hands was trained on the door.

It opened.

Two rubber-suited figures came into the room, peeling off their masks.

He took in the look of total amazement as their eyes focused on the weapon in his hand.

'Sit in the corner and put your hands on your heads.'

They did, bewilderment and fear in their eyes.

'Are your patients dead?'

They nodded dumbly in unison.

'What happens now?'

Silence.

'The procedure. Tell me.' Bruno spat the words. The gun in his hand trembled. 'Tell me.'

'Dr Grubber is phoning for the burial party.'

'When will they come?'

'Immediately. They are disposed of without delay,' stammered the Swiss researcher.

'How many in the party?'

'Three, sometimes two. It varies.' The man's eyes darted nervously. 'Are you going to kill us?'

'If I have to.' Bruno's words came rapidly. It was as if he heard someone else speaking them. Then the significance of what he'd said dawned on him. He had threatened to kill someone. And he had meant it.

Bruno spun to face the door as it opened. Dr Grubber stood there.

She had long blonde hair and pale blue eyes. She was one

of the staff Bruno had been introduced to when he'd first arrived at the clinic. She looked at her two colleagues sitting on the floor, hands still on heads, then coldly at Bruno.

'This is utter madness, Dottore Rossi. Have you taken leave of your senses?' she said.

'Get over there with the others.' Bruno motioned with the carbine.

'Certainly not,' she tossed her head.

With one hand on the trigger he grabbed her roughly and slung her across the room. She crashed into a metal changing locker. The door flew open. Her face said: This is not real.

Bruno said to Lucia, 'See what you can find in the locker to tie them up with. Quickly.'

The blonde doctor moved for Lucia who peered through her mask into the locker. She reached inside and took a pair of women's stockings, the doctor's, and a white cotton shirt. She bound the doctor's hands behind her back.

'It's too tight,' she complained and winced.

'Too bad,' Bruno said. Then he told her sitting colleagues, 'Stand up.'

They did hurriedly. Lucia used the second stocking to bind the taller of the two. Then she strained to tear the shirt into shreds. When all three were tied, Bruno placed the carbine up against the wall and used strips of the shirt to gag them. Only Dr Grubber struggled. As Bruno made her fast she kicked back and connected with his shin. He bundled her into the open locker, slammed the door shut and locked it.

'You next,' he said as he opened the door of a second locker. 'The pair of you.'

They obliged. He locked the door, moved to the window, opened it and tossed the key out into the snow. He glanced towards the cable car and saw the electric tug and truck winding along the path towards him.

'They are on their way,' he said as he grabbed a mask. Lucia fastened it for him. She fumbled nervously and he could feel his own heart pounding.

*

There were two of them. Bruno, Lucia at his side, met them at the door to the lab.

'You have completed your programme?' The disembodied voice was distorted through the mask filter. 'How many?'

'Three of them,' Bruno said.

'You have not been into the room or touched them?'

Bruno shook his head.

'Fetch the bags,' the voice crackled. The owner wore a leather holster on the hip. The other unslung his rifle, leant it against the door and went back into the night. He came back, three canvas lace-up bags over the arm.

Bruno moved back to the locker room as the figures pushed open the swing doors to the testing lab to begin their gruesome task.

Bruno jumped. Dr Grubber began to kick the locker door. Her mumbled protests echoed as her feet pounded the metal door. Bruno kicked it with all his might. The vibrations rang in his ears.

'If you have lost all interest in life then just keep that up,' he snapped hoarsely, his lips pressed tight against the crack in the still ringing door. The blonde doctor fell silent.

Minutes later he saw the guards pass the open door. One at each end of the canvas bags. A lump came to his throat. He noticed Lucia turn to the wall and he clenched his fists.

Then they bore the second corpse.

Then the third.

Bruno watched as they laid the last bundle alongside the other two in the open-back truck. He felt sick.

'You,' he called. 'Come here.'

The guard pressed his finger to his chest and angled his head for confirmation.

'Yes, you.' Bruno turned from the front door as he heard the guard's footsteps crunch on the snow behind him. He heard the other press the starter button on the tug. It whirred to life with a soft hum, as Bruno re-entered the locker room. Lucia, her head resting on her arms, leant against the far wall.

He picked up the carbine and gripped it. It felt totally unfamiliar, alien in his hands. He noticed they trembled.

This was it.

He positioned himself behind the open door.

The guard came in, pushed the door shut behind him, and looked around. Bruno jabbed with the carbine, he felt the barrel sink into the rubber suit above the guard's kidneys. There was a strangled cry as he sank to his knees clutching his bruised side.

'Get up.' Bruno raised the gun to his shoulder. The guard rose, bent double, and cursed through the filter mask. Bruno motioned with the gun. The guard slowly raised his arms above his head.

'Lucia,' Bruno said, 'get the other one in here.'

She turned and faced him. Hesitated, as if she was unable to comprehend what was going on. Then she dashed from the room.

He heard her call, 'One moment,' to the guard.

She was back in the doorway. She nodded. Bruno indicated to her to stand back and Lucia moved nervously to the corner.

The guard marched briskly into the room, then halted as if confronted by an invisible wall.

Bruno pointed the gun from shoulder height. He glanced quickly at the second guard, then back to the first.

'Take off your masks,' he snapped.

The first obeyed instantly, tearing it from his face. He looked terrified. The mask dropped at his feet.

The second guard did not move.

'Your mask,' Bruno yelled.

The guard laughed, then snatched at the hip holster, rubber fingers tearing at the fastener.

Bruno froze. His fingers refused to tighten on the trigger. The holster flap tore open. He saw the black handle of the pistol leave the guard's hip as the figure swung, knees bending in slow motion.

'You've got your safety catch on,' the disembodied voice

taunted him as the hand holding the gun levelled itself. He felt his grip on the carbine slacken. The pistol facing him was almost level.

Then Bruno swung out like a baseball player, the carbine his bat. He swung in a vicious arc. The air whistled as the carbine cut through. There was a sickening crack as the metal barrel connected with the bone beneath the rubber mask. A scream was stifled in the filter as the pistol flew from the guard's hand.

Guard and gun hit the floor at the same time. From the corner of his eye he saw the second guard scramble on all fours after the bouncing pistol. His hand closed around the butt.

Then Bruno raised the carbine like an axe above his head. He brought it down with all the force he could muster and caught the man on the shoulder. He jerked as Bruno heard his collar bone snap. A second clout to the side of the head left him unconscious.

Bruno rested his hands on his knees. Head bowed. He'd let the rifle slip as he felt his strength ebb from him.

He saw Lucia tear the mask from the prostrate figure of the first guard. It was the harsh-faced woman who had met him from the train.

'You've broken her jaw. She's out cold.'

'So she is,' Bruno said, 'and we've no time to care.'

Together they dragged the guards and laid them in the corner.

From the locker room came the sound of the blonde doctor sobbing.

Bruno and Lucia walked calmly out into the snow towards the waiting tug and its human cargo.

The tug shuddered as Bruno eased back on the throttle. He neared the cable car and saw the hoist was already in place. He reached out and felt Lucia's hand. She still trembled.

'Easy,' Bruno said. 'We are almost there.'

He saw there was just one guard. The other was patrolling

the perimeter fence. It was then Bruno realized with horror that he'd left the test laboratory door open – with the lights on. The patrol was skirting the fence in an anticlockwise direction. That was something. He had three-quarters of a lap to go before he stumbled on the lab.

That, Bruno reckoned, gave him fifteen minutes.

He hoped.

They neared the waiting guard. The Doberman began to snarl. It foamed at the mouth, white teeth standing out against the black fur. The guard hauled the beast back as he retreated towards the control building. Bruno guessed the man wanted to distance himself as far as possible from the three limp bundles in the back. The guard, he noted, wore just a balaclava, not a filter mask. As Bruno took a deep breath to steady himself he could taste the antiseptic from the filter. Somehow it tasted sweet.

He pressed the brake as the guard raised a hand. The dog snarled furiously.

'That's far enough. Wait until I start the cable car,' the man called through cupped hands.

Bruno raised his arm in acknowledgement.

'Don't fancy lending a hand?' he shouted.

'Not for what I'm paid.'

Bruno watched the guard unlock the door and haul the dog in after him. The lights came on.

They waited in silence.

The generator inside the control building coughed to life. The throb of its motor sent grey smoke from the thin metal stack on the flat roof.

'All clear.' The guard's head appeared around the door. He waved them on, then retreated to the safety of the building.

'Shut up,' his voice snapped. There came the sound of a slap and the dog yelped.

The tug was gearless, much to Bruno's relief. He stabbed the accelerator and it shot forward. It jerked to a halt alongside the hoist.

'You know what to do?'

'I've watched them many times.'

'Right,' said Bruno. He jumped down into the snow. It was hot inside the protective suit. The sweat stung his eyes. It was like a sauna.

He moved towards the canvas shrouds and looked down at the lifeless bundles. A sad anger washed over him. He wondered who these people had been.

'No more than animals.'

Zeiss's words ran through his mind. It was beyond his understanding. There was no sadness now. Only anger remained.

'No more than animals.'

He looked across at Lucia who was next to him. Just like her?

It was beyond all comprehension.

He noticed the guard and dog on patrol near the ridge of pine trees alongside the clinic. The dog cocked its leg then moved off back towards the fence. Time was short.

Bruno hesitated for a moment, then reached down for the first bundle. His mouth dried.

'I'll take the arms,' he breathed through the filter. He saw Lucia tense. 'Come on,' he urged.

She took the legs.

Together they lifted the corpse. It was no more than a bag of bones.

They placed it on the hoist.

When all three lay side by side they climbed the platform steps. Once on top, Bruno began to winch the handle. The hoist rose. They carried the bodies and laid them on the car's floor.

When done, Bruno saw the guard come from the control.

'Take her away,' he shouted.

Bruno took Lucia by the elbow and ushered her into the car. He drew the door shut, fixing the metal peg in the bolt to fasten it.

The car swung.

Above, Bruno heard the wire scrape over the pulley and they began to move. They lifted clear of the fence. He looked down and saw the drop was sheer. The virgin snow glistened – diamonds of frost.

The car followed the cable down the cleft of the valley. The clinic, built at the head, grew smaller. Lucia threw herself against him and began to weep.

'I can't believe it,' she sobbed.

Bruno looked over her shoulder. The car was picking up speed. Sparks flew as the overhead pulley scraped down the wire rope. He saw the down station getting closer.

He closed his eyes and sank his fingers into Lucia's shoulders.

He had done it.

It had been easy. For the first time in his life he had held a gun on someone. Something he'd never imagined he would be able to do. And, because he had had to do it, he had almost brained them with it. He wondered what he would have done if he had known about the safety catch.

The down station neared. Two hundred feet below, he guessed.

One hundred and fifty.

'We'll have to walk to the railway. We can follow it down to the village, then somehow get help.' He heard himself thinking aloud.

Lucia nodded numbly.

One hundred feet.

There was a white vehicle parked in the down station clearing. A red cross on its side.

'An ambulance.'

He strained his eyes. It was unattended. It had been left for the burial party.

Would the keys be in it?

He should have searched the guards he'd laid out.

Fifty feet.

There was no sign of life in the clearing.

Forty feet.

A wire rope screeched. Sparks danced against the night sky. The car slewed from side to side and rocked crazily as it slowed. Up above, someone was straining on the brake lever.

The patrol had stumbled on the testing lab. A klaxon sounded. It screamed in the night.

Alongside a bank of snow gave way because of the sound of the klaxon. Boulders of snow rolled in the abyss. Then the side of the adjacent valley moved like a great white sheet. Thousands of tons of snow began to slide. It rocked the pine trees like corn in the wind. The night was clear. Snow from the slide swirled against the car windows like an Alpine blizzard.

The car tilted and swung through ninety degrees. The bodies in canvas shrouds flew against the walls. Their bonds did not break – this time.

Bruno and Lucia rolled helplessly along the walls, then the floor of the lurching car. Then the walls again.

The wire rope above them stretched as it became taut. Bruno heard the strands snap. They cracked like gunfire.

The head of the valley burst into light as the searchlights sprang to life. The beams from a dozen giant electric eyes played through the darkness until they rested on the hanging car.

It had come to a halt now.

The bodies rolled from side to side across the floor as it swung in the air. Bruno heard more wire strands snap. He grabbed the wall rail and hauled himself to his feet. He looked down from the window. Below him the snowfall swirled through the blackness, great white twisting clouds on their way to the valley floor.

He threw himself to the other window, grabbing at the wall rail.

Red tracers flashed past the window. He ducked as one passed clean through. The blurs of elongated red lights were followed seconds later by the sound of the guns that fired them.

A voice was lost amid the mountains. It came from a loudhailer.

There was no time for fear. Bruno was thinking clearly. As clearly as he'd ever thought in his life. He tore the peg from the bolt holding the sliding door. He hauled it back. The cold air whistled through the car. It had slowed to a slow tilt.

He looked down.

Thirty – forty feet at the most to the down station snows.

A fusillade thudded into the wooden lower half of the car. The force rocked it.

Bruno lunged at Lucia. She was stunned, half-covered by a canvas shroud. Bruno pulled her free and, arm around her waist, hauled her to her feet. He draped her arm around his neck and lumbered towards the door.

The intensity of fire increased as the car hung helplessly in the trained beam of light.

They were at the open door. He looked down. The edge of the down station clearing gave way to the depths of the abyss. The snow on the clearing was deep from the previous day's fall.

Bruno looked into Lucia's eyes through the round circles of glass set in the rubber mask. In them he saw fear.

'Jump,' he pointed to the clearing.

The fear grew. She shook her head.

Another fusillade rocked the car.

'Jump,' he screamed.

The fear grew as her eyes widened.

He grabbed her tightly around the waist. He felt the bulge of her hitched skirt beneath the rubber suit. She tried to push him away.

Crack.

Splinters flew as another burst smashed into the car.

Lucia began to struggle. The car swung again, like a soundless bell. A canvas shroud slid slowly across the floor to the open door where Bruno fought to restrain the terrified Lucia.

The body passed between them as he tried to hold her at arms' length. She kicked and screamed with fear.

Bruno's stomach churned as the body rested briefly at the open door.

Then, as Lucia struggled to be free, the car tilted again. The body fell into the night.

Bruno watched it spin into the vast emptiness, its outline stamped against the snow. It hit the edge of the clearing, half on land, half over the abyss. Then it toppled into the darkness.

The car juddered. It began to move.

Upward.

They were hauling it back to the Clinic Ascha.

Bruno snatched at Lucia.

He lifted her above his head with a strength his instincts summoned from the depths within him. He tottered slightly, then threw her into the night.

He dived headlong after her just as a fresh burst of gunfire whistled past the dangling car.

CHAPTER THIRTEEN

Bruno hit the soft snow with a force that drove the breath from him. He rolled onto his back and felt he was suffocating, the bitter-sweet taste of antiseptic in his mouth. He ripped the mask from his face. His lungs filled with mountain air. Above him the cable car swung precariously on the wire. It was being hauled back to the clinic at full speed. He saw another canvas shroud slide through the door and spin head over heels into the bottomless night.

He sat up and realized with horror he was only feet from the edge of the precipice.

'Lucia,' he yelled and scrambled to his feet in desperation. He looked around him frantically. She's gone over the edge, he thought with dread.

Then he caught sight of a grey shape rolling and sliding down the ridge towards him leaving a shower of snow in its wake. A tumbling ball of arms and legs.

Lucia.

She was gathering momentum dangerously, pushing the snow aside as she slithered down the slope. There was no way she could stop herself. The gap between her and the precipice narrowed sickeningly.

Bruno ploughed up the slope to head her off. He stumbled and bent double before he regained his balance. Then he took giant leaps, bringing up his knees waist-high.

She was sliding far to his right.

He dived arcoss the snow, arms at full length. He slid on his belly like a sledge. She slipped past. He shot out an arm in a final desperate effort. His fingers closed around her ankle. They spun like acrobats in the snow, highwire artists on ice. He grabbed her other ankle. They began to slow. He saw she was conscious and using her hands as brakes. They crashed into a drift and came to a tangled rest.

He helped Lucia to her feet and removed her mask, tossing it aside. Her lips were cut and swollen. A bruise had begun to show under her left eye. To Bruno she looked simply fantastic, her hair tangled and wet with perspiration, her dark eyes wide.

Bruno stilled her as she was about to speak.

'Later,' he said, 'there is no time now.'

He took her by the wrist and, half stumbling, they moved through the snow towards the clearing and the parked ambulance. Bruno looked back. He could see the glow from the searchlights bright against the night sky.

Bruno shuddered at the thought. But he knew then he would have to return to Clinic Ascha.

He also realized that three men would have to die.

Pini.

Werner.

Zeiss.

Perhaps four. His own cousin, Rossi. He thought coldly about it, and was aware that the thought did not bother him in the slightest.

They'd reached the old ambulance.

Bruno tried the door. It was locked. He dug into the snow, found a rock and smashed it through the window. He reached inside and opened the door. He climbed into the driving seat and scanned the dashboard.

There were no ignition keys.

Again he cursed himself for not searching the guards he'd laid out. He thought for a moment, sucking his cheeks with worry.

The cable car would return soon, full of armed guards. He remembered Rossi's warning and knew that he and Lucia faced certain death. He'd read about people cross-circuiting ignition systems. He did not have the faintest idea how. Yet he knew the ambulance was their only chance.

'Got it.' He snapped his fingers, satisfied.

He knocked the ambulance out of gear and released the

handbrake. He leapt to the ground.

'We,' he told the startled Lucia, 'are going to push.'

'Push?' Her eyes widened.

Bruno moved to the back of the vehicle and shoved his shoulder against the door. 'Push,' he confirmed as she joined him. 'If we can get this thing moving we don't need an engine. We are already on a downward slope. It's just a few yards to the road. If we can get it that far, then it's downhill all the way to the foot of the bloody mountain.'

He dug his heels into the snow. It was packed hard on the clearing. His heel marks left deep ruts. They strained until they thought their hearts would burst.

Slowly, the ambulance shifted. Just a few inches.

But it shifted. The slope down the road was steeper than it looked. It began to pick up speed. They were running behind it now, pushing as the momentum increased. Lucia pulled up, panting.

Bruno stumbled.

His hands fell away from the back door. Behind him he heard the cable car wire begin to hum. He heard it vibrate.

They were coming.

He ran headlong and realized with dread the ambulance was pulling away from him. He sprinted wildly after it, fists clenched as they pounded the air.

His chest swelled as his legs moved like pistons. He threw back his head, his mouth grimacing, as the tendons on his neck stood out with effort. He began to draw alongside the door. He threw out a hand and grabbed the handle.

He lost his balance, but his grip on the handle was true.

He was being towed along by the ambulance now. He summoned all his effort and leapt onto the running board.

He'd done it.

They were almost on the road.

The start of a steep hill, the edge of the precipice, yawned ahead. A vast chasm of darkness.

He wrenched open the door and flung himself into the cab. He took the wheel and stabbed at the brakes. They were good. They'd have to be on these roads. The ambulance slowed. He played the brakes until it slowed to walking pace.

In the mirror he saw Lucia, hair flying. She was running like the wind. He flung open the passenger door, leant across the seat and held out his hand.

She gripped it tightly. He heard her gasp with effort. She was on the running board. She flung herself onto the seat.

The door slammed as Bruno took the first bend. They were picking up speed.

He pounded the steering wheel with undisguised glee.

The back wheels shimmied as Bruno rounded the bend noiselessly. It was the fifth hairpin along the twisting road from the down station.

He looked up and saw the black outline of the cable car come to a halt above him. The echo of voices carried through the mountains. He saw a flash of light, then others. Then the sharp reports of the carbines sang through the night.

They were shooting at them.

Bruno noted with satisfaction that was all they could do. There was only one vehicle. He had it. And he was fast moving out of range.

Steering the ambulance without the use of the engine was more difficult than he thought. He could not use the gears to slow him down and it was difficult to gauge the speed without the noise of revs to guide him. The speedometer remained rooted at zero.

They reached the fringe of the pine forest. They moved through arcades of trees broken only where the road curved perilously around the edge of sheer rock face.

'They must have people further down the road,' Bruno decided, 'and they must have radioed ahead.'

'Yes,' Lucia agreed.

Bruno eased the brakes. They stopped on an incline. He rammed on the handbrake. Steering the ambulance needed all his concentration. And now he needed time to think ahead. Clearly.

He bit his thumb as Lucia eyed him nervously.

Bruno recapped on his journey to the clinic. He and Rossi had been driven from Vipiteno, the first town on the Italian side of the Brenner Pass, to the small village of Udanzi. The Alpine railway, a private line, began the first leg of the journey to the Clinic Ascha a few miles from the village. Bruno guessed the clinic would have staff there. Someone had to organize and supervise the human cargo.

He turned to Lucia. 'Put yourself in the position of the guards at the clinic. What would be your next move?'

She thought for a moment, frowning. 'Radio down to the railway terminal and send men up the line by train to head us off.'

'Yes,' Bruno said. 'But the chances are they'd be too late. We would have gone beyond the halt by the time they arrived.'

'True.'

'But if I was in their shoes, I'd still send the train. I'd also send men by road. They must know we have no chance of survival if we took to the forest or tried to leave the road. They would close in on us from each end and we'd be caught in the middle.'

'Then that's what they'll do.' Lucia looked troubled.

'As long as we agree,' Bruno smiled. He touched her knee, then released the handbrake.

The ambulance rolled on.

He noticed the sky was getting brighter. Dawn was not far away, he thought, as faint pink tinges seeped across the horizon.

They sat huddled together and waited. Bruno cupped Lucia's head to his shoulder. His eyes were closed.

'Look,' she cried.

Bruno stirred.

'Where?'

'They've disappeared behind the trees,' she blurted and sat bolt upright, squinting into the gloom. 'No, wait,' she pointed. 'There they are again.'

Bruno saw them.

Pinpricks of light flashing through the trees hundreds of feet below them. The headlights of advancing trucks. He thought they'd be crammed with guards.

'I hope we're right about them sending the train too,' Bruno said uneasily.

'We are. Listen.'

Bruno stuck his head through the broken window and cocked his ear. He caught the chug of a toiling steam engine. Then its shrill whistle shrieked. Seconds later he saw sparks fly into the air above the dense pine forest as the train pulled nearer.

'Right.'

He leapt to the ground. Lucia joined him.

'When I say – push like hell,' he said and she vanished around the back of the ambulance. Bruno pressed his shoulder against the door frame. His eyes switched to and fro between railway and road.

The trucks were getting nearer.

The pinpricks of light were now beams. He saw them light the trees as they flashed past.

Then the train rounded the bend and came into view. He heard the wheels slip as it fought its way up the last gradient which would take it to the end of the line.

He prayed they had lookouts watching for the fleeing ambulance.

'Push,' he screamed as he ripped off the handbrake. He heard Lucia gasp as her effort expelled the air from her lungs. With one hand on the wheel Bruno shoved with all his might.

The train hooted furiously.

A signal, he hoped. Let it mean they've spotted the ambulance.

He was running beside it now.

'Let go,' he yelled.

He looked behind.

Lucia stood panting, head bent and hands on knees. Bruno twisted the wheel. The nose of the ambulance swung towards the gap in the trees. Beyond lay the sheer drop.

He threw himself clear. Hands on hips, he snatched back his breath as the ambulance slewed uncontrollably towards the edge of the road, just before the hairpin bend curved to the right into the dense foliage arcade.

He watched as the ambulance left the road.

It seemed to shoot straight ahead, as if it was flying without wings. The doors flew open. The nose dipped. It plunged from sight.

There came the sickening thud of searing metal. Glass smashed. Then came a mighty whoosh.

Bruno felt the heat from where he stood as the petrol tank exploded. Sparks from the crashing metal set it alight. The flames engulfed the whole vehicle. That was when the lethal drums of quicklime and acid exploded in the back. The roar from the burial fluid was deafening. Seconds later the echo was drowned by the avalanche it triggered across the valley.

'Holy mother,' Lucia breathed. She was at his side holding onto his arm as if she feared the rumble would blow them both from the road.

'What caused it to go up like that?'

'Corrosive that kills Wildfire,' he said darkly.

They began to run as if their lives depended on it.

The train's wheels locked and sent out a shower of sparks as it thumped to a halt against the red buffer.

Bruno and Lucia crouched in the pines above the halt.

'Motorbikes,' he whispered and pointed.

The machines were stacked in an open sheep truck hitched to the rear of the coach. Bruno saw men vault over the observation platform to the ground. Two lowered the side of the truck.

It formed a ramp.

They scrambled onto the truck after four of their companions and kicked the bikes to life. Bruno recognized the song of their engines. They were the British-built BSAs solid old workhorses with low-geared side-valve engines. Unmistakable.

Bruno pulled Lucia low as they roared off in line. One turned and accelerated off towards the approaching trucks. The others swung left up the mountain road.

'Give them ten minutes,' Bruno said.

They sat in the half light until the sound of the engines died. The bikes, Bruno guessed, had arrived at the bend where the ambulance had left the road.

What was left of it had come to grief on a ledge fifty feet down the cliff. The men would now, he reasoned, be trying to reach it to see what, if anything, was left.

He grinned at Lucia. She looked adoringly at him. It made him feel like Errol Flynn. A few months ago he would have worried about breaking the speed limit. He amazed himself. And was proud of it.

'Come on,' he said fliply, 'or we'll miss our train.'

Lucia giggled, girlishly. It made him feel warm inside.

He grabbed her hand and ran from the trees to the waiting train, its long stack smoking softly against the lightening sky.

The driver was polishing the brass pressure gauge with a clean rag. He looked at Bruno and Lucia with surprise.

Bruno barked at him in Italian, a passable imitation of his cousin Rossi. He reasoned the driver would not have been given the reason for his journey. He would only have been told to make it. Quickly.

'Get up steam,' Bruno snapped. 'We are from the Clinic Ascha. We have to report to Udanzi at once. Hurry, man. Hurry,' he was bellowing. His nervousness made it come easily.

The driver wiped his nose with his sleeve and stared back hard at Bruno. His heart sank. The man had tumbled them.

He knew.

His eyes fell on the stoking shovel. He would have to brain him with it.

It was Lucia who spoke. 'He can't understand you. They speak only German in this part of Italy.'

She then translated, in rapid German, Bruno's command. The man nodded repeatedly. He said something in German and began to pile logs into the boiler. Furiously.

Bruno followed Lucia to the coach.

He closed the door as the train began to move backwards down the mountain. Lucia turned to him.

He saw the tears stream down her face as she threw her arms around his neck.

The train rocked slowly. The light in the coach came from an oil lamp which swung from the wooden ceiling. The seats were made from slats of unvarnished pine.

Bruno listened intently as Lucia spoke. He said nothing as she paused and lapsed into long silences. She closed her eyes and swayed with the motion of the train as she recounted her nightmare at the Clinic Ascha.

'I thought at first they were going to kill me,' she began, 'just like poor Maria. But Pini said I was fortunate. I had a powerful friend which meant I lived. I guessed it must be you.'

No, Bruno thought. He wanted to tell her about Fulgoni but he remembered the old man's oath to Lucia's mother. If she was to know then the Cavaliere had to tell.

Lucia continued. 'They brought me to the clinic in this coach. I was, they told me later, heavily sedated.' She opened her eyes and indicated the coach. 'It was just like a cattle truck then, full of those poor demented people. Hopelessly insane, all of them. And I thought I had become one of them.'

'At first that's what they wanted you to think,' Bruno said softly. He reached across and took her hand.

'What made it worse was that I knew what was going to happen to them. I *knew*,' her voice rose bitterly. 'I thought that was what was going to happen to me. I was going to be sacrificed just like them.

'Every week they would bring a fresh train load, men, women and children. Every day I would watch from my room as the burial parties carried their bodies from the testing lab. It was horrible. You just cannot believe that this was being done to people.'

'I can,' Bruno said gravely. He felt her squeeze his hand.

'In the beginning, I was kept under sedation. Then, one day, they discontinued it. That was when Pini came to see me. He showed me around the clinic. Everything. Then he tried to persuade me to join the research team.' She pointed to herself incredulously. 'Me. Pini said it would make my life easier for me. The alternative was to be held a virtual prisoner in the clinic.'

'You refused?'

He was taken aback by the look she shot him. It said – how dare you?

'Lucia,' Bruno said, 'I had to know?'

She nodded, fighting back the tears.

'It's over now,' he said, although he knew it was not.

The train whistled and began to slow.

'We must be almost there.' Bruno rose and pulled up the hood of Lucia's rubber suit. Then his own.

'What are we going to do now?' she asked earnestly.

His cheerful grin disguised his doubts.

'Sightseeing,' he said. 'I want to show you a mountain village in Tuscany called Perino Maggiore.'

'Where?'

'My parents were born there, and there are some people I want you to meet.'

He stepped out onto the observation platform.

She followed.

The train hissed to a halt and was enveloped by its own steam. Bruno gripped the handrail and felt the first twinge of doubt as he took in the scene.

The place seemed deserted.

There was a long shed made from sheets of black corrugated iron. It was windowless and the doors were bolted from the outside.

Twenty yards from the single track stood what he guessed

was the office. It was a low building built from roughly hewn logs. The roof was angled to take the weight of the winter snow. Although, now, at the foot of the mountain the ground was covered only by a thin powdery blanket.

As they stepped cautiously to the ground the train puffed slowly towards a water tower beyond the black shed.

Bruno saw a face appear briefly at the office window. Then vanish.

His apprehension grew.

They should have left the train further up the track, skirted the halt and made straight for the village of Udanzi, he reasoned. It was too late for that now. He'd thought every available man would have been sent on the mountain chase. He had not counted on someone being left behind.

Bruno decided not to make a run for it. They would not get far on foot before the alarm was raised. They needed transport.

'We are going to have to bluff it out,' he told Lucia. 'Stay outside,' he said and began to stride boldly towards the office, Lucia a few paces behind. Bruno threw open the door and marched in.

He looked down the barrel of a Mauser.

It was being held by a small fat man in his mid-fifties. He was bald and obviously very frightened. Behind him, on a long wooden table, was a radio transmitter. Bruno assumed the man was the operator.

'I'll shoot if you cause any trouble,' he said and licked his lips. His pate glistened with sweat. He gripped the pistol with both hands as if he was afraid he'd drop it. He added theatrically, 'Put up your hands and stand and face the wall.' The gun in his hand began to shake.

Bruno moved to the far wall, more afraid of being shot by accident than design.

'You're the intruder from the clinic.' He made it sound like an omen. 'Where is the other one who got away?'

Bruno could not believe his ears. The fool had not seen Lucia.

Then he saw the reason on the table next to the transmitter. The man's glasses. They had wire frames and thick pebble glass. He must have been as blind as a bat.

The crack was ear-splitting. Bruno winced.

It was followed by a thump as the man crashed to the floor.

Bruno spun around.

He saw Lucia standing over the figure on the floor. She had a snow shovel in both hands. It was still raised above her head.

The fat man tried to raise himself for a second, then slumped face down.

Bruno knelt beside him. The gash on the back of his skull was bleeding profusely. He saw she'd caught him with the edge of the shovel. He eased the gun from the limp, stubby fingers. A pool of blood seeped into the bare floorboards.

He placed the gun on the radio table.

'If we take that out it will buy us time.' He pointed at the radio – the sole link with the men on the mountain and the clinic.

He peered at the mass of wires. He looked puzzled.

'Stand clear,' Lucia said.

He did.

He watched, almost in awe, as she threw the shovel over her shoulder.

She swung.

Sparks flew from the radio. The wires frizzed. Valves exploded. A haze of blue smoke filled the air.

He nodded with admiration. She'd destroyed the communications link with the clinic and the search teams with one blow.

He saw the train driver swing the trunk hose from the water tower. Water cascaded over the tank of the little engine. He decided the driver was no problem.

He turned to Lucia. She let the shovel fall.

'What is happening to us?' she asked as she looked down at the bleeding heap at her feet.

'We are surviving,' Bruno said. 'Staying alive.'

The fat man on the floor began to gurgle. Bruno turned

him onto his back. He laid his head to one side. Blood poured from the corner of his mouth.

Bruno recognized the signs. The man was dying.

He turned to Lucia and put his arm around her shoulder.

'Let's get out of here.'

She turned for the door.

'Wait.'

Bruno scanned the room. The man's overcoat hung on a peg near the door. It was dark blue, woven from heavy cloth.

'Take that,' he pointed, 'and let's get out of these suits. We don't want to freeze to death.'

He watched Lucia step from the tight-fitting rubber suit. She hitched her skirt from her pants, let it fall and tossed her head. She ran her hands over her jumper and skirt to smooth the creases. Bruno noted it had little effect.

He helped her on with the fat man's overcoat. It almost reached to her ankles. She buttoned it up to her neck and flicked her hair outside the collar.

Bruno paused and went back to the dying man. He laid the operator's arms above his head and pulled his jacket from him. He repositioned his arms on his chest. He took off his suit and put on the jacket, then put the pistol into the pocket. He felt unclean.

They walked from the room.

Bruno saw the driver had filled the train's tanks. The powdery snow kicked at his feet as he walked towards them.

Bruno pulled the office door tight behind him. He took Lucia's arm and advanced to the driver.

He acknowledged the couple by raising his hand.

Bruno smiled. From the corner of his mouth he told Lucia, 'Tell him we have to get to Udanzi. Urgently.'

She translated.

He pointed to the log office.

'He says there are some motorbikes at the back. He wants to know if they'll do. Otherwise he says to radio for a car from Udanzi.'

'The bikes will do fine.' Bruno's grin spread from ear to

ear. 'Now tell him to take his train back up the mountain and wait for the search teams.'

He heard the man mutter.

'And apologize for the trouble we've caused him,' Bruno added.

Lucia did.

The driver shrugged, looked at Bruno as if he was the original pain, and ambled back to the engine. He gesticulated to the train as he did so.

He may speak German, but he thinks like an Italian, thought Bruno.

He turned and saw Lucia was already heading for the back of the log office. He raced after her.

The train whistle blew as the wheels spun. Bruno clicked his fingers as he rounded the building. Then his face fell.

There were three motorcycles, each in various stages of repair. They were trusty BSAs.

The first was stripped of petrol tank and carburettor. They lay on a sack on the snow beside it. A tool kit was spread on a sheet of oily canvas.

Bruno looked at the other two machines. The innards of their engines and gearboxes spread around them.

But both had petrol tanks – and carburettors.

He dived for the tool kits.

The transplant took him almost twenty minutes.

Then Lucia carefully drained the contents of the one petrol tank into the other, now fixed on the complete machine. They had a full tank.

Bruno rummaged through the tool kits. He found a set of feeler gauges. He selected one and slid it into the ignition lock. It fitted. He turned it. A faint red glow glimmered on the speedometer.

'Sod it, flat battery.'

He grabbed the handlebars, hauled the bike from its stand and ran with it. He picked up enough speed and leapt onto the BSA side-saddle. He cocked his leg over the tank. His foot kicked into second gear.

He let out the clutch.

It fired and shot forward.

He re-engaged the clutch and shouted over his shoulder, 'Come on.'

Lucia, coat around her ankles, ran and jumped on behind.

He felt her arms tighten around his waist as he shot forward.

They flew down the road.

The signpost at the first junction read: 'Udanzi. 6 Km. Vipitena – Brenner Pass – 46 Km.' It indicated right.

Bruno crouched low. Lucia held tightly.

He swung to the left.

He followed the sign to Verona.

And opened the throttle wide.

CHAPTER FOURTEEN

Bruno sold the BSA in Verona.

They had ridden all day without a break, taking rough roads through villages off the beaten track. It was late afternoon when they entered the city and the shops and smaller bars were reopening for the evening. They crossed the river Adige, a sluggish green ribbon through the centre, and headed for the Piazza Bra, in the heart of the old city.

They wolfed a large dish of lasagne verde and paid for it with the handful of change and notes he found in the radio operator's jacket. They counted it out on the table. It came to just enough for the meal plus a jug of rough red wine.

Bruno left Lucia in the café and headed for the backstreets on the other side of the river. That's where all towns house their small garages and repair shops, usually run by one man and a boy, and not too particular. He found such a place without difficulty.

The man was swarthy and unshaven, a red handkerchief tied around his throat. He put down a wrench and wiped the grease from his hands on his blue overalls.

He walked around the BSA several times, kicked the tyres then started it up and held the throttle wide open.

'It's seen better days, no?' he shrugged indifferently.

'It's less than a year old, and it's been looked after,' Bruno said. He was grateful that papers were not needed for motorcycles in Italy. He had no doubt the man would still have bought it, but for even less than he now offered. It was half what the BSA was worth.

Bruno took it.

He watched the man count out the large lira notes from a greasy tin on his cluttered work bench. The mechanic stuffed them into Bruno's open hand. He put them in his pocket without counting.

He took an ancient black taxi back to the Piazza Bra. Lucia waited, smoking nervously.

'How much did you get?' she asked looking up.

'Enough for some new clothes and a week in a cheap hotel with some to spare.'

'Good.'

Bruno ordered a beer and a coffee for Lucia.

They decided to buy clothes first. They picked the most anonymous they could find. Lucia chose a plain sweater with a high neck, a dark jacket and slacks. Bruno suggested she also bought a handbag and some make-up. He bought a plain wool shirt, cord trousers and a strong casual jacket. It make him look anything from a junior librarian to a low-grade civil servant, not like someone on the run from *Il Duce*'s secret police.

But he did look like someone who could check into a small family hotel without arousing suspicion.

It was one of many in a side street in the heart of the old city. The kind used by hard-up lovers and commercial travellers for less prosperous companies.

Bruno guessed the owner's wife thought they were lovers.

He signed the register in a false name and could have kicked himself when she asked if they wanted their luggage taken to their room. He should have bought a suit-case.

'We don't have any,' he mumbled.

'Ahhh,' she said knowingly and winked.

They all laughed as she led them up a narrow staircase to the room, but Bruno realized she now had good reason to remember them if she was ever asked.

The room was small and neat with two single beds. There was a rug and chair with a rail on the wall to hang their clothes. There was the obligatory crucifix and a picture of an unsmiling pope.

Not a place to spend an evening.

He suggested a meal.

Lucia agreed.

Bruno chose a large restaurant. It was crowded with families and large groups as well as couples. Waiters with white aprons and black jackets wove incessantly between tables and kitchens with trays held above their heads. The noise inside was almost a din and the menu prices were much higher than the trattoria a few doors away. That was small and intimate with candle-lit tables. It was also half empty which was why Bruno did not choose it.

The waiter tucked them away at a table in the corner. Bruno sat facing the door. Just in case.

They ate leisurely, skipped the pasta and settled for veal in a cream and mushroom sauce. It was excellent. Bruno put down his fork and felt Lucia reach out for his hand. She clasped it.

'Do you think we have much of a chance?' She lowered her long eyelashes. 'We can't run forever.'

'I don't plan to. You will see things differently once we get to the mountains. They are safe.'

She looked uncertain. 'Who are these people waiting there for us?'

'Friends. Some I think you know, but please don't pressure me for names.' Bruno knew he dare not risk telling even Lucia the members of the *Noantri* – the different ones. He was more than aware, God forbid, just how ruthless Rossi's OVRA could be if they ever laid hands on either of them. He shuddered at the thought. He knew Rossi would be mounting a massive search for them at this very moment.

Perhaps it was the thought of that which made him glance up. He felt his colour drain. He gripped Lucia's hand tightly. Her dark eyes darted as she sensed his dread. He glanced down at the table.

Then his eyes were drawn back to the man reading a newspaper a few tables away.

It was not the man who frightened him.

It was the newspaper.

Bruno's picture was reproduced on the front page. The headline screamed: ENEMY OF THE STATE. The smaller type read: Massive Hunt for Fugitives.

Rossi had wasted no time. Bruno guessed his picture must now be in every evening newspaper in Italy. By morning he should be among the best-known faces in the country. The photograph was the one taken for his new passport. At least they did not have one of Lucia.

'Turn your head slowly and don't panic,' Bruno whispered.

Lucia turned and quickly looked away.

'Oh my God, what are we going to do?' she asked.

'Get out of here for a start. They have not got a photograph of you. You pay the bill and I'll meet you outside. Give me five minutes and watch if anyone follows me. If they do I'll try to lose them. If that happens meet me back at the hotel room. At least we'll be off the street.'

The restaurant he'd carefully chosen was now working to his disadvantage. They were at a corner table furthest from the door. He looked at the mass of crowded tables between him and the street. Bruno saw two people reading the same newspaper as the man a few tables away. Suddenly it felt as if every eye in the place was just waiting for him to walk past and be recognized. The crowded street seemed miles away.

'Give me five minutes,' he reminded Lucia as he got to his feet and pushed the chair from the table. 'Then leave. Just walk off.'

Then he saw the door to the toilets. He would not have to risk walking the length of the restaurant. Just a few feet to the door. He walked calmly towards it and pushed it open.

The toilets were set at the end of a passage. He ran, burst into a cubicle and locked the door.

He listened for the sound of the outer door opening. That meant someone would be following.

'Don't be a fool,' he told himself. 'You're panicking. All it would mean was that someone else wanted to use the toilet.'

But he listened. Just in case. No one came. He moved from the ill-lit cubicle.

There was a window set in the wall just above his head. It had frosted glass with wire running through it. He reached up and undid the metal catch. The night air hit his face as he flung it open. He hauled himself up, straining and grunting until one leg was through the window. The rest followed. It was a tight squeeze but he scrambled through.

Bruno found himself in a narrow side alley. If he had stood sideways with arms outstretched he would have touched the walls each side of it. He disturbed a cat rummaging in an overflowing bin and it screamed at him.

Millions now knew his face. It frightened him. He moved slowly towards the street. It was swarming with people. He joined the strolling throng. He moved with the crowds for forty yards then crossed the street. Angry drivers hooted him as he dodged through the slowly moving traffic.

He moved in the opposite direction until he came to a shop opposite the restaurant. He gazed into the window. It was a food shop. The window was crammed with hanging salami and long sausages. Great bottles of olive oil encased in wicker baskets were stacked among the cheeses and brightly coloured packages.

Bruno saw Lucia's reflection in the glass. He watched her leave the restaurant and scan the crowd. She turned and walked off. He waited until he was sure no one had followed her, then went after her.

He crossed the road and caught her up. She jumped as he touched her elbow.

'Just keep walking. We are not being followed.'

He steered her through the narrow streets back to the hotel. He looked through the plate glass window into the foyer, then bundled Lucia into a doorway.

There were two *carabinieri* at the desk, machine guns on their shoulders. The hotelier and his wife stood behind the reception desk. She was gesticulating silently towards the stairs. He pored over the newspaper spread out on the desk with Bruno's picture on the front page.

But it was the third man who captured Bruno's attention.

He was talking urgently into the phone on the desk.

Bruno had seen him before.

He was one of the OVRA men who had been at Rossi's side when he'd come to the villa after the abortive raid on the underground lab at Bologna. He was minus the trilby, but still radiated an almost tangible air of menace.

Lucia recognized him too.

'I've seen the one on the phone before. He's been to the clinic with Pini. He made a special request to watch an experiment. He told Pini he needed to put it in some report.'

'I'll bet he did,' Bruno said.

He saw the man put down the phone and snap his fingers. The *carabinieri* followed as he drew a revolver and dashed up the stairs.

Bruno moved.

He ran headlong down the street, Lucia at his side.

Verona railway station was seething. Uniformed soldiers mingled with passengers in the concourse, they were waiting for a troop train. Some drank from bottles of beer, others ogled the girls, catcalling in the mindless tradition of soldiers on the move.

Groups of passengers pushed and shoved each other to get to the ticket kiosks. Mothers clouted, children bawled, the scene was of ill-tempered chaos.

Bruno eyed the departure board. There was a train to Florence in forty minutes.

'We'll take it,' he told Lucia. They were standing amid the hand trolleys piled high with luggage. Bruno scanned the crowds from behind the suitcase in front of him. He checked the ticket barriers. The plainclothes men standing alongside the *carabinieri* were easy to spot. Each held a photograph as they scanned the faces making their way to the waiting trains. He noticed they occasionally stopped someone for a closer look.

The OVRA men hovering on the fringe of the crowd around the ticket kiosks were not hard to spot either. Bruno wondered why plainclothes men also tried to ape in real life the men who played the role in movies, even to the width of the baggy trousers and the angle of the trilbies on their heads. The same length of handkerchief showed from their top pocket and they all carried rolled-up newspapers. If it had been raining they would all have worn the same colour trench coats.

He also noticed none of them shifted position, the only ones not pushing and shoving to get tickets. They were just waiting.

For him.

'They are so obvious,' Lucia commented.

'And dangerous,' added Bruno.

'Only because they know your face,' she said. 'I'll buy the tickets.'

'Forget it,' Bruno snapped. 'You can't be certain they have not got a photograph of you. It's too big a risk.'

'If they had one then it would be spread over the papers alongside yours.'

He knew she was right. He hated the thought of her having to take the risks just because of a stupid bloody snapshot. But he also knew the train was the fastest way south.

To Fulgoni and the *Noantri*.

There was also less chance of them being caught on the train. The tactics seemed to be to check them before they boarded, not once they were on the train.

'Buy three tickets, one for a child,' Bruno said. 'They will be paying attention to people buying two.' He gave her a fistful of lire. 'Be careful.'

She kissed him on the cheek. 'Wait for me here.'

He nodded.

He watched her take her place in the milling crowd. His heart was in his mouth.

He felt his jacket pocket for the Mauser he'd taken from the radio operator. His fingers curled around the grip as if they had a will of their own. His eyes drifted from Lucia to the waiting OVRA men, then back again. Constantly shifting, watching for a sign that she'd been recognized.

Lucia had worked her way to the centre of the crowd. She stood shoulder to shoulder with a nun, her white headdress standing out like a starched butterfly.

Bruno noticed other members of the order standing near one of the entrances to his left. There were four of them. They must have been from an orphanage or convent school, for scurrying around their feet were at least a dozen children of all shapes and sizes. And all looked under seven. They were giving the nuns a hard time to try and keep them in some form of order. The strain showed on the nuns' faces.

The first nun was at the kiosk now. Lucia behind her. He saw her collect the tickets and follow the nun towards him.

'Where was that nun going?' he asked urgently.

'Rome, I think.' Lucia looked baffled.

'Give me an adult and child ticket. I'll see you on the train. It's safer you are not seen with me.'

'But, Bruno . . .' He stilled her protest by placing his fingers on her lips.

'Go quickly.'

As she turned for the train Bruno headed for the nuns and children.

'You look as if you have got your hands full. Let me help with the children.'

All five nuns smiled and bowed their heads gracefully. Bruno placed the tickets in the corner of his mouth. He snatched two children, a girl aged two and a boy about four. He cradled them chest high so they obscured his face. He followed the scolding nuns towards the train. They ushered the remainder of their brood before them like serene goosegirls.

As they neared the barrier, Bruno pinched the little girl on the inside of her leg. Hard. She began to kick and scream.

'Why did you make my sister cry?' the boy said.

'I didn't,' Bruno reassured him.

'You did,' said the girl reproachfully through a flood of tears.

'See,' said the boy smugly. 'I bet you couldn't make me cry. My sister is a girl and they are all cry babies.' He began to taunt the girl.

'I'm not. I'm not,' she screamed.

Bruno held her face next to his to comfort her. The boy tugged a lock of her hair. She began to wail.

Perfect, Bruno thought.

He was past the plainclothes men and at the barrier. He offered the tickets in his mouth to the collector.

'The girl's with me, the boy is with the nuns,' he said through clenched teeth. The collector grunted. The girl yelled at the top of her lungs in his ear.

'No, she's not with him. She's my sister,' the boy complained.

Bruno's stomach churned.

But the boy's words were lost in his sister's screams. Tickets back in mouth Bruno caught up with the nuns. He handed the girl over. Then the boy.

'Sister,' she sobbed, 'this horrible man pinched me.'

Bruno smiled.

'Oh you wicked girl,' the nun said and smacked the child on the arm.

'Children,' Bruno grinned.

Bruno made for the train, the girl's wailing ringing in his ears.

Lucia left the train at Modena.

Bruno watched with trepidation as she walked across to the station bookstall. She bought a large-scale map and two newspapers. She headed back to the train clutching her purchases.

It was then Bruno spotted them. Three stood like statues at intervals along the platform. He saw them study faces that rushed past them.

There were two more at the ticket barrier. Each held a photograph. His.

Lucia must have spotted them too. Bruno saw her stop.

She had been half running. Now she stood rooted to the platform.

'Keep going. Walk,' Bruno willed her. 'Damn you. Walk.'

He clenched his fists as Lucia bit her lip and looked anxiously in all directions. It seemed she and the OVRA men were the only people standing still in the flowing sea of rushing passengers.

Bruno heard the carriage doors slam. He risked a look and stuck his head through the open window. He was standing in the corridor next to the toilet. He saw a railway porter at the far end of the train. He was making his way towards him pushing doors shut. Bruno looked up the platform. The signals on the overhead gantry were on green. The locomotive whistled. A grey cloud of steam billowed from the piston valves.

The train shuddered. It began to move.

Lucia still froze on the platform.

An electric baggage car hauling empty trailers hooted its klaxon as it snaked through the crowd. Lucia was in its path.

Lucia dropped the papers and elbowed her way towards the train. Then, his heart pounding, Bruno saw her begin to run. He eased the door handle, and held it.

She was alongside the carriage, running blindly. Bruno flung open the door and grabbed her. He hauled her onto the metal step and pulled her into the corridor. The door slammed shut behind her.

Bruno saw one of the OVRA watchers move. He rushed along the platform and grabbed a colleague by the elbow.

The man pointed towards the train.

Then they ran towards the ticket barrier, knocking people aside in their haste.

Bruno half closed his eyes and put his head through the window. He squinted as a shower of red-hot sparks flew past his face. He breathed from the ribbon of smoke the powerful locomotive spat out behind it. The squares of lights from isolated houses flashed by. As did the telegraph poles alongside the line.

He was frightened out of his wits.

He knew the OVRA operatives would have rung ahead. They'd spotted them. The doom spilled over him. He pictured his cousin, Rossi, eyes bulging, pacing his Rome office. The man wanted his blood. He would bring the wrath of frustrated ambition down on Bruno's head.

He turned to Lucia.

'They will be waiting for us at the next stop – Bologna.'

'It's all my fault. I panicked.'

They were still standing at the door in the corridor. Bruno yearned for sleep. He looked at his watch. It was almost two o'clock in the morning. They had been on the run for twenty-four hours.

A door slid open up the carriage. A man stepped out of the compartment. He stretched and yawned and rubbed the stubble on his chin. Bruno stood Lucia in front of him and turned to face the window. He placed his hands protectively on her shoulders.

He heard the man's footsteps near. The toilet door opened and shut behind him. Lucia placed a hand on his. She realized he was shaking.

The train began to pick up speed and Bruno realized they had no chance of jumping from it. Earlier he had looked in vain for a British-style communications cord or emergency lever to pull. To his despair he realized they were not fitted to Italian trains.

The toilet flushed. The door slammed. The man grunted and trudged back to the compartment.

The train whistled. Red lights from a road crossing winked briefly and were gone.

Bruno's brow knotted in concentration. He had to stop the train. He felt the bulge of the Mauser. It hung heavily in his pocket. There was no other choice. They were doomed the moment they reached Bologna.

He turned Lucia to face him.

'Listen,' he said. 'We are going to have to get off the train. It's our only chance.'

'How?'

Bruno took the gun from his pocket. He toyed with it uncertainly.

'Force the driver to stop.'

Lucia looked blank.

'Let's go to the head of the train. I'm going to have to try and climb over the tender and reach the cab.'

'Bruno,' she looked aghast. 'That's impossible. At this speed you'll be killed.'

He remained expressionless. 'All that is certain is we will both be killed if I don't try. I'll force the door of the end carriage. I noticed a ladder on the back of the tender. Once I've climbed that I can crawl over the coal to the cab.' He took the safety catch off the gun. 'The driver will stop,' he said with certainty.

He turned, gun in hand, and led her up the train. Blinds on the compartment windows were drawn as the passengers inside slept. They moved forward stealthily.

The only noise came from the rush of the train and its wheels as they clicked rhythmically over the rails, eating up the distance to its next destination.

They entered the last carriage.

Bruno stopped and cursed.

It was the guard's van.

Mail sacks and crates were piled high behind a wire wall. The guard and his mate sat playing cards at the far end, a bottle of wine and half-eaten sandwiches on the table beside them.

Bruno raised the gun.

'Get up,' he barked.

The look of astonishment on the men's faces turned quickly to fear. They sat with open mouths, not able to believe their eyes. They slowly rose to their feet as Bruno and Lucia moved forward. He prayed they would offer no resistance. He had no desire to harm them.

He indicated the last door on the train.

'See if it's locked,' he told Lucia.

The two men backed aside as she rushed forward and tried it.

'Yes.' It would not budge.

'The key,' Bruno snapped.

The guard's mate fumbled in his trouser pockets. He produced a ring of keys.

'Which one?'

The man fumbled and held one up.

'Open the door.'

He shook as he tried to fit the key in the lock. At last he succeeded.

Bruno pointed the gun at the padlock on the wire door of the mail compartment.

'Now that.'

The man approached timidly, his face stiff with fear. He opened the lock. Bruno snatched the keys from him.

'Inside. Both of you.'

They obeyed.

He snapped the lock shut behind them.

Then the floor bucked under Bruno.

Mail bags and crates flew in all directions knocking the two rail men to the floor. Lucia was sent flying and crashed into the table as the bottle of wine smashed against the wall.

Bruno bounced off the wire wall and fell to his knees.

The sound of metal wheels screaming on the rails filled the air. Bruno saw sparks fly past the window like scarlet fireballs and heard the mighty locomotive hiss and groan as the driver tugged the massive brake. Bruno slid on his back as the train bucked and rocked like a tormented horse. He crashed against the door at the far end of the carriage with a force that winded him.

Lucia bounced off the wall and he heard her gasp.

With the gun in one hand Bruno hauled himself to his feet.

Then came the sickening crash. The sound of metal splintering like matchwood. He felt the train lift from the tracks then crash back onto the rails. He felt the force would snap the bones in his legs.

He saw the cab of an ancient lorry sail past the window in a cloud of debris.

The train shook again. Bruno was sent crashing. His arms flailed. The gun in his hand exploded involuntarily into life. It jerked crazily as aimless bullets burst through the window. He saw the crimson tracers fly from his hand and light the darkness.

The train screeched to a halt as if it had experienced some dreadful agony.

Then came silence except for the soft hissing of steam.

It was broken by the sound of gunfire. A line of bullet holes punctured the carriage walls. The window caved slowly inwards.

Bruno crawled to Lucia and threw himself on top of her. He heard people begin to scream as voices barked commands in the darkness.

There were three more bursts of gunfire.

Screaming filled the air from the terrified passengers. Bruno lifted Lucia to her feet. He tried to open the last door. It had buckled tight in the collision.

He could see shadowy figures running alongside the track. Sinister shapes in the darkness.

Bruno's sole instinct was to run. He grabbed Lucia by the wrist and plunged headlong back up the train. He tore open the door to the next carriage. Passengers who spilled into the corridor were now elbowing and shoving to scramble back to their compartments as the sound of a shot echoed through the train.

They had to run for it, seek refuge in the darkness on the other side of the tracks. He wrenched the door handle and kicked open the door.

He looked down on the man with the gun. He was dressed in black. A balaclava covered his face.

'Let's get the hell out of here.'

Bruno recognized the voice of Seldon.

CHAPTER FIFTEEN

Bruno's knees bent as he hit the ground. He stumbled forward and regained his balance. Lucia was framed in the open door. He held his arms out. She looked confused and frightened.

He saw her cringe as Seldon raised his sten gun and fired four short bursts into the sky.

'Come on,' Bruno yelled as Seldon's signal rang through the night. Lucia jumped. He caught her under the arms. She winced as she twisted her ankle on the gravel by the side of the track. Lucia flung her arm over his shoulder as Seldon motioned with the gun for them to follow.

They hobbled after him as three figures in balaclavas responded to Seldon's signal with the gun and leapt from the train. One of them unleashed a rapid burst of gunfire over the carriage. People inside screamed.

The *Noantri* sprinted towards the level crossing with Seldon hard on their heels. Bruno dragged Lucia in an effort to keep up.

Ahead he could see the remains of the truck they'd placed on the line. Its innards lay strewn either side of the track. Fulgoni's Facel Vega stood with its engine running at the crossing, its headlights lit the scene of the wreckage.

Bruno saw the others reach the car.

'Move it,' Seldon screamed.

Bruno increased his effort but Lucia was dragging her leg badly. 'It hurts,' she cried out in pain as Bruno stumbled. He stopped and hoisted her over his shoulder in a fireman's lift. His shoes crunched on the gravel as he began to run. His chest heaved like a long-distance athlete.

He saw the Facel Vega send a shower of dirt into the air as it swung in a circle. The lights dazzled as it bounced along beside the railway towards him.

It swung to the left and broadsided. He heard the throaty engine roar as it accelerated after him. It passed, its thick front bumper nosed into the ground as the brake lights flashed. The back door flew open as it reversed towards him. Seldon, gun still in hand, leapt out.

He grabbed Lucia and flung her into the back seat and bundled Bruno in after her. He dived beside them and pulled the door tight. Bruno gasped for breath as he looked through the back window. He saw the train driver in the light of the firebox. He was leaning out of his cab and throwing up.

The tyres screamed as the car came in contact with the road. It swung hard to the right and ploughed through the remains of the truck on the level crossing.

Bruno saw the red warning lights dangle on the broken crosses each side of the track.

The driver took one hand from the wheel and tore off his balaclava. He tossed it onto the floor and turned his head. 'Franco,' Lucia said in astonishment.

'*Ciao.*' He smiled through his wild beard.

His companions on the front bench seat removed theirs. They were women. They tossed their hair free in unison. Bruno recognized them from the camp. They were white-faced with fright.

Bruno turned to Seldon.

The man he held responsible for his father's death smiled back weakly as only English public shoolboys can.

'Dear boy,' he said, 'that was a close thing. After he'd smashed through the truck I didn't think the damn driver was going to stop.'

The sound of the thin voice banished any brief sense of gratitude Bruno felt.

Seldon added in English, 'You can never tell with Italians.' One of the girls in front turned her head and smiled nervously. Obviously none of them spoke English.

'*Grazie, signorina,*' Bruno said.

They shrugged and smiled coyly.

Bruno spun on Seldon. He would never understand the attitude of some English to foreigners.

'These Italians probably saved our lives,' he said pointedly. His fingers tightened around Lucia's shoulders. She was still shaking.

'Easy,' she whispered as if she sensed Bruno's feelings for the man next to him. He squeezed tighter.

'How did you know we were on the train?' Bruno asked.

'Because we are efficient,' he said curtly.

Franco looked over his shoulder at Bruno. 'Carla told us.'

'Carla?'

'She is exploiting your cousin Rossi's strange tastes,' he said bitterly. 'And provides us with information from the inside.'

Bruno saw the hurt in his eyes and remembered the first time he'd seen her with the blonde bar girl.

Franco added: 'She was with him at the Villa Marco when Rossi took a call from Modena to say you were on the train. They were waiting for you at Bologna. The place was swarming with his thugs. Rossi wants to nail you to the wall. Carla says she has never seen anyone so obsessed with revenge.'

'He hasn't seen anything yet,' Seldon said.

Neither have you, Bruno thought.

They changed cars in a deserted mountain clearing. The sun was just inching its way over the horizon. Bruno and Lucia watched as Franco knelt and felt under the Fiat's door sill. That was where the key was strapped. He got it and started the engine.

'Let's go,' said Seldon.

Bruno and Lucia climbed in the back seat. Seldon got in the front and wound down the window.

He called to the two girls in the Facel Vega.

'Take it away and burn it. Someone on the train could have spotted the number.'

They drove in silence along the twisting road. They passed

through villages waking to meet the needs of the day. Men fixed donkeys to carts and eyed the Fiat as it sped past.

Franco, fingers drumming impatiently on the steering wheel, had to pull over occasionally for a herd of goats or long-legged, thin mountain sheep.

Bruno noted this was not the road to Perino Maggiore. They rounded a bend, and over Franco's shoulder Bruno saw a man waiting by the roadside. He held a string of four patient mules.

The Fiat pulled up.

The man was unshaven, a battered hat pulled down over his eyes. The mules stirred uneasily as Seldon got out of the car. Bruno could not hear what was said. The conversation was animated and the peasant made much use of his hands. He saw Seldon press a wad of lire into his hands, then turn on his heels and walk towards them. He pointed to the mountains.

'We'll take the mules across to the camp,' he said. 'The less conspicuous we are the better.'

They got out of the car and walked to the animals. Bruno lifted Lucia onto the back of a grey mule. There was no saddle and the reins were rope. He noticed she took them expertly.

Bruno mounted.

With Franco in the lead they set off in single file. Seldon, sten gun on his lap, brought up the rear. The mules stirred as the Fiat, the peasant at the wheel, roared past.

The animals were sure-footed and, unlike Bruno had always believed, responsive. They followed the lead mule off the road and up the boulder-strewn hillside without difficulty.

The early morning mist lifted as the sun rose in the sky. It was lined with thin white strings of cloud. The air was crisp and fresh. Bruno breathed it deeply to stop himself dozing off. The weariness washed over him as he was lulled by the steady swaying of the mule beneath him.

The road was far below them. It was lost from sight when

they crossed the ridge. The naked mountains stretched out ahead.

Bruno saw no sign of life.

He had been three hours on the bareback mule. The inside of his legs began to chafe and the small of his back hurt. He tugged the rope reins. They were crossing a shallow, swift-flowing stream. He noticed Lucia in front of him. She was hunched forward over the animal's neck. She had begun to slide off its back. Bruno dug his heels into his mule's flank and urged it alongside her. She'd fallen asleep. He grabbed her by the shoulder and shook her.

'Wake up.'

She jolted upright and blinked with surprise.

'We need a rest.' Bruno looked over his shoulder at Seldon. The Englishman shook his head.

'Not yet. This area is patrolled by the *Milizia*.'

Bruno swung his leg over the mule. He was ankle deep in cold rushing water. He placed his hands on Lucia's waist and lifted her down. Her arms locked around his neck.

He bent, cupped his hands and filled them with water. He splashed his face. He shook his head and refilled his hands.

'Here.'

He doused Lucia. She gasped as the water ran down her face.

Franco's mule twisted, its back legs kicked, as he tugged the rope halter. The animal's legs stuttered over the slippery stones on the stream bed.

'Let's move,' Seldon said.

Bruno glowered.

'She's beat,' he said.

Lucia held her hands to her eyes.

Franco stilled his mule. He patted the straining muscles of its neck. 'There is a *baracca* three kilometres ahead.' He pointed to a cluster of trees on the next hill. 'We shall rest there.'

Bruno saw Seldon tense.

'It belongs to a goatherd. We can eat. The mules can rest.

The next mountan to Perino Maggiore is a hard haul.'

'So let's go,' Seldon snapped impatiently.

Bruno's loathing grew.

He lifted Lucia back onto the mule. The dark-haired girl looked exhausted. Franco reached out and took the rope reins from her hands. He clicked his tongue and stabbed the mule with his heels.

'Hah,' he yelled.

He towed Lucia from the stream. He drove the mule up the bank as Bruno steadied his mount and swung onto its back.

Bruno heard Seldon slap his mount's flank and, splashing through the stream, it pranced, eyes rolling and ears flat, past Bruno. Its legs scrambled for a foothold sending back a shower of loose stones.

Bruno followed, his fingers entwined around the rope. The mule took its head. The rope scorched his fingers.

They slowed to a fast trot and followed a rough path down one side of a valley and up the other side. At the brow of the hill Bruno saw smoke.

Franco saw it too.

'The goatherd,' he yelled and levelled his hand at the grey pall drifting from the ravine the other side of a small copse.

They galloped in line, Franco's arm straining at the socket as he towed Lucia.

Bruno held an arm to his face to ward off the branches as they rode through the copse.

He saw the goatherd rise from his haunches and shield his eyes. The wire-coated dog at his feet braced its back legs and began to bark. The goatherd kicked out at it. The dog yelped, and continued barking.

Then the goats scattered down the ravine; the dog, still barking, chased after them.

Bruno was the first to dismount. Franco's mule bucked and Lucia grabbed its mane. Bruno took it by the halter and held it firm as it lashed out with its back legs. He steadied it, then helped Lucia down. Franco gathered the mules and led them to a tree and tethered them.

The goatherd had vanished into the *baracca*. He re-emerged carrying a white enamel jug and two thin mugs in one hand, the aroma of coffee was stronger than the smell of goats.

Bruno saw the man smile toothlessly. He held a hard chunk of goat cheese in his other hand. He motioned with it for them to eat.

They flopped on the grass. The man filled a mug with coffee and handed it to Lucia. She sipped gratefully.

He handed a second mug to Seldon who passed it to Franco. Bruno took the mug Lucia offered and caught the blank expression of Seldon's face as the goatherd blurted rapidly.

The sentences were incomprehensible to Bruno's ear. He saw they also made no sense to Seldon or Lucia.

They did to Franco whose face dropped as he followed the man's finger. He continued speaking in the word-spitting dialect of the mountains as he pointed.

Bruno caught the words *Guardie Forestali*, amid the man's incomprehensible ranting. He saw Seldon tense as he looked to him for explanation.

It was Franco who provided it. 'They are worse than the *Milizia*. The Forest Guards are all mountain men born and bred. They would sell their own mothers for their weekly wage packet. Last night they raided a *carbonari* camp. Four charcoal burners were killed before they realized their mistake. The *guardie* thought they were partisans – *Noantri*. They are still scouring the area.'

Seldon seethed. 'Blast. Where are they now? Does the old fool know?'

The old man's dog answered by rushing up the side of the ravine panicking the goats it had rounded up. It barked and snarled furiously.

Three men's heads came into view over the brow of the ravine.

Bruno recognized them by their feathered caps. They were

modelled on those worn by the crack mountain regiment his father had served in during the Great War. The Alpine.

'*Guardie Forestali*,' the goatherd breathed in fear. Bruno saw Franco try to restrain him.

He was too late.

Bruno watched the old man leap to his feet. He ran headlong down the rock slope towards the copse.

A shot rang out.

A *guardi* looked down the sights of his carbine.

Bruno saw the old man's dog lift into the air. It somersaulted and rolled over the rocks. It yelped once and died.

Bruno ducked, hands over his head, as a second shot rang out. He turned as he heard the old man scream. He saw his arms fling out in a gesture of surrender. A red smudge seeped through his jacket and spread across his back. The third shot lifted him off his feet. It hurled his dead body into the bushes which fringed the copse.

Then came the rapid spit of sten gun fire.

Bruno saw Seldon spraying the air. He was backing towards the *baracca* as he fired.

All three *guardie* returned the fire. They'd dived onto their bellies.

Seldon mouthed as he fired, his words lost above the song of the sten.

Bruno grabbed Lucia and scrambled, bent double, for the *baracca*. Like Franco, he did not need to be told what to do.

Bruno felt Lucia stumble.

He feared her grip was slipping away. Stones danced at his feet as *guardie* bullets pitted the ground.

Now Bruno, dragging Lucia, stumbled.

He felt Franco's shoulder drive into the back of his thighs. He saw his arm wrap around Lucia's waist as the bearded *Noantri* drove them through the open door of the *baracca* like a marauding rugby forward.

All three crashed onto the dirt floor as Seldon, sten singing, backed in behind them.

Bruno hurled Lucia into the far corner as his hand dived into his pocket. The Mauser he'd taken from the railway radio operator was in his hand.

His rage reached boiling point. He rushed to the doorway and fired blindly. The gun jumped crazily in his hand as, for the first time in his life, he shot to kill.

He felt Franco's fingers tighten around his wrist. The Mauser fired into the sky. Once.

Then Bruno was pushed aside.

Franco's beard was in his face.

'Don't waste your shots. They are out of range.' Franco released his wrist. 'You too,' he yelled at Seldon.

Bruno saw the line of dirt kicked up by Seldon's sten as it fell way short of the *guardie*. Seldon stopped firing.

'He's coming,' Bruno screamed.

One of the *guardie* was on his feet. He was crouching low as he wove down the hill.

'There's two more. No, three,' Bruno pointed as they came into view. Then he thought his ear drums had burst as a deafening roar filled the *baracca*. The wooden hut's walls shook. His hands thumped the side of his head as he covered his ears.

Then came the second blast.

He turned his head.

Lucia had found the old goatherd's *lupara*. She was framed in the window beside him. It had no glass. She lowered the sawn-off double-barrelled gun.

Bruno saw the advancing *guardi*'s carbine fly into the air. The man screamed and clutched his face as the lead pellets tore out his eyes and half his face.

'He's in range now,' Seldon shouted.

There was a burst from the sten.

Bruno's eyes followed the dancing dirt. He saw the man pirouette in death as the burst scythed through him. The dust at his feet turned crimson as he fell to the ground.

Bruno crouched at the window as Franco took the *lupara* from Lucia. He broke the barrel and two empty cases, still smoking, fell onto the floor. Franco pointed to a cluttered shelf.

'Fetch more cartridges. There's a box next to the jar of salt.'

Seldon shouted, 'We've got to keep them back. Prevent them from surrounding the hut.'

Bruno's head popped above the window frame. 'Too late.'

He saw the *guardie* had already begun to fan out. Four were moving forward in a wide arc, using boulders as cover.

The mules began to bray, the whites of their eyes rolled as they tugged and strained to free themselves from the tree.

Beyond them Bruno noticed the fifth guard remained just below the brow of the hill, he was out of their weapon range. The man knelt and took aim with his carbine. He fired.

Bruno ducked as the bullet thudded into the hut and sent a shower of splinters into the air. The rapid carbine fire continued.

Seldon responded with a short burst. They fell short.

'The bastards have got us pinned down,' the Englishman yelled. 'Concentrate your fire on the *guardie* behind the rocks.'

Franco emptied both barrels of the old man's *lupara*.

Bruno raised the Mauser and squinted down the barrel. He knew he had to make each and every shot count. He trained it on the rock shielding one of the *guardie*. He would wait for the man to raise his head. He thought Seldon's wild bursts were wasteful. At this rate they would soon be out of ammunition.

Then he noticed the covering fire from the man on the ridge had stopped. He allowed his gaze to shift to the brow of the hill. The man was on his back, face to the sky, with arms outstretched. The carbine lay on the grass.

Bruno could see the garrotte wire around the man's bloodstained neck quite clearly.

A figure was scrambling up the hillside on his hands and knees. Bruno watched speechless as the figure reached the top. He stood outlined against the clear sky and signalled with his arms. Seconds later more figures appeared on the skyline, rifles in hand.

'The *Noantri*,' Bruno spoke in no more than a whisper. Then he yelled the words.

It was lost in the sound of fire from the partisans' rifles. They were trained on the backs of the four *guardie* crouching behind the rocks.

It was over in seconds.

The men lived only as long as the sound of the shots that killed them. The *Noantri* had not even moved from their positions on the brow of the hill. Bruno saw them raise their rifles into the air. A gesture of victory.

The force of fire from the MIs had hurled the dead *guardie* from behind the boulders. Their bodies were strewn on the hillside of the rocky ravine above the *baracca*.

The line of *Noantri* on the skyline parted. Franco and Seldon were already rushing towards them yelling and waving. Bruno put his arms around Lucia's shoulder.

'Come on,' he said quietly. He walked from the hut and froze.

There was a man on horseback on the ridge.

It was the Cavaliere Fulgoni.

Bruno held Lucia tightly as the Cavaliere came slowly towards them. He noticed the look of awe in Lucia's eye as they watched the old man on the horse.

Bruno saw it was a mountain pony, a sturdy, short-legged animal with a coarse brown coat. Fulgoni handled it with confident and expert ease. He wore his leather jacket and a broad-brimmed hat. There was a pistol in his belt and a rifle on his shoulder.

The brim of the hat cast a shadow over the craggy face. His legs were tucked high against the squat horse. He dismounted in front of them and removed his hat. The lion-mane shock of silver hair tumbled about his ears then lifted in the wind. He twisted the hat nervously in his large fingers. His shadow stretched across the barren earth and fell on

Bruno and Lucia as the sun rose higher in the sky. Bruno noticed the gaze from the weary, lined eyes fall on Lucia.

Bruno felt uncomfortable. There was a sense of wonder in Fulgoni's eyes and Bruno realized he was intruding on a private act of pure love. Lucia shifted uncomfortably at his side. He felt her cling to his jacket as if she'd sensed it too. The old man's eyes began to fill.

Fulgoni shook his head. 'She's alive.' His deep voice cracked in disbelief and he turned, for the first time, to Bruno. 'You brought her to me.' He lowered his head. 'I thank you.'

He felt Lucia tug on his sleeve. 'Bruno?' her voice questioned.

'The Cavaliere Fulgoni,' Bruno said awkwardly.

'*Ciao*,' Lucia mumbled. She sounded uncertain. Bruno felt the grip on his sleeve tighten as the girl's face was drawn to the old man's. Fulgoni's eyes were wet.

The Cavaliere raised his arms, started forward, then halted. Bruno saw the look of agony as the old man's arms fell to his side.

'Tell her,' Bruno said flatly.

'Tell me what?' Lucia's voice rose in protest. 'What is going on?' she demanded.

'Her mother's child,' Fulgoni mumbled and lowered his head. He pawed the ground at his feet like a caged bull.

Bruno freed himself from Lucia's hold. He walked to Fulgoni and placed his hand on the broad shoulder.

'Tell her. She must know,' his voice low and firm.

'Bruno?'

He turned and stilled the girl by raising his open hand. He motioned her to silence. She looked puzzled, almost afraid.

He brushed past Fulgoni and moved slowly towards the others.

'Bruno,' he heard Fulgoni's voice crack as he called his name. He did not answer or look back. He stepped over a *guardi*'s body and picked his way up the steep ravine. Behind him he heard Fulgoni's pony neigh.

He walked on.

He shut his ears to everything except the crunch of his own boots on the stones beneath his feet.

He had no part to play in the scene behind him.

He stopped just before he reached the others. He saw they'd gathered up the dead men's weapons. They were laid out in a row along with their identity warrants.

Seldon seemed in charge.

'Right,' Bruno heard him say. 'Strip them of their uniforms.' It gave him an idea. Four of the *Noantri*, still wearing balaclavas, walked towards Bruno.

He held up his hand.

'Wait,' he jerked his thumb over his shoulder. 'Give them time.'

'It's something we don't have too much of,' snapped Seldon.

The *Noantri* hovered uncertainly.

'Move,' Seldon barked at them.

'I said give the old man time,' Bruno roared back at Seldon.

'He's right,' echoed Franco.

The *Noantri* mumbled assent and sat down on the grass.

Seldon seethed. He pointed a finger. 'Don't push your luck too far.'

'Luck,' said Bruno calmly, 'is something I have never believed in.'

He turned and looked back to the *baracca*.

He saw Fulgoni on his knees in front of his daughter, his arms around her waist like a child.

Lucia cradled his head, her hands pressed against his silver hair as she soothed him.

He guessed they both wept.

He turned back to the red-faced Seldon.

'As I said, give them time.'

They approached the camp near Perino Maggiore in the late afternoon. Bruno could smell the charcoal on the air before he saw the glow of the pits in which it burnt.

Franco and Seldon led the band down the mountain towards the encampment. Bruno rode behind Lucia and Fulgoni. The rest of the *Noantri* followed wearily on foot. They all looked exhausted.

A girl sentry with a sub-machine gun greeted them at the entrance to the cave on the ridge above the clearing.

Franco asked, 'Any news of Carla?'

The girl shook her head. 'Not since the first message that they were waiting for the train at Bologna.'

Bruno saw Franco's disappointment as they all dismounted.

'See to the animals,' boomed Fulgoni, his arm around Lucia. As the mules and pony were led after the *Noantri* down to the camp Bruno felt a pang as he climbed to the entrance of the cave behind Lucia and Fulgoni.

He realized it was called jealousy.

He chided himself for being foolish. But as Seldon and Franco clambered past him he realized he felt it deeply. He did not want to share her.

Then he saw her wait for him as the others vanished into the cave. He took the hand she held out.

'He explained everything.' She spoke with obvious delight. 'I can't thank you enough.' She kissed him lightly on the lips.

The pang twisted inside him. The kiss had felt like that of a sister.

Then she kissed him again. He felt her fingers curl into his hair as she reached up for him. He responded as her tongue found his. Their eyes closed. Her breasts were firm beneath the sweater. He could feel each contour as they rose and fell and she pressed herself against him urgently. He felt the line of her hip bones as she breathed in snatches and his body seemed to melt into hers.

He wanted her desperately. There on the ledge outside the cave.

He had never wanted anyone so much. His temples

pounded. He shivered as her fingers played a frantic tune with the skin on his back.

'Lucia.'

Fulgoni's voice bellowed and echoed through the cave. Their lips lingered as they slowly drew apart.

'My father,' she whispered through a gentle smile.

They laughed.

'Make love to me soon. Please,' she pleaded. 'Like you have made love to no one before.'

'I promise.' He stepped back and looked lovingly at her. He saw she was blushing furiously. She turned and dived for the darkness of the cave.

Bruno grinned foolishly. He felt like a gawking teenager. And he didn't give a damn.

He brushed aside the sack draped over the entrance and climbed down the makeshift ladder to join the others.

The oil lamps were lit. The shadows of the figures sitting around the table loomed on the damp wall. Lucia stood behind Fulgoni, hands on each shoulder. Bruno thought, there in the half light, the old man looked ten years younger. He understood why. He shared it.

It was Seldon who spoke. He said simply, 'The clinic.'

Bruno saw Lucia lower her eyes. Her lashes almost touched her cheek.

Seldon snapped his fingers impatiently. 'Tell me about it.'

Bruno had had enough. 'I'll tell you when I'm ready.' He looked at Fulgoni. The Cavaliere's head moved imperceptibly. It was enough to tell Bruno the old man was on his side. If he had Fulgoni then he had the *Noantri*.

He had means to destroy Wildfire. He was in control.

Suddenly, Seldon leapt to his feet and banged the table.

'Now look,' he yelled at Bruno, 'you are just an amateur who has had a lucky escape. If you had followed the plan we agreed then you would have left the clinic with their blessing thinking they had you in their pocket. Instead, you are responsible for the biggest manhunt anyone can remember in Italy for a long time. If we had not hauled you from the train you would have been dead now. Don't you forget it.' He fumed.

'And don't you forget you too would have been dead at the *baracca*,' Fulgoni said slowly.

'Remember I trained that mob for just such a situation,' Seldon snapped back.

'This is not a bloody schoolroom, Seldon,' Bruno interrupted quietly, 'so stop acting as if you are in one.'

Seldon glared, first at Bruno then at the unflinching Fulgoni, his lined face like stone. Seldon sat down and clasped his hands on the table.

All eyes turned to Bruno. He felt he was back in a lecture theatre.

'Let's examine the problem. It is a very simple one. We must destroy all stocks of the mutant strain of Black Death – Wildfire. We must also destroy the men behind it who are trying to turn it into a weapon of war.

'We shall begin with the underground laboratory at Bologna. We shall end by razing the Clinic Ascha to the ground.'

Seldon said, 'We've tried the underground laboratory and . . .'

Bruno cut him short. 'And you failed. Now we are going to do it my way.'

The truck was a Mercedes. It was painted brown and had an open back with high slats. It powered through the night from Florence to Bologna with a load of melons. The road crosses the Apennines then falls steeply onto the plain of Emilia Romagna after it passes over the tall bridge over the River Reno.

The detachment of *Guardie Forestali* waited on the bridge. Bruno and Lucia watched from the shadows of an olive grove on the far side. Traffic had been light and the night was filled with the sound of the rushing river as it swept down to the plain.

Bruno pointed as the truck, headlights blazing,

approached the detachment. Their uniform was the jaunty feathered cap, green jacket and brown trousers tucked into thick socks with heavy boots. To anyone who did not know their ruthless reputation they looked like amiable mountain guides, except they carried carbines, not ice picks.

They formed a line across the road. A figure moved forward and raised his hand. The truck slowed, then stopped. Two of the *guardie* flung open the truck's doors and dragged the driver and his mate onto the road. The others covered them with raised carbines. The short struggle was stilled by a jab from the butt of a carbine.

As the truckers were bound and dragged into the bushes the truck was driven off the bridge and reversed to the edge of the gorge. Hundreds of melons splattered on the rocks as the *guardie* opened the tailgate.

The truck swung back onto the bridge as Bruno and Lucia moved from the olive grove. In the glare of headlights Bruno saw Franco remove his feathered cap and wipe his brow. He shrugged his shoulders at Bruno.

'Wearing a dead man's uniform makes me uncomfortable,' he said as he tugged the jacket he had taken from one of the *guardie* killed at the *baracca*. Crude stitching patched the two bullet holes just below the shoulder.

Bruno inspected the truck. 'It's almost new. Better than I expected. Will it pass for an official *Guardie Forestali* vehicle?'

'It will have to. The back will be full of men wearing their uniform.' He grinned through his beard.

Franco climbed into the cab. Bruno and Lucia joined the five uniformed figures in the back. They leant on the roof of the cab. Bruno banged it with his fist and the truck moved off.

'What did you do with the driver and his mate?' Bruno asked Luigi, the *Noantri* he'd first met wearing a clown's costume.

'Tied them to a tree like a cannibal's lunch,' Luigi said. 'They are far enough off the road to be hidden for hours.'

'I hope you're right.'

The truck left the mountains behind and headed for the university city of Bologna. Traffic was still sparse, a few cars, but mainly heavy trucks on their way to Rome from the industrial centres of the north. Their tyres sang on the concrete road.

No one spoke much in the back of the stolen truck and Bruno felt the tension mount as it left the main road and turned for the underground laboratory. Seldon's abortive raid had left its mark on the *Noantri*. The attempt to storm the place had been beaten off with little difficulty. Bruno hoped to take the place without having to fire a shot. With luck they would be back in the mountains before their handiwork was discovered. His main worry was Lucia.

'I wish you hadn't come,' he told her as the truck slowed because of the rutted road.

'I thought we'd been through all that back at the camp. You need someone with you who knows what to look for.'

He knew she was right. This would be the last chance to destroy the Wildfire stock and test cultures. They would have to work quickly. He looked at the luminous dial on his watch. It was almost midnight. The *carabinieri* guarding the laboratory began duty at ten. They were relieved at six.

The truck took the track that led to the main gates of the laboratory. Bruno must have travelled it a hundred times, it always seemed sinister because of what lay at the end of it. Now, because of what he knew, because he had seen what happened at the clinic first hand, he felt a sense of repulsion. It looked different somehow.

It was.

A light bobbed ahead where there should have been no light. It came from a torch. It was signalling them to stop.

Bruno tensed. He pulled Lucia to the floor as Franco ground the gears. The truck shuddered.

'*Carabinieri*,' Luigi said.

'How many?'

'Just one.'

The truck stopped. Its engine throbbed.

'*Guardie Forestali*,' Franco yelled as he stuck his head out of the window, his hand on the wing mirror.

The beam of the torch played on the truck. It lit the uniformed figures around Bruno.

Franco shielded his eyes. 'Put that bloody thing out. It's blinding me,' he complained.

'*Avanti*,' the *carabiniere* yelled. He still trained the torch.

Franco let out the clutch and the truck crawled up the track.

Then Bruno and Lucia were covered by sprawling *Noantri*. They lost their balance as he felt the surge of power as Franco's foot hit the accelerator, driving it hard against the floor. The Mercedes screamed forward.

There was a dull thud, the truck bucked twice and Bruno winced when the man's bones crushed as the wheel rolled over him.

The truck halted.

Luigi vaulted over the tailboard and ran back up the track. Bruno saw him inspect the heap in the road and dash back for the truck. He leapt on the running board and into the cab.

'He's dead,' he called as he slammed the door shut.

They moved on.

Seldon had tried to storm the main gate from the darkness. They'd been beaten back by the sheer accuracy of the firepower guarding it.

Bruno planned to drive straight up.

Lucia still sat on the floor, her back against the truck's cab. Bruno, fingertips between the slats, pulled himself up and peered through them over the cab roof.

The truck rose out of a dip and he saw the wire gate.

They have changed the bloody system, Bruno thought to his dismay.

There were four *carabinieri* outside the main gate. Another stood with a German shepherd dog behind the gate. The sixth sat on the entrance steps to the underground laboratory smoking a cigarette. Previously the place had been guarded by just four men. Bruno should have guessed things were different when they were stopped up the road.

His mind raced.

The *carabiniere* on the steps was the main threat. At the first sign of trouble he'd lock himself inside the lab. He'd phone for help. There was no way they could stop him.

Bruno thought, Seldon would have thought of that. He'd have cut the phone wires.

Now it was too late for that. The men at the gate had unslung their rifles. He saw the *carabiniere* on the steps stub his cigarette and stand up. The dog started barking.

Franco killed the engine and leapt from the cab. He darted into the beam from the headlights so they could see his uniform. He walked to meet the *carabiniere* who advanced towards the truck. They were forty yards from the gate.

Luigi was behind the wheel now.

Bruno saw Franco take his warrant from his pocket. He showed it to the guard. He would be telling him they had been sent to inspect the fence around the laboratory and note possible places where it could be scaled. From the *carabinierie*'s gestures Bruno saw there was dissent. His heart was pounding.

'Just stay down,' he told Lucia.

He saw Franco and the guard turn and walk back to the gate, arms waving. He turned to the *Noantri* at his side.

'Guido,' he asked, 'could you hit the *carabiniere* on the entrance steps?'

Guido fingered his weapon. 'He's well in range.'

'I asked if you could hit him?'

'Yes.'

'Get him in your sights. Now,' he rasped nervously.

The guards at the gate would not be able to see beyond the truck's headlights.

The barrel of Guido's gun inched through the slats and poked out over the cab's roof.

'Don't fire until I give the word,' Bruno said.

The bolt clicked as it was rammed home.

'*Avanti*,' Franco called and beckoned them forward. Luigi gunned the Mercedes. It crawled towards the gate. Three of the *carabinieri* stood in front of it in a line, their backs pressed against the wire.

'Choose your target,' Bruno barked hoarsely.

'The one on the left.'

'Centre.'

'Right.'

The three *Noantri* moved to the back of the truck. It slowed to a halt as Fabio and Nino unhitched the tailgate. The third, Steffi, jumped down. The others joined him. They spread out on each side of the truck.

'Now,' Bruno yelled.

The report from Guido's shot almost deafened Bruno. He saw it lift the guard on the steps off his feet and slam him against the laboratory wall before he fell, face first, onto the ground.

The first report was followed by three cracks in unison from behind the truck. Their chosen targets spun and twisted against the wire. One clawed it as he slid to the ground.

Bruno leapt from the truck. He was met by Franco. The Alpine hunting knife in his hand was stained red up to the hilt.

Luigi's foot hit the throttle and the truck surged forward at the gate. The wire closed around the truck like a net. The Mercedes ploughed into the compound dragging some of the fence and uprooted poles behind it.

The sole surviving *carabiniere* had dropped the dog leash and fled headlong for the lab. Fabio's first shot smashed into his shoulder and sent him sprawling. He scrambled on all fours until the second shot stilled him.

Then Fabio screamed.

The snarling German shepherd dog had leapt over the trail of wire and was at his throat. He fell backwards as the dog's jaws ripped into his throat. Its teeth pierced the jugular vein as it shook Fabio like a rat.

Lucia, hands to her face, screamed as Guido, standing at her side, took aim and fired. The dog slumped over Fabio. Franco dragged it away by the tail.

Bruno knelt by Fabio. There was sheer terror in the dead man's eyes. Half his throat had been torn out. Bruno had not planned it this way. He threw up.

Franco hauled him to his feet.

'We must go,' he urged.

Bruno nodded dumbly, then shook himself to action.

Inside the underground laboratory Bruno worked in a frenzy. It was better, far better, than he had dared hope.

After Seldon's raid and his own escape from the Clinic Ascha, Rossi and Pini had moved everything connected with the Wildfire Project from the main university to this lab. It was now all under one roof.

Box files of research papers were stacked. Filing cabinets full of notes were crammed into every available space.

'Burn the lot. Everything,' he said.

He'd already fired the incinerator until the dial on the wall registered white hot. The *Noantri*, tottering with their arms full of papers, scurried in an unending procession down the steps to the incinerator. The oven door lay open, the heat was almost unbearable as the flames devoured the secrets of Wildfire.

Bruno was with Lucia in the experimental laboratory. They had emptied the lead-lined store of the Wildfire bacilli. The sealed culture slides were arranged in orderly piles on the laboratory benches. The antidote protein cultures they stacked on the floor.

Guido, sweat pouring from his forehead, came through the door.

'The papers from the files and cabinets have all been destroyed,' he blurted.

'Good.' Bruno looked down at the sealed slides. He knew they contained enough bacilli to wipe out half mankind. 'We'll take the mutant strain stock first.' He indicated the slides on the benches. There must have been two hundred.

He picked one up and turned it over in his hand. Just to touch it now filled him full of horror.

'Get the others up here,' he said and indicated a large wicker litter trolley. It was full of waste paper. 'We'll load them into that.'

Guido ran headlong from the room.

'How much more is at the Clinic Ascha?' Lucia asked.

'Ten times as much. They provide shipments for the experiments here.' Bruno shivered as he thought of the risk involved in transporting the stuff to Bologna.

A careless driver.

An overturned lorry.

Guido returned with others. They loaded the trolley, each gingerly carrying two slides at a time. They stacked them neatly, two rows high without a centimetre between them.

Guido and Steffi lifted the trolley. They carried it carefully down the narrow steps to the incinerator room. Bruno followed with the others.

The blast of heat hit them as they entered the room. It scorched their eyebrows. One by one they tossed the slides into the white flames. The needle was almost off the dial on the wall.

When it was done Bruno looked at Lucia. She closed her eyes. He shared the look of mute relief on her face.

It was done.

'What now?' Franco asked.

Bruno looked at his watch. It was half past four. The new shift of *carabinieri* would arrive in ninety minutes.

'Empty the contents of the desks in the offices. They contain only administration papers but it will throw the whole system into chaos if we destroy everything we can lay our hands on.'

'Move,' barked Franco and bolted for the stairs. The others followed leaving Bruno and Lucia.

He took her by the hand and led her back to the laboratory. They stood in the doorway. Bruno heard the others kick the office doors off their hinges.

The laboratory was littered with empty slide trays. Cupboard doors hung open, the contents spilled over the floor.

Bruno leant on the work bench. His eyes ran over the experimental equipment before him. Suddenly he grabbed a large microscope stand. He began to smash every piece of equipment in sight, racks of test tubes, Bunsen flasks and glass jars.

'Bastards,' he yelled as he swung the brass stand. Broken glass filled the air. He wrecked everything. The glass-fronted cabinets caved in and he swept the bottles clean off the shelves with his arm.

'Bastards,' he screamed at the top of his voice.

Lucia watched dumbstruck until the place was in ruins. Bruno slumped against the wall as Franco burst past Lucia. He was wild-eyed.

'Bruno,' he yelled.

Bruno looked over his shoulder slowly. He recognized the haunted look of Franco's face. The look he'd seen before.

La paura. The ultimate fear.

'Come quickly,' he shouted.

Bruno made for the door and grabbed Lucia's hand. He saw Franco shake his head. He released her. 'Stay here.'

He dived after Franco who pointed to the door hanging off its hinges. It led to Pini's office.

Bruno walked slowly towards it, Franco at his heels.

He peered in and choked on what he saw. He shook his head numbly.

It was Claudia Mattucci. Her dead eyes gazed coldly at the ceiling. She was naked except for her suspenders and torn stockings. Her legs draped over the arms of the swivel chair. He head hung grotesquely.

Bruno saw she'd been badly beaten. She was covered in red weals and bruises. Her breasts sagged and bore the mark of cigarette burns.

Bruno walked slowly towards her. He reached out to touch

her then pulled away. He held his head in his hands.

He heard Franco say: 'Recognize this?' He opened his eyes and peered through his fingers.

Franco held a test tube. There was a syringe on the desk behind the swivel chair. Bruno read the words of the test tube label.

'It's scopolamine,' he mumbled.

'What?'

'A mixture from belladonna. It's a hypnotic, used as a truth serum.' Bruno pressed his knuckles to his mouth. 'Jesus Christ.'

'OVRA,' hissed Franco.

'Rossi.' The name sounded bitter as Bruno spat it out. He remembered Rossi asking how he knew about the meeting in Venice between Pini and Werner.

But he recalled with greater horror the drunken night he told Claudia about the Cavaliere Fulgoni.

Guilt swept over him.

Claudia had been tortured, raped and killed by Rossi because of the secrets he'd exchanged with her. He cursed himself. He was a fool. He wanted to curl up and die. Bruno knew just how effective the drug scopolamine could be.

Rossi now knew everything that had passed between them.

'It's finished. Everything is destroyed.' It was Luigi. He called from the door.

'Go,' Bruno said quietly to Franco. 'Take Lucia, I'll join you in the truck.'

Franco nodded, adjusted his feathered hat and spun on his heels.

Alone, Bruno sank on his haunches in front of Claudia. 'I'm sorry,' he mumbled. It sounded inadequate. He remained motionless for what seemed like eternity.

Then he got up.

He lifted Claudia from the chair and laid her on the floor. He walked to the lab and returned with a white coat. He covered her.

Bruno closed the door and walked, head bowed, to the waiting truck.

CHAPTER SIXTEEN

They buried Fabio in the soft ground near the wood below the encampment. The soil there was damp and deep, unlike the sparse earth covering the bedrock where they'd built the *baracca*. The *Noantri* piled the grave high with stones to deter wolves. They left no cross. The broken mountain rocks were his monument. When it was done they drifted back up the mountain in small groups.

Bruno, head bowed, trudged behind Fulgoni who held his daughter's hand. He left them outside Lucia's *baracca* and passed through the encampment and climbed towards the labyrinth. Franco, a burning brand held high, stood inside the entrance.

'Carla is back. She left Rossi's bed this morning. All hell has broken out after our efforts last night. The OVRA are arresting everyone they can lay their hands on,' Franco spoke rapidly.

'Is she all right?' Bruno asked.

'She's all right,' Franco said ruefully, 'now that she's back.' Bruno detected the resentment in his voice and remembered the scene in the sacristy.

'It must be hard for you,' Bruno said. 'Is there no other way we could get information from Rossi?'

'No. Not as well as Carla does.' His voice fell as he added, 'Besides, I think she enjoys it. Come.'

Bruno followed him through the labyrinth to the main cave. Carla eyed them both as they came in. He sensed an atmosphere between the two lovers.

He saw Carla's clothes piled on a creased blanket set out on the floor. They were the ones she'd worn when he'd first seen her at the Villa Marco. Now she wore the rough garb of the *Noantri*.

Carla drew deeply on a hand-rolled cigarette.

'I was wrong about you,' she said to Bruno.

He just nodded.

'Enrico Rossi wants you dead more than anything else in the world. And he is going to tear it apart to find you.'

Bruno stirred uneasily. He was involved in a vendetta with his own bloodline. He knew exactly what that would mean.

'Then we must kill him. Get him before he gets you,' Franco said.

The words rang in Bruno's brain. He knew they made sense and was suddenly aware he was shaking his own head.

'He's right,' prompted Carla. 'Rossi has become obsessed with revenge. Ever since you fled from the Clinic Ascha he has been acting like someone demented. When he heard the news he paced the floors ranting and raving. The only time he stopped was to bawl instructions down the phone. He is even threatening to arrest his own people if they do not get results. He says you have wrecked his world, and for that he wants your head.'

'I cannot be party to his murder,' Bruno said.

Carla snorted her contempt.

Bruno spun on her. He pointed a shaking finger. 'You will never understand. Not in a million years.' He thought of his father's life in the village across the valley. 'You do not know what poverty can do to a man.'

'I know what Rossi's obsession for you can do to us,' Carla snapped back. 'He plans to hunt you to the end of the earth. That puts all of us at risk as long as you are with us – or he still lives. The man's hate for you has possessed him like a disease, for the last few days I have lived with it.' Carla leapt to her feet and banged the table. Her eyes burnt fire. She seethed. 'That I do understand.'

'You're both wrong.' Seldon's voice wafted coldly through the gloom.

Bruno turned as he came out of the labyrinth. He took a newly lit cigarette and stubbed it underfoot. 'Why should we take unnecessary risks to take the sod out of the game? His own people will do that now that his scheme is falling apart around his ears.' He turned to Carla. 'When you left the Villa Marco how well was it guarded?'

'The place was crawling with *carabinieri* and plainclothes OVRA,' she mumbled.

'Of course it was, my dear girl. Rossi expects us to attack. Let him stew in his own fear. There are more important fish than Rossi.'

'Don't underestimate him,' Carla snapped. 'He's clever and dangerous.'

'So are we,' Seldon replied.

Bruno never thought he would be grateful to Seldon. He was now. The thought of killing Rossi, despite his feelings about the man, cut deeply.

'Pini and Werner are more important,' he said quietly.

'Exactly.' Seldon avoided Bruno's stare. He turned to Carla. 'What do you know?'

'Pini has left for Venice,' Carla said.

'To meet Werner?' Seldon asked.

'I assume so.'

'Do we know where?'

'No.'

'I do,' Bruno said flatly. 'The Europa, on the Grand Canal.'

'You are sure?'

He felt Seldon's eyes bore into him.

Ask Claudia Mattucci, he thought.

He said, 'Yes.'

At that moment Fulgoni's frame blocked out the light at the entrance to the cave. He picked his way heavily down the ladder and drew up a chair and sat at the table. He looked tired.

'You did well,' he told Bruno.

'We destroyed the Bologna end of the project,' Bruno said.

'That leaves the Clinic Ascha,' Fulgoni replied wearily.

'And Pini and Werner,' Bruno added. 'They must be taken care of. Soon.'

He turned to Carla.

'Do you know how long they plan to be in Venice?'

She shook her head, drawing hard on the cigarette. 'Rossi arranged the meeting. I was in his bed at the time. It was when they rang from Modena to say you were on the train. He told Pini to . . .' she paused, her brow lined with concentration, as she tried to remember details, 'get in touch with Werner himself and not to go through his secretary, Claudia Mattucci.'

Bruno bit his knuckles. He leant towards Fulgoni. 'I'd like to speak with you alone,' he mumbled.

The Cavaliere grunted. Bruno saw Seldon glare as he followed the old man into the tunnel at the back of the cave where the radio transmitter was kept.

'Once, when I was very drunk I mentioned your name to Claudia Mattucci. After Rossi had used scopolamine on her you can be sure he now knows too. I'm sorry.' Bruno looked downcast.

'I am not afraid of rats like Rossi,' the old man said firmly. 'I knew the moment I began to get involved with this business that things could never be the same for me again. They never will be until Italy rids herself of the rodents that rule us. That's why I have transferred all my affairs to Stockholm. Mussolini's thieving minions will not be able to lay their hands on them. I have even made sure my art collection is beyond their reach.' He paused and sighed. 'I'm an old man, when this war is all over I know I'll no longer be here. It will all be Lucia's.'

Bruno felt the fingers close tightly around his wrist. 'You will look after her.' Fulgoni's hoarse whisper was a command, not a question.

Bruno nodded.

'Good.' Fulgoni spat on the floor through clenched teeth. 'Now we take care of that duo in Venice. When?'

Bruno turned back to the cave. He scanned the faces sitting around the oil lamp on the table. He looked back over his shoulder at Fulgoni, then fixed his stare on Seldon.

'We leave for Venice at first light,' Bruno said. Then he turned, brushed past Fulgoni, and vanished into the darkness of the labyrinth.

Bruno lay huddled in his sleeping bag, curled up on the floor of one of the tunnels near the mouth of the labyrinth. He was aware of the sound of water dripping from the roof, it pinged regularly on the rock floor. The air was heavy with the smell of charcoal from the encampment below.

He did not hear Lucia approach, but he did feel the warm fullness of her lips on his forehead. He opened his eyes and saw her kneeling beside him. Her long hair hung below her shoulders. She wore a rough flannel shirt and corduroy trousers bagged tight by a leather belt.

Bruno rolled on his back as he watched Lucia rise.

'Your promise,' she said softly. 'I am asking you to keep it.' She moved the storm lamp to one side. It cast her shadow large on the wall behind her. She unbuckled her belt and dropped it on the floor. His mouth dried as she removed the trousers. The coarse shirt came just above her knees.

On the wall her shadow danced as she unbuttoned the shirt. She started at the bottom and lowered her eyes as the cloth opened around her. His mouth dried as she let it fall from her shoulders. She stood naked above him, her arms at her side.

The sight of her made him feel weak. Her breasts were proud and firm. She covered them with her arms, her hands rested on her shoulders.

'Love me,' she whispered.

Bruno rose. He drew her to him and wrapped his arms around her. He could feel the rise and fall of her breasts against his skin. His breath snatched as her taut stomach pressed into him. He kissed her hair then lifted her face to his.

Slowly he drew her down onto the sleeping bag. They knelt, embraced in each other's arms. He felt her eyelashes on his cheek as her mouth sought his. The kiss was timeless.

He savoured her taste as he eased her back. She moaned softly as he pulled away, her fingers sinking into his arms as she tried to draw him back. He leant on his side and ran his hand over her face.

'I just want to look at you,' he said. 'And touch you.'

He moved his hand slowly down the contours of her body and caressed her undulating hips. He pressed his palm gently onto her stomach and his tongue teased her breast. He felt her tremble and writhe slowly beside him. Her back arched as he took her breasts against his mouth. Her eyes closed and her arms locked around his neck. She tossed her head and groaned as he parted her legs. His lips moved to hers and she convulsed as his hand gently moved downwards.

As her fingers sunk urgently into his shoulders he could hold back no more. Their bodies slowly merged as one. They became part of each other, neither willing to be the first to separate.

At last, when all they could do was gaze at each other, they still did not want to break their bond.

They slept as one, each wanting to be part of the other.

Forever.

The light was fading slowly. Bruno sat alone on the fishing quay at Chioggia. Watching.

He looked across the lagoon towards Venice. The domed outline of St Mark's basilica and the pointed campanile stood out like a dark ribbon between the sky and sea. The last rays of the sun spangled on the flat waters as fishing boats, nets hoisted high, returned to port. Large tankers rode at anchor beyond the Lido waiting for berths at the oil port of Mestre. The refineries scarred the horizon. Bruno's attention was focused on the *motoscafi*, the fast launches that plied their trade around the island city. One was heading towards him pushing out a distinct bow wave as it wove through the returning fishing fleet.

He guessed it was the one which would take them to the safe house in the city. There were police checks on the causeway from Mestre, the only road access to the ancient city. That's why they had cut south of the lagoon to the fishing village of Chioggia. They had arrived in an aged bus. It was parked in a steep side street above the quay where Bruno sat on a fish crate watching the launch approach. He squinted into the dying sun and picked out two figures standing behind the windshield in the prow of the vessel. They would be members of the city's GAP partisan cell. Fulgoni had contacted them by radio from the camp at Perino Maggiore. They had been instructed to begin a surveillance on Pini and Werner and provide a safe house for the *Noantri*.

Bruno could see them clearly now as the launch slowed and entered the harbour. The man behind the wheel was young and muscular, his arms bulged through a blue and white hooped vest. The other was small and timid looking with curly hair and wire-framed glasses. The flag on the stern was the winged lion crest of St Mark, symbol of Venice. Bruno had been told it would be flying upside down. It was.

The launch pulled up at the quay. Bruno watched the small man leap onto the landing steps. The launch reversed into free water and sat bobbing alongside a string of moored fishing boats. The man climbed the steps to the quay and looked around anxiously.

Bruno rose. He picked his way around the fishermen mending nets and approached him.

'Is the *motoscafo* for hire?' Bruno asked.

'It depends.' The man's eyes darted behind his glasses.

'On what?'

'The number of passengers.'

'Six,' Bruno said and waited for the agreed reply.

'Two women and four men.'

'Right,' grinned Bruno and pumped his hand. The little man smiled nervously.

'The others?' he asked.

Bruno indicated the parked bus.

Seldon, Franco and Carla were already walking down the

hill. Lucia climbed from the bus followed by Luigi.

As they all followed Bruno and the small man down the landing steps the launch swung in an arc and, throttles down, came alongside, its engines throbbing. They climbed aboard and sat themselves on the wooden seat which ran around the well of the craft. Its nose lifted as they left the harbour and the helmsman pushed the twin throttles forward. The surge of power was enormous as it cut through the waters of the lagoon towards the city rising from the sea.

'It seems Pini and Werner have a routine,' the small man began. He said his name was Salvatore. No one cared to question it because it was safer that way. 'They lunch at the Europa in their suite where they spend the entire day. Then, at eight o'clock every evening they take a gondola along the Grand Canal to the Piazza San Marco. They have a table booked at the Florian. They dine. Werner takes a gondola back to the hotel. Pini spends the rest of the evening at the Blue Dolphin.'

'A night club?' Bruno asked.

Salvatore laughed. 'A high-class whore-house.'

'How do you know all this?' Seldon asked.

Salvatore eyed him impatiently. 'We have a man who works as a porter at the Europa. He arranges it.'

Seldon grunted.

Bruno walked to the window. He looked down onto the narrow canal. It ran past the safe house and linked the Grand Canal to the Lagoon of Death and the island of San Michele where Venice buries its dead.

The *motoscafo* launch was moored to a string of old gondolas. The murky waters were slicked with a thin film of oil which held driftwood and litter. The shuttered buildings opposite were damp with decay. This was not the Venice of the tourist guides.

Bruno looked at his watch. It was eight thirty. Pini and Werner would now be eating at the Florian. They were only a few hundred yards away.

'How long do the pair plan to stay in Venice?' he asked Salvatore.

'They have an open booking. It means they could leave at any time.'

'Then we have to move now,' Bruno said.

The others murmured assent.

Bruno moved to the large map of Venice spread out on the table. The *Noantri* gathered around him. He fingered the Piazza San Marco.

'The Florian is here,' he said and traced the route along the Grand Canal to the Europa Hotel. 'Where is the Blue Dolphin?'

'On the Mazaria.' Salvatore pointed to a narrow street on the map that ran from the Rialto Bridge to the Piazza San Marco.

'That means Pini has to walk to the whore-house from the restaurant,' Bruno decided.

Salvatore nodded.

Bruno frowned with concentration. He was planning a murder yet he felt no sense of guilt. He saw it as just one more step along the path to the ultimate destruction of Wildfire. That path was already littered with dead.

He turned to Seldon. 'We'll take them one at a time. Pini on the way to the whore-house, Werner on his way back to the hotel.'

'Agreed,' Seldon said. He moved to Bruno's shoulder and stabbed the map with his finger. 'Here.'

He pointed to a canal, the Rio Fume. It flowed onto the Grand Canal before the Europa. 'I'll take Werner. We are going to need a *motoscafo*.'

'We have Gino's, the one that brought you from Chioggia,' Salvatore said.

'No.' Bruno shook his head. 'It will be safer to steal one. It can then be dumped and there can be no way it can be traced back to us.'

'No problem,' Salvatore said, 'there are dozens moored at the Paglia Bridge, under the Gondoliers' Madonna.'

'Good. We'll divide into two groups,' Bruno said.

'I'll take Lucia and Luigi,' Seldon said.

Bruno hesitated. He wanted Lucia with him, but there was no time to argue. 'Take Gino too. You are going to need an expert helmsman. When you have . . .' he faltered for a second, 'killed Werner I want you to get back here as quickly as you can. They will expect us to flee the city. We won't. We'll sit tight for a week if need be. Any questions?'

'No.'

'Right. Let's go.'

Bruno found the Blue Dolphin first. There was a discreet brass nameplate on the door. It stood between a jeweller's and a shop specializing in the traditional black and gold Venetian furniture. There were two carved ebony negro torch holders outside.

Bruno nodded to Franco and Carla. They were toying with lace set out in a tray in front of a shop on the other side of the narrow street. He set off through the milling crowd towards the Piazza San Marco. Franco and Carla followed, one each side of the street.

Bruno's mouth was dry, he could taste the acid of fear which rose from his stomach. One hand was in his jacket pocket, his fingers curled around the Mauser pistol. It was hard for him to think that half of Europe was locked in war as he elbowed his way through the crowds. American tourists and Swedes seemed everywhere. He saw one mid-west matron swing out with her handbag at a man who rushed past her pushing a barrow of vegetables.

He halted at the edge of the Piazza. The sight had always filled him with awe. The three massive flags hung limply outside the basilica. They were momentarily lost behind a flock of pigeons who flapped into the sky like one grey blanket.

He saw the Piazza was crowded. The cafés under the covered galleries were full. Bruno glanced over his shoulder and beckoned Carla. She came, her face impassive.

Bruno indicated the Florian. 'See if Pini is still there. He does not know your face.'

Carla said nothing. He watched her amble through the crowds and admired her calm. He felt on edge. He even felt suspicion in the innocent glances of passers-by.

Keep moving. Don't stand still, he told himself and strode off across the marble Piazza towards the Grand Canal. He waited for Franco under the huge columns crowned with winged lions. His hands ran with sweat as he turned over the pistol in his pocket.

'There's the Englishman,' Franco hissed in his ear.

Bruno scanned the canal. He saw Gino in his blue and white vest at the helm of the *motoscafo*. Seldon lounged in the back between Lucia and Luigi. The craft entered the lagoon and began a slow arc.

He saw Gino turn his head and point in his direction. The wake boiled as its bows lifted through the water. Bruno glanced at Franco who indicated the silver-haired man striding towards the quay. He was flanked by four men in double-breasted suits and trilbies.

One of them broke into a trot and moved ahead of the group. He moved out onto the wooden pontoon and waved in a gondola.

'Werner's got an OVRA bodyguard,' Bruno said.

He and Franco moved to the other side of the column. 'Get back to the Florian. If Pini moves, tail him. Tell Carla to wait for me on the corner of the Mazaria.'

Franco moved quickly into the throng and headed back towards the basilica.

Werner and his escort had their backs to Bruno now. He watched them climb into the gondola. The gondolier swung on the single oar as his passenger settled under the central canopy. The man swung and found his rhythm. He propelled his craft slowly from the quay and followed his course up the Grand Canal. It was dotted with gondolas. A *vaporetto* waterbus slowed to give way as Werner's gondola cut across its path.

Bruno shot a glance towards the lagoon. Seldon's *motoscafo* began to close on the gondola, stalking it up the canal like a deadly predator. Seldon now stood alongside Gino.

Bruno spun on his heel and walked quickly back across the Piazza. He cursed himself for not calculating that the two scientists would be given a bodyguard. It was too late to do anything about it.

Carla waited on the far side of the square.

Bruno took her by the elbow. 'Has Pini gone?' he asked urgently.

Carla nodded towards the narrow street. 'Franco is on his heels. But Pini has OVRA company.'

Bruno cursed silently. 'How many?'

'Just one. The others went with Werner,' Carla said.

'I saw them,' Bruno mumbled, his concern growing. The execution of Werner was not going to be the single sharp shot he'd planned.

Carla was already making her way back up the Mazaria towards the Blue Dolphin. Bruno caught her up. He was aware of the urgency in their step. Everyone else seemed to be ambling. Even the tourists. They had taken on the Venetian *far niente* – the idleness of a city where the sundials proclaim they only count the happy hours. Bruno increased his stride.

He slowed when he saw Franco standing outside the door of the whore-house. He looked exasperated.

Bruno raised his eyebrows.

'You have to make an appointment.' Franco pointed to the brass mouthpiece of a speaking tube set in the door frame. 'We should have been told. There is no way they will let us in.'

'Then we can hit him when he comes out.' Carla's eyes blazed as she spoke. Bruno could feel the wrath the girl harboured for her murdered sister. Vendetta. Just as his cousin had for him.

'No.' Bruno turned, shoulders hunched, he walked slowly up the street, the others at his side. 'We have to act now.'

He looked apprehensively at his watch. 'The moment Seldon strikes then all hell is going to break loose.'

He looked back to the Blue Dolphin's door, sandwiched between the jeweller's and furniture shop. The whore-house must occupy all the upper floors. He doubted they would share it with a firm of accountants.

Time was running out.

'You two stay here,' Bruno said. 'Wait until someone leaves and stop them. The moment that door opens I want the pair of you inside with your guns at the ready. Stay in the passage until you hear from me.'

He held up his hand to ward off Carla's question. 'Just do as I say.'

He moved up the street alone until he came to a dank side alley. It was narrow and cobbled. A Madonna was carved on one wall and songbirds hung in wooden cages from the balconies. It led to a thin canal.

Bruno stood on the brink. The building to his right was an undertaker's. A funeral gondola was tied to a pole at the back of the building. It was painted black like the drapes and tassels which hung from the central canopy. It bobbed silently on the murky water.

Bruno reached out for the mooring rope and pulled the gondola to him. He dropped into the stern and undid the knot. He used his hands to propel himself along the rear of the buildings. They were mellow and faded with age. He could hear the faint sound of music coming from the whore-house less than twenty yards away. A girl shrieked with laughter.

He reached the back of the building. A short flight of worn stone steps led to a small patio, stacked with crates of empty wine bottles and cardboard boxes. Bruno made the gondola fast and climbed the steps. He tried a windowless door. It was unlocked. It opened into a kitchen. There was a charcoal-burning range piled high with unwashed copper pots and pans. Plates were piled high in the sink.

Bruno drew the Mauser from his pocket. He realized he

was shaking as he moved towards the narrow stairs. He could see a light under the door at the top and heard girlish laughter.

At the top of the stairs he froze with fear, rooted to the spot. The realization that he had to kill a man gnawed at his brain. He willed himself forward and pushed open the door.

It led to a plush salon. Two girls on a period sofa stopped chatting and turned towards him, a look of horror on their faces. Another, sitting on a stool at the small bar, stubbed out her cigarette with wide-eyed amazement. She wore a low-cut dress with black fishnet stockings. She rose from the stool, her eyes fixed on the gun in Bruno's hand. Her fingers covered her painted mouth.

Bruno turned to the girls on the sofa. One wore a blue satin dress, the other a transparent negligee over a red basque. The cocktail glasses on the low table in front of them were stained with lipstick. The girls looked terrified.

'I am not going to harm you,' Bruno said, aware of his own voice cracking as he spoke. He scanned the room. It had the ritzy feel of an art nouveau hotel reception from the 1920s, complete with potted plants in large china tubs. The jazz record on the wind-up gramophone began to slow, the strangled tones of the high-pitched singer filled the salon.

Bruno prayed silently none of the girls would scream.

Then came chaos.

He felt a sharp crack in the ribs. He spun round and saw an old crone with a knotted walking stick. She was dressed in widow's black from head to foot with a face like creased leather. A wart perched on the end of her Roman nose. She lashed out again with the stick and yelled obscenities. Bruno warded off the blow with his arm, holding the gun in the other.

The girl at the bar screamed and bolted for the door that led to the stairs and street.

'Stop,' he yelled, but she was gone.

The crone struck him again, then aimed a blow at his head. He ducked back and she lost her balance. She crashed into a potted plant and ended up in an oath-spluttering heap on the floor between the two remaining girls.

There was a piercing scream from the stairs. The fleeing whore had run into Franco and Carla. Then came the yells and curses of a vicious struggle as the girl was bundled up the stairs. He saw Carla shove her back into the salon. The girl's face contorted as Carla held her by a twisted knot of hair.

The girl in the basque fell back on the sofa in a dead faint.

'Leave her,' he yelled at Carla as she dragged the girl across the room by her hair. Carla shot him a venomous look, then flung the girl on the sofa. It overturned.

Bruno saw Franco snatch the crone's stick as she struggled to her knees, her lips pinched in a vicious pucker as she screwed up her eyes in rage.

'Where is Professor Pini?' Bruno yelled. He recoiled as she spat at him. He turned to the girl in the blue satin dress. She was white faced.

'Where is he?' he said as he grabbed her arm. She just shook her head in dumb terror.

'Tell him,' Carla yelled. He saw her ram the muzzle of her gun into the young neck.

The girl pointed to the door.

'Show me,' Bruno barked and Carla shoved the girl forward. She half stumbled. Bruno caught her. 'No one is going to hurt you. Just show me where he is.'

He saw the girl look at Carla and caught the reflection of fear in her eyes. Carla trembled. The girl mumbled incoherently and led Bruno to the double door. He kicked it open and froze.

The OVRA bodyguard was framed in the stairwell above him. Bruno saw the man's hand dart for the shoulder holster beneath his jacket. Like a true professional he spun sideways to lessen the target.

Bruno pushed the girl aside. He raised his gun and, as Seldon had taught him, took aim.

'Squeeze the trigger, don't pull. The gun will snatch if you do,' Seldon's instructions from the *Noantri* camp echoed in his head. 'Shoot,' he told himself as he saw the bodyguard draw his gun. Bruno's finger tightened around the trigger. But it would not respond to his own commands.

'Shoot.' The voice that yelled was Franco's.

Bruno felt a shove in the back as Franco pushed him clear. The two shots rang out almost simultaneously. The guard's bullet thudded into the stairwell wall. The plaster spat at Bruno.

He saw Franco's bullet hit true. Blood gushed from the OVRA man's mouth as he tumbled down the stairs after his gun and trilby.

'Next time shoot,' Franco screamed at him.

Bruno shook himself. It was as if he was dreaming all this. The cacophony of screaming whores behind him told him he was not.

He stepped over the dead guard and bolted up the stairs. He kicked open the first bedroom door. He had something to prove.

The girl next to the fat man screamed. He trembled as he peered at Bruno from behind the bed covers. Then squealed as he drew the covers around the contours of flab.

Bruno slammed the door shut.

'Bring that girl up here,' he yelled to Carla at the foot of the stairs. She pushed the girl forward as Franco burst into the next bedroom along the corridor.

'It's empty,' he yelled.

The whore wept with fear as Carla jabbed her with her pistol. 'He may not harm a hair of your head but I'll blow it off your shoulders.'

'Where is Pini?'

'Next floor. Third door on your left. Angelina's room,' she blurted.

Bruno noticed the whole place seemed to be filled with screams as he bounded up the stairs to the next floor, Franco and Carla, guns drawn, hard at his heels.

Naked couples bolted back to the safety of their rooms as

the trio ran headlong for Angelina's room. Bruno, breathless, pressed himself against the wall next to the door. He held his gun aloft.

'Kick it in,' he barked.

Franco did. The air filled with splinters. Franco, gun at the ready, moved forward. Bruno stopped him.

'It must be me,' he said softly and stepped into the room.

Carla followed. Franco remained in the corridor.

Bruno saw the barefooted Pini was dressed in vest and pants. He stood against the window overlooking the canal. His whore stood in front of him. She was naked, except for the silk stocking Pini had tied around her neck. He held both ends.

'One step further and she dies,' he hissed. The terrified girl choked as he pulled the stocking tighter.

Bruno shook his head in disbelief. 'You bastard.'

He heard Carla kick the door behind her.

'Let her go,' Bruno said.

Pini grunted. His face was like a wax death mask.

'Put down your gun, Bruno Rossi,' he said softly. The girl's eyes bulged as he twisted the stocking. 'We can both become very rich men. Your cousin and I will sell Wildfire for millions. Part of it can be yours. You need no truck with the savages who wrecked the Bologna laboratory.' His gaze shifted to Carla who now stood alongside Bruno. 'Kill that little cow and we can be away from here. Your past foolishness can be forgotten. I will see to it.'

'Let the girl go, Pini,' Bruno said slowly.

He saw her wince and her breasts lift as Pini tightened his grip.

'Let her go,' Bruno snapped, 'she's going blue.'

The girl's eyes began to roll. Bruno drew back towards the door, he reached out and pulled Carla with him. She trembled with rage.

Pini moved out onto the balcony.

The girl's knees began to buckle. Her whole weight was now supported by the stocking around her neck. A low gurgle rumbled from her throat.

'For Christ's sake let her go,' Bruno screamed.

Pini grinned.

'Toss your guns on the floor. Towards me,' he barked.

'Do it,' Bruno rasped.

The guns thudded on the carpet.

Bruno jolted as Pini hurled the girl at him. He caught her under the shoulders and her body convulsed in spasm.

He saw Carla leap towards Pini as he dived for the guns. She bounced sideways as Pini punched her full on the face with a clenched fist.

Bruno heard the door crash open behind them. A shot rang out. It richocheted off the balcony where Pini now was.

The girl in Bruno's arms twitched. He knew she'd died. He looked up in rage as a second shot rang out just as Pini vaulted into the night air.

He laid the girl down and grabbed Franco by the sleeve as he brushed past him.

'He's mine,' he said.

Franco stopped dead as Bruno scrambled for his gun. Carla nursed a bruised mouth in the corner.

Bruno leapt onto the balcony, arms flailing. He looked down. Pini had crashed through the canopy of the funeral gondola. He lay swathed in black drape. Bruno raised his gun as Pini struggled to his feet.

Their eyes met.

For the first time he saw emotion in Pini's reptilian gaze. It was terror.

Bruno fired.

Pini's bald pate flew through the air in fragments. Still clutching the black drape he tumbled into the canal.

Bruno leant over the balcony, looked over his shoulder at the strangled girl and back towards the canal.

Pini, arms outstretched, floated on the black mantle.

Bruno gripped the rail.

Then he threw up.

*

The man who said his name was Salvatore opened the door of the safe house.

Bruno knew in an instant that something was wrong, very wrong.

'They have killed Gino and taken Lucia,' he mumbled as if he disbelieved his own words.

Bruno felt weak. He turned to Franco and Carla on the step behind him. They were open-mouthed. Bruno brushed past Salvatore into a small hall tiled in marble. Standing in shadow halfway up the stairs he saw Luigi, his face as sad as any he wore as a clown.

'What happened?' Bruno said quietly.

Luigi shook his head. 'We did not expect the bodyguards,' he mumbled.

'What about Werner?' Franco asked.

'He's dead. Seldon shot him,' Luigi said.

Bruno turned and walked to the drawing room off the hall. He beckoned Luigi and held open the door as he walked into the room, shoulders stooping and head bent. He looked at Franco who took Carla by the hand and led her upstairs to their bedroom.

Bruno closed the door.

'Where is Seldon?' Bruno asked.

Luigi shrugged. 'I am not sure.'

Bruno felt like screaming his rage from the rooftops. Once again he felt Seldon had cocked things up. Only this time he'd left Lucia in the hands of the OVRA. 'I want to know what happened,' he said slowly. 'Everything.'

'We followed Werner's gondola up the Grand Canal, the water traffic was much heavier than usual. There were craft everywhere, Gino had his work cut out to keep close enough to make a sudden strike.

'Seldon decided we would have to make our play earlier than we planned. He leant over the side, and held his gun in both hands. He emptied it into Werner and blew him to pieces. Seldon was so fast Werner was dead before his guards had a chance to fire back. Gino looked back and opened up the throttles. Then the guards fired back. Gino at the wheel was the only standing target. His back was riddled with bullets. The force threw him forward through the windscreen into the water. The launch was now out of control. It was weaving about like a demented fish. I tried to grab the wheel but the air was still thick with bullets.

'I looked up and saw the bows of a waterbus heading straight towards us at speed. We were side on to it. It sliced the launch in two. I dragged myself onto the quay and looked back.

'I saw the bodyguards haul Lucia into the gondola. She was struggling furiously. There was no sign of Seldon and nothing I could do for Lucia.'

Bruno thought hard. Somehow they had to free Lucia. For him that was paramount. But he was also responsible for the others.

He opened the door and yelled for Salvatore. The little man crossed the hall and peered at Bruno through his wire-framed glasses.

'We are going to have to move house,' Bruno told him. 'Can you fix it?'

Salvatore shrugged and cupped his hands. 'It's possible,' he drew out his words slowly, 'but is it necessary? This house had served us well for months.'

Bruno snapped at him. 'Look, those bastards have Lucia, Christ only knows what they will do to her.'

He thought of the drug Rossi had given Claudia Mattucci. It made him feel sick.'They also have Gino's body. It's only a matter of time before they trace him back to this house. He is a licensed *motoscafo* operator. His face will be in the records and I don't have the time to argue the toss. So move.'

Salvatore hesitated. 'You're right. But it won't be easy.'

'Then let's not waste any more time. Get up to the attic and use the radio to contact other cells. Find us something. Fast,' Bruno said.

Salvatore bolted up the stairs.

Bruno turned to Luigi. 'Gather up all the hardware you can find in the house – weapons, ammunition and explosives.'

He moved to the back window and looked down on the canal. Gino's *motoscafo* still bobbed alongside the gondolas moored on the wooden *pali* that rose from the water like a decaying tree. He felt an idea stir. He looked at his watch. It was ten thirty. He wondered how long the OVRA would take to identify Gino.

He raced for the stairs and took them two at a time. He paused outside Franco's room. The sounds Carla made were identical to the ones he'd first heard in the funeral chapel in Bologna. He called her name.

The groans grew louder. His voice was lost in her necessity. He threw open the door. Carla screamed agonizingly as Franco drew himself from her and spun towards Bruno.

'We have got to get out of here. Get dressed. Quickly.' He closed the door and headed for the attic.

Salvatore frantically twisted the dial on the radio.

'Any luck?'

Salvatore shook his head.

'We are going to take Gino's *motoscafo*.'

'That's madness. You won't get any further than the end of the canal.'

'We can't risk staying here.'

Bruno knew if he was caught now, then Wildfire could still become a reality. Rossi, Zeiss and the Clinic Ascha still existed.

'But where can you go?' Salvatore asked.

Bruno told him.

The little man grinned. 'You will be safe there, at least for tonight. I'll stay here until I can find you a refuge.' He rose and opened the skylight. The ancient rooftops were clear against the sky. 'My way out the moment they break down the door. *Ciao* and good luck.'

Bruno thanked him with a hug and was gone.

The others were waiting in the hall. Carla, her face flushed, was still buttoning her shirt. A canvas sheet containing weapons lay tied at Luigi's feet.

'Do you think you can handle a *motoscafo*?' Bruno asked.

'Yes,' Franco said.

Bruno led them to the wooden landing stage at the back of the house. They climbed aboard the waiting launch.

Franco toyed with the controls. 'No problem.' He gunned the engine.

Bruno caught Carla around the waist and lifted her down. Luigi tossed in his canvas bundle and jumped down after it. The launch rocked, oily water came over the low transom and spilt over the slatted deck board.

They headed slowly up the canal. The sleeping houses slipped by silently.

The launch floated under the last arched bridge and entered the Lagoon of Death off the city's northern shore.

A red light blinked in the distance. Bruno knew it came from the beacon on the Isola San Michele, the island cemetery half a mile offshore inhabited only by centuries of Venetian dead.

He pointed to the light.

'Head for that and give it all you've got.'

The bows lifted from the water.

It began to rain.

CHAPTER SEVENTEEN

'It's sacrilege,' Luigi complained.

'It's dry,' Carla retorted and smashed the pane of glass in the side door of the English chapel. She reached inside and turned the key in the lock. The rain had become a downpour. Her hair hung in wet strands.

Bruno, soaked to the skin, was past caring. He pushed open the door with his foot. The others followed him inside. He saw the chapel was small, simple and sparse. It had been built a hundred years earlier to meet the needs of Venice's English community. It had a pointed slate roof and a belfry in the square tower. Except that it had been whitewashed it looked as if it could have been transplanted from a Hampshire village. It was out of place among the rows of family vaults set in high walls. But, as Bruno pointed out, it had the belfry which looked out over the lagoon.

Franco volunteered to take first watch. He climbed the tower steps as the rest of the group tried to sleep on the wooden pews of British oak. They used hassocks as pillows.

Bruno found sleep impossible. He thought of taking Franco's watch but dismissed the idea. He needed to think. He shuddered at the idea of Lucia in OVRA hands.

What would Rossi do with her?

He tried to picture his cousin at that very moment. He would be in Rome. At his home, white with rage.

Grazziani, his father-in-law and superior officer, a man who hated his guts, would have had to pass the news of the assassinations on to higher authority.

Il Duce himself.

The reaction would be awesome. Mussolini's hand of cards to use Wildfire as a lever of influence on Hitler was looking weaker by the moment.

Bruno was the key behind the impending collapse. Rossi was responsible for him coming to Bologna.

And Rossi would be on the rack.

Bruno would have rejoiced at the havoc – if not for Lucia.

Suddenly, Franco was on the belfry steps. Bruno looked up as he leapt to the floor.

'There's a boat,' Franco blurted, 'it's heading straight for the funeral quay.'

'Wake the others,' Bruno said and made frantically for the belfry.

The rain had ceased and the air was sweet and clear. He looked across the lagoon to Venice. The outline of the boat was clear. It was a large motor yacht and showed no lights. Bruno guessed it was no more than a hundred yards away.

He moved back down the steps.

The group were waiting, carbines in hand. Bruno picked up a weapon from the canvas bundle spread out beneath the altar. He chose a Mauser pistol.

'Let's go,' Bruno said quietly.

He could hear the low throb of the yacht's engines as soon as he stepped from the chapel. It echoed through the vaults.

Bruno ordered the group to fan out and take up positions behind the tombs overlooking the funeral quay. It was a straight stone structure that jutted out into the black sea.

'Don't fire until I do,' Bruno called as they positioned themselves, rifles trained on the empty quay.

Bruno ducked behind the low cemetery wall which enclosed the whole island. He flicked the safety catch off the Mauser and glanced quickly out to sea. The cruiser had cut its engines and was drifting on the current towards the quay. It was a British-built Rampart with a fly bridge and cabins above and below decks. A shadowy figure came out onto the deck and walked to the bows. He jumped out onto the quay and made fast. Bruno watched from the cover of the wall as the man signalled to someone else on board. A second figure leapt onto the quay. Both wore caps pulled low over their faces. The second had a pistol.

Perhaps there are others, Bruno thought as the two men walked towards the high cemetery gates. He ducked low and skirted a row of ornate tombs to bring himself to the main path. Bruno heard the gates creak open and footfalls echo as the men approached. He looked down towards the yacht. There was no sign of activity.

Bruno saw Franco crouching between a row of vaults on the other side of the path. He touched the pistol in his hand and shook his head. He did not want to risk the sound of shots. He indicated a garrotting movement. Franco nodded his understanding.

As soon as the two men came into view Bruno sprang. His arm locked around a throat as he kicked the first man's legs from under him. He felt the air leave his opponent's body as he crashed to the ground. He rammed the pistol's nose into the soft flesh of the underjaw. The man's gun fell from his grasp and clattered on the path.

Bruno turned him on his back.

It was Seldon.

His eyes were wide with fear. Bruno withdrew the pistol.

'Idiot,' he snapped as Seldon ruefully rubbed his throat. Franco was standing over the other man. Bruno saw it was Salvatore.

Luigi and Carla, rifles raised, came into view.

Bruno watched Seldon, still rubbing his throat, struggle to his feet. He seethed with anger.

'You've lost me Lucia,' Bruno said coldly. He grabbed Seldon by the sleeve and drew him roughly until they were out of earshot.

Bruno still had the pistol. His wrath for Seldon was cold and deep. He eyed him vengefully. 'You have cost me both the people on this earth that I loved dearest.' Despite himself he dug Seldon hard in the ribs with the pistol. He winced.

'Easy, Bruno,' Seldon said slowly, his hand raised to ward off a blow he obviously expected. 'We both need each other. I also need Fulgoni's daughter which is why I plan to get her back.'

Bruno snorted contemptuously. 'I don't think I'd trust you to walk my dog.'

Seldon shook his head and sighed with resignation. 'Maybe not. But you are going to have to trust me to lift Lucia from the OVRA.'

Bruno felt his anger rise. 'If anyone is going to get Lucia then you'd be the last man on earth I'd choose.'

'But you're not doing the choosing,' Seldon snapped impatiently, 'and I do not have the time to argue. You are too valuable to risk on any rescue attempt. You and Lucia know the Clinic Ascha. If anything happens to you then she is the only one who can show us what we are looking for when we get there.' He shrugged his shoulders. 'I'm expendable. If I'm taken out of the game London would send someone else without batting an eyelid. If anything happened to you or the girl they'd have a fit. It's that simple.'

Bruno thought, Oh no it's not.

He still suspected Seldon would try to get the Wildfire stock.

Bruno said, 'All right. You were responsible for her getting caught, how do you plan to get her out?'

'Tell your people to gather their arms and join me on the yacht,' Seldon said sharply. 'They are Fulgoni's orders.'

Bruno watched him spin on his heels and walk through the gate towards the waiting yacht.

He followed slowly. On the quay he paused to look at the name painted in elaborate scroll on the vessel's bows.

Francesca.

The name of Lucia's mother.

He stepped aboard.

Bruno waited for Seldon in the *Francesca*'s stateroom. The rest of the group snatched a few hours' precious sleep in the guest cabins below decks.

A lamp swung above his head. He turned it on. There was gleaming brass everywhere, from the closed porthole covers to the rails around the tables. The walls were highly polished mahogany panels and the seating which ran along them was deep brown leather. This was a real ship not a floating gin palace. Bruno thought that's how it should be. He settled in a swivel chair with a heavy oak base. A short flight of stairs led to the bridge. Seldon came down them and ducked under the cross beam.

Bruno eyed him cautiously. Seldon had just been on the ship's radio to Fulgoni at his villa. Bruno saw Seldon looked fraught.

'Things are moving fast,' Seldon mumbled. 'Too fast for my liking. The bastards have hit the camp at Perino Maggiore.'

Bruno's stomach churned as he leapt to his feet.

'What?' he bellowed.

He was quelled by Seldon's raised hand.

'No one was taken,' he said wearily. He looked strained, Bruno thought, his face taut with tension.

'I think you had better tell me what's been happening.'

Seldon slumped on the leather bench seat. 'We got Werner . . .'

'I know. And they got Lucia. Then what?'

'There was chaos after the waterbus cut through the gondola. I just swam for the gondola landing stage at the Rio Vento and made myself scarce. No heroics,' he said quietly.

Bruno looked at him scathingly. He said nothing.

Seldon continued. 'I dared not risk going back to Salvatore's. I made for one of the back-up safe houses on the list. I got on the short wave radio as usual. I could not raise the camp so I called up Fulgoni at his villa and told him what had happened. He told me to go to this yacht. It was moored at the Lido. It's owned by one of his companies.

'Salvatore was already on board. Fulgoni had radioed him. He said that his contacts had found out that Lucia was now in the hands of the *carabinieri*. They plan to fly her to Rome this morning. Fulgoni has one of them on his payroll. We will take her on the Mestre causeway. It's all arranged.'

'Just like before,' Bruno said darkly. 'Now what about the camp?'

Seldon hunched his shoulders and clasped his hands. 'There was a shoot-out with a detachment of *Guardie Forestali*. None of the *Noantri* were hit.'

'Thank Christ for that.'

'Details are scarce but they retreated from the camp and vanished into the caves. All twenty got clear. Fulgoni has sent them to a camp in the Dolomites. We will join them there and then try the clinic.'

'We destroy the clinic,' Bruno corrected, 'and the last of the Wildfire strain.'

He saw Seldon's eyes flicker. For just a moment. It was enough to put Bruno on his guard.

'Now tell me how we free Lucia,' Bruno said.

Seldon picked up a map and spread it on the table.

Salvatore cast off from the quay at dawn, Gino's *motoscafo* in tow. Bruno was on the bridge with Seldon, Franco at the wheel. He pushed the twin throttles forward and the Perkins engines responded throatily.

Bruno glanced down into the stateroom. Carla and Luigi sat smoking nervously. Luigi gave him a thumbs up and Bruno smiled back faintly. His heart was in his mouth. He picked up the Lieberman and Gortz binoculars from the console. They had a powerful 25 x 52 magnification. He focused as Franco swung the *Francesca* in the direction of Mestre, the oil port on the mainland.

Bruno counted five ships in the port's roads. Their lights flickered in time with those on the oil refineries. He could pick out the vehicles crossing the three-mile causeway to Venice. A goods train steamed alongside them towards the mainland. The sky was turning pink. It tinged the lagoon, already criss-crossed with small trading craft.

The ugly skyline of Mestre neared.

The *Francesca* cut her engines half a mile from the shore and the end of the causeway.

'It's time,' Seldon said. Bruno gave him the binoculars. Seldon focused and scanned the causeway and the mainland. He paused, his face screwed in concentration, then handed back the binoculars.

'Waiting at the road junction leading onto the causeway,' he said.

Bruno looked. He saw a red mechanical road digger, its metal arm like a claw, parked between two heavy construction trucks. He could see the group of men standing alongside.

'Is it them?' Bruno asked lowering the glasses.

Seldon nodded. He moved out onto the open wing of the bridge and turned the chrome searchlight towards the shore. He pulled three times on the light's handle.

The leading truck flashed its lights in return. Seldon brushed past him and disappeared into the stateroom. He glanced at Franco, still holding the wheel.

'It will be all right,' he mumbled through his beard. 'It is the Cavaliere Fulgoni's idea. It will work.'

'It has to,' Bruno replied.

Seldon, Carla and Luigi were on deck now, Salvatore had untied the *motoscafo* and brought it alongside. The three boarded gingerly. They all carried pistols.

Bruno scanned the lagoon as the *motoscafo* cut through the waters like a knife towards the shore. There were no police launches, as far as he could see.

Through the glasses he saw the *motoscafo* pull alongside a jetty. His eyes followed the three ashore as they ambled to the waiting vehicles. The assembled men huddled around them.

Bruno shifted the glasses back to the *motoscafo*. Salvatore was standing at the wheel as the craft idled halfway between the jetty and the causeway.

Bruno felt impotent. He should have been there.

'Please?' Franco held out his hand for the binoculars. Bruno handed them to him.

'It's happening,' Franco yelled suddenly.

Bruno snatched the glasses.

He focused frantically.

The trucks and digger had gone.

'The causeway,' Franco barked.

Bruno swung the glasses along its length. He picked out the convoy. It was led by a black and white Fiat, the word *Carabinieri* painted on the door. There were four men inside.

Then came the armoured prison van. Bruno pictured Lucia handcuffed inside. His stomach turned.

The van was followed by a small bus full of armed *carabinieri*. He could see their raised rifles clearly.

Bruno's gaze shifted.

The digger was a hundred yards from the approaching convoy. The huge construction trucks, twenty yards apart, crawled slowly towards their target.

The gap closed.

Suddenly, Bruno saw the second truck veer into the opposite lane. It had put itself between the leading car and the prison van whose path it now blocked. He saw the van's brakelights glare as it stopped dead in its tracks.

Then the second truck switched lanes as the bus bringing up the tail slowed. Bruno could see the men inside jostling for the door.

He winced as the truck rammed it. The bus folded like a metal concertina as the massive truck smashed it into the iron parapet of the causeway. The truck reversed, then charged a second time. The twisted bus was pushed on its end, its torn sides touching each other in the centre. Bruno knew there could be no survivors. The truck hit it again. The bus bent into a giant hook and toppled over the parapet and vanished into the lagoon.

The truck reversed towards the prison van. Its tailboard pressed hard against the rear doors.

Bruno switched to the lead car. Its doors were open. The four men it carried now lay still on the road. He saw Seldon and Luigi, pistols in hand, running towards the van. Carla stood in front of it, gun blazing. Bruno saw chips of glass fly from the windows. They were bullet proof. But the van's escape path was still blocked by the first truck.

He saw Seldon wave an arm. The mechanical digger crawled alongside the van. Its claw was raised. It dropped suddenly, its metal teeth tearing into the van's roof. It ripped it open as if it was nothing more than a can of sardines. The claw rose again. This time it came down slowly and the teeth closed around the top of the van's side where the roof had been a few seconds before. Bruno saw the van tilt slowly onto its side as the digger pulled back.

'Lucia's in there,' he spat through clenched teeth. He turned away in desperation. He felt Franco grab him by the shoulder.

'Look,' he yelled.

Bruno focused on the figures standing on the parapet. His heart skipped. Seldon held Lucia by the waist.

He pushed her over the side and leapt after her into the water. He saw him bobbing alongside her, holding her head above the waves.

Salvatore's *motoscafo* was bouncing over the waves towards them, engine at full revs, leaving a curved wall of water in its wake.

He saw Carla and Luigi leap into the water.

On the bridge the partisans from the trucks were piling into a car. They sped off. The causeway was completely blocked by the wreckage. There was chaos.

Franco's finger hammered the ignition button. The *Francesca*'s engines roared. He pressed the automatic winch and the twin anchor chains slid across the deck.

Bruno bolted for the deck. He leant over the side as the *motoscafo* circled alongside.

Carla helped Lucia to her feet, her hands were cuffed behind her. Bruno reached out and slid his arms under her shoulders and lifted her on board.

He wrapped his arms around her and pressed her to him. As the *Francesca* swung towards the open sea Lucia began to sob. Over her shoulder Bruno watched the Venice skyline slip lower into the early morning sea.

Lucia had been beaten under interrogation. She had told them nothing. Bruno was grateful they had not used scopolamine. He looked down at her as she lay asleep in the oval bed in the master suite. He smiled fondly and closed the door. He walked out onto the deck.

He breathed deeply and filled his lungs with sea air. The *Francesca* was out of sight of land. She rose and fell as she nosed her way north through the choppy Adriatic swell. The crests of the waves turned crimson under the last rays of the setting sun. It was time to make an agreed radio contact with the Cavaliere Fulgoni at his villa.

He made for the radio room. It was housed under the bridge. He ducked through the low door. The set took the whole of one wall. He sat before it and put on the headphones. It was already tuned to Fulgoni's frequency. He lifted the hand microphone and turned the set on. It whistled piercingly as the valves glowed red, then cleared to a mild atmospheric crackle. He reached upward and flicked the switch which would send out the automatic signal telling Fulgoni to prepare to receive.

No response.

He tried again.

And again.

Then came the return signal – three long shrill bleeps followed by four rapid short ones.

Bruno switched to transmit. He bent over the microphone.

'The *Noantri* are calling home. Come in please.'

He flicked to receive.

'Get off the air.' Fulgoni's deep voice bellowed through the speaker. 'Break transmission. Now.'

Bruno heard a thump. There was the sound of a struggle. He heard Fulgoni cursing faintly in the background. His cries were strangled as Bruno, now white faced, heard another scream to get off the air. It came through above the sound of breaking glass. Bruno was on his feet. He stared in horror at the radio. Then he froze.

'You treacherous bastard.' The disembodied voice filled the room. It was his cousin Rossi's.

He was at Fulgoni's villa. Bruno felt his bowels turn to water. He was transfixed to the crackling radio, unable to do more than stare.

'Speak to me,' Rossi's voice screamed.

Bruno was dumbstruck.

'Do you hear me?' his cousin spat the words.

The background commotion grew louder. Fulgoni was booming at the top of his voice.

Then came silence. It seemed unending.

Rossi's voice broke it.

'Bruno,' he said urgently. His tone had changed. 'In the name of God, help me.'

Bruno stared silently. His cousin's voice filled with desperation. He was pleading.

There was a frenzy of static. Then Rossi came through again.

'Please understand. My life is on the line because of what you have done. Unless you stop this madness it is you or me. They have given me no option.'

There was a long pause. Then a screamed 'Answer me'.

Bruno slumped into the chair in front of the seat.

'Answer me,' Rossi yelled again.

Silence.

'Look,' Rossi urged. 'I know what you are planning to do. It's impossible. You cannot destroy the clinic. Cease this madness now. I can help you, give you immunity, anything. Anything you want. Name it and it's yours.' His voice rose. 'You must or I am a dead man.'

Bruno's brow glistened with perspiration.

'Please, think of Paola and the children . . .'

Bruno heard a crash. Someone grunted in pain.

Fulgoni's voice filled the room. 'Get off the air, you bloody fool. They are trying to fix your position.'

Bruno jerked upright. He killed the switch. The glowing valves dimmed.

'Do we tell the others?' asked Seldon looking up from the navigation table in the chart room.

Bruno hesitated. He walked to the porthole and lit a cigarette, inhaling deeply. He wondered just how much he could rely on the *Noantri*'s total dedication without Fulgoni. With the Cavaliere gone he feared Seldon might try to take command.

He could not let that happen.

Bruno looked over his shoulder at the Englishman. His former friend looked ashen after the episode on the causeway. The stress showed. The certain gratitude Bruno felt was still overshadowed by what had gone before.

'No. We do not say a word about Fulgoni,' Bruno said firmly. He expected Seldon to argue, but he simply poured himself another drink from the almost empty brandy bottle on the table beside him. 'Go easy on that stuff,' Bruno said. He noticed Seldon's hand shake as the glass moved to his mouth. Seldon grunted.

Bruno left him hunched over the empty glass and made for the bridge where Luigi sat in the captain's chair chatting to Franco. The *Francesca*'s course had been set on the automatic pilot. She was heading for the Bay of Aquileia, a great rocky bight between Venice and Trieste.

Bruno watched with fascination as the wheel corrected itself to keep the yacht on the course Fulgoni's people had set.

'We are almost there,' Franco said checking his watch against the brass ship's clock. 'There are the lights of Grado.'

Bruno saw them flicker faintly on the horizon. He saw that Franco now had the wheel. He swung the yacht's nose away from Grado and headed for the lonely shore.

There Fulgoni's people waited. The *Francesca*'s crew would get their yacht back in exchange for fast transport to the mountains of the north.

'There,' Luigi pointed. 'The signal.'
Bruno saw the red light flashing.

The driver was a girl. She had long chestnut hair and milk-white skin. Bruno thought she would have looked perfect in Shakespearian costume.

He was in the lead car, a black Lancia. He sat in front. Lucia, Carla and Franco were squeezed in the back. Seldon and the others followed in an old Citroën with sweeping mudguards. They had travelled through the night from the coast.

'How much further?' Bruno asked as he passed the girl a cigarette he'd already lit.

'About half an hour.' Her name was Gina. She put the cigarette in her mouth and squinted as smoke got into her eyes. It was mid-morning and they were well into the mountains, despite skirting major towns like Udine and Cortina.

Bruno looked out of the window. The tops of the rugged mountains were still covered in snow. Belts of pine forest punctuated Alpine pasture which swept down steeply to the fertile valley floor. Below he saw a thin silver line which was a river. Above, a herd of chamois stood like carved sentinels on the rocks below the snow. An eagle circled above them, menacing against the clear blue sky.

The girl swung off the track they were travelling for a lesser one which was even more pitted and rock strewn. She hit the brakes as a man appeared from the trees ahead.

He had a gnarled expression and wore a heavy fleece jacket with no sleeves. He waved a rifle in his burly arm. The cars slowed to a halt.

'Mario,' Gina smiled.

Bruno wound down the window as Mario lumbered towards them. He caught the smell of goats as he leant out.

'You Bruno Rossi?' he asked gruffly.

Bruno nodded. He shook the offered hand.

'I'll show you the rest of the way,' he said. 'You can drive right into the camp.'

'*Ciao.*' Bruno smiled as Mario climbed onto the Lancia's running board and cupped his arm through the open window. The smell of goats grew stronger as the car bumped slowly down the track. Behind him Bruno heard Lucia and Carla giggle.

The car passed through a glade, damp with moss and ferns which grew alongside a gushing stream.

'Leave the track and turn right when we are the other side,' Mario called to Gina. Bruno caught the garlic off his breath as Mario peered through the window. The grey stubble on his chin stuck out like wire bristles.

'The camp is in the trees the other side of the hill,' Mario said as the Lancia's wheels spun when it left the track for the soft earth of the gentle hill.

Bruno leant forward in his seat and rested his hands on the dashboard. In the rear view mirror he saw the Citroën follow as it rode and dipped on the soft suspension.

In the mirror he could see his own apprehension. His eyes shifted slightly so he caught a glimpse of Lucia. He dreaded telling her about Fulgoni.

He thought nervously of what lay ahead. God only knew what was in store.

He shuddered as the Lancia dipped over the brow of the hill. Before him he saw the camp. A vast green canvas awning had been rigged up in a cluster of trees, to provide a roof over the neat rows of camp beds. Brown tarpaulin had been pegged to stakes to form three walls. The front wall was rolled and tied with rope to the sagging roof.

Bruno could see some of the *Noantri* inside sitting on camp beds. Some cleaned rifles, others lay reading. The rest sat in groups, backs propped against the tall pines. As all heads turned towards the approaching cars Bruno nodded appreciatively. The camp would be impossible to spot from the air. Even the two open-sided trucks were slung with bracken-covered nets. After the attack on their last camp no one was taking any chances.

'Drive the cars into the trees,' Mario yelled as he jumped

from the running board.

Bruno wound up the window as Gina negotiated her way between the tree trunks. In the wood Bruno could see several other, smaller canvas shelters rigged. They even had a mobile field kitchen – it was Great War issue. Steam hissed around it.

Fulgoni has considered everything, Bruno thought. He shot a glance to his daughter as she stepped from the car. Lucia was smiling. Bruno's gut churned.

He turned and walked to the main canvas structure. He waved his arm for Seldon to follow and strode, head down, towards the rows of camp beds.

Franco was at his shoulder.

'Get everyone together,' Bruno said quietly.

Franco passed on the order to those nearest him. They rose from the beds and moved out among the pines.

Bruno turned to Seldon as the rest of the *Noantri* moved under the shelter of the awning.

'We are going to have to move,' Bruno said, 'and move fast. The quicker we strike the less time they are going to have to prepare against us.'

Seldon nodded, almost imperceptibly. Bruno noticed the brandy still hung on his breath, and his pallor was like damp chalk. At that moment he realized Seldon, the SIS man from London, the expert, was afraid.

And Bruno realized he was not. He felt strange because of it. He should have been terrified of the prospect that the next few hours held. But all he experienced was a detached but uncomfortable calm. Seldon's fear showed.

For the first time since their Cambridge days Bruno believed he understood the man. The arrogant bravado and cutting sarcasm was a front. He remembered the failed first attack on the laboratory. Yet Seldon had put everything on the line the previous day to save Lucia from the certainty of the firing squad. That had been cold courage, the kind not born of the anger and desperation Bruno harboured. It was Bruno's motivation – the unquenchable thirst to destroy

Wildfire. But for Seldon it was a duty, a duty which overrode his now obvious fear. A duty the man had put before their friendship, that had begun the path to his father's death. Bruno did not know whether to pity or admire him. For he also knew Seldon saw it as his duty to acquire Wildfire.

Bruno despaired.

The *Noantri* had gathered around him. Their faces engraved with sullen determination. A few were new. Others he recognized from the camp near his father's village.

Steffi and Guido had been with him on the final raid at the Bologna underground lab. They were in their twenties, student actors, and wore the haggard look of veterans.

Bruno watched silently as they hung a map from a large wooden easel they'd erected. It was a blow-up of the one Bruno had drawn of the clinic and its surrounds the last time he'd left Fulgoni. He swallowed hard and could almost feel the old man's crushing handshake. Bruno moved to the map. He was back in the lecture theatre where he really belonged.

'Are there any reports from partisan groups in the areas between here and the clinic?'

Guido raised his hand.

'We have been in contact with all of them by radio this morning,' he said. 'There has been a lot of government activity. A detachment of Alpine troops has been drafted into Vipiteno near the Brenner Pass. They have been billeted with local families.'

'The *Alpini* are crack troops,' Bruno commented.

'The best,' echoed Franco, 'hard bastards.'

Guido agreed. The face he pulled said so. He added: 'Some of the troops are being used on patrol with the *Milizia* who are based in Udanzi, the village near the end of the railway. They have pitched a camp on the outskirts. *Guardie Forestali* are on constant patrol in the area from the railway to the cable car station. It is all heavy stuff.'

Bruno paused. 'But is there word of what they have done to reinforce security at the clinic itself?'

'No,' Guido said sombrely. 'No one has been able to get anywhere near it. The risk is too great.'

'Of course it is,' Bruno said.

Seldon and Franco frowned.

'Make no mistake, Rossi knows that we plan an attack on the clinic and he has prepared for it in the best way possible. He knows we cannot destroy the clinic if we can't reach it. The only way to the clinic is by cable car and the only way to the cable car is through the forces he has put there to stop us. We can't.'

'So how do we get there,' Seldon snapped, 'fly?'

Bruno shook his head. 'We walk,' he said simply.

'Walk?' It was Franco who raised his voice in astonishment.

'Yes,' Bruno said emphatically. 'We will walk across the mountains and scale the heights to the clinic from the rear.'

'Impossible,' Seldon interrupted.

'Difficult,' Bruno corrected. 'These mountains are formidable but they are not the Matterhorn. It is possible and I see no alternative.'

There was a murmur of assent from the assembled *Noantri*. Only Franco and Seldon looked doubtful.

Bruno shared those doubts. He did not let it show. He would have to depend on the enthusiasm and youthful idealism of the *Noantri*. In the end it would account for everything.

'Get the large-scale map of the area,' Bruno said.

Steffi produced it from several rolled up on the bed. He unfurled it and spread it out on the floor. Bruno squatted and the others gathered around.

Bruno saw the railway and single roads were marked. The clinic was not. He drew it in. Then his finger traced a line to the north-east which led from the rear of the clinic, across a valley and down the other side to a broken red line on the map.

'A goat track,' he said.

That in turn led to a black line denoting an unmade track.

It curled along the contours of the map until it reached a thin unbroken red line.

'A road,' Bruno beamed. He turned to Steffi. 'How long would it take us to get there from here?'

'Four to five hours.'

Bruno grunted. 'Good. We leave at dusk.'

CHAPTER EIGHTEEN

The two trucks came to the place marked on the map as an unmade track. That was an understatement.

Bruno, behind the wheel of the lead truck, saw a rough line stretch out before him. It was marked by irregular lichen-covered boulders. No one had trodden it for years, let alone driven across it. This was desolation at its wildest.

In the wing mirror, Bruno saw the other truck stop. He pulled up, left Lucia in the cab, and ran back.

Franco was already peering under the vehicle. The bearded face looked up.

'The back axle has gone. It's snapped in two,' Franco explained.

'Sod it,' mumbled Bruno. 'Pile everyone and their equipment onto the other truck.'

The others transferred while Bruno and Franco covered the broken truck with a camouflage net. Bruno decided to bring the nets after an Italian Air Force spotter plane had overflown the last camp the previous afternoon.

They drove on until the going became so rough it was quicker to walk. They covered the truck and set off in single file along the goat track.

Mario in the sheepskin fleece led the way. He'd torn a living from this land since a boy. He was a mountain man through and through. He was strong, silent and uncommunicative; and proud of it.

Despite his bulk, he moved as nimbly as the chamois whose pelts he once sold. Bruno realized he was a godsend. The big man fixed the pace. It was steady and relentless, always moving at the same speed, set so the three girls could keep up with their back-packs and weapons. They rested every hour for ten minutes and ate chocolate washed down by a swill of water with a dissolved sugar cube.

Bruno had chosen twelve for the assault on the clinic. They would scale its mountain lair in two teams of six.

Seldon was in charge of one, though it would be Mario who would lead the climb. With him would be Franco, Carla, Gina, the girl with long chestnut hair and her brother, a hill farmer called Marco.

Bruno had Lucia in his team. He'd also chosen Guido, Steffi and Luigi who were with him on the Bologna raid. The sixth was Salvatore.

Ahead Bruno saw Mario raise his arm. The others stopped and thankfully sank to the ground. Bruno eased off his pack, the straps had cut into his shoulders and his back ached. He moved to Mario's side, breaking off a slab of chocolate. The mountain man pointed.

Bruno saw the landscape rising before him. His eyes moved from where the coarse grass gave up its fight against the steel-grey rock. It slanted upwards at an angle, clefts and gullies sprawled over the surface in deep scars, spreading down from the ridge like tendrils.

It would be a murderous haul. But then, he'd climbed the mountains of Wales since a boy.

'Beyond that ridge is the valley,' Mario said. 'The other side is the mountain face that will take us to the clinic.'

Bruno looked at his watch. It was noon. They had been on foot for four hours.

'How long will it take to clear this first ridge and into the valley?'

Mario shrugged. 'Me an hour. The rest of you maybe two.'

'Then let's rest and eat.'

'We'll take an hour.'

Bruno scratched his nose. 'I want to begin to climb the face to the clinic before dark.'

'We still take an hour's rest,' Mario said, 'or no one will make it. Including me.' He thumped his chest.

Bruno grinned. He took the mug of water Lucia offered and flopped beside her.

*

Awesome.

It was the only word Bruno could think of to describe the mountain above them. It had a frightening magnificence and rose out of the pine and spruce which grew in the shelter of the valley. He counted two waterfalls. They fell vertically, then carved their way through the trees to the stream on the valley bed below.

The peaks were still covered in snow. Some of the rock faces were sheer and shone as if they had been polished. Others had been twisted by the ice age into giant sculptures.

Bruno pointed out a gully to Mario. It cut diagonally through the rock face changing directions to form a zig-zag route to a distant ledge.

From the ledge was a vertical climb to a short ridge which ran between two rounded peaks. Somewhere beyond that ridge lay the Clinic Ascha.

'We'll scale that gully in teams of six,' Bruno said.

Mario nodded grudgingly.

'I go first,' he said.

'Sure,' Bruno agreed and was in no doubt what Italians meant when they joked about mountain pride. 'Everybody check your equipment and weapons. Then rope up.'

Bruno bent to check his own pack. A pick, snow shoes and shovel were tied to the back.

'Bruno.' It was Luigi who took him by the arm. 'This is for you.'

Bruno took the sealed letter. 'It is from the Cavaliere Fulgoni. He said you were to have it just before the attempt on the clinic. I guess this is the time. It is not to be opened until it is all over. He wrote it after you left for Venice in case he never saw you again.'

Bruno took the letter in silence. He stuffed it inside his jacket. He moved towards Lucia and checked her rope.

'Nervous?'

'No,' she said and kissed him on the cheek.

He thought, Jesus, I don't believe she is.

'I just want to help remove that place on the other side of

the mountain from this earth,' she added as he turned to check the rest of his team's rope. One bad knot and they could all be dead.

Mario and his team were already scaling the gulley. Bruno watched in silence as they reached the first stage. He noticed the two girls, Carla and Gina, were doing well. Carla was assisting Seldon who seemed hesitant. He watched her steady him as he faltered.

Bruno remembered the climb in Wales when Seldon was almost killed. The man was terrified of mountains, yet here he was attempting something Bruno was awed by. Duty was a strange master, Bruno decided.

'It's no problem,' Mario called down.

'Tell that to the birds,' complained Steffi as he joined the others in fixing the packs.

Bruno's team began. His awe left him the moment his limbs began to work on the rock. He began to relish the challenge.

Bruno reached Mario's team resting on the ledge at the top of the gully. They were still roped together and looked tense. Seldon was grey, his eyes fixed to the ground.

Mario indicated the rock face to the ridge above. It was sheer. Bruno unroped himself and told Mario to do the same. 'We'll climb to the ridge alone. Get the equipment up then come back for the others.'

'I still go first,' Mario said.

'*Prego*. You're welcome.' Guido laughed nervously.

Bruno watched Mario check the pitons in his belt. 'Enough,' he said, satisfied with the metal spikes. He had a hammer in one hand and his *lupara* on his back. He slung the rope over his shoulder and reached for a hold.

Bruno fed him out from the coil at his feet. He knew he was watching an expert. Nothing was rushed or risked as Mario drove the pitons into the rock.

He waited for the tug on the rope, followed in the same style, driving home a second chain of spikes. At times his fingers ran over the rock so softly it felt as if he caressed it. His eyes never moved from his fingers as they sought out each new hold.

He looked up only when he felt the rope around his waist slacken. The gnarled, unshaven features of Mario peered down at him over the edge of the ridge. The grin was huge.

Then suddenly Bruno heard Seldon scream out in warning. He froze on the rock face, his fingers tightened and his muscles strained painfully as he pressed his feet firmly to the narrow hold. He felt Mario take up the slack, and felt a familiar gnawing inside at that signal of trouble. He looked up.

Mario's face had gone. But the rope was still tight. Bruno glanced sideways and winced in horror.

At first he thought the bi-plane's wheels would take his head off. It was flying at a 180 degree angle only yards from the rock face. It banked away steeply and the sudden rush of air almost lifted Bruno into the sky after it. He hung on grimly, resisting his instinct to swing his head suddenly in the direction of the noise from the engine. His face was pressed side on to the cold rock. He could feel every contour against his skin.

Seconds later the little plane screamed back into his view. It was an Italian Air Force spotter plane. He saw the pilot and observer clearly in the open cockpit. They wore goggles and leather flying caps. The pilot had a flowing white scarf around his neck.

The plane vanished above the ridge and he heard its engine change pitch. He guessed it was banking to make another run to confirm what the pilot had seen.

The grey underbelly flashed into view. It was so close he could see the rivets in the bodywork. The noise was deafening. The wind from the propeller rushed at him viciously and stung his eyes.

This time Bruno carefully turned his head to keep it in view. He did so slowly, so as not to foul his balance. As he shifted a pungent smell drifted past his nostrils.

The smell of oil.

He heard the plane splutter.

Bruno's eyes slowly followed the trail of black smoke which drifted into view. He saw it pour from the plane's engine. It had enveloped it before it passed from view.

He glanced up.

Mario, smoke wisping from the twin barrels of his *lupara*, looked down. As he raised the gun into the air in triumph Bruno heard the plane explode in the hills behind him.

Bruno remained motionless.

Below him he heard the others cheer. He cursed them for their stupidity. The pilot could have had a radio. He might have had time to use it. The crash might have been seen. A slim chance in these mountains. But a chance.

Bruno cursed again.

Then slowly continued to climb.

He used Mario's offered hand to scramble onto the plateau. Bruno turned to look for the wreckage. He could not see it.

'In the woods on the far hill,' Mario pointed.

Bruno screwed up his eyes. He could just make out a thin pall of black smoke seeping from the dense foliage.

'Thank Christ for that,' he mumbled.

Mario just shrugged as he reloaded the gun. He appeared to think as much of his action as if he'd just shot down a pigeon for supper.

Bruno said, 'Let's get the rest of the gear up here.'

'Sure.' Mario cleared his throat and spat on the ground. He tossed the tackle over the edge as Bruno took in the landscape. The ridge opened out for three miles to a snow-covered plateau which shelved steeply until it fell away against the clear blue sky and an unending vista of snow-capped peaks.

A deep, low rumble caught Bruno by surprise. He looked up at the cliffs each side of the ridge. Then at Mario.

The mountain man's eyes narrowed.

The rumble grew louder and Bruno followed Mario's gaze to the peak behind him. A great sheet of snow seemed to push itself slowly from the mountains with the noise of a lingering explosion. It crashed through the air towards the valley floor and disintegrated into a thousand white boulders. Behind it the crisp white powder hung on the air like thick mist.

'The noise of the plane.'

Bruno caught the unease in Mario's explanation. 'Then let's move.' They worked frantically until all the equipment was stacked on the ridge. Bruno refastened the rope around his waist while Mario hammered a holding spike into the hard ground. He tied the end of Bruno's rope to it. He held it firmly as Bruno made the descent to the ledge a hundred feet below. He reached it without difficulty.

He pointed to the pitons they'd driven into the rock face.

'Use those like a ladder. I shall be in the lead and Mario is on top as an anchor.'

They all looked terrified.

Bruno began the ascent cautiously. His movements were deliberately slow. He called them out so those below could imitate his actions. His team moved in unison, Bruno urging encouragement at every move.

It was an agonizing haul.

He reached the top.

One by one he helped the others onto the ridge.

Lucia first. She'd climbed with her eyes closed, using only touch. Then came Guido and Luigi.

Salvatore next.

It was Steffi who froze, just three rungs from the top. Bruno looked down on him. He was ashen and locked with fear. His eyes were filled with terror.

'Close them,' Bruno said reassuringly. Steffi trembled as he did so. Bruno lay on his stomach and reached down. His fingers just touched Steffi's.

'Bring up your left leg – slowly . . .' he urged. 'Just raise it until your toe touches the spike.'

Steffi, eyes still closed, did.

'Now stand on it and push yourself up.'

Bruno was now able to grab his wrist.

'Again,' Bruno urged. 'And again.'

At last he hauled Steffi onto the ridge beside him.

'I'm sorry,' he choked. 'I just couldn't move.'

'It happens to everyone,' Bruno reassured and made way for Mario's descent.

The mountain man lowered himself over the edge as Bruno and Luigi took the strain. As they played out the rope Bruno saw the light was fading. Once the mountain sun sets dusk is rapid. He silently urged Mario's team on.

Then it came.

Without warning.

There was no rumble this time. Just a noise which sounded as if the mountain behind them had burst. The setting sun vanished behind a waterfall of white. The whole mountain moved.

The avalanche was deafening. Snow rushed down like a tidal wave. The air was as thick with snow as any blizzard.

It was blinding.

Bruno felt the rope burning across his hands. He and Luigi were being hauled forward. Bruno dug his heels into the ground as if locked in a deadly tug of war with unseen opponents. He screamed for the others to take up the rope as he was dragged towards the edge.

He knew Mario's team had lost their hold. Behind, the others took up the rope. His heart sank as he felt it go suddenly limp in front of him.

It tightened again. Someone on the team had regained a hold.

Great balls of snow now began to break around Bruno, hurled through the air from the main seat of the fall on the peak half a mile away.

The hold on the rope was firm now.

'Keep it tight,' he yelled above the roaring mountain. He let go and rushed to the edge.

He looked over and his stomach turned.

He saw Mario clinging to the pitons in the rock. Behind him Carla and Franco also held on. Their faces twisted in agony.

Below them Seldon swung through the air like a pendulum. The rope around his waist trailed away to nothing.

There was no sign of Gina.

Or her brother.

Bruno's eyes moved to the foot of the gully. Their broken bodies lay twisted grotesquely, arms and legs askew.

He moved back from the edge and grabbed the rope.

Bruno screamed at the top of his voice, 'Pull.'

The others needed no urging. They toiled until it seemed their arms would leave their sockets. Slowly, very slowly, they began to make ground. From the feel of the rope Bruno knew that the others had regained some control.

'Stop pulling, but keep a tight rein,' he shouted.

It was up to Mario now.

Bruno could feel Mario's team moving up the rock face.

The big man's arms appeared over the edge. Then his gnarled face. Bruno rushed forward to help him.

Together they hauled the others to the top. They were in a state of shock. Their comrades helped them away from the edge.

Only Bruno looked back as they stumbled away. His eyes rested on Gina and Marco.

Then he turned and followed sadly after the others.

They wore snow shoes now as they trudged forlornly across the plateau. Roped together for safety, desolation shown by their hunched shoulders and lowered heads.

Bruno insisted Mario led the human trail. He was number two in the depleted line and paused as Mario prodded the snow in front of them with his ice axe searching for hidden danger beneath the packed snow.

He saw the big man raise his hands and wave them forward. Bruno glanced over his shoulder. There were at least twenty yards between each of the *Noantri*. It was the safety margin for being dragged after someone who fell into a chasm. Bruno waved Lucia on. He saw the raised arms repeat the signal down the line.

The ascent was almost over. He saw Mario pause on the skyline and motion him forward. He slipped the rope from his waist and, arms pumping, moved to the crest of the incline. He dropped on his belly next to Mario.

There it was.

The Clinic Ascha.

It lay serenely on a white shelf just below him, bathed in light from the searchlights on top of the fences. The snow in the compound glistened like priceless gems. It sparkled blues, reds and greens.

All the searchlights were trained towards the cable car station and the clinic. The approach to the rear fence was in total blackout.

He pushed himself back and slid towards the waiting line of *Noantri* crouching in the snow. Bruno rose on one knee.

'Seldon.' The urgent whisper carried on the May night. He checked his watch as Seldon stumbled towards him. Snow shoes were alien to him.

It was seven twenty. Two hours until the rest of the *Noantri* and partisan cells began the diversions.

Seldon grunted breathlessly as he flopped at his side.

'Take a look,' Bruno urged with relish.

They crawled towards Mario.

'There,' Bruno indicated. 'Not one light trained in this direction. They thought access was impossible.'

'So did I,' mumbled Seldon.

'Right,' Bruno grinned. He'd read Rossi as well as if he'd shared his mind. 'Get the others up here.'

Bruno eased off his pack, dug inside and produced binoculars. He trained them on the compound.

He took in the laboratory blocks first. A light burned in one. He could see the staff moving about. Their shadows on the curtains. The clinic was in darkness.

He swung the glasses towards the cable car station. He saw the outline of the car hanging in the sky. Two spotlights were trained on it. Rossi knew that as long as it remained at the top of the mountain no one could cross the abyss from the down station to the clinic. Bruno smiled. No one had to anymore.

They were there.

Bruno shifted. He saw four armed guards on the raised platform next to the hoist. They wore the boiler suit uniform with balaclavas. There were more guards milling around outside the cable car control station. Bruno tried to count them. In the end he had to guess.

He estimated eight. Some had Dobermans.

Bruno corrected himself.

He spotted another guard, with dog, on perimeter patrol. He was skirting the fence behind the conifers that acted as a windbreak to the clinic.

He saw the guard pass into shadow, out of the line of lights on the fence. He remained in darkness for a few seconds. The dog barked and the man cursed it. Then Bruno saw the beam of a torch. It played along the inner of the two fences. Not once did it go beyond.

The rest of the group were now lying along the crest of the ridge beside him, their eyes just above the snowline. He motioned Seldon to follow, ducked down and crouched along to Lucia.

'The bloody place still sends shivers down my spine,' she hissed. He squeezed her warmly by the arm. 'What do you think?' she said.

Before Bruno could reply there was a blinding blue flash followed by a sharp crack and sparks.

The dog growled ferociously as a sudden shaft of light swung through the night. It came from the cable car platform and swept over the snow towards the sound of the dog.

Bruno saw man and beast caught in the glare. The guard raised one arm to his eyes. In the other he held a white mountain hare.

'That's four this week,' his voice echoed back from across the mountains.

The light died instantly and was replaced by the eerie sound of hollow laughter.

Bruno watched in silence as his eyes followed the torch beam until the patrol returned to the light field.

'How often do they patrol?' Seldon asked hoarsely.

Bruno turned to Lucia.

'Every half hour. On the hour. It takes them thirty minutes.'

Seldon frowned. 'Are you sure?'

'You're damn right she's sure,' Bruno snapped. 'She's had time to count.'

Seldon mumbled an apology. 'I'd forgotten.'

'I haven't,' Bruno said. He clenched his fist and grabbed a handful of snow. He let it fall through his fingers. Then he snapped them.

'Steffi. Luigi.'

They were at his side.

'You know what to do.'

They nodded as one.

'Dig your hideouts first. You spend twenty minutes under the wire then back to the hide until the patrol passes. Good luck.'

'*Ciao*.'

Bruno watched them slide down the slope on their bellies like human sledges, the snow shovels fixed to their backs.

'Will it work?' Seldon asked anxiously. Bruno could feel him knotting beside him. The toe of his boot stabbing at the snow.

'Sure it will work,' Franco snapped. He, too, sounded tense.

'Easy,' Bruno said. His stomach was beginning to knot with last-minute doubts. He tried to sound confident. 'All they have to do is scrape enough earth from under the fences for Carla to squeeze under.'

Seldon sighed.

Bruno felt Lucia tug his sleeve. The patrol emerged from behind the screen of trees.

Steffi and Luigi had seen it too. They dived for the safety of the hides.

When the guard passed, everyone on the ridge breathed again.

Two patrols later they'd done it. Bruno saw Luigi raise his shovel in triumph.

Seconds later they were back.

Carla was already at his side. He sensed the animal in her. Her eyes were wild. The skin on her face seemed to have tightened. Her eyes narrowed.

'I'm ready.'

'OK,' Bruno said. 'Let's go over it again. The power house is behind that door.' He pointed at the back of the main building.

'It's held by a single padlock. You unscrew the bolts on the hinges, get back in and blow the fuse. When I was shown the security arrangements by Zeiss he pointed out that each section of the fence is on a different circuit, each shown on a drawing. It's the same with the lights.'

He felt Carla's fingers tighten in his hair as she kissed him unexpectedly. Hard on the mouth.

'I misjudged you,' she said quickly, wiped her mouth and was gone.

'I pray to God she is small enough to get under that gap,' Steffi said.

'So do I.' Bruno crossed his fingers.

He watched anxiously as Carla neared the outer wire. She knelt to inspect the gap before dropping onto her stomach and pressed herself hard against the ground. His mouth dried as she wriggled forward. The bottom strand of electrified wires swung to and fro only inches above her. One touch and she was dead.

Her luck held.

'Come on; slowly,' Bruno urged as she disappeared into the snow before the inner fence. It was worse now he could not see her. He half expected the blue flash which would spell disaster.

'She's done it,' Lucia said.

Bruno raised his head.

He saw Carla's outline against the snow.

She was moving like a cat towards the clinic.

Eight minutes later Carla was framed in the doorway. Bruno felt a buzz of anticipation as she raised a victorious fist in the air then retreated back inside and closed the door.

'The fence is dead,' he announced.

'You hope,' Seldon muttered.

Bruno glared. 'It's dead.' He turned in the snow and produced a pair of wire cutters from his pack. He asked Lucia: 'How long before the patrol returns?'

'Six minutes.'

Bruno hesitated. 'Have we got enough time to get us all inside?' He was thinking aloud.

'There is no choice,' Lucia replied. 'Look,' she pointed, 'the tracks in the snow.'

Bruno saw the trail Carla had left. He knew he could not afford to waste a second. He slid down the bank towards the fence on his stomach. He rose and stared at the wire. What if Carla had pulled the wrong fuse? There was only one way to find out.

He moved forward and raised his hand, wire cutters poised.

He jerked as the fingers tightened around his wrist, squeezing. He spun round. Seldon's mouth breathed on his face, the blue eyes darted.

'Not you,' Seldon said. 'I don't want to risk you.' He still held Bruno's wrist. With his free hand he snatched the wire cutters. The grip slackened.

Before Bruno could move Seldon reached out and took the wire. His eyes closed as he touched it.

Nothing.

'Good girl,' Seldon sighed. He began to tear at the wire with the cutters.

They were through to the second fence.

Bruno waved the others down as Seldon cut through it. He looked at his watch.

Four minutes before the patrol. He watched the raiders wriggle through the gap. His brow creased as he looked again at Carla's tracks, then at the shreds of wire hanging from the breached fences.

'Everyone to the power house. Follow Carla's tracks and move in single file. Quickly. Mario and Franco stay with me,' Bruno said as he grabbed a snow shovel from Steffi's pack.

'Can you handle the dog?' he asked Mario. The others ran for the clinic.

The big man grunted. 'It cannot be more difficult than a wolf.'

'Good.'

Bruno sank the shovel into virgin snow. It was three foot deep.

He began to dig.

The patrol was two minutes late.

Bruno looked through the power house window. Behind him came the succession of metallic clicks of weapons being checked for the last time. Guido hummed a few bars from a folk song and the oil-fired generators whirred steadily. The vibrations shook the window. Bruno wiped the condensation from the glass and was aware of Lucia at his side. But his eyes never moved from the empty whiteness leading to the torn fences. The outer one sagged badly.

'Stop that row,' Seldon snapped at Guido and the humming stopped. Then Lucia snatched her breath.

Bruno saw the torch beam sweep through the darkness. Then the guard came into view. His Doberman suddenly strained on the leash, its front paws left the ground and its ears flattened. It had caught the unfamiliar smells on the clear night air.

The guard halted as the dog tugged urgently, choking on the chain. It went wild. Bruno followed the torch beam as it cut across the ground. He stepped back from the window as it lit up the disturbed snow, then the gaps in the fences.

Bruno blinked as the torch dazzled him. The guard had traced the tracks to the power house. The beam played briefly on the window, then swung back to the fence.

Bruno tensed as the guard slipped the dog's leash. It lunged for the fence, the guard hard on its heels.

The dog sniffed feverishly in circles around the tell-tale marks. It yelped and snarled as it picked up a scent and followed its nose towards the fence. Bruno crossed his fingers as the animal began to dig the snow with its front paws, the rear kicking in unison. The dog buried its black head into the snow it had disturbed. It hauled a dark shape clear and shook it venomously, raising itself on its hind legs.

It was Mario's jacket.

Suddenly two figures erupted from beneath the snow before the astonished guard. They sent a white cascade showering into the air as they emerged from where Bruno had buried them; Mario eighteen inches beneath his jacket which Bruno had used to lay a trail for the dog; Franco three yards away.

Bruno saw the guard go for his rifle as the dog tossed aside the bait and flew at Mario. He saw the mountain man sink to one knee and hold out his arms. His hands closed around the Doberman's front paws and yanked them apart with a fearful strength. The animal's lungs must have caved in like punctured rubber, Bruno thought. He noticed the dog could not summon enough air to yelp as it died soundlessly.

Bruno, pistol in hand, was out of the door now and ploughing through the snow, Seldon and Guido behind him. He slowed as Franco eased himself from under the guard, knife in hand. The snow had turned crimson from the slash to the jugular.

Bruno pulled up and looked down at the dog. Its tongue lolled from the still curled mouth.

'Wolves are harder,' Mario grunted and picked up his jacket.

Bruno nodded and turned quickly to Seldon who wiped his mouth with the back of his hand. 'When Steffi kills the lights around the cable car. You know what to do.'

Seldon sucked his cheeks.

Bruno stood silently as Seldon and the *Noantri* fanned out across the snow. They kept to the shadows, out of the line of lights, and crouched in a drift yards from the first of the six laboratory buildings.

He turned back towards the power house. Steffi gave him a thumbs-up sign and smiled faintly as he re-checked the line of fuses on the wall. They were clearly marked to indicate what they controlled. Lucia and Carla stood each side of the door. Lucia's pistol was shoved in her belt, Carla had tucked her sten under her arm and stood akimbo.

He looked up at the first floor balcony. It was below Lucia's old room.

'Right,' he said and Lucia stepped forward. He cupped his hands to take her foot as Carla moved to his side. He felt her shift to take some of Lucia's weight as he hoisted her high.

'Got it,' she gasped as she gripped the balcony rail. Bruno bent at the knees so she could place her feet on his shoulders. He reached up for her thighs to steady her.

'The rope,' Bruno said through clenched teeth as he took the strain. He tottered as Lucia's weight shifted when she caught it. 'Come on,' he urged, swaying slightly.

'It's tied.' She gasped and he felt relief as she clambered onto the balcony.

He followed Carla up the rope and looked down at Steffi standing in the snow. Bruno caught the back-pack he hurled. It contained the plastic explosive and fuses. He slung it to Lucia and skirted the building, ducking below the shuttered windows. No lights showed. He reached the corner next to the line of trees and motioned the girls to him.

Briefly he looked back at the motionless figures lying on the drift.

Waiting.

Then he turned and counted the shuttered windows facing the row of pines.

The fifth pair covered Zeiss's office.

Bruno moved to the third. The shutters were unlocked. He eased them open.

'Knife.' He clicked his fingers.

He took it from Carla.

Carefully he eased the blade through the crack in the full-length window and raised it slowly so it lifted the catch. He handed back the knife and drew his pistol.

They were inside.

The room was bare. He padded softly across the polished pine floorboards and eased open the door to the corridor.

Night-lights burnt dimly through glass saucers set in the ceiling. Potted plants trailed from stands set outside the doors.

An electric clock was fixed to the wall at the end of the the corridor. The red second hand moved silently. Bruno saw there were seven minutes to go before Steffi threw the lights.

That's when it would begin. The whole clinic complex would be blacked out for just three minutes. It would be Seldon's cue to move. His group had that long to take up position in the snow. They would form an offensive arc between the cable car station and clinic.

In the blackout Luigi and Salvatore would storm the one laboratory still working. Then they'd fix plastic charges in the other five.

After two minutes Steffi would restore the lighting trained on the cable car control. The rest would remain in darkness. The guards assembled there would be illuminated targets. They would not see who was firing at them from behind the blaze of light. Dogs were prime targets. The guards next.

There were to be no prisoners. The *Noantri* under Seldon would then take the cable car control. Once the car was immobilized they were immune from any counter-attack from Rossi's forces below.

The clinic and its stocks of Wildfire would be razed to the

ground. It would be destroyed forever.

The *Noantri* would then leave by the way they came.

That, at least, was the way Bruno had planned it.

He closed the door on the corridor and turned to face Lucia and Carla. The room was still lit by the arcs from the fence. The girls looked up. They knelt on the floor fixing fuses into the grey lumps of plastic explosive. Lucia had arranged them in a row next to the cluster of grenades they'd emptied from the pack.

Bruno carefully picked up three lumps of plastic and eased them gently into his jacket pocket.

Carla laughed mockingly. He winced as she rolled a ball in her hand and threw it at the outer wall.

'It's harmless until you prime the fuse,' she chided. Her voice trembled with nervous excitement.

Bruno glared.

'I know,' he growled. He could have kicked her. He saw Lucia's face make a gesture of appeasement. He realized then just how much he loved that girl. He should have sent her packing – back to the plateau above the clinic. She could wait there for him in safety.

It was impossible.

She was needed to destroy what papers remained in Zeiss's office. If time deserted them then she alone would know what was important enough to obliterate.

He thought, God forbid.

Carla was also vital. The animal in her would take Zeiss.

He would destroy the Wildfire stock in the vault.

The room suddenly plunged into darkness.

Steffi had hit the switch.

'Lucia,' Bruno called softly. Lights danced in the blackness before his open eyes.

He felt her touch him. His hands were on her shoulders. He drew her to him and kissed her briefly on the forehead and felt her cling to him.

Then he was gone.

*

Bruno felt for the outer door to the vault in the darkness. He remembered it was to the left of the first flight of stairs below the ground level. Arms outstretched he found the wall. His arms moved along it.

There was the door. It was locked.

He took out a lump of plastic explosive, broke a piece off and slapped it on the lock. He fumbled for a fuse, rammed it home and groped for the stairwell. He found it as the lights came back on.

He ducked into the well and cowered, hands over his ears.

The flash was blinding, followed by a searing roar as the plastic lifted the door from its hinges. The walls stained black. Bits of wood burnt on the tiled floor. Smoke filled the air.

He covered his eyes and moved forward. The solid steel door to the vault itself lay at the end of the passage. It was opened by combination operated by a large spoked wheel. He fanned away the smoke and recited aloud the combination he'd memorized when he'd watched Zeiss open the door for him to inspect the stocks.

'A4593. A85327. S49. J561.'

He began to wrestle with the wheel. Beyond lay a wall ladder. It led to the Wildfire stock that was kept in sealed trays.

The steel door opened.

As it did so, the whole floor under him seemed to shake from the effects of a massive explosion. The roar was distinctive. Bruno had heard it before. On the mountain below the abyss, when the ambulance they'd used to flee the clinic had gone over the cliff. It was the corrosive used to destroy Wildfire. It seemed as if the whole stock had blown.

A brief lull followed the echo.

Then came the sound of gunfire. The firefight had begun.

He dived for the ladder, clambered desperately for part of the way down, then dropped the rest. He winded himself as he hit the steel floor. It felt ice cold on the palms of his hands.

There it was.

The Wildfire stock.

All that now existed, stacked casually in sealed slides on metal shelves. He felt numb at the horror of it all. His eyes followed the line of grey shelves, then rested on a glass-fronted section. A red skull and crossbones was painted on the front. His unease grew.

Bruno rose slowly. He walked hesitantly towards it, one heavy foot in front of the other, his dread growing with every step.

He knew.

Instinctively.

They'd done it.

He peered through the thick glass. There were twelve slim lead boxes. Each was stamped with a label.

It said 'Ready for Use'.

He closed his eyes and trembled.

Zeiss had finished what he started. He had grafted Bruno's antidote to the bacillus.

They had their bomb.

That explained why there was only one light burning in the laboratory block. There was no need for further experiment.

It was done.

Here. At the Clinic Ascha.

He realized all that had gone before was a total waste, unless this could be destroyed.

The papers would be in Zeiss's office. That's where Lucia was.

He had to destroy the stock before him. The incinerator was in the experimental laboratory.

Bruno turned for the second exit. It was set in the wall at the top of the flight of steps above him and opened out directly from the side of the clinic opposite the laboratories. Both doors and combinations were identical. He'd made a play of commenting to Zeiss during his conducted tour. The Swiss had made light of Bruno's feigned concern.

Now he thought, Thank Christ.

Bruno tore up the steps, his footfalls echoing hollowly. He

wrestled with the wheel on the door.

He knew he had to get everything in this vault to the incinerator, even if he had to do it alone. He must.

As the wheel turned, each click of the lock seeming like an age, an image flashed through his mind. It made him shiver.

It was not the experimental photographs.

Or the wretches he'd watched die.

It was of the Rhesus monkey twisting in agony at the Bologna laboratory. He doubled his efforts.

The door unlocked. He shoved it open with his shoulder, straining and grunting.

Cold air swept over him as it moved. He shoved harder. Then stopped dead in his tracks.

His gaze fixed where the laboratories should have been.

In their place lay a mountain of smoking debris.

That's what the explosion had been.

Now there was no incinerator. He willed himself not to think of Luigi and Salvatore.

'Bruno,' the voice shrieked behind him, 'Bruno.'

He turned.

Carla stood at the foot of the stairs.

'All hell has broken loose. Everything has gone bloody wrong.'

He saw the tears of rage streaming down her face.

There was the sound of gunfire and a man screaming.

Bruno ducked back inside. He dropped to the vault floor.

Bruno slapped Carla across the side of her face. The girl stopped ranting. They were on the stairs leading to Zeiss's suite of offices.

It was chaos. The sound of heavy firing came from the ground floor. That meant armed men were in the clinic. Bruno could not tell if they were *Noantri* or guards. There was still shooting outside, punctuated by exploding grenades.

Bruno grabbed Carla.

'What the hell is going on, where's Lucia?'

'Seldon's got her,' Carla spat. 'He's in Zeiss's office going through research papers.'

'What?' Bruno screamed. It contained all the anger he'd ever felt. 'The bastard is supposed to take out the cable car.'

Carla snorted. 'He never went anywhere near it. The moment Steffi fixed the lights he left the others to it and doubled back to the clinic. I heard Lucia scream when I went to see what was happening. The moment I stuck my head around the door Seldon tried to shoot it off.'

Bruno controlled the hate welling inside him. He now needed to think more clearly than he had ever done in his life. 'What about Zeiss?'

'I shot him.'

Bruno paused. 'Keep this corridor covered. I'm going to get Seldon.'

Carla cocked her sten.

Bruno bolted towards the suite of offices. He tried the handle of the secretary's door. It was warm and sticky.

Blood.

He wiped his hand on his jacket and eased the door open with his foot.

The room was a shambles, drawers ripped from desks, files all over the floor. Some of the papers were heavily blood-stained. The door to the washroom was ajar.

Bruno swallowed hard. He moved cautiously towards the door of Zeiss's main office. It was frosted glass. He raised his pistol and kicked it open. It was a mistake.

It gave Seldon time to grab Lucia. His gun rammed under her jaw. Bruno saw she'd been beaten. Dried blood ran down her face in stripes from a wound to her head. He mouth was bruised.

Bruno took in the room. Zeiss's wall safe was open and empty. Seldon had been in the process of stuffing every paper in the office into four canvas sacks. They lay against the far wall. Somewhere in that lot lay the key to the horror in the steel vault. The only key. He knew there would be no other.

Once Zeiss had it he would not share it.

He saw Seldon was frightened, and knew he dare not risk panicking him for a second. Not if Lucia was to live.

He let his pistol fall.

'Get over there against the far wall,' Seldon said. His voice cracked.

Bruno obeyed. Seldon and Lucia now faced him. Their backs to the door.

'Empty those drawers and put the contents in the empty sack,' Seldon snapped. Bruno saw he was pointing to an open cabinet.

'No,' Bruno said. He noticed Seldon's eyes widen.

'Do it,' he screamed.

'No.'

'I'll kill her.'

'Don't do it, Bruno,' Lucia blurted. Seldon pressed his hand over her mouth and dug the gun deeper into her underjaw.

'It's no use to you, Seldon,' Bruno said quietly. 'There is nowhere you can go with that lot. You need us to get you out of here. You know you could never make it alone.'

Seldon sneered. 'Look, old chum,' he said. 'The arrangements to get me out with what I came for were made in London months ago.'

'That's nonsense, Seldon, and you know it. Just think of the situation we are in. Think, man, think,' Bruno urged.

Then Bruno's jaw locked.

It was Zeiss. He swayed in the door behind Seldon. He had the pallor of a corpse. The front of his white shirt was saturated in blood from the wound in his stomach. But Carla had not killed him. It was his blood in the secretary's office.

Bruno remained motionless as Zeiss leant against the door. Bruno could see the effort written on the dying face as he struggled to raise the gun in his hand.

It was level now.

Zeiss fired.

His shot coincided with the burst from Carla's sten behind

him. It hurled him through the air, into the office.

Seldon pushed Lucia aside as he swung instinctively towards the sound of the shot. He fired at the shape flying through the air.

He was still firing into Zeiss's body when Carla's second burst cut him to pieces.

Bruno was already emptying the sacks onto the floor. Sheets of loose paper fell on the dead men.

Carla had vanished.

'Plastic,' Bruno yelled at Lucia, 'all you have got.'

The office filled with the sound of sten gun fire from the corridor as Bruno helped Lucia with the explosive charges.

Carla backed through the door, firing wildly.

'Get out,' she screamed.

Bruno kicked in the French window to the balcony and dragged Lucia after him as Carla fired from the door. Then he saw her kick it shut and sprint towards him. She leapt straight over the balcony and sprawled onto the snow below.

Splinters flew from the office door as Bruno and Lucia dived into the night.

As Bruno hit the snow he felt the blast of the explosion. He looked up.

A tongue of flame licked through the office window. It was tinged with swirling black smoke.

He saw Carla and Lucia ploughing through the snow towards the cable car station. He guessed the figures lying down in front of it firing at the clinic were what was left of the *Noantri*.

Then to his horror, Bruno realized something was missing.

The cable car had gone.

'We were too late,' Franco said desperately. He pointed to the wrecked control unit in the station house. 'It's a dual system. They smashed this after the car had gone. It's now controlled from the down station.'

Bruno bit his lip.

He stepped over the dead guard in the doorway and Franco followed him outside.

Bruno counted six more boiler-suited bodies in the snow. They lay amid their dogs.

Behind him the fire raged in the clinic. If he burnt it to the ground he knew the Wildfire stocks would still be safe in the steel vaults.

But he could still fight his way back to it through the second door he'd left open.

Bruno turned to where the laboratories and incinerator had been.

The ruins of twisted steel and plaster still smoked after the blast. There was no sign of the incinerator.

'That,' he indicated the rubble, 'means we have no way of destroying the stocks. The vault is steel. It will not burn and all a plastic explosion would do would be to release Wildfire into the air.' He shook his head forlornly. He could not have felt more desperate than at that moment.

He'd lost. Civilization had lost.

He looked out across the snow. The *Noantri* were still raking the clinic with spasmodic bursts. It was being returned. He saw the flames leaping into the night were still confined to the area around Zeiss's office.

'How many of us are left?' he asked as he noticed more corpses, their black outlines clear against the snow.

Franco rubbed his wild beard. 'Six. Mario, Guido, Carla, Lucia, and us. Guido's wounded.'

'Steffi?'

Franco shook his head. He pointed to the rubble. 'Luigi and the Venetian.' Then he added defiantly indicating those left: 'We are still fighting like *Noantri*.'

Bruno smiled weakly. 'How many guards do you think are inside?'

'Who knows? They broke through us and fought their way back inside. Some of the staff are armed too.'

'Tell the others only to fire when they have to, just enough to keep those bastards inside,' Bruno said.

He watched Franco run crouching towards the four *Noantri*. The firing stopped.

Bruno climbed the cable car platform. He looked across the abyss and saw tiny figures milling around the down station. Then he heard the wire above his head creak and groan. It began to slide through the pulley. It was moving.

So was the cable car. It was coming back up the mountain.

Bruno spun and yelled for Franco.

'Bring me a sten,' he called.

Then as he turned back to look at the cable car something caught his eye. It was the small electric tug used as the clinic transport. It was hitched to three small trucks.

Bruno's smile was from ear to ear.

Not all the deadly corrosive had gone up with the test laboratories.

Five large drums were stacked on the trucks.

The cable car was just out of range. Bruno saw the red tracers from his sten fall just short. There was no return fire.

Franco was scaling the girders to the top of the lift. There he would place the plastic charge which would destroy the structure and send the car crashing to the valley floor. If there was time.

The car neared.

This time Bruno saw his burst thud into the woodwork and it slewed crazily on the wire. Then, before he could fire again, it stopped, swinging silently in the air.

He lowered his sten.

The only sound came from the flames crackling in the clinic.

'What is it?' Franco called down from his perch.

'I don't know,' Bruno said quietly as something stirred in his gut.

The car just hung there, as if it was mocking him.

Then came a low scraping noise as the car door was pulled slowly back.

'Bruno.'

His name echoed through the mountains from the loudhailer. The hairs on his neck prickled. It was Rossi's voice. 'I've got Fulgoni.'

The amplified words filled the night. It was eerie.

Bruno glanced over his shoulder. He saw Lucia rushing towards him. He looked up at Franco straddling the girder.

'Keep her back,' Bruno said quickly.

Franco dropped onto the platform and leapt to the ground. Bruno watched him head off Lucia. He took her by the waist as they fell into the snow.

Bruno's eyes returned to the car. Slowly, very slowly, it began to move again. He lowered his sten.

Alone on the wooden platform he felt vulnerable and exposed. He watched the car. It stopped twenty feet from him.

Suddenly, Rossi was framed in the open door. He stood aside and two OVRA heavies shoved Fulgoni into sight. He was bedraggled, his head slumped onto his chest and his silver hair hung down. His knees bent. Bruno realized the men on his arms were supporting him.

'I want to trade,' Rossi said through the loudhailer.

'You are too late,' Bruno bawled. 'It's done. We've destroyed it.'

'Liar. If you had you would not still be there. Now let's talk trade.'

Bruno did not respond. He could not take his eyes off the old man. The Cavaliere hung there like a broken bear. He dreaded to think what Rossi had done to him.

'You and the girl I can save. This old goat too.' Bruno saw Rossi jab Fulgoni. The old man raised his head and looked up towards Bruno.

'He lies,' Fulgoni boomed as he straightened. 'He's done for. He must kill you or they will kill him.'

Bruno realized the effort that must have cost Fulgoni. He clenched his fists as he saw Rossi hit him.

Then his cousin raised the loudhailer to his lips. 'This is the deal, Bruno. It is just between you and me. The authorities will never know. You, Lucia and Fulgoni go free. The others I must have. I'll give you three safe conducts and a fortune. You hear me, a fortune. All I want are the Wildfire stocks. Don't give me any shit that you've destroyed them.'

Silence, except for the distant flames.

'Well?' Rossi's echo rang from the mountains.

Then came a low drone from the sky. It grew louder. It was a plane.

'Look behind you, Bruno,' Rossi called hollowly.

Bruno turned his face to the sky.

He saw one white puff first. Then another.

Parachutes opened in a line across the clear sky. They were dropping on the plateau between the ridge they'd scaled and the clinic.

'See,' Rossi said triumphantly. 'You have no chance. You will be overrun. Now I can still save you. We can trade.'

Bruno thought, Why?

'He has to get you himself or he's a dead man,' Fulgoni's voice filled the night. It did not have its familiar power. But it was unbent.

Bruno saw the car suddenly rock violently on the wire.

He caught his breath as he saw Fulgoni loom up behind Rossi. The old Cavaliere enveloped his cousin in a bear hug. As big a man as Rossi was, Bruno saw Fulgoni lift him from his feet. Rossi kicked frantically as the grip tightened.

Bruno, rooted to the spot, watched helplessly as the two men swayed in the open door. Then he saw Fulgoni launch himself into the abyss, Rossi still held firmly in his grip.

Bruno could only look in horror as the men spun in the air. Slowly.

And over.

Turning.

Until they were lost in the nothingness.

Bruno was transfixed.

Then the bullets smashed around his feet.

He blasted back at the car with his sten. When he'd emptied it there was only silence.

Then he heard Lucia screaming.

She was still struggling with Franco in the snow. She broke free, and ran towards the platform.

In the sky above her the parachutes billowed over the plateau. He counted ten. Slowly drifting towards the earth.

He jumped to the ground and Lucia ran into his open arms. He held her, letting her weep. Then he held her firmly by the shoulders.

'I'm going back into the clinic. The stocks must be destroyed. I need you to cover me. Understand?' He shook her.

She nodded. Her eyes were red.

'It was what he would have wanted,' he said. She freed herself and turned for her gun.

Franco was at his side now. 'The parachutes?'

'All that matters now is that bloody bacillus,' Bruno said. 'Can you get the tug to the vault entrance?' He pointed to the round steel door set in the clinic wall. It was half open.

'I can try,' Franco said simply. And was gone.

'Cover me,' he screamed at the surviving *Noantri*. They began to move forward slowly, firing as they went.

Bruno headed for the shadows, out of the line of light that still blazed from the arcs on the fence.

Breathless he stood under the balcony, his back pressed against the white wall of the clinic. Beside him hung the round steel door of the vault.

The covering fire from Lucia and the others was intense. It was being returned with equal ferocity. Bruno saw one of the *Noantri* jerk upwards, arms raised, then fall back in the snow.

It was Guido.

He looked anxiously for Franco. The tug and trucks slipped out of the shadows into the light from the fences.

The bearded *Noantri* was taking the shortest route to the vault door.

'Get back into the shadows,' Bruno screamed. He saw

bullets pit the snow around the tug.

Bruno knew if one hit a drum then they would all be wiped off the mountain, including the clinic.

Then the only victors would be the microscopic bacilli that would float unseen on the air.

Bruno wiped his forehead. He could feel the heat from the flames that raged over the balcony above. He guessed they were spreading.

The tug was snaking now, weaving towards him over the snow. He could not see Franco who was crouched low in the small cab.

The others were doing their best to draw the fire. He saw Lucia on her feet spraying at the clinic. So was Mario.

'Get down,' he screamed. His words were lost in the fire play. Then came the sound he was dreading. The sound of bullets against metal. He knew the tug had been hit.

He spun towards it. It had stopped in its tracks. Franco hung grotesquely over the side. The snow around him was stained red. The fire from the clinic was now concentrated on the *Noantri* who were falling back.

He saw one of them break away from the group and toss a sten aside.

'Carla,' Bruno breathed.

He watched impotently as she ran to her dead lover. She slid the last few yards on her stomach. She pulled Franco from the tug cab, left him on the snow and climbed into his place.

The tug moved again.

Five yards away. Three.

Its snub nose bounced to a halt against the clinic wall.

Before Bruno could move, it reversed and completed a tight turn. The whole train was now under the shelter of the balcony.

Carla leapt out.

He looked at her.

There was nothing either could say.

Bruno strained and opened the steel door fully.

Together they unloaded the five drums onto the path. Then rolled them to the open door.

'If we topple them down the steps will they explode?' Carla asked simply.

Bruno shook his head. The girl amazed him. 'They need to be ignited.'

'Good.'

They pushed the first drum through the door. It bounced noisily on the steel floor.

'It will be quicker if you roll them into position in the vault,' Bruno said. 'I'll send them down.'

He pulled a lump of plastic explosive from his pocket. He handed it to Carla with a fuse.

'Is that all?' she asked.

'It's enough.'

Bruno turned for the second drum as Carla went down into the vault.

Then it was done.

Carla was still in the vault when Bruno heard Lucia yelling. She was in the shadow.

'Come on,' he called to Carla, then turned and ran headlong for Lucia.

Mario was still blasting at the clinic. His fire was directed at the front door, pinning the remaining guards inside. Bruno saw two dead bodies on the step. The flames now had spread to the roof.

He stumbled on Lucia. She pointed at the sky. Bruno looked up as a small plane swooped over their heads. It banked out of sight above the flood of light.

'It's got skis,' Bruno mumbled. 'And that bastard is making a landing approach.' He thought of the parachutists. They, too, would have skis, and at that very moment were using them to cross the plateau towards them. God only knew what, or how many, were in the plane. He looked up and saw a single light falling slowly out of the night.

It was going to land behind the trees on the far side of the clinic.

'Move.' He shoved Lucia towards the section of the fence they'd reached.

'Bruno,' she protested.

'For Christ's sake move.' He shoved her again. 'Wait for me at the fence. Once we're outside at least we have some chance. It's more that we have here. Go.' He was yelling.

She went.

He sprinted back for Carla, screaming for Mario to come as he ran.

He reached the vault door and froze. He thought it was closed. Bruno looked again and saw it was slightly ajar. Just.

Carla's voice trailed from the inch gap.

'The fuse is dud.'

Bruno dug into his pockets, twisting urgently. They were empty.

'Will it ignite if I tap a drum?' Her voice was barely audible.

'Yes,' Bruno croaked hoarsely.

'Then I'll set fire to it. I have a lighter. I'll use my shirt as a torch. I want to stay here with Franco.'

The vault door thudded shut. The combination clicked. He banged the door until the side of his hand bled. It was no use. Carla had sealed her own tomb.

Then the firing suddenly stopped.

'Mario.'

He saw the mountain man stumble into view, raise his sten, then collapse face down in the snow.

It was over.

He turned and ran headlong for the fence. He could see Lucia standing near the guard and his dead dog. She was pointing skyward.

Bruno fought for breath as he looked over his shoulder. He thought his lungs would burst.

He saw the single landing light of the plane falling out of the sky. He put down his head and ploughed on. The strength was ebbing from his limbs.

A voice inside said, 'It's enough.'

The sound of the plane's engine rang in his ears. Louder. And louder.

The voice said, 'Rest. Just fall down in the snow. The cold will ease the aching. It's over. Take your rest.'

The blood pounded in his temples. He felt dizzy. His heart felt as if it was leaping around in a wild dance inside his chest. It was going to burst.

Another voice told him, 'Keep going. Reach the mountains. There's a chance.'

He fell flat on his face. The first voice was right. The snow felt good. Cold. Soothing. It was in his mouth. Up his nostrils. It was good.

Hands were on his face. He raised his head.

Lucia's face.

She was tugging at him now. Pulling him to his feet. Pleading. He was on his knees.

Then he stood uncertainly.

He turned as if in a dream. The plane slithered into view from behind the trees. It swung on its skis and came slowly towards him. The single propeller blew snow in all directions.

The slap on his face was vicious. So were the next three. They came in rapid succession. Then Lucia screamed his name.

His head cleared. He pulled the Mauser from his belt.

He swung it towards the plane as it came to a halt. The pilot jumped out and ducked under the overhead wing. He wore a leather jacket with a fur collar and knee-length boots. He pushed up his goggles as Bruno raised the gun.

'For Christ's sake, Seldon, move it. I've not got all bloody night.'

The English accent rang sweetly in Bruno's ears.

'Seldon. Move,' the pilot yelled.

Bruno began to laugh. Seldon had been serious. This plane was his way out. He grabbed Lucia by the wrist and stumbled towards it. The pilot was back in the cockpit and the plane turned to face the way it had come.

It was a two-seater British Auster. Yet Bruno noticed it bore no markings of any sort. It was painted brown. The passenger door was flung open.

Bruno looked up as the pilot leant over the seat towards him.

'Just you, Seldon. No passengers.'

Bruno lunged and held him by the throat. He thrust the Mauser under his nose.

'My name is not Seldon and we are taking her,' Bruno said. He climbed aboard. Lucia clambered after him and squeezed into the gap behind the seats and fuselage.

'What the hell is going on?'

'If you don't get out of here you can ask them.' Bruno pointed to the back of the clinic. Three boiler-suited guards, rifles in hand, rounded the corner.

They began firing.

The pilot needed no second bidding. The plane swept across the snow and lifted steeply to clear the perimeter fence.

Bruno looked down as it swooped out over the abyss.

The burning clinic, still bathed in light, grew smaller as the Auster climbed.

Then the whole complex vanished in a billowing ball of smoke and flame. The force reached up and rocked the plane. It tilted momentarily from side to side, then straightened.

Carla, Bruno thought. She was with Franco now. He imagined her alone, lighting her shirt, and winced.

She had not failed him.

None of them had.

It was over.

'Heavens above! What the hell was that?' the pilot asked quietly.

'A lot of lives being saved.'

Bruno reached out and touched Lucia's cheek. He looked back, smiled, then turned to the pilot. 'I assume you are with Seldon's lot in London?'

'SOE actually.'

'Well, when you get back you can tell them Wildfire is destroyed.'

'So who the hell are you and where is Seldon?'

'My name is Bruno Rossi and he's dead.'

'Bad show. But you are British, with us I mean,' the pilot said.

'No,' Bruno mumbled. 'I'm not with you. I'm not with anybody.'

'I see,' the pilot said flatly. His eyes fell on the gun in Bruno's hand. 'You would use that if you had to, wouldn't you?'

'If I have to.'

'Thought you might. So what's to do?'

'You are going to fly us to Switzerland.'

'I'm supposed to fly to Nice. Switzerland is neutral territory.'

'Exactly,' Bruno said.

The pilot shrugged. 'I don't suppose I have much choice.'

'None at all.' Bruno handed the gun to Lucia. She sat with her knees tucked under her chin.

They all lapsed into silence as the plane banked into the night and changed course for Switzerland.

It was later Bruno remembered the letter Luigi had given him from Fulgoni. He felt for it inside his jacket, opened it and read it by the light of the navigation lamp.

He whistled softly and glanced at Lucia. The old man had kept his word. All of his immense wealth had been shifted to Sweden. It was Lucia's now. There was also a letter of credit for him at the Sverige Norsk Bank. They were both to remain in that country until the war was over. That was a condition. He then hoped that they would return to Italy and build a life together.

'That's Switzerland,' the pilot pointed down.

Bruno noticed Lucia's eyes well.

'Bruno, will we ever be able to go back?'

'When the madness ends.' His voice was reassuring.

'Together?'

The plane began its descent.

'Together,' he said and squeezed her hand.

Together, he vowed silently.

They would pick up the strands his father and Fulgoni had left untied. A new generation. A new beginning.

In the mountains of the north.

When the madness ends.

Duncan Kyle

'One of the modern masters of the high adventure story.' *Daily Telegraph*